DRE
AS JULIA

SIMON POTTER

T-O-P

2022

"Dressing As Julia" was first published in Great Britain by *Trans-Oceanic-Press* 2022

www.simonpotterauthor.com

ISBN: 978-1-9164295-1-2

A catalogue record for this book is available from the British Library.
Cover design by Trixie Wirrell

Printed and bound by Witley Press, Hunstanton, Norfolk, PE36 6AD

Like wanton boys we follow bubbles….
Pleasure? What is it?
Only the good hours of an ague.

(John Webster: *The Duchess of Malfi*)

CONTENTS

oOo

February 2020: *REQUIESCAT IN PACE*

'Stop! Stop, Janek. I want to check myself.'

Lindy Franitza jabbed on her lipstick. When she frowned at the car's vanity mirror her nose wrinkled up. Janek had loved her nose once, but now it often repulsed him to see how the pigginess of her mother was settling on her.

'You look fine.'

'I don't care what you think. Just stop.'

Janek had hoped to reach the abbey quickly because he was beginning to feel the familiar bursting sensation in his bladder. With what Lindy called 'one of his flounces', he drew to a halt.

'If we're stopping for you to primp yourself, I must just….,' he muttered, clambering out of the car and gazing at the roadside trees.

'As usual,' she said, more to herself than to him, 'All in the mind.'

When Janek returned, Lindy was compressing a tissue between her lips to get the gloss off the lipstick. She then patted on some powder. She had rosacea, one of several complaints, which required a special hard compact that had to be ordered at $78.

The bright sterility of a clear day in February lay along the hood of the car and paled the tame landscape of southern Connecticut. The road sign read: East Hartford, Rockville, Stafford Springs.

Janek came back out of the trees and stood looking in on his wife before sliding into the car.

'East Hartford. Surely we're nearly there?' said Lindy, patting her hair and flipping back the interior mirror. 'If we're not, we'll be late.'

'We're not late – not that anyone would mind if we were.'

He moved off, looking for the gates and beyond them the abbey among the trees. The Satnav suggested a winding drive from the road but gave no real indication of the building's whereabouts on it. Janek peered out. A sudden wall of grey stone came into view. Ten minutes later, he and Lindy were walking through the abbey church door under the waves of a bell.

A monk came up to greet them, rubbing his hands together.

'I'm Father Luke, the hospitality master. Let me show you where to sit. Have you come far?'

'From Yonkers, Father,' said Janek. 'Not too bad today after White Plains.'

'Are you his pupils from New York? His ex-pupils, I should say.' Dom Luke looked at each of them in turn.

'I'm the pupil – from St Matthew's – from, oh, well, from when he was teaching there nearly thirty years ago. Janek Franitza. This is my wife, Lindy.'

'And NOT one of his pupils,' crinkled Lindy with a keep-your-distance smile, shaking the priest's hand.

'You are not the only one from his St Matthew's days. I'll show you up to the top on the left. There's going to be a gaggle of you, I believe. A sad death, painful and before his time. But he was very brave.'

Dom Luke whisked up the aisle, his habit hissing. Janek and Lindy followed and were shown into a row of pews already nearly full. The occupants turned to look at them and Janek studied them. He didn't recognise a single face.

'Excuse *me*,' said Lindy, pointedly expecting an elderly couple to move up. They did so, and the Franitzas took their places, opening their black coats and letting the material flow on each side of them.

They gave attention to the catafalque, draped in mourning, which stood high in front of the altar rails. Janek began to remember more about the man who lay inside and why he had felt compelled to drive up from New York this morning. The dead Benedictine brother had given him – unintentionally – one of the astonishing memories and one of the sad regrets of his youth. Those few days in far-off Nova Scotia with the high school play..... How distant the confident happiness he had found there seemed, how incoherent the immediate fierce misery. Those days had seen a ridiculous misunderstanding, a hopeless mistake, and the shattering of certainties; and they had had far-reaching echoes.

There were more noises, muffled conversation and

the clicking of heels from the back of the abbey. A brusque voice, accustomed to off-hand authority, was saying,

'No, no. Don't bother them. I guess we'll just slide in here.'

Something about the tone chimed with the part-suppressed memories in Janek and he turned round. Several pews back, a grey-haired, heavily-built man and a pretty middle-aged woman were seating themselves. But he didn't think he recognised them.

'These requiem Masses can be very long, I've heard,' whispered Lindy.

'Pretty long,' replied Janek. 'He was one of the brothers here for more than twenty years. They're bound to make something of it.'

Onto the altar came a boy server. He lit six tall candles which ran across above the tabernacle. He then came forward to the lectern, looked out into the body of the abbey, and busied himself with opening a missal and draping ribbons down the right pages. Janek's heart gave a sharp jump. Two regrets collided simultaneously. The treacherous past! How it inserted itself into you now and then, like chilly fingers creeping under a coat for warmth. Why could Francis not have lived? His habitual wave of depression gurgled round him as his eyes followed the boy out into the sacristy. His darling son would be thirteen now if.... And then, linked to that competence with taper and missal, came thoughts about Jem. Jem – and all those years without contact. A dry pricking behind his eyes and a familiar blocking of his nose warned Janek that a tear would soon creep from his eyes. Francis was too recent, too raw. Jem, though his name was as comfortable still as old leather, came from layer on layer of time back. And those lines from a poem for Jem, never shown, still remembered: *"You take me upstairs on a peach-flavoured skate-board; you do it. That's just what you do."* Janek murmured them – for they were never far from the surface, from that lost time when he had loved Rosa and Jem, so differently – and brushed his eyes with a hand.

He forced himself to think of something else – of what exactly the dead man had worn in Canada nearly thirty years ago, when Janek had last seen him. It was while he was engaged in this, and the stifled sob had quieted, that there was another clatter of new arrivals.

With aluminium tappings, a handsome, Latin-looking man, with a mane of dark hair going silvery in parts, came up the aisle supported on one side by a crutch and on the other by a youth in his late teens or early twenties. Lindy hissed,

'That suit cost a bomb. Who is he? He looks Italian, or Spanish.'

Janek was about to say that he had no idea, when he realised that he did find the man with the crutch familiar. He took in the massy gold ring, the tinted spectacles, the gleaming shirt; took in too the attentiveness of the youth who had his arm linked in to an elbow.

'I do feel I know him, but I can't think where from…...'

The two, one limping, one holding, were taken right to the top up by the catafalque.

The final arrival was noticeable only as a shadow out of the corner of Janek's eye. Opposite the Franitzas, over the broad aisle and several rows behind the teenage helper, was an empty pew. One moment it had nobody in it, the next there was a figure. Janek turned a bit further and stole a quick glance at what, in that instant, seemed one of the loveliest women he had ever seen. As he did so, the oddest feeling came over him that he did know this tall, impressive woman. He couldn't take in her details without turning obviously round, which seemed rude and unsophisticated, so he feigned interest in the architecture of the abbey church. She put a hand up to her breast in a fluttering gesture which immediately gave life to ghostly memories – memories of a past also inhabited by the dead Benedictine brother – so that he was put to work feverishly linking these people.

Surely the woman couldn't be…. Rosa? That flutter of the hand…. no, not her, of course…. too tall and different nose….but so familiar …..

The congregation was standing, a choir sang and the sanctuary filled with twenty or so monks in dark habits. Janek forced his attention back to the Requiem

Mass. Yet that gesture! The hand fluttering at the breast, and the strange memories it stirred! Out of the mist of plangent singing, he seemed to taste, rather than see, two red lips kissing a poisoned Bible and to hear an hysterical voice, terrified of Hell, scream: *"Oh! I go. I know not where!"* It was so tantalising, so sharp, that he forgot again where he was in his efforts to bring it back.

Janek realised that he would have to wait until the reception before he got any further with the funeral guests' identities, and, however much Lindy wanted to get back to the city, he determined he would make an opportunity to speak both to the man with the crutch and to the beautiful woman. As the service moved on, he looked forward to setting in train the release of ghosts.

8

28 YEARS EARLIER
January: JUST ONE OF THOSE DECISIONS

'I just don't want the semester to stumble to a halt with a whimper. We can't let St Philomena's scoop up whatever focus and praise that's going round here.'

Mr Howard, who held the Chair of the English Faculty, nearly banged the table with his mug to emphasise his remark. It seemed theatrical and might have cracked the mug – so he didn't. His second in the faculty grunted,

'Well then – what are we going to do? A big musical is out, because all the girls will be involved in their pom-pom crap, the older kids will be obsessing about who they're gonna take to the Prom, and no one is going to want to sit through a Brecht, or fidget through yet another ham version of *The Importance of Being Earnest*.'

'It's January, David, and we've got five months. There's an eager little mob of Luvvies out there, so we need a play with twenty or so guys and hardly any women's parts – and I've got an idea.'

'Will it interfere with the Regents or the Advanced Placement? You're not thinking of using Seniors, are you?' asked Jeff.

Mr Howard gazed out past young Louise's attractive head to the globe of the Queens Museum etched onto icy air. He stood up and sat on the low window-sill, a large-framed man back-lit, and regarded his faculty team.

'No, I don't believe so. What I've got in mind *is* in fact one of the AP texts.'

'Jeez, not *King Lear*!'

'Nope. But close. Webster.'

Mr Howard's colleagues gave a collective gasp and all began speaking at once.

'Not *The Duchess of Malfi*?' hooted David.

Mr Howard cut across their jabberings.

'What's the big problem? Three, four or more who wanna perform it are studying it with me, *and* loving it, may I say. The rest of the cast will be fourteen-year-olds or Sophomores. I reckon it'll be the making of many of them. AND,' he continued, 'it needs only four girls: the Duchess, Cariola the maid, the old lady, and that slut Julia.'

'It's very demanding – for school kids, isn't it?' asked Mateusz.

'Yes. But demanding is good. AND,' added Mr Howard, ramming home his next argument, 'it's out of copyright, so we can cut, add, prune, invent, modernise – whatever we like. AND we have God knows how many copies in store, so it'll be cheap. Cheap – but classy.'

'And you've got time to direct it?' smiled Jeff.

'I have.'

'And you don't mind if it's the biggest fiasco since

Pearl Harbour?' said David.

'I don't.'

'And will the Theatre Studies people at St Philomena's *let* four girls come over to be in an end-of-semester horror show?'

'They will. I phoned yesterday. Besides, one of my kids in the Juniors knows two St Phil's girls who can't wait to come over to St Matthew's and be with lotsa new boys. Natural, huh?'

'OK, so we've got a bunch of ego-maniacs and some boy-mad groupies,' grunted David. Then, catching Louise's eye, he murmured, 'Sorry, Louise. Nothing against the gals. But what about costumes, the set, you know, all that.'

'Costumes from Stacey's over in Lower Manhattan as per usual,' replied Mr Howard, detaching himself from the window-sill and going over to a dry-board, 'and for period and setting I've had a brainwave. What are the play's main themes?'

'You mean, a poor virtuous woman hounded to death by her two evil brothers....?' said Louise.

'And....?'

'We don't all teach AP 17th century Eng Lit to Seniors,' murmured Harry Doyle, the TLA.

'OK, Harry. I didn't mean to sound like a wind-bag intellectual snob,' laughed Mr Howard. 'But in addition to the poor young Duchess being banished and murdered at the orders of her brothers, one of those brothers is a Cardinal of the Catholic Church, the other becomes a lycanthrope.'

'Popularly thought to happen to a guy who lusts after his own sister, eh?' said David.

'And a lycanthrope is…?' asked Harry.

'A werewolf, man. What an idea. And then there's the hired killer, Bosola, and the wicked Cardinal's mistress, Julia, and a big troupe of crazed loonies, which Webster would probably have borrowed from Bedlam, as Middleton did in *The Changeling.*'

'And – excuse me for being the ignorant hired help – what is Bedlam?' asked Harry.

'The St Bethlehem Hospital for the insane in London, England,' replied Mr Howard. 'You could hire loonies back then to caper at weddings and such-like, and Londoners would go along to chuck buns at them for entertainment, when they weren't at bear-baiting, cock-fighting, or at the theatre.'

'Nice lot,' grinned Jeff.

'So, I thought, don't let's have a load of kids in sagging tights, like in the usual private school's Shakespeares, but update the whole thing to a time of fascination with werewolfism, with gangster murders, with doubts about the Catholic Church's clerical hierarchy, with the rise of feminism – ie; to *now.*'

'Webster in modern dress?'

'Trendy, eh?' muttered Harry.

'Webster in Marvel comics, stylised, sorta *Blade Runner, Batman* modern dress. Long leather coats, high collars. Stunning frocks in silver. Lotsa metal.

Whaddya think?'

'And the set? Our stage is pretty trad, you know. Fine for debates, concerts....'

'Metal themed. With tiny black revolving rooms on castors, and mirrors everywhere.'

'And Webster's language?

'They'll master it – with cuts here and there.'

'I'll help,' twittered Louise. 'I quite like the sound of it.'

'Count me in, somewhere,' said Mateusz. David Lomax nodded. Jeff and Harry gave non-committal grunts.

The meeting of the six colleagues of the Faculty broke up. Mr Howard seemed to have gotten his way. *The Duchess* began rehearsals.

June: **PLAYS CHANGE LIVES**

Jem's diary lay open in front of him. In absorbed excitement, his eyes gleaming through his reading glasses, he was scribing a single letter against today's date. His heart beat unsteadily. Single letters appeared on several days of the week – some more than once.

Mon 6th: R

Tues 7th: A, R

Wed 8th: F, F

Jem had begun to write these in the week of April 6th - 12th and was still at it four weeks later. The satisfaction of counting them had not yet palled.

Next to him, Janek Franitza was also scribbling, but, unlike Jem's, his breathing was not shallow and unsteady; nor was his face flushed.

'Clarke. You DO know what you have to do?'

Mr Scott's tolerant voice suspended the biro in Jem's fingers.

'Oh! Ah, er….,' muttered Jem.

'I mean – you do understand the task?'

Jem's hand hovered over the diary, obscuring it.

'The task,' Jem replied. 'Certainly, Mr Scott. To – um – finish noting the chapter on tectonic plates and attempt exercise eleven. It's on the board, Sir.'

'Oh, I *know* it's on the board, Mr Clarke. After all, I put it there. I was hoping it might also go in your diary – as you've got it open – so you won't forget.

14

You seem to be stuck on one letter.'

'Sorry, Sir. I – I won't forget, Sir. I'll pop it down now.'

'Pop away, boyo.'

Honestly, thought Jem, I must get a c-o-m-p-l-e-t-e and utter grip on myself, or someone's going to poke their nose in and start asking questions. Why ARE you putting letters against dates in your diary, Clarke? Why an R? What's with the A? And why an F? Secret code, Clarke? Mind you, he thought, who would care? No one is all that intrigued by other peoples' little mysteries. Even Janek (who had sat next to Jem in every lesson since their Freshman year, and, now they had moved up into 11th grade, did some topics of the IB with him) had passed no comment, and he must have seen now and then over the last four weeks. The thought of anyone knowing made Jem writhe and go hot and cold with horror, even though he couldn't stop himself adding an R, or an A, or an F and keeping a running tally of each. He had, while ornamenting one of them, before Mr Scott's interruption, been mulling over the steady change from all As, to As and Rs, and recently to Fs. Whatever the letters meant to him, they brought a flush to his oval face and a glister to his eyes.

As the Geography class came to its end, Jem began to allow the tang of anticipation – which he had repressed since waking up at home that morning – to rise in him.

Rehearsal.

'See you tomorrow, Jan,' he said to the reserved, quiet Pole, whose company, seated always at his left, was as familiar as the clothes he wore. He slipped the diary into his trouser pocket and grabbed up his bag.

'And it was exercise eleven, Clarke,' came Scotty's ironic voice.

'About plate tectonics, Mr Scott, Sir. I'll be doing it at home after rehearsal.'

'Oh, re*hear*sal,' said Mr Scott, with just that top-note of disparagement which Geography and Physical Education teachers almost always managed to inject into a reference to the high school play. It was, Jem thought, as if he'd said, 'Oh, *hair*-dressing.'

The hall was dark, its drapes pulled against the glaring sun. Dim paintings of former alumni stared down from the rear wall, the grand piano gleamed, a savoury whiff hung in the air – a fading bouquet of pizza – for, since recent rapid expansion, the auditorium had been pressed into service as a secondary canteen for eighth and ninth grade.

Jem was the first of the cast to arrive. Dragging a chair from the stacks of ten, he placed it in the centre of the shiny floor and sat astride it, his folded arms along the top, his chin resting on them.

Ahead of him was the stage-set.

He had helped to heave much of it into place. He had secured permission to miss lessons (some of them with Scotty) to help Mr Lomax to paint the jet-black frontage. A prosaic eye would have taken in the superannuated gloss-black doors with their faux-Victorian etched glass, $10 each in a housebreaker's sale, the sheets of plasticised garden mirror, the heavy gilt throne cut from spare timber in the Craft Rooms, the lighting gel covering the pointy Gothick apertures at the back, the swivelling, rubber wheels at the bases of three matt-black rotating room sets and calculated it at two hundred dollars the lot.

To Jem's eye, twinkling like a water-sprite's in the curtained gloom, it was his new world and he loved it. His clear-complexioned face resting lightly on his arms, Jem gave himself up to the happiest of reveries, and let images of what that stage meant to him circle in his mind.

First was his part.

Julia.

John Webster wrote The *Duchess of Malfi,* after the poorly-received *The White Devil,* sometime in 1613 for The King's Men's Company, and it was first performed in the theatre at Blackfriars. The plot, as Mr Howard had explained to his young cast, had come from the true story of Giovanna d'Aragona who had married, in 1490, aged twelve, the heir to the Dukedom of Amalfi. When he died, the Duchess, still young, had, secretly because her brothers despised his low social status, fallen in love with her major-domo,

Antonio Bologna. Astonishingly, their later marriage was kept secret for years, as was the birth of children. The Duchess disappeared and Antonio, after being exiled, was murdered. Matteo Bandello wrote the tale up in his *Novelle* of 1554, then Francois de Belleforest recounted it in *Histoires Tragiques,* the first to make it a story of a woman murdered by her own brothers. William Painter's *The Palace of Pleasure,* printed in English in 1567, was no doubt the version that Webster read, and upon which his play was based.

Mr Howard had impressed on the cast that it had been Webster who had painted the Duchess as a girl of purity and integrity, who had created the monstrously evil brothers – with a not untypical tilt at the Catholic church, so unpopular in England since the Gunpowder Plot against James I – and who made so much of the complex assassin, Bosola. Webster also was the first to include *the lustful Julia*, as he called her, married to the impotent Castruchio, mistress to the Cardinal, and moral counterpoint to the Duchess.

'I think it's going be necessary,' Mr Howard had said, 'to have not just one but two drag parts this year.' He spoke in his nearly British Bostonian voice, humorous and authoritative, which Jem rather admired. The boys assembled for auditions back then in January had given each other sidelong startled glances. The two young ladies who had come over from St Philomena's Girls' Catholic high school, also looked surprised. 'It's this dance and variety evening in the final semester,' Mr Howard had explained. 'It's taken virtually every girl who isn't a cripple or who has identity problems or a speech impediment, or all three – except, of course, you *very* welcome poppets,' he had added, as usual well aware of the mixture of exasperation and amusement which his condescension brought about in his girl actors. 'So – there are, for this year, some opportunities for those guys among you who are never happier than when snuggling into panti-hose and strapping on the English Faculty's size J bra.'

Julia.

That's how it had started – partly a joke, partly expediency.

As auditions had gone on, Aisha Keating, a Senior with exams in the summer, had landed the part of the Duchess, and Rosa Voss, a year younger, who wanted a small role, the part of Cariola, her maid. As it turned out, a third girl, Susie, who had originally turned up, had done so in the hope of working backstage with the boys' lighting and stage team.

And then had come Jem's moment.

'Jem Clarke, dear thespian,' Mr Howard had drawled. 'I do remember what fun you were as Mrs Joe in your chunk of *Great Expectations*.' Jem had been thirteen in 8th grade at the time of that end-of-term Christmas Drama competition. 'Yup. You've got a clear voice, and that's half the battle. Can you have a falsetto go at Julia? Don't strain if you find it hard to sustain a high screech. But just see how it goes. It's how they did it in Webster's time. No gals.'

To his own surprise, Jem had read two of Julia's scenes, including that of her death, with such lascivious vividness that the others had clapped him.

'Wow,' Mr Howard had murmured. 'Well, we've got our Julia then. You won't recognise yourself, Jem, when we've finished with you; tumbling wig, our giant Marilyn....'

'Marilyn, Sir?'

'Our Monro. The most stunning bra in the cosmos – well, in the Drama cupboard – and lashings of war paint. I think we can say you're gonna look sexy and G for gorgeous.'

For a moment, Jem had wondered whether he wanted to look like a gorgeous woman, but that spatter of applause had worked a small transformation in him. For another moment, as the applause died away, Jem had wondered if it was quite normal and right for Mr Howard to think of describing him – a boy pupil – as sexy and gorgeous, but his matter-of-fact tone and obvious admiration were reassuring; and they too worked a little transformation of their own. Julia's was not, perhaps, a very big part, but it was a challenge for a boy, and Jem saw himself bowing complacently in front of an amazed audience.

That *would* be rather wonderful!

There was, as Mr Howard had announced earlier, another drag act in the play: the part of an old hideous woman insulted by Bosola. Mr Howard had thought of cutting her, but Bosola's cruel taunts were, he felt, necessary to establish that character's malign presence. A 12th grade Senior, Greg McManus, who had been already given the part of Delio, had cackled and grimaced amusingly, and he too had been enthusiastically clapped. Jem, therefore, did not have to feel alone about cross-dressing. Since that time, Jem had learned Julia's lines, and found no discomfort in being the play's slut.

On a damp day in May, when Act V, scene ii came to an end, Mr Howard had suddenly spun on his heel, clapped a hand to his bow, gave a great whoop and cried,

'My God! I'm a genius!' He had then shouted, 'Jem! Jem! Come over to the piano, I want to try something out.'

Jem had swayed over to the piano and draped himself on it. He was aware, in the oddest way, that there was both a Julia and a Jem in his personality nowadays. Mr Howard's eyes, he felt, were appraising him in a manner difficult to define: friendly, admiring, amused, tolerant, protective – perhaps what might have been ordinarily expected from a teacher towards a favourite pupil – but with just a whiff of something warm, intimate even, onto which Jem couldn't quite latch. The Julia in him seemed to react with natural flirtatiousness to that whiff, in spite of other instincts.

'I've had a completely, but *completely* brilliant idea, Jem, though I say it myself,' smiled Mr Howard. 'How are you on sleight-of-hand movements?'

'Well, I can do a few card-tricks, Mr Howard, but....'

'When the Cardinal gives you the Bible to kiss, Webster assumes that poison on it kills you. But how would it be if we used the same idea as in *The White Devil*?'

'Um, what idea, Sir....?'

'I forgot you haven't studied Webster's other great play. Well, Clarkie,' – sometimes Mr Howard called Jem Clarkie, which Jem liked very much – 'I think we have the makings of a sensational *coup de theatre* if you can pull it off.'

'How do you mean?'

'In that other play, a girl kisses the painting of the man she loves and her face sticks to it and is eaten away by acid. At least, that's what happened when I last saw a production of it off-Broadway. So – how would it be if the Bible eats away your face? You would need to kiss it with your back turned away, then, with some sorta trick of the hand, bring from inside the Bible part of a mask to clap onto your face – and that mask would be a face eaten away by acid.'

'Ugh, Sir!' squealed Aisha and Rosa. 'Gross!'

'But effective – if it works,' smiled Mr Howard.

Jem smiled with that intelligent humour which Mr Howard found so appealing.

'I guess I don't mind trying that, Mr Howard.'

'OK – but how about my *other* idea? You're so realistic as a girl that I thought: suppose we put you down on the programme under a different name....?'

'What? Totally different....?'

'No, no. say, an anagram of your name... Oh, like, like...'

Mr Howard paused, faced with the difficulty of thinking of anagram of Jem Clarke. Clea Krmej seemed forced, as did the masculine Kel McJame. And nothing better came to mind.

Jem's forehead wrinkled.

'What about my middle names?' he asked. 'They're Oliver and Andrew, after my grandfathers,' he added, as if to excuse them.

'God, that's lot more vowels. Wait! I've got it! Let's just use the O and A. Er, what about Cleo Rajmeka?'

'What about Cleo Jakemar, Sir? That sounds less Bulgarian or something.'

'Cleo Jakemar? Yeah, it sure sounds actress. How brilliant of you, Jem. Okay, so Cleo Jakemar it is, and we put it on the programme to *totally* convince the audience that you are a girl...'

'All right by me, Sir.'

'And you have a frantic, gasping, hysterical death.

We might cut some of the lines after *You are poisoned by that book. Because I knew you could not keep my counsel, I have bound you to it by death.* And have you writhing on the ground trying to tear the Bible from your mouth before you have that vision of going to Hell, *Oh! I go, I know not where.*'

Aisha wrinkled her brows. As the cast's only Afro-American, she had to keep her end up.

'Hm. It's a lot more dramatic than my death.'

Mr Howard looked distressed. She was a lovely girl, but he hoped she wasn't going to be ornery.

'But you've got a long, long death, my dear. The executioners strangle you, then Bosola orders your children to be strangled.'

'Yes, but then Cariola fights and scratches and screams *I will not die. I must not. If you kill me now I am damned. I have not been to confession these two years* – and then Bosola's executioners throttle her. That's a good stage death too, while I…..'

'You remain alive for a hundred and twenty lines, Aisha, gasping on the stage floor, and you have a death that is not despairing, remember, because you do not know Antonio is dead and you think the Pope has brought him back from exile. It fits what Webster wants from your part. What does Bosola call it…?'

'*Sacred innocence, that sweetly sleeps,*' quoted Riccardo, who played Bosola.

'Exactly,' said Mr Howard. 'All of a part with how you have portrayed her from the start, Aisha. Tears guaranteed from all around. Trust me.'

'OK, Sir.' Aisha's face relaxed into a smile.

'And as for Julia's death, it's just a bit of fun in the school play, you know. And I thought that when you take your bow, Jem, you might remove the wig and amaze the punters by showing that you're a guy, not a gal. Fun all round.'

After that rehearsal, Aisha came up to Jem and said,

'If your part's going to work, you'll need to be more than a pretty face, Jem. We haven't seen you in a frock yet. You'll need to have good legs, you know.'

Jem looked sharply at her. Was this a barbed comment, or not? After her recent objections to his death-scene, he couldn't be sure.

'What's it to you?'

'I think we ought to check. Come on. Pull up your trouser leg.' She crouched down in front of the chair he was on and, before he could stop her, had rolled up a trouser leg. Jem's skin responded with a shock to her fingers holding back the dark material to reveal his calf and knee. Mr Howard, catching what she was doing, ambled over.

'They're pretty good, Aisha, don't you agree?' he smiled. 'Jem'll be as lovely as you are, dear girl. Julia has to be quite a swinger. Of course, it'll be seeing him in tights that'll be the acid test.'

Jem had resisted a crazy, perverse impulse to ask Mr Howard if he thought his face was also as attractive as a girl's, but, six weeks on – and this seemed to date from those few exchanged phrases – it really did matter to him that Mr Howard considered him – how could he put it? – appealing. Julia's ways had (and Jem no longer felt ashamed of how much he liked them) become ever more dominant in him.

Riccardo Parisi was a Senior at the end of his time at the school. He had taken the great part of Bosola after considerable thought and debate with his teachers about the impact it might have on his examination performance. Mr Howard, who taught him English Literature, had persuaded him that actually being in one's set text could only enhance one's understanding of it. It had been an amusing moment of irony in audition to find out that Riccardo, an Italian, was best at playing that ultimate Italian villain, Bosola. Joey Docherty and Liam Madden, Juniors who had landed the Cardinal and Francisco, the evil brothers, were both Irish.

Jem had suggested they make something of this.

'Couldn't they really put on the Oirish?'

'I suppose they could, but…'

'Begorrah and begob, it'll come tremenjus easy to me, Sorr. 'Tis how me grand-daddy speaks….,' said Liam.

'When he's had a few, bejeezus,' grinned Joey.

'Hm. Let me think about it. I like the idea – if it doesn't crucify Webster too much, begob.'

'Mind you, Irish people aren't automatically funny-farm types, Sir,' said Joey.

'Point taken, Mr Docherty,' said Mr Howard. 'Above all, the two wicked brothers must *not* be comic figures. That would screw Webster's theme completely.'

'You mean it would tennis-balls up the play completely?'

'I surely do.'

Whenever members of the cast appeared in the auditorium together, they would cry, *'We are the stars' tennis-balls!'* – a line from the play, and the sort of in-joke which made life at rehearsal so absorbing. The ordinary grind of high school seemed to be merely a tame diversion from the main purpose of existence: the preparing of *The Duchess of Malfi* for performance at the end of the academic year.

Rick, as Bosola, had assumed a large importance in Jem's life. Jem had worked to differentiate his everyday, easy-going side from his voluptuous Julia side. He had begun to incorporate, quite naturally, however, such important female mannerisms as keeping his knees together when seated, letting his legs fall naturally at an angle to the floor, to flutter his hand helplessly, and to peer up, shyly, under lowered eyelashes. These were directed at the Cardinal, upon whose arm Julia's hand fell, towards whom she swayed sinuously across the wide stage, in whose embrace she draped herself, then to lie back on the set's day-bed – a siren adulteress, and, later in the play, directed at Bosola, whom she seduces, feigning that she has had a love-potion put into her drink.

Jem only partly analysed the various emotions these stage contortions generated in him. In fact, if he had been asked, he would have said it was all a huge joke – guys fooling around, having fun – but on one occasion he was genuinely surprised to feel quite aroused in Rick's tough grasp, looking up with parted lips into Rick's brown eyes.

That was when an R began to appear in Jem's diary, day after day, keeping a tally of the times he submitted to secret self-pleasuring while fantasising about doing it with Rick Parisi. Sometimes he asked himself: what the hell am I up to? But his consciousness of possessing an approved figure, powerful drag-acting ability and the undivided attentions of Mr Howard and Rick at least three times a week at rehearsals, prevented him from examination of changes being wrought in him. It was easier to bathe in honey.

The darkly menacing set glowered in the auditorium and Jem continued to gaze at it – alone with his readiness to become Julia again.

His right hand slipped from the chair back and he

laid it on his leg. His eyes closed. For a moment he smelt Rick's jacket and the scent of his unsubtle Brut after-shave – or fancied that he did. Then the image was overlaid by that *other* particular moment when Aisha had kissed his lips.

The cast followed Mr Howard's absolute insistence on a chronological pattern of rehearsal for his plays. Not for old Howard the trendy drama teacher's method of taking bits from here and there, exploring the characters and only bringing it all together in the last week.

'Jumping Jehosaphat!' he had exclaimed when early in rehearsals Liam Madden had asked whether there would be any time given over to explorative extemporisation of one character with another in situations outside the plot. 'We're not on some kind of Brechtian actors' philosophy course for pseuds and St Matthew's is not The Royal Shakespeare Company. I'm a simple English teacher and you're a pack of brats who will go on discovering subtleties, even in a creaky old revenge melo like this, right up to the last performance. I'm not risking any of you not knowing the story-line, either. We'll rehearse pages 1 through 6, then 7 through 12, then 13 through 18 *ad infinitum*. Then you'll know where you are, when to come on, when to go off.'

Aisha and Rosa were on different stages of elective Theatre Studies for Advanced Placement exams, and had been studying modern theatre, starting with Christopher Fry and going on to Sam Beckett and Caryl Churchill. They had started *The Duchess of Malfi*, an old play by someone far less famous than Shakespeare, with every appearance of slumming. What had drawn them in was that St Philomena's in Flushing, a quick bus ride away, had no tradition of end of semester theatrical productions. In fact, Aisha had informed Mr Howard that their Drama teacher was of the opinion that the chief interface was not between play and its audience, but between actors and script. Mr Howard had guffawed shortly but given no comment.

Yet, thought Jem, there was something in both opinions. Only last week had he grasped the point of Julia's line in Act I, *Your laughter is my pity* after Delio had made a joke about her husband Castruchio not having *a good back.* Mr Howard had gently suggested that it should be spoken directly out to audience. Of Course! It generated pity for Julia's sexual frustrations, and, as the point that Castruchio, in spite of *pitifully sore buttocks*, was oftener riding his horse than his young wife, made a nice theatrical pun.

Mr Howard succeeded in teaching his cast four truths: (a) Nothing is easy, (b) There's always more to everything than at first appears, (c) Actors should not shuffle about when speaking and (d) Inconsequential conversation in plays is harder to master than long speeches.

'Anyone can stand, tights sagging round their ass, ruff sticking out, and spout *Is this a dagger I see before me?* or *To be or not to be? That is the question.* And they always get away with it in school plays. Parents don't expect Big Will or anyone else in the 17th century to make sense anyway; they just congratulate themselves that their kid is at a school which does the Bard for its end of year play. To have parents crying, "That was brilliant! You'd never have thought it a high school play – it was as good as Broadway!" you *have* to master timing and know when to be still and pause.'

And, thought Jem, after he'd told us that….she….Aisha kissed me. We'd just got to that moment in Act IV when she cries *What hideous noise was that?* and Cariola sees *the wild consort of madmen* and we stopped for the day, and the lights went out, and she put her arms around my neck. What did she whisper in the dark? 'You are rather a darling, Jem….. a darling'…. And she lent right into me…. in the blackout….and her lips touched mine…. She pressed them hard…. Her lips were sherbert and plump-feeling…. Her tongue flickered…. In my mouth…. Inside it….

Jem felt a familiar excitement rising. He realised that his breath was coming rapidly. Rick's hard arms, then Aisha's kiss drifted one after another through his thoughts. I must be excited by dark skin, he thought.

He considered the letters – what they meant. Those As, those Rs. Suppose Rick and Aisha got to know too? Would they be excited too if he were to confide in them – in Julia's voice, so much huskier and more full of desire than his own....?

'Julia,' he whispered, feeling his lips rounding, pouting on the 'u'. He ran his tongue over them, his hand stroking his thigh. 'J-u-l-i-a. Oh, Julia....'

Slam!

The auditorium doors opened and Rick (Bosola), Liam (Ferdinand), Joey (The Cardinal), Mat (Antonio), Greg (Old Lady and Delio), Tony (Malateste and A Doctor), Peter (Pescara), Guy (Silvio), Dominik (Castruchio), Mike (Roderigo) and the prompter, Pharhad, tramped in. The various 10th grade sophomores whom Mr Howard was using as crowds, Lords, Madmen, Pilgrims, and Executioners were not required at every rehearsal, so that the main characters could concentrate on their scenes without hangers-on becoming bored – and noisy.

'You're early, Jem,' cried Dominik.

Rick sought his eyes and winked.

'Old Howard's on his way,' said Greg. 'He's just taking some books up to Faculty.'

'Why are you in the dark, man? Hey, Pharhad, put the lights on.'

In the open doorway the girls were suddenly framed. They came forward, arm in arm.

'Hey, Jem,' said Rosa.

'Jem darling,' smiled Aisha. She ruffled his hair.

Jem grinned back at them all. He got to his feet circumspectly. The violent desire he had felt to go into the foyer washrooms, and relieve that surge of excitement, ebbed away. He stood behind the chair, holding the back closely to him casually while his tensions died.

The little cast – his fellow conspirators, closest to him in all the world – regarded him.

'Act II, scene iii to the end of the act, isn't it?' he asked.

OK. First came this delight of rehearsal and Julia's part in it; but he promised himself the most luxurious abandonment to his fantasies as soon as he got home.

June : SOME OF MR HOWARD'S MANY DIFFICULTIES

Having put his annotated copy of *Macbeth,* grade-book and a clutch of essays onto his cluttered desk, Mr Howard reached up to his top shelf for a Lipton's tea-bag. He was about to carry it next door to get his mug and hot water from the new device in the Faculty kitchenette, the EVABOYL, when the constrained voice of Louise Carrbridge wavered into his ear like the sighing of breezes over an upland graveyard.

'Mon, you couldn't spare one of those, could you? My throat is frightfully dry and I've run out.'

Mr Howard waved a hand at the box,

'Sure, Louise. Help yourself.'

'And, Mon, do you need me for tonight's rehearsal? I think you said you might, but I can't remember.'

Mr Howard looked into her face. What a pretty girl she is – or rather, would be, if she didn't have that permanent expression of strain and self-doubt. He hardly liked to tell her that of *course* she was damn well needed. She had volunteered to help with costumes, had she not? – and it was costume afternoon for trying out what the school possessed, *and* he wanted a woman's touch where make-up, dresses and buying tights were concerned.

'Not the whole thing, Louise. But you were going

to bring some suits and coats and hats over from Theatre Studies and decide who we're taking to Stacey's tomorrow.'

'Is it tomorrow? Oh God, thank God you reminded me, Mon. I haven't let Harry Doyle know. Do you think he'll be able to cover my classes? It's rushed up terribly quickly, hasn't it?'

'The show is only a month off, Louise. In fact, four weeks today is the penultimate night.'

'Gosh. It's like *Chariots of Fire*, isn't it?'

'Is it? I guess I didn't get round to seeing that one. I sorta missed it. It'll be doing the rounds in art movie theatres for ever. I'll catch it one day.'

'It's very good, Mon.'

'Right. Well, tea now, and then off to Amalfi. They're waiting.'

'Sorry. Sorry. I'm wittering, aren't I? Have you arranged your lesson cover for tomorrow?'

'I have. I thought we'd take a few representative catch-all size boys and the two girls and let them do the trying out for the whole cast. I've booked a minibus to get the stuff back. All you need to tomorrow is to meet us at nine by the statue.'

'I'd better set work. Thank God I've only got two 8th grade lessons over in the Junior High; the 11th grade can write essays. I'm sure Harry can help out. He's still in the TLA office. I'll go see him now. Good job you put it back in my mind. I'm sorry to be a drag, Mon.'

'Typical girlie-type incompetence, Louise. Think nothing of it,' smiled Mr Howard. 'See you in the theatre – just for twenty mins or so – when you've had your tea.' He turned back at the door. 'And don't forget you were going to bring a costume or two. It would save us dough at Stacey's if we can fit some of them out.'

With his *America Kicks World Ass* mug in his hand, Mr Howard pushed open the double doors and came into the auditorium.

'Afternoon, Luvvies!' he cried. 'All here, I see. Please – no courtship, no ceremony. No need to abase yourselves as if in the presence of a God. Resist urges you have to throw yourselves at my feet. Quite unnecessary. Rosa – I take your adoration for granted. Quite *de trop,* Aisha – I know your secret yearnings.'

The cast grinned, as they always did. Mr Howard was popular. None noticed that, in spite of his jocular greetings to the girls, it was Jem's eye that he sought. And he met it, too, for Jem – by now quite himself – returned his glance with that peculiar quick quality which Mr Howard found it difficult to pin down, but liked so much. Jem was never over-familiar, in the cheeky sixteen-year-old's manner, but he seemed to infuse into his exchanged looks a sort of....closeness, a sort of....intimacy and understanding which, every time it happened, gave Mr Howard the illusion that he and Jem were alone in the room. This non-verbal communication had grown into a frequent exchange, whether at rehearsal or not.

As Chair of English Faculty, Mr Howard had tried – subtly, he hoped – to get Jem transferred, as he went from up to 11th grade, into his own English class, although that was a highly unusual thing to do. Back in February, he had come up with the idea that the English sets should be of equal size; that was what had worked the trick, and Jem, with his pal Janek Franitza, had moved from Jeff's class of 12 to Mr Howard's of 8. With fluttering heart, he often went miles out of his way to pass rooms from which he knew Jem was about to emerge – seeking thirstily that intimate exchange of eyes.

He knew that he was in for a bad time again. Monson Howard – so named because his parents believed they had conceived him while honeymooning on a trek in the Appalachians at what would become the start point of the Hundred Mile Wilderness in Maine at Monson – was not, as most of St Matthew's believed, an American. He had been born in Toronto, Canada; his father was Glaswegian Scots and his mother Canadian, from far away in Vancouver. But they had emigrated to the 'States, and he had been schooled in Bangor, Maine and had gone on to Boston University. American demotic had had not quite obliterated the tell-tale Canadian pronouncement of 'about' and 'out', but to most of his colleagues, and in Queens at any rate, he was thought to speak like a classy New Englander.

A spell in the seminary at Georgetown to train for the Catholic priesthood had caused him surprising pain. A young man of deep religious conviction, he had been sure that he had a vocation since his late teens. But, as happened to so many others, his deepest wishes foundered on his deepest emotions. Fleeing from self-knowledge, he left before his final vows and married a nurse from Virginia. She desired to go home to Roanoke, so, as a couple they settled there for a short, disastrous time, in which he discovered that she slept around. He suffered yet another blow to his self-esteem and his convictions.

He had done his training as a teacher in the state, but, as his marriage fell apart, he felt he had to put several hundred miles between his treacherous wife and himself. He got secondment at a public school in New Jersey, then, keen to serve in the Catholic school sector, a post in the English Faculty at St Matthew's, Queens. When Edmund O'Malley retired, Mon applied for, and got, the Chair of his subject. The popular Senior high was expanding and developing a large academic 12th grade year, and Mon found that his love of the English classics: Chaucer, Shakespeare, Milton, Pope, Keats, Wordsworth, Tennyson & Co made him the man to handle the Advanced Placement courses in the Senior years. He loved his job and he hadn't seen his wife for seventeen years. She had never contacted him about the divorce, which he knew, as a Catholic he could never hope to have. Annulment was possible, perhaps, but was difficult to get. Mon Howard did not miss intimate life with a woman and his Chair of Faculty post and his frequent drama productions absorbed most of his thoughts and energy.

He would have been utterly happy had it not been for Jem Clarke.

When he had been a seminarian, Mon had had trouble with that particular bugbear of aspirants to the Catholic priesthood: celibacy. It was never that he desired to leave the precincts after lights out and daggle after girls in the downtown bars and diners. He knew of one or two who did, but not him. Never that. His difficulty lay with other young men who were on the course with him.

A completely honest person, Mon Howard had, in recent years, admitted two things about himself: firstly, that he was probably, no damn it, *definitely* homosexual; secondly, that his young wife Yvonne had slept around because he had not satisfied her as he should have done. There, he had said it. He had been a failure as a trainee priest and then as a husband because he was *queer*. And, oh, the relief of admitting it, facing it, even if only to one person – himself.

He liked the company of young men and boys. He warmed to their approbation, admiration, and he knew how to charm them into thinking him delightfully roguish and unconventional. Yes, yes, he had to admit it – he almost flirted with young men. He realised that he never looked at a girl in the room if there was a youth to look at instead. Oh God, yes, he used to murmur internally, I have always been excited by the beauty of boys. I can admire the loveliness of girls, as I might relate to a sunset; but I don't study the curve of limbs, the contour of face, the complexion and movement of any creature that is not a youth. I need to be in an all-boys' school.

In these periodic fits of 'facing himself', as he liked to put it, he realised how fatal to his teaching career would be the slightest hint of this; fatal too to his faith in his church and its teachings, if he let his secret thoughts hold forth too loudly in his internal debating chamber. And he did debate the unfairness of things sometimes. There were many years to go before same-sex marriage, gay pride and greater tolerance and understanding later in a new century would go some way to soothing the agony of the hidden.

So he went to Mass regularly at the Jesuit Church in Manhattan, boyish, modish, good looking for his years, devout, compassionate in eye and face; on friendly terms with the Choir Master, with three or four other men who were teachers in the Catholic school sector; friendly too with several of the Jesuit priests at the church; happy to spend weekends in religious retreat with the Benedictines at Hartford Abbey in Connecticut, or to take occasional trips abroad to Europe with groups of elderly bookish acquaintances.

Sometimes he saw the tightrope he walked: the witch-hunt of newspapers, the infrequent public hysteria about paedophilia (not yet associated strongly with the Catholic church, as was to happen in later years), the abuse and ridiculing of old queens in public places who couldn't keep their hands to themselves. Then his private categorising of the beauties of some of his pupils withered away. Then he forced himself to remember that (a) he was still technically married, (b) that he was '*in statu parenti*' to other peoples' children, (c) that the Pope condemned any form of homosexual expression as disordered and a grave sin, (d) that he could lose his livelihood and (e) that he wasn't like that, anyway.

When he appointed Louise Carrbridge to the Faculty – the only woman the St Matthew's Senior High English team had ever had – he did so partly on the grounds that her unusual beauty might later tempt him into a healthy affair with her. But that had been in one of those increasingly rare periods of denial of his real state and, moreover, now he had got to know her, he realised that she too had private problems of her own, and something in him shrank from the thought of intimacy deeper than that of supplying her with occasional tea-bags.

Often he knew he was morbidly unfair on himself. A chronic, perceptive loneliness – except during semesters – and a grown-up understanding of the world, told him that, by comparison with many, he was a good, decent, moral person. In fact, he had recently come to believe that it wasn't adolescent males in general whom he found attractive and whom he desired. It was only one of them: Jem Clarke. This seemed an important distinction. For a start this sort of – hey, call it by its name – this sort of *love* had only affected him three times before in his life. There had been his hopeless, violent attraction to Patrick at Bangor State High. He had been eighteen and Patrick fifteen – and nothing had happened, except contrived meetings and solitary desperate nights in his cubicle in the agony of the unrequited. And there had been Clive at the seminary. They had talked together about their feelings night after night, the conversation irresistibly growing more focussed on the physical, until each had retired to his cell-like room to release pent-up yearnings. These releases were about the only events that Mon Howard remembered from his priestly training. Only once had Clive tried to touch Mon and their eyes had met, and, yes....yes – it had to be admitted – something would have happened, had not Father Swire barged in with one of his funny looks and some nonsense about a change in lecture times. Old Peeping Tom!

Finally – at St Matthew's – had been that very bad time over James. Eight years ago! My God, the boy must now be twenty-six!

Patrick, Clive and James. Only three violent loves

– and none consummated, all unrequited, all lost. Oh, and Yvonne – the bitch. Mon supposed he had once loved her, but not as he loved his three young men. In some difficult to define way she couldn't have entered the Pantheon, even if she hadn't betrayed him. And wasn't it strange? Of all of them, only with her had he experienced physical love. But the fantasies he had entertained for the others had all the vivacity, all the fireworks that his marriage duties had lacked. When alone with himself and with *their* images, he had sometimes been taken to a strange Eden of nerves, a communion so intense that he had cried aloud in painful joy and had later sobbed as if the cauterising of tears would rip frustration and thwarted completeness from his brain.

And his church? He knew too well that such feelings, such actions were regarded as grave sin – but the greater part of him did not believe they were sinful. He reasoned that, in Stone Age times, men ate to stay alive, clothed to stay warm, walked to follow prey, impregnated women to maintain the species. Now, thousands of years later, food had become a matter of choice and delight; clothing the subject of fashion, design and ornament; transport the choice between sedans, coupes, pick-ups, motorcycles, Rolls Royces to Plymouths. Why should the reproductive urge not be regarded in the same light – mulled over, subject to variation and dreams and experiment? Mankind had grown up and developed tastes, choices, subtleties. The Catholic Church did not see the gourmet, at the wheel of his Aston-Martin, in his high-end branded leisurewear, as a sinner. Why, reasoned Mon, should it see his dreams of union and his personal delight in images of his loved youths as worthy of damnation?

Then – he wasn't sure when – then, like his young parents breasting the clean upper slopes of a mountain and leaving the incult forest behind, it had all stopped. All of it: the longing, the lonely physical release, the guilt.

Patrick, his sweetest memory of all, with shaded eyes under long, dark lashes and smooth, white skin, Clive, a sense of a laughing, ironic face and a sturdy frame, James, forgotten, except in a curling photo on his desk – and all three so obviously changed by time that they existed in picture-form only, like Snow White in her cartoon.

It had all stopped – and Mr Howard, calm, amusing, acerbic (in a cuddly, non-threatening way), adept at explaining the great canon of Eng Lit, and dedicated to producing at least one school play a year, had arrived in paradise. It was a slightly tame one, perhaps: a haven of calm, selective TV viewing, Mass with the Jesuits, good meals with his few close friends in publishing and education, being something of a *doyen* to an increasingly numerous young staff at St Matthew's High, driving his rare British Morgan sports car, becoming interested in Democratic party

44

politics; a paradise of low-level ease.

But then Jem Clarke had bobbed up, unheralded, unexpected, dressing as Julia in *The Duchess of Malfi,* and had now become necessary to him, and it was beginning all over again.

'Act II, scene iii, isn't it, Sir?' someone was saying.

'Are any costumes going to be tried out today, Sir?'

'Yup,' said Mr Howard. 'Now, how about getting that curtain straight and moving the table out from the wall? That'll be part of the setting.'

'Shall I put some stage lights on, Mr Howard?' asked Pharhad. 'It helps me read the prompts, Sir, behind the flat.'

'There shouldn't *be* nearly sixty prompts per act for you to read by this stage,' grunted Mr Howard. 'Thank God my name's not on the programme.'

'What, Sir? Not on it anywhere?' cried Guy (Silvio).

'Nope. I'm having them printed with: *Director: Robert Mugabe* on them.'

Mt Howard saw, of course, Jem's appreciative smile directed at him. As usual, for a second, it seemed as if they were alone in the auditorium marvelling at the charming naivety of kids. 'Well, let's get going, shall we? I mean, we've got a whole three and a half weeks, thank God – so we're just not pushed for TIME, or anything.'

'Sir,' came Rick Parisi's grown-up, slightly drawling voice. 'I've really got a whole heap of revision to do for my next exam. Are we going to be long?'

'We need up to two in the morning, but I guess we'll stop at 5.15 as per usual. But I see what you're getting at. Let's start with your entry with a dark lantern. *Sure I did hear a woman shriek* – a soliloquy which I hope you know, Rick. Stand by, Cardinal, Delio and Julia. It'll rattle through if Pharhad doesn't have to read the whole act line-by-line first.'

Pharhad, sitting behind the glass screen at the back, heard his name, clicked on a dimmer pack and lifted a few lanterns, as yet unfocused, with his desk sliders.

There was a gasp from those of the cast on the stage and screwed-up eyes.

'Not *too* high, dear boy,' called Mr Howard. 'Let's (a) avoid skin cancer and (b) save the bulbs, shall we?'

As soon as the warm ambers at stage front centre, the blues of the rear wall and two strong par-cans at stage left and stage right came up, the whole, quite large and complex set of separate black rooms became the magical and self-sustaining place which had warmed Jem's mind so much when he had sat alone gazing at it in the gloom.

The stage! It made a world entire from nothing.

The cast were now starting from the beginning of

Act II. How young they looked under the lights. Even Riccardo's dark-shadowed Italian face was revealed in its postures, uncertainties, its helplessness. The other boys and the two girls, not matured by costume and stage make-up, touched Mon Howard with something lovely and fragrant he had once dreamed about and could no longer fully recall.

Babes in the wood. *See, see the little victims play, regardless of their fate.*

Jem, he believed, was – for a boy – genuinely lovely. His clear, oval face, the profile of nose and jaw, his happy, open smile and fine teeth, his clean brown hair, the poise of his tallish frame, the aura of contented involvement in his task, made Mon suddenly yearn to have a child like that of his own.

Youthful voices, interspersed by prompts, bounced off him. Oh, you lying bastard, he told himself. It's not as a father you are looking at him. Self-deluder. How can you *kid* yourself like this?

Yet there was not, at that instant, a shred of impurity in the protective urge he felt for the young human beings in front of him; just tenderness, and an understanding which had the sound of a sigh.

The Duchess of Malfi proceeded and Mon stared unseeing at his troupe, his script remaining unturned.

Clive, he knew, was a parish priest over on the West Coast in Sacramento. His wiry hair would be greying, perhaps going, and his figure thickened. He'd by fifty – no, forty-nine, this year, getting to be

an old man, sighed Mon inwardly, and all that I felt
for him came to nothing. Patrick, fragrant in the brain
as a summer's meadow, well now, he'd be just about
forty. Why had they ever lost touch? How criminal he
had been in permitting that sacred love to float away
on the ocean. He recalled again how, on his own
fortieth birthday, he had decided to spend hundreds,
thousands of dollars if necessary, to track Patrick
down and see him once more. Their old school in
Bangor had no record of where he had gone, but hey
– there's radio stations, there's detectives.....

Jem's clear voice, trilling in honey-smoke falsetto,
came to his ear: *You told me of a piteous wound in the
heart and a sick liver when you wooed me first.* Oh
yes, I had a piteous wound that first time – and it has
never healed, thought Mon; and his mind responded
to the Cardinal's retort, comparing his affection to
lightning. Terrifyingly deep love *is* like lightning; it
scorches, and the burn cannot heal....

Patrick would now look his age, wouldn't he?
Might he have stayed artificially boyish? Suppose if I
met him again I found I didn't – couldn't – love him
at all? And in vain Mon tried to recall exactly what
the boy he'd adored had looked like, but he got no
further than a heart-shaped, smooth-chinned face and
a crew-cut. He had seemed romantic in his cardigan
of the period and tight slacks. Mon tried to recreate
the precise sequence of nervous impulses that had
once over-loaded his brain whenever Patrick's image

jumped into it. But it was too long ago. Twenty-five years were just not bridgeable. However hard he strove to see Patrick's face and figure, he only saw Jem's.

With a jump, Mr Howard realised that the cast had finished Act II. He strode into the surround-glow of light.

"Darn good," he said. "I may have dropped off once or twice there, on account of hearing the deathless words of this play every other day for four months – but I say you did what you did when you oughta have done it, an' with no prompts."

'Erm, well, I prompted seventeen times, Sir,' said Pharhad, popping his dusky head round the stage-right wing.

'I didn't hear them, so it must be going pretty faultlessly. A credit to your director, I'd say.'

'To Robert Mugabe, Sir,' said Peter.

'To Robert Mugabe *at the moment.* You forget that Act IV stinks.'

'Can I shoot off now, Mr Howard?' murmured Riccardo. 'I guess I've a whole bunch of work I've got to do tonight.'

'Yeah, scram, Bosola – and don't forget you are required next Tuesday, precisely three weeks from curtain up.'

'Oh, yes, Sir.'

'And go over your lines for Act IV and V.'

'I will, Sir.'

Riccardo left. Only Mon Howard noticed Jem's eyes following his tall frame into the square of sunlight beyond the auditorium doors. Oh, that is interesting, he thought. That's something I've gotta think about.....that's....

He forced his attention back to the rehearsal.

His voice was easy, though his mind hummed.

'Okay, survivors. We can finish up to Act III, scene ii, line 227-ish without Bosola – and without Julia, which is lucky, because here is Miss Carrbridge to discuss costumes.'

Louise Carrbridge and Susie, the backstage volunteer, appeared in the foyer doorway clutching three carrier bags each.

'Oh, Mr Howard, I'm sorry I'm late,' came the familiar, indecisive voice. 'I've got a few things here.'

'Pharhad! House lights and save the stage lanterns. We'll pause for fifteen mins.'

The claustrophobic world of Webster's paranoid city state disappeared as unflattering neon tubes flickered on above them and everyone immediately looked tired and pale.

'What have we got here, then?'

'I – I've – we've brought over a couple of period dresses for Rosa, Aisha and Jem, of course, to try on, and a cardinal's red robe and a Shakespearean-style Hamlet-ish tunic for Bosola. Although I see he's not here. And some other bits and pieces.'

'No, he's gone. Not to worry. We'll try the tunic before we go to Stacey's tomorrow.'

'Can I help you put them out, Miss Carrbridge?' asked Jem.

'Oh, thank you, Jem. That would be a help.'

'I'll put these tables together and we'll have a flat surface for everything.'

With economy of action and typical good sense, Jem arranged the contents of the bags deftly along the tables: hats at one end, dresses and tunics in the middle, tights and accessories, including some slipper-like shoes, at the other end.

'Tiny little shoes,' he smiled. 'Like Cinderella's.'

'Size isn't everything, Jem,' smiled Louise, and then stopped, suddenly aware that she had nearly made a suggestive remark. Aisha and Rosa poked each other.

'Isn't it?' murmured Joey in Aisha's ear.

Louise blushed prettily, thought Mon. Poor girl.

'Help! Door!' came a shout from the foyer. Rosa and Susie ran over to pull the heavy doors back. Mr Lomax strode in holding up a tray full of little sandwiches and doughnuts.

'Thought the ravening wolves would like these, Mon,' he grinned. 'They're left over from the Principal's lunch for other Queens Top Dogs. They don't seem to like tuna or doughnuts.'

'Pity the whole cast isn't here. There's just *we few, we precious few*,' quoted Mon.

'More to go round then. Ain't all bad noos!'

David Lomax was chunky, reddish, loud, vital, laddish and unfailingly good-tempered. An ex-pupil of Mon's, he had been second in the Faculty for four of the eight years he had taught at St Matthew's. He was the one member of the team who could be relied on to help with the obvious and the non-obvious: what Mon called "the edu-ordure" which came their way from the Principal's office. 'Yeah, I sorta intercepted these going over to the Faculty lounge. Everyone's gone home, except you Luvvies, and there's no point in them curling up in the ice-box overnight. Come on, girls. C'mon Clarke, Miss Carrbridge. Have a doughnut!'

The remaining cast and Pharhad took two or three sandwiches and at least one doughnut each and perched on the edge of the stage to eat them.

'Hang on! I wanna take a photo!' cried Susie, who had constituted herself the chronicler of the production. Immediately Peter lay back on stage and balanced three tuna sandwiches on his forehead, Jem held a doughnut over his upturned mouth, Aisha and Rosa came together, shoulder to shoulder with genteel little fingers stuck out.

'And you, Mr Howard!' called Aisha.

Mon selected a doughnut.

'Make room, Jem,' said Rosa. 'Why don't you go between Jem and us, Sir?'

Mon Howard perched on the stage edge, a dangling

leg touching Jem's, his eyes turned to Jem's face where the sugar crystals from the doughnut were spangling his laughing lips.

My lips are nine inches from his. I wonder if he can scent me.

Partially despising himself and partially finding it stimulating – like dressing up for a ball – Mon had taken to sloshing on some Old Spice before meeting Jem at rehearsals. He feared terribly that Jem should find him unattractive. He stared at the bloom of Jem's cheek, the clean fall of his hair, the striking loveliness of his straight forehead and nose. More than anything he had wanted to do for twenty years, he yearned to lick the sugar crystals from those kind, mysteriously understanding lips. Lick….and feel the sweet wet sand of them crunch between his teeth.

What would they all say? What would Jem feel as my tongue followed the curve of his lips, licking….?

What would happen to me?

Aware of Mr Howard's eyes on him, Jem stopped laughing and turned to bring his gaze to meet his teacher's. Mon thought that he read at least a dozen messages in the boy's stare. Had something advanced or retreated in that moment?

Ping!

Susie's camera flashed and caught them all revealed in their thoughts and glances and actions – Jem and Mon Howard in the centre – and locked them up on film forever.

June : **LOUISE CARRBRIDGE, VIRGIN**

'Oh, I don't know, CoCo. I can't make up my mind. I mean – I've things to prepare and I've still got to get up at 6.15 tomorrow....'

Louise Carrbridge and CoCo D'Souza, her flat-mate and oldest friend, sat facing each other over a table at Wojtek's Polish café on Bleeker St. Louise cut precise chunks from the triangle of chocolate *sacher torte* she had asked for and CoCo sipped lemon tea from a glass in a metal cradle. They raised eyebrows at each other in the café's dim, artily distressed interior.

'You're the one who's made us late, dear heart. I've been sipping glass after glass, fearful of making a puddle on the floor, for over an hour. I've read *The New York Times* from cover to cover twice, including the sport.'

'I'm sorry, CoCo. Mr Howard asked me to help at rehearsal tonight. It just went on longer than I meant it to. I didn't get to Parson's Boulevard 'til well after five and it's sixteen stops to West 4th Street. It'd have been easier for *you* to meet *me*, as it happens, than the other way round.'

'Well, never mind. Are we going to Barnaby's, or aren't we? It's too late to get home and cook now, and I can't stand another KFC, pizza or something slithery from the deli, for at least a fortnight. Barnaby will have some decent eats.'

'I feel a bit tired, CoCo….'

'Why you don't tell your precious Mr Howard to stick himself up his own play script, I simply don't know. I mean, God, Louise, I thought the whole point of teaching – apart from having sixteen weeks holiday a year and getting poked by bookish History professors – was to get off work at 3.30 every day. If you go on slaving over your hot little boys until 5.30, you might as well be in the real world at a merchant bank or a realtor's.'

'I don't mind helping, CoCo. And it's all very well for you to sound all worldly-wise. I know darn well that you'd be revelling in it if you were at St Matthew's; the boys are so nice and it is fun doing the play – really it is. Mr Howard makes everything fun, I think. He has a sort of gift for it.'

'I wonder if, unbeknown to yourself, you're falling for this Daddy-O, Louise. Has he said, done or hinted at doing anything to you that gives you the impression he's interested?'

'Oh no, CoCo!' gasped Louise, blushing. 'What an idea! Mr Howard….why he's an old man, and, well, I never thought he….' Louise stopped, nearly understanding why it was absurd to think Mr Howard was attracted to her, but not understanding enough to make the final jump and see why he wasn't. 'He's just too dedicated to the boys.' She added lamely.

'Hm. Is he? I've got to meet this guy,' muttered

CoCo. She pushed her cup away. 'You are a difficult person to do things for, you know.'

'Honestly, CoCo, I'm grateful to you about Barnaby and everything, but I just don't feel....'

Louise looked up at her friend in her Princess Diana-ish way which was, in her case, shyness, and not at all coy. CoCo stared back, on the edge of an all too common exasperation. CoCo's father had come to America from Catholic Goa and married an Anglo-Indian. Privately Louise found CoCo strikingly beautiful and had done since those Senior High years at The Immaculate Conception in North Bergen where they had first become close.

CoCo held her friend's gaze and shook her head slowly.

'You've still got that problem, Louise, dearest one. You know you have.'

'Yes, but it's only been....'

'It's been two years. You've got to be brave and take the first step. And one of those steps is coming over to Barnaby's. If you don't like things, we'll just come on back early to the apartment, and that'll be that.'

'I'm a bore, I know,' sighed Louise. 'Thank God you're so nice and understanding. Without you I don't know what I'd have done.'

'Pals at dee-ar old Immac; pals for life, what, what?' grinned CoCo, putting on her funny Brit voice. 'I've said it a hundred times, but you should have experimented at sixteen like the rest of us nice convent gals. That's where your troubles began. Too virtuous for too long.'

'Well, it's hardly "troubles",' smiled Louise. But even as she framed the mild objection, she thought of her mother eagerly questioning her about the men at St Matthew's, her father patting her absently whenever her great failure was alluded to.

Aged just eighteen, Louise had left The Immaculate Conception Catholic High where she had been Head Girl and leader of The Apostleship of Prayer. She had exchanged New York for Salem, Massachusetts, entering the dwindling order of The Sisters of Perpetual Succour as a postulant nun. This order had struggled to maintain her own school and several others in the USA and Louise had sensed that it was fighting a losing battle against lack of vocations. Louise had made the classic mistake of the early twentieth century postulants: leaving the world before knowing anything of the world. Probably if the Sisters had not been so chronically reduced in number they would never have acceded to her request to become one of them at her age. By the 1980s, it was unusual for Roman Catholic male orders to allow young men to join straight from school. Too many broken vows and years of unhappiness lay along that road. Louise had been strongly religious (which pleased her Irish mother), never contemplating any other life than a nun's after the age of fifteen. She might have been influenced by the example of two of her aunts on her mother's side and by a Dominican friar on her father's. The joining of the order had not seemed to Louise the inexplicable walling-up that it appeared to her contemporaries. One of those was Chantal – CoCo – D'Souza who had done her best to dissuade her.

Then, in misery so acute she hadn't wanted to live, Louise had decided, at the age of twenty-two, that she had no vocation.

She had read English with Theology within the seminary as an external student of St Ignatius College, Harvard, and she had also learnt the job of nurse-sister. She had thought she would be good with the old and the dying, the convent nursing-home's main intake, but she found she was deluding herself. Age and sickness revolted her. Deep depression had begun to settle on her and, five weeks before her twenty-third birthday, in the year she was awarded her degree, she screwed up courage to tell her Mother Superior that she could not contemplate moving on towards her final vows. After that momentous decision, it had all been easy. The convent made no attempt, as she had feared, at insistence that she stayed, and, less than a month later, she was on her way back to New York.

She had no desire to go to her parents' house. To live once again with them in North Bergen seemed too much of a reversion to girlhood. It would have rammed home her wasted years too cruelly. The faithful Co-Co had immediately offered her a room in her little apartment in Jackson Heights, on Louise's insistence that they would share the rent as soon as the ex-nun found a job. She, unlike CoCo, began regularly to attend Mass at Our Lady of Mount Carmel. It was a sadness to her that CoCo had seemed to have fallen away from the faith, but she was wise enough not to reproach her, and hoped that CoCo might return through her example.

Louise enrolled, late, on a post-grad teacher-training course at The Institute in Manhattan – where she was thought attractive, if weird and reclusive. Her teaching practice, at a private girls' high school in Montclair and then in a boisterous co-ed public high in Yonkers over the Hudson, had been unexpectedly successful. She was kind and knowledgeable and not the pushover that her contemporaries had expected. Her lack of social life had left her with plenty of time for thorough preparation and assessment – and that made its own impression. And the key thing she had taken away from the Yonkers school was a liking for boys and their humour. The girls' high had, somehow, reminded her of the convent at Salem. At both schools she had found it easier to deal with children than with adults.

One legacy of her girlhood and postulant time she recognised as absurd: she was cripplingly shy with men. Some ex-nuns, realising that the current of their lives runs more freely down the channels of passion and self-expression than those of self-abnegation and prayer, become promiscuous when the door is opened. Louise was the other kind. At ease, confiding and sympathetic with kids and with her few women friends, she was idiotically tongue-tied with men – especially those young men friends of CoCo's who noisily visited the apartment specifically to meet her, or clamoured to take the two girls out to the movies.

One event remained like an alternating hot and cold douche in her memory: the AoT Christmas Ball. CoCo, who had graduated in Electrical Engineering at the Academy of Technology and was engaged in a two-year post-grad research assignment there, had asked the ex-nun to the thrash. It was Louise's first Christmas out of the convent and CoCo, eager to break the ice, had invited the nicest young man she knew at AoT and his best friend (who was between girls) to go with them. Such was her concern that Louise should enjoy herself that she paid for the tickets. The young men accepted gratefully, for, unlike CoCo, who was on a research grant, they were broke. The beginning of the evening had been a success. Louise had looked pretty and relaxed. She clearly interested CoCo's friend's friend, and he monopolised her in conversation and kept her plate and glass full.

When they started dancing, things began to go

wrong. Louise had little notion of disco but jigged away near him. Then the DJ put on *When a Man loves a Woman* and Louise's companion took her in his arms, held her to his chest, and smiled richly in her face. At one point he put his lips to her cheek and slid his hand down her waist towards her bottom. She scented the wine on his breath and his after-shave. She got panic-stricken and wriggled away with a choking cry. The young man asked what was wrong. Had he trodden on her toe? When he put his arm apologetically round her shoulder, she had screamed, lashed out, catching him a stinging blow across the face, run across the hall, barged into several couples, tripped, crashed to the floor, torn her dress, and stumbled sobbing down into the women's rest-rooms. CoCo, who had seen the flight, had dashed after her to give comfort. It was no good; Louise would not go back. In the end, gritting her teeth and dedicating it as another burnt offering on the altar of friendship, CoCo had taken Louise home and made tea. The next time she saw them, she had told the ball-goers that her flatmate was terrifically highly-strung and had not been well. A total freak-out and fiasco.

Louise had felt for weeks that she would never be able to hold her head up anywhere near AoT – anywhere on Manhattan Island, in fact – in case she was recognised. 'Quite right too!' had snapped CoCo, understandably put out.

They left Wojtek's and made their way back over

the river to the apartment. CoCo had gotten her own way and Louise began to put on her party dress (chosen for her by CoCo) and to apply make-up (CoCo's choice). CoCo barged into her room and perched on the bed.

'Well? Are you going to go on like this forever? You look as if you're going to a funeral.'

'Oh,' sighed Louise, brushing her long hair, 'I don't know. Sometimes I feel I don't belong anywhere now. I can't go back to the Order, but I don't seem to fit in out of it. Except at school. I thought that there I might, perhaps…..'

'The Order was *in* the world, wasn't it? You make it sound like Outpost 16 on Mars.'

'You know we were taught to think differently about things, CoCo. You remember….from school….'

'Huh. The Immac! I remember a load of drivel from the old biddies about the sins of the world. I didn't take much notice of that, as you know. What do you suppose God gave us the world for?'

'I don't mean to sound like a twisted prude, but it's just that…..' Louise tailed off.

'What do you suppose is going to *happen* at Barnaby's tonight?' asked CoCo.

'I don't know. You said there was this other guy….'

'Yes. There is this guy. His name's Josh. He's a friend of Barnaby's at Henderson Finance. He's not deformed or liable to vomit on you. He's not a certified rapist or woman-beater. He's just a nice, normal Joe who's happy to meet you *because*, Louise, I've said how nice and attractive you are.'

'But suppose…?'

'What?'

'Suppose he….?'

'What?'

'You know what I mean.'

'Suppose he finds you attractive? I hope he does. That's the point.'

'Well, what would happen?'

'While we're eating? Nothing. D'you think he'll want to poke you over the dessert?'

'CoCo!'

'What are you vapouring about?'

'But if he wanted to see me again?'

'If you like him, see him. If you don't, tell him to take a jump.'

'If I saw him, like, again on, say, a couple of dates, wouldn't he expect…..?'

'Yes, probably.'

'That's what I – I – think is – would be – a sin. Do you see?'

'He might not expect anything for a while, CoCo. Not all young men are uncontrollable fiends. But if you got fond of him, what is so sinful? Murder, yup; torture, OK; slave-trafficking, naturally; stealing, depends what it is – I wouldn't count a cookie, but a car or a $50 dollar bill, but….'

'You know what I mean.'

'Sex.'

'Yes, yes. Sex. We weren't taught that it's sinful *per se*, of course…'

'We damn well were,' murmured CoCo.

'….but outside marriage, outside the having of children. I don't need to spell it out.'

'You still disapprove of me, don't you, Louise?'

'Of course I don't.'

'You do.'

'No.'

'Yes, You diddie-diddie-do.'

'Well….'

'Aha!'

'You've led such a different life since we left school.'

'I have, thank God.'

'And you've done such different things.'

'I haven't taken a vow of celibacy, no. And, if you won't be hurt by my saying so, I think it's rather a Middle Ages thing. God, Louise, there's little enough pleasure nowadays. You smoke, you get cancer; you take drugs, you get arrested; you eat, you get fat. What's left *but* making love? Oh, and there's alcohol, and then you get cirrhosis or DTs.'

'You see….'

'AND there's shopping – but not on a research grant.'

'I wish I could think like that. You've engaged in intimacies with men, but you seem so at ease…'

'Jeezus! It's so mincing the way you put it, Louise! Really! I've made love a few times, if that's what you're driving at. I'm hardly Madame Bonka from Bangkok, doing it in threes.'

'Did you ….care for them?'

'Yes, I did; all four of them. At the time, anyway. One was in our Senior Year at High School, and you knew him – it was Erica's brother.'

'Not Jerry! Wow, I never realised…'

'….and one of them I saw a lot of on the AoT course, and one was a quick fling in the summer you were coming out of the convent, and the fourth, although I'm over him, was at the AoT Ball with us – so you know him too.'

'Oh, don't remind me of the ball,' shuddered Louise. She puckered her eyebrows. 'I don't think I could clock up four men, just like that.'

'I started at sixteen, remember. The Scarlet Vamp, the Insatiable Tramp. And yet, if you saw me in the street, would you take me for a wicked person? Am I one of the Evil Ones?'

'No, of course not! You're one of the kindest people I've ever known.'

'And yet I seem to have disobeyed most of our girlhood teachings. Explain that.'

CoCo smiled, amused by Louise's expression.

Feeling there was a logical impasse here, and that

she was losing an argument which she had not wanted to have, Louise took another tack.

'But....what I mean....when you are with a man....like that....how do you manage to feel at ease?'

'You mean "with" as in "making love with"?'

Louise blushed hotly, the Irish side of her complexion helping to spread the blood. She had taken great pains not to talk about this particular topic all year, even though she knew that CoCo thought her agonising shyness had its origins in this fear and had often tried to get her to open up about it.

'Yes,' whispered Louise.

'There's not much mystery. Erm, you feel like you do when you're doing it to yourself, but sometimes it's better, and sometimes it's definitely worse.'

Louise, who had let her dress fall to the floor while she perched on a chair, stared at the rug. This is where this conversation must stop, she told herself. We've never talked like this before. It's too awful, too shaming....for me, not her. She's at ease. I'm not. In spite of not wanting to say it, however, Louise found herself murmuring,

'I know you're going to laugh and make me feel like a Schmuck from Schmucksville, but I may as well tell you that I have....never.....done.... it....to myself, as you put it.'

CoCo gazed at her. Amazing, she thought. There was always a little more to learn about her friend.

'Never? Not in your room at school, or in the bath?'

'I might have felt the urge, I suppose you might call it, but not to do anything about it. It's because it didn't seem right, or natural.'

'I think, given that it's practically a hundred per cent common activity, that it's natural. I guess boys are more obsessed by it, perhaps, than girls, so I've heard, but it's not against nature, surely?'

'Perhaps not, but....'

'But the idea of ending up stark naked in a bed with a guy just seems embarrassing, without any compensating enjoyment?'

'I suppose so. You see, I like the *romantic* idea of love. In fact, there's a boy at St Matthew's – I mean, he's obviously too young, he's only sixteen. But, well, I could see what love of him might be like. He's in the play. Actually he's playing a woman's part, dressing as Julia, the Cardinal's mistress. He's wonderfully good-looking. You'll see him in a few weeks in it. But what I'm trying to say is that he's the sort of man, because he's gentle and kind, that, when he's grown up, that I could really like....that I could love, I think....'

'You think, but you don't know. If I can quote a play tag back at you: *There is no art to find the mind's construction in the face.*'

'*Macbeth*,' murmured Louise.

'Exactly. Your boy may not be what he seems.

Anyhow, Louise, I thought that lusting after the pupils was what got teachers into the scandal-sheets.'

'Oh gracious, no! That's not what I meant!' cried Louise.

CoCo thought: she is a lovely girl. She talks of good looks but seems unaware that she's a cracker. Her face is regular, her teeth white and even, her smile gorgeous because it doesn't come very often and lights her up slowly. She has those Irish colleen's eyes that go flat along the bottom and long lashes. Her hair is glossy, her skin good, her figure slender and tall. CoCo, who privately thought that she herself was a smasher, was able to admit that her friend matched, perhaps even outdid her. What a pair they made! No wonder they were always being asked out.

How dense Louise was being. Really!

And then compassion came over her. Never known pleasure! At her age! So surprising and, well, rather sad. Oh God, she thought, I'm going to say something I'll probably regret. She took Louise's hand.

'Dear CoCo,' sighed Louise. 'I'm such a bore to you.'

CoCo knelt down by the bedside.

'You're not. I love you dearly. We old girls must stick together and help each other. Look, if what I'm going to say next distresses you, tell me straight away and I'll never mention it again. Just remember I'm trying to help in my way.'

'What on *earth* are you going to say?' smiled

Louise.

There was a silence

'I think I should show you what you can feel.'

'*You and me?*'

'Why not?'

Louise's eyes widened. There was another silence – a dreadful one.

CoCo smiled encouragingly.

'Us?' gasped Louise.

'Yes. We'll get ready. We'll go to my bed, as it's a double. And I'll teach you a few things you need to know.'

'Oh, really – I – I – I don't know. Oh, CoCo, I never thought….I never meant…'

'And why not? We girls are all alike. Nothing about you is going to surprise me, and vice versa, I should imagine.'

CoCo got to her feet. She reached for Louise's hand and drew her up. 'Come on,' she said, trying to keep urgency out of her voice. Louise allowed herself to be led to the door. CoCo turned.

'I'm going to take this dress off and dab on some perfume. You do the same and we'll meet in two minutes.' As Louise hesitated, she added, 'Think of it like a driving lesson. What you learn will be useful when the crunch comes later.'

'Pity you put the two together,' said Louise, with an attempt at levity and with a half-formed smile. Yet she went back into the room, sat on her bed, plucked at her slip, stopped, and then methodically removed it, then her bra, then everything else. She freshened herself with cologne, shuddered, and then realised that she was having the same sensations she had sometimes felt in her late teens – a desire to be naked, and a yearning which she had not known how to consummate.

It couldn't be her friend CoCo in there, waiting. It was a stranger.

Louise was staggered to think that a quarter of a hour earlier she had not dreamed that such words and feelings could be generated between them, and now.... She suddenly longed for the irrecoverable simplicity which had been theirs before CoCo's astonishing suggestion. And, thought Louise, nerving herself to cross that passage into her friend's bedroom, this is not something I can back out of with my usual wooliness. Suppose I never did go into that room – and the minutes lengthened to half-an-hour? What then? Would CoCo come back for me and beg me, order me into her bed? How could we meet, constrained and ill at ease at breakfast, finding that things were never going to be the same? But if.... If I do go into her room, go to her bed and do....that, whatever it is, with her, won't things never be the same anyway? How can we go back to what we were before?

And so Louise, faced, like countless billions before her, with the bewildering heightening of the stakes that sexual intimacy always brings about, stood up, slipped a dressing-gown on, took one of two appalling choices, and prepared to meet her future.

CoCo too, in her room, preparing herself with absurd care, as if for a new husband, was full of qualms. She knew, though, with a worldly person's conviction, that she could not stand by and see her friend go on into frigid aloneness, afraid of others' desires, and, more worrying, afraid of her own. Surely the sympathy of a friend – a high school friend, and her oldest – and another woman, would be a gentler entry into her awakening than the clumsy fumbling of some would-be stallion, probably the worse for drink and intent only on his own needs?

She too had done nothing like this before – not since that one far-off experiment with Suzanne at school. It must, she decided, be partly that Louise is strikingly attractive – not conventionally pretty, perhaps, but in a classical, almost rural and natural way was very handsome. I see her as boyish, maybe. And finally, there is the love I do honestly feel for her; a sort of purity of feeling and a need for ever-deeper union.

One fear did trouble her as she slid, unclothed, into the double bed. By awakening Louise, am I condemning her to a hopeless yearning for *me*, or, worse, for other women? Like Louise over the passage, she too wondered what would happen if she called it off, treated it as one of those jokes…. Oh, I can't do that, she thought, not if she's getting ready for me....

And before she could continue oscillating between alternatives, the door opened.

Louise walked firmly – just as if a long-deferred decision had been made at last – into the dim bedroom towards her.

June : **TRIBULATIONS OF A SEX-GOD**

Jem left the rehearsal with a brain overflowing with 17th century words, a flushed face and an ache in his stomach that was like a craving for food – but wasn't that.

The miracle had occurred again: he had, for short moments, *become* Julia – had felt himself outwardly alluring and pliant, inwardly hard and scheming. It was as if, when in that small but decisive role, both sides of himself – ordinary, gentle high school kid and aching striver after experience – blended, each overlaid by a magnification and disguise of itself. '*Jem and Julia; weigh them, they are as heavy; sound them, they are as fair*', he murmured.

Miss Carrbridge had conjured from the Theatre Studies treasure trove an evening gown in deep cream satin studded on the breast with opalines. In no way was it Jacobean in design, but its appearance was the fruit of Mr Howard's envisaging of his production in variants of contemporary dress. That dress was the beginning of what was to be a startling modernism in the St Matthew's *Duchess of Malfi*. It had a long slit up one side, so that walking in it was easy. The department "Marilyns" had fitted after being stuffed with cotton-wool, and Jem found he could just balance in the high-heeled evening shoes which Mr Howard had helped him fit.

'They'll be less difficult to get on, Jem, when you're wearing tights,' Miss Carrbridge had explained. Jem had smiled intimately at her and liked the reflection of himself which he read in her eyes.

Oh, but what warm waves of embarrassment had flooded him when he had removed his trousers, socks and shoes in the wing area to the side of the stage and had pulled the dress on over his underclothes! When he thought of the number of times he had, in fantasy, wished that he'd had an audience on which to practise the shedding of libido and sway sinuously....as Julia, but now felt so vulnerable, he was forced to adjust the easy commerce of the imagination to reality. In the presence of diffident Miss Carrbridge and among the shaded ironies of Mr Howard, he had found himself shy and horribly conscious of the filminess of the dress and of the length of leg revealed by its slit.

The high-heeled shoes had been difficult to force on, but he could see that the sheen of tights would make a difference. Eventually they had settled on him, the curve of their uppers pressing redly into the arch of his right foot especially, but he could sway upright, clutching one of Mr Howard's arms for support. The heels gave him a new height; his face was now a little above Mr Howard's and he had smiled sheepishly into his teacher's eyes.

'It's bit tottery, Sir. Like being on stilts.'

'Hey, glam rock groups manage it every night,' retorted Mr Howard.

The gown had clung to his hips, his arms were held out to poise himself; the gown's slit revealed his left leg from mid-thigh to ankle – and that is what Riccardo Parisi saw when he came round the wing edge.

'I've finished the work I had to do, Mr Howard. Greg told me you were trying out some costumes, so I thought I'd come back and....' He had stopped, his startled eye falling on Jem's leg, then on his flushed face, to his bust and to his revealed leg again. My God, he had thought, just *look* at him! Unbelievable! Gorgeous, isn't he? Those shoes make all the difference, they push his calf up and point his ankle bone. He is absolutely believable as a girl – even without a wig.

Mr Howard had breathed incense on Jem.

Riccardo now breathed a stronger incense on him.

Miss Carrbridge, sorting through wigs, had not noticed either of them.

Jem had caught Rick's eye, started and, aware of the revealing dress, had twitched the material over himself. His face flamed, and he knew, as if Rick had spoken aloud, what the older boy was thinking. He realised he found it startlingly pleasant.

A current of something exciting had flashed between them.

'*Confess to me – you put love powder into my drink*,' smiled Jem, quoting Julia to Bosola in Act V, and he swayed elegantly up to the senior and then tripped as his ankle turned in the high heels. He had been caught by the waist and, metamorphosed by the costume, his feminine side uppermost, had allowed himself to fall against Rick's chest. Through the satin, he liked the muscular arm that supported him. As it had been with Mr Howard, his face was on a level with the dark-haired Italian's. He had been amused, then stimulated, by Riccardo pouting his lips and puffing him a kiss through the little space between them.

'Take it easy, sweetheart,' the senior boy had grinned.

Miss Carrbridge had by now found a wig and came up to him, saying,

'Head forward, Jem.'

Jem had left his hand on Rick's arm for as long an instant as made it significant and had bent towards her. A moment later he lifted upright with a Titian bronze wig transforming him. Its locks fell to his shoulders. Miss Carrbridge nodded in satisfaction. One character complete – only thirty to go.

Jem, with the wig on, floated out onto the stage. Wolf whistles from the boys and clapping cries from the three girls had come to him from the auditorium.

'Nice legs, Jemima!'

'Great dress, shame about the knees!'

'Gimme a kiss, Jemima!'

'Oh, can it, you schmucks,' Jem had smiled. 'And *you* ought to try these shoes. It's like torture in the Spanish Inquisition.'

Miss Carrbridge looked out.

'Jem. That's enough. Come on back and get that lot off before you burst a seam or fall off the stage.'

'That's got to be Jem's costume for Julia, Miss Carrbridge,' Aisha had said. She'd come up the front steps and taken Jem's hands. As Miss Carrbridge turned away, she had whispered. 'I think you're even better looking in a dress, if you must know. You really do something for me.' She had kissed him on each cheek and, before he could stop her, fully on the mouth.

As before, he had felt her tongue flicker between his lips, pushing them apart.

She had whisked back to Susie and Rosa to look through accessories. Jem stumbled off to change, enwrapped in the aura of interest in him. He was too young to interpret Mr Howard's mingled air of anguish and pride, but he could sense the bond that had effloresced between Rick and himself; and he longed to feel the sherbet spangle of Aisha's tongue between his lips again.

'No problem about your basic costume, then,' had come Mr Howard's level voice. 'Let's get that dress on a hanger, the bra with it and the shoes on the floor under it. And Jem, you're gonna have to shave those legs before you get tights on them. Okay? And I think you need a topcoat. We'll sort that out tomorrow at Stacey's'

'Am I coming to Stacey's?' Jem had asked breathlessly. He suddenly wanted to go to the big costumiers, even though his costume was virtually complete, and he hadn't thought to be required.

'I wanted you to come, Jem, because you can be one of our identi-kit boys. Miss Carrbridge and I find that your measurements are those of at least seven others in the cast – so, if you don't mind being a clothes horse, you can try on stuff for them. We only need to go with a few of you. Indenti-kit girl and three or four boys should cover everything'

'Is Riccardo coming, Sir? To get a costume for Bosola?'

'No. He's my size in chest and height, and he's got work to do. He'll wear his own trousers and white shirt under what I have in mind for him.'

Jem had been surprised to feel quite let down at this news. He'd obscurely felt that if he could have had Rick, Aisha and Mr Howard at Stacey's with him, he would have three of the four people he found most fascinating at the moment. He'd briefly fantasised a scenario where he stood in his underclothes, trying on dress after dress – even though he loved the cream satin one – at the centre of an admiring group, encircled by the perfume of desire they sprayed on him, a perfume he sensed, rather than acknowledged rationally.

Louise was more right than she realised when she had said to Mon Howard as they left the hall together,

'All this attention is very bad for Jem Clarke. He'll get quite a big head.'

'Not to mention a lifetime's psycho-sexual disorders brought on by cross-dressing, eh?'

Louise had not noticed an indefinable excitement in her older colleague's voice – but it was there, and Mon knew it was.

Jem had then set off home alone. He lived south of Kissena Park, a precise twenty-minute walk from St Matthew's, just before the Long Island expressway, along Jewel Avenue, over Utopia Parkway and up 172nd Street. The glimpses of his parish church, The Holy Family, with its low gingery bricks and statues under the tree in the distance, were, he knew, five minutes before he could get up to the bedroom landing, enter his room, close the door, and give expression to his desires.

Walking quickly, with inward-seeing eyes, his elegant motions forming and re-forming in shop windows, his mind was taken up entirely with his sensations.

What did he feel about Aisha? What did he feel about Rick? Which of them did he like best? At different points of his journey he felt that it must be Aisha for whom he felt the strongest desire. He was haunted by the longing to feel her tongue moving in his mouth again and, now he had leisure to turn it over, by the precise sienna of her skin against the bright green T-shirt she wore, and the slow resonance of what she had said: 'You really do something for me'. Lingering common-sense reminded him that, as he was not quite seventeen and she was over eighteen, she could hardly be all *that* interested in him. He imagined that College students or young men who already had jobs would be her natural partners. But had she not kissed him passionately? Perhaps she had only been excited because he had been in drag. It had something of the delicious whiff of gender puzzlement that hung about *Twelfth Night* – Jem's sophomore year play which he had liked very much, although not many of his class would have agreed with him.

It must be Aisha he desired then. He tried to imagine her chocolate breasts and bare legs.

Besides, she was a girl – so that was all right.

Rick, of course, wasn't, and Jem hardly dared go deeply into the reasons for his excitement when he was with the senior boy.

Aware of the risk, like making a trail of petrol and igniting it, Jem still couldn't refrain from constructing little intimate scenes in which he and Rick featured; couldn't stop revolving the details of that muscular body and olive-skinned face in his mind. And he called me, 'sweetheart', reflected Jem.

When Jem, last year, careful in his bed to make no noise in his pleasurings that might find its way into his mother's or sister's room, had drawn up one of his legs far enough to embrace it and kiss his own knee-cap, it had been a *Twelfth Night*-like creature – a Viola in boy's disguise – that he held in his arms. Now, this term, he had become that creature! His role as Julia marked a heightened level of self-intoxication. Before rehearsals had started he had had, if anything, a rather low opinion of his looks and personality. He knew himself to be self-effacing, to be shy, to be unwilling to quarrel, to hate having scenes explode round him, to like to take account of others' views. Everyone who taught him and had occasion to mention him, always prefaced or subjoined the comment: 'He *is* a nice boy.'

He read a great deal, and a great deal of what he read would not have passed muster under Mrs Clarke's eyes; but she was too busy to be aware of what Jem was up to in a fantasy life as real as his actual life. Sometimes he longed to escape from the day-long pressure of his desires and dreams. These often beset him at inopportune moments. He had been impressed by the comment made by an elderly man in a 1930s English novel he had started, who said: *I see no reason to mourn for my lost youth. Now I am old, I am at last free from the torments of desire.* Jem hadn't understood at the time what that implied – it was nearly two years since he had abandoned the book – but it had stuck in his mind and the force of it came to him often now, and it was why (so ironically) he envied the calm, passionless Mr Howard, whom he thought the epitome of cool.

Perceptive – possibly more so than the average sixteen-year-old, because he was attentive to the feelings of others – he knew that two, perhaps three people in his little world had interest in him warmer than that of ordinary friendship. He *knew* it and was amazed more than disturbed by it.

His old interests: the electric radio-controlled cars which had caused problems in the family finances before his father had left home for good, the skates he'd used for speeding to school (until his Year Principal had banned them on safety grounds), his yellow and chrome-framed Schwinn chopper-style pedal bike, no longer claimed his attention. They were vapour-trails of his childhood; Jem's discovery of his fellow beings offered excitements far in excess of children's playthings. The little chopper bike, in particular, seemed pathetically *jejeune*, gauche and silly and he often rotated in his mind the best way of selling it. A strain of gentility in his make-up had never really favoured things that, like his bike, seemed "flashy". It was why he didn't have a skateboard. The new craze for these was "flashy". For Jem, one of the negative attributes of "flashy" was the annoyance-value things had for others, and Jem was one of those rare teenagers whose need to seek attention didn't automatically involve being a pest. It was why adults favoured him so much and accorded him a steadiness and maturity he didn't quite have. It was also why, if not particularly popular with his high school fellows, he was respected by them. They had got used to his aura of calm competence and grown-up way of looking at things, and they seldom took advantage of his well-known kindness.

Ewan Clarke, Jem's father, had been on the verge of leaving his marriage and the house with the green roof on 172nd Street for as long as Jem could remember, so when his departure actually came, it was a relief – as when a train pulls out at last after too long a period of farewells on the platform – as much as it was painful and disturbing.

Jem had set himself the task of being a support to his mother; he had known she had leant on him since Ewan's affair with Catherine had begun. 'You're not really old enough to understand, Jem, but....' she would begin. And Jem would hear all about the trips his father made to Florida and about the hotel suites that he and Catherine Ferrier designed and how Catherine had tempted Ewan and how he had been lured by her to a doom that included living together in Miami. And how, thank God, he was paying school fees. He had gone when Jem turned fifteen, nearly two years ago, so a further accretion of maturity had been added. Jem was man of the house as well as party to his mother's miserable bewilderment. For some time, he had been both man-support and woman-confidante: a demanding double-act.

His younger sister, Betsy, had developed her own

brand of self-obsession and had grown annoying; she operated on a parallel line from Jem, and he had little to do with her. Baking, painting, embroidery and creating bright odd jewellery out of molten plastic seemed to make up her entire existence.

Things had settled.

Jem's mother threw herself into her work as a hospital receptionist and needed him less. He didn't miss her possessiveness. No, now it was the new-found wonder of inter-personal relationships with those in his little world of high school which dominated Jem's thoughts. Mom's OK now, he told himself.

When he trod the long sidewalks between St Matthew's and home he felt his steps buoyed by – well, by a sort of *love*. Every spring off the concrete which his rubber-soled shoes made was propelled by that secret new knowledge of his own desirability. Had not Aisha kissed him? Twice! Had he not responded to her lips with an interior flame which dizzied him? Had not Rick held him tight – his right hand low and casually placed on Jem's buttock – and looked into his eyes with a lingering meaning which, incredibly, could not be missed? Had not Miss Carrbridge, at the costume try-out, said to him, 'You are a very good-looking boy, Jem'? And had not old Howard added, ''Yup, you'll make a gorgeous woman when we've finished with you'?

The mysterious As, Fs and Rs which marched

across Jem's diary pages seemed hardly sufficient as coded confirmation of this universe of love. Furthermore, though Jem had started with As a few weeks back and had not intended to add more, he had recently begun encoding more and more Rs, and, as a result of another impulse, a succession of Fs – about which he felt ashamed. Yes, that was rather shaming when he faced up to his feelings about it.

He had involved Janek Franitza's little brother, Francis, in *The Duchess of Malfi*.

Janek, quiet and dignified, was, to observers, Jem's best friend. They never disagreed with one another, they had utterly divergent interests, were on the best of terms, and usually ate their lunch together, occasionally murmuring, or wrapped in disassociated reading – Jem conning Julia's lines or deep in a novel, Janek studying a hi-fi or car magazine. Janek took others as he found them, not seeming to delve beneath appearances, so Jem felt obscurely that he was taking advantage of old Jan's simplicity when he began yet another erotic obsession with Jan's brother.

Francis Franitza was in the 9th grade, only just fourteen, but he had the vivacity and challenging looks which Janek lacked. Jem had been made properly aware of his existence when he had gone home to Jan's house for supper earlier in the semester. Francis had taken to Jem immediately and they had a hilarious game of rude scrabble, sitting on Francis' bed among his copies of music mags and the various knives he collected. Jem had found himself being unusually and noisily witty. He felt, by comparison, that Janek appeared taciturn and distant. It was only when he got home that it occurred to him that Jan saw Francis every day and hardly needed to make an impression. It puzzled Jem all that evening why exactly *he* had felt it necessary to make an impact. The next morning, Jem could not help asking Jan what Francis had thought of him.

'Oh, he was going on about you for ages after you left – asking this question and that.'

'What sort of questions?'

'Silly ones mainly, Jem. I don't know what's in his mind. Stupid kid.'

'Well, what *sort* of silly questions?' Jem had persisted, aware that he ought not to let his peculiar interest show too strongly, but unable not to.

Jan had been embarrassed.

'Oh, heck. Forget it.'

'Come ON!' Jem cried, in spite of his sensing that Jan was finding it odd that he was asking this so pressingly.

'He….he wanted to know – would you believe it? – whether you were circumcised, among other things.'

' God! What other things?'

'He asked if you had hair….down there. You know….'

'God Almighty! What did you tell him?'

'Well, I said that as far I knew, you were

circumcised, and that you had hair that was normal –
I mean at your….at our age. What was I to say?'

'Oh, Jeez!' Jem had whooped; amazed and thrilled
that Francis' questions should have taken such a
personal tack, but oddly horrified that his friend had
known how to answer them. 'How do *you* know what
I look like?'

'I saw you once, coming out of the changing-room
showers, round about Easter, didn't I? Not that I took
a bit of notice,' added Jan quickly.

'Fancy a squirt like that knowing what
circumcision is,' smiled Jem.

'He's a dirty-minded little shit sometimes,' his
fond brother had grunted. 'I wouldn't pay any
attention.'

But Jem had paid attention – a lot of it. St
Matthew's Junior and Senior High were on the same
campus, so from that time on he'd sought Francis'
profile in the crowds of boys outside school, several
times contrived to be outside his classroom at time of
dismissal and had managed, by slow questioning of
Jan, to piece together Francis' timetable so that he
could, in theory, find him whenever he wanted. He
forced down into a deep recess the undoubted
homoeroticism in all this. It's what they call a crush, I
suppose, he told himself. It'll pass.

Since last month, with the obsession gripping him,
he had suggested that Francis get involved in *The
Duchess of Malfi* on the production side – giving

assistance backstage – and this had been arranged with Mr Lomax. Jem dreaded Jan suspecting his new fever, fearing the accusation of being queer. He worried constantly that everything about Francis attracted him: the easy bend of his slim, black trousers, the neatness of his hands, his dark gold hair, his sultry, cheeky expression and compact shape. Bolts of lightning shot through Jem when their eyes met across rooms.

Jeez! A fourteen-year-old Polish boy more attractive to him than a beautiful, sophisticated eighteen-year-old Afro-American girl who obviously fancied him! Was he insane?

Images of Francis peopled Jem's self-pleasuring fantasies as least as often as did Aisha's. And so the Fs appeared day after day. He forced himself to concentrate on Aisha so that he could get back to writing As in his diary margins. But so often her image vanished, and it was Francis' face and form that filled his inner eye.

Jem's favourite fantasy was that Francis had yet to discover sex, and it was he – Jem – who had to teach him; first by example, closely watched, then by helping him.

No passers-by bothered to guess what was passing through the mind of the handsome, oval-faced youth hurrying towards the privacy of the green-roofed house on 172nd Street, with his hands thrust into his pockets, but Jem fancied they did. As sometimes happened on the walk home after rehearsal, Jem – his thoughts like a relay on alternating current, swinging from Aisha's tongue in his mouth to Francis's black-trousered legs – understood just what Keats meant when he wrote that he yearned to be *awake for ever in a sweet unrest,* which Mr Howard had explained was just this sense of arousal, endlessly prolonged. Like the poet, Jem too longed to lie *pillowed on my fair love's ripening breast.*

He walked up the short driveway, glancing at his watch. 5.50. No one should be home for another twenty-five minutes; he knew that his mother had gone to collect Betsy from her dancing lesson. Drawing in his breath with anticipation, he fumbled his key from his pocket and was about to insert it in the lock when a voice came over the hedge from his neighbour's.

'Oh, hello, Jem. Your Mam's not back yet,' said Mrs O'Meara.

He looked over at her pleasant Irish face. Invariably polite and considerate, Jem forced himself to stop and reply.

Damn!

Only twenty-odd minutes left!

Boring old COW!

He prayed inwardly that Mrs O'Meara – a formidable gabbler if given encouragement – was in a hurry herself and would let him get inside and upstairs.

'Ah – yes. I – er – I'll just have to put the kettle on myself, Mrs O'Meara.'

'Nothin' like a well-trained man,' she said. 'And 'tis better for you to be having tay than a bottle of Coke. I'm always telling Sean that very thing. But does he listen?'

Jem had removed his light jacket as the June afternoon was warm. He was conscious of his hard nipples visible through his white shirt, of the bulge in his trousers under the hand in his pocket. It seemed to him that Mrs O'Meara could not fail to take in these details of his aroused state – could read like a book what he intended to do the moment he got indoors.

But her expression showed nothing other than kindly concern. She smiled at him.

'Well, have a nice cup o' tay. I'm off now to Safeway's, so I'll be on me feet for an hour yet. See you, dear.'

Mrs O'Meara went across to her old Plymouth, looking for her keys in her bag. Jem nodded at her pleasantly before turning back to the door. Once in the house, he called, just to be on the safe side,

'Erm – anyone in?'

Silence. Thank God.

He darted upstairs, flinging his jacket on the banister rail as he passed.

His bedroom was meant to be a castle, but neither Mrs Clarke nor Betsy seemed to recognise the importance of its large notice: KEEP OUT! IF YOU

MUST ENTER, KNOCK AND WAIT!!! More than once Jem had had a narrow escape during the day-time, although he knew he could generally rely on being left undisturbed at night. The trouble with the nights was the utter silence of the house. The O'Meara's were quiet neighbours, there was little traffic after eleven o'clock, Mrs Clarke went to bed before ten-thirty, and Jem thought that every sound reverberated from his bedroom. He had, as a result, grown expert at pleasuring himself in silence. Since he had turned sixteen, though, he had wanted to experiment with more complex versions of the same act. Some of these could, potentially, be noisy, so that he used more and more the precious time after school before his mother, who collected Betsy from one of her many girlie activities after her work, arrived to start making supper.

5.55.

He slowly removed his shirt, stepped from his jeans and flipped off his socks. Wearing only his under-garment, he took silent steps into his mother's bedroom. Jem had no full-length mirror of his own and he lacked the nerve to ask for one – believing Mrs Clarke would guess what he wanted it for – so he used hers to gaze at his own body. She had a classically-styled make-up table in the window. This piece of furniture stopped anyone seeing in, as Jem knew, but he twitched the curtains over a little, just in case. He liked to angle this mirror and the full-length one in the wardrobe so he could see himself from behind as well as from the front.

Jem did not really approve of what he saw between his mirrors. He was, on the whole, a modest and self-deprecating youth. But now, after this afternoon at rehearsal, he felt less displeased with his image. He thought his legs were a little too plump, which irritated him, considering that he walked for forty minutes every day, but he considered them long enough, quite well-shaped, lacking boniness, and having a sheen to calf and thigh. He wished he had slimmer ankles, a characteristic he admired in others. Mr Howard's comment about having to shave his legs came back to him and he longed to smother them in foam and razor away the light delicate hairs. He turned this way and that, feeling that he was fairly well-muscled, although not sporty, but disliking his pale, hairless chest. His body hair was anything but excessive, and less dark than that on his head.

Jem put his hands behind his neck and stood for a moment longer, his legs slightly apart, his hands behind his head. Miss Carrbridge thinks I'm good-looking, he mused. I'm going to be G for Gorgeous.

He pulled the remaining garment down. Jem wasn't particularly confident about his penis; it seemed adequately, if not spectacularly, formed. He knew that Shakespeare had sneered at someone for being a "three-inch fool" in *The Taming of the Shrew*, and Tony Greene, a friend of his in the sophomore year, had daringly read (and showed Jem) a novel in which a man had "a twelve-inch rod". Careful measuring at the right time had assured Jem that his was longer than Shakespeare's character's, and he suspected (rightly) that the fictional article's length had been given authorial licence.

He tilted the dressing-table mirror to reflect his side-view and then lay back on Mrs Clarke's bed. So, Rick thought him sexy, did he? Suppose Rick were with him now, and just suppose he took his clothes off too? Suppose I were not to find his nakedness repulsive? Suppose Rick manipulated me and he didn't shrink from doing it? Would it mean that he….that I….? Just as a clear mental picture of Riccardo and himself sitting in the set of *The Duchess of Malfi* exploring each other formed, so an interior conversation with Francis Franitza began to take place in which Jem was instructing the younger boy.

The pleasure of having Francis actually with him in the room, on the bed, would have been almost unbearable, but as Jem could never, of course, dream of asking his friend's brother to come home alone with him, such a situation had to remain a fantasy.

He knelt in front of the mirror, leaning back on his heels, legs apart. So good is the imagination when it needs to be, that Jem almost saw Francis kneeling on the bed beside him. He grew more excited, and had begun operations, concentrating on varying touches to himself, was arching backwards and gazing into the mirror to drink in the tautness of his leg muscles, and the near readiness of his whole body to reach pleasure, when….

Crash!

Voices!

'Jem darling! We're ho-ome!'

'Jem. Look what I've made!'

6.10

Oh! They're ten minutes early!

Jem jumped from the bed, closed the wardrobe door, re-tilted the make-up table mirror, drew the curtains back and dashed across the passage to his own room. Downstairs he could hear things banging in the kitchen.

'Jem? Je-em? Have you had some tea?'

He bundled into his jeans and shirt.

'Er, hello, Mom. Hi, Betsy,' he called, his voice a little trembly. 'No. No. I came straight up to do some – some work. I'll be down in a second.'

He zipped his jeans, took a look in his small round table mirror (My God! My pupils are dilated, my lips red; they'll know what I've been doing!) and tucked his shirt in. He then remembered that he'd left his underpants in his mother's room. Once again he whisked across the landing, darted in and retrieved them, hastily smoothing his mother's bedclothes flat. It was too late to get out of his jeans again and put them on, so he kicked them under his bed.

Betsy appeared at the turn of the stairs.

'You look hot,' she said. 'I've made a model of a witch's cavern.'

'Oh great!' gasped Jem. 'Let's see it.'

'It's in the kitchen. I'm getting my head-band.'

'I'll – er – I'll go downstairs.'

Jem took a further look at himself in his little mirror before he went down to greet his mother. All seemed well, although his cheeks were still flushed. He put his spectacles on, feeling they made him look calmer. Surely no one would guess at his heightened state of the last quarter of an hour? That was always the miracle. No one, he thought, ever seemed to spot that he went through such explosions.

'Tea, dear? Rehearsals go well?' asked his mother.

'Oh, fine. Very well, really. I'll – I'll just wash my hands,' muttered Jem, crossing to the little lobby washroom. On return, his took his mug when the kettle had boiled and had a long, grateful swig of Lipton's while his nerves gradually settled down.

That night, after the others had gone to bed, Jem had a much more satisfactory act of self-pleasing. He imagined that his hands were tied behind his back and that he had to reach orgasm without touching himself at all. He had never yet managed this feat as a result of pure auto-suggestion and had always succumbed to the desperate need for release.

The whole evening leading up to bedtime had become a long, jumpy state of part-arousal for Jem, watching a quiz show and a comedy on TV, helping his mother to clear up dishes, listening to Betsy's account of her day. Without his underpants on, he felt nearly unclothed, as had been the case earlier in the year when, in a history class, and Jan away with a cold, he had secretly and unwisely pleasured himself under his desk. He had thrown away his dampened undergarment and walked home without it. On that occasion too, he had felt an extraordinary sense of being naked in public.

He was, therefore, in a state of almost frantic looking-forward to the moment of fulfilment, the outcome of the afternoon having been such a disaster. At last his orgasm came, with a perfect crackle of light and violence which seemed to implode inwards through to his backbone. He couldn't repress a cry of delight, which he immediately turned into a cough. He lay on his back, his chest heaving, and with the longed-for, amazing, warm tingling in his naked limbs. A minute later there was a tap on his door.

'Are you okay, Jem?' came his mother's voice. 'I thought I heard you call out.'

Jem flipped the sheet over himself and pretended to yawn. The door opened a crack.

'I'm fine – fine,' he muttered, rubbing his hand in his eyes. Mrs Clarke looked down at him. 'I didn't hear anything, unless it was in the road,' he went on. 'I think I coughed.' He coughed again, in a high-pitched way like the sound he imagined his orgasmic cry had made.

'Get some sleep,' said his mother, gazing in at him. The door closed.

Jem sat up in bed, dabbing himself with a Kleenex. Now WHAT had she meant by that comment? What was she hinting at? He felt himself go hot and cold with embarrassment at the thought that she might *know* what he had done.

He just couldn't sleep.

Triple, lustful images of Aisha, Rick and Francis danced in his brain. He had written up his diary for that day. Not a single A for a week! Oh, Aisha!

As he dozed off, he knew he would have to sort out this question of his privacy. He would be seventeen in September – practically grown up – and too old to live a secret existence in his mother's house. Just suppose I did ask Francis home with me, and I casually hinted that we came up to this bedroom? Or just suppose that Aisha came back after rehearsal and – in this room – took her clothes off, and I took mine off…. Or what if Rick and I came back here to go over our lines? That's more likely really. I would act Julia's part, and he would have to hold me to his chest, on line 162, Act V, scene ii, and then on line 165 I have to kiss him – on the mouth; yes, we could try that – and whisper *Now you'll say I'm a wanton….* And then suppose, as we were kissing, mother or Betsy walked in on us…..?

Although Jem's love life was totally imaginatively constructed and he could not, in reality, believe in any other person in his bedroom with him, it irked him to think that he might never be able to have a full relationship with anyone (even supposing anyone ever showed an inclination to go that far) except on a purely conceptual level. And why? Because of the pathetic skimpiness of the house on 172nd Street – that was why.

He would leave!

Yes! When he was seventeen.

Why not?

He could take a part-time job as a soda-jerk, perhaps, or in a supermarket after school, and rent a tiny room of his own.

Ever since his and Betsy's father had left them to live with Catherine in the sun, his mother had clung to him. At fifteen he hadn't minded. At sixteen, nearly seventeen, it gave him a suffocating feeling. Jem accepted dicta about TV programmes, smoking, loud music and tidiness with his customary humour, but recently....recently he felt he was living for a particular pleasure, and he was always being hounded out of the bathroom, or tapped at in his bedroom at moments which should not be interrupted. He wanted to see the adult films and read the magazines some of his friends spoke about. He knew he could never hide these activities from his mother, who seemed to be always in his room tidying and taking clothing in and out, and his spirit squirmed again with the horror of it being known by her that he did things to himself in bed. (He neglected to remember that his mother had been brought up in Chicago with her brothers, his uncles, and knew from them and their friends exactly what teenage boys were obsessively interested in, sometimes talked about and were always doing.)

He woke again, sighed, and snipped his light on. It was on a dimmer switch, so that its glow barely reached the crack under the door. 4.20. It was going to be one of those nights. He propped himself on his elbow, plumped his pillows and lay back again.

Hm, those qualms I have about desiring Rick and Francis.

As with the biz of leaving home, he knew he had to grasp that other nettle one day of deciding if he was gay or not.

He had begun to debate this often since *The Duchess of Malfi* rehearsals had started – and more so than ever tonight, since he had dressed as Julia. *Why* did he find Rick so powerfully attractive? *Why* didn't he have a girlfriend? Now that was worth asking. Quite a few youths of his age group had; he hadn't. He just wasn't sure if it was a matter of orientation or of 172nd Street. Homo or home? A few of his classmates lived in houses no bigger than his, and openly spoke of taking girls up to their rooms.

Not long ago he had looked furtively into a paper for homosexuals in a shop near the Queens Museum. He had been amazed by the number and variety of the private adverts in it. Now, he occasionally imagined putting – when he was seventeen, of course – an ad in for himself:

Young Caucasian male, 17, cultured, interested in Jacobean drama, seeks active fun and fellowship.

Then would follow his phone number......

Jem gave a huge yawn.

Young Caucasian male with yellow chromed Schwinn chopper for sale. Well-used but kept polished.

He smiled faintly and yawned again.

As he was falling asleep, he saw Mrs Clarke, a duster in her hand, lifting the receiver to speak to an unknown caller about "active fun with a young male Caucasian", and the advert's image shattered like a mirror.

June : A RIDE IN A MORGAN

Stacey's – costumiers to so many Broadway shows – is mighty impressive. Long passages, formed by row upon row of hanging clothes, march parallel to each other through the old candle factory which Somerville Stacey and Abel Korzeniowski had converted when Tutton's Candles gave up manufacture in the 1930s.

The select team of costume hunters had left St Matthew's after lunch and travelled in convoy, occasionally getting separated by traffic lights and barging vans. There were six in the high school minibus and Mon Howard and Jem in Mr Howard's Morgan sports car. Stacey's is one those civilised stage outfitters which permits you to take costumes away when you have chosen them and lets you have up to three weeks with them before the show in which they are to be worn. For these reasons several rows of seats were left empty in the bus for the boxes of clothes and accessories. Mr Lomax drove, with Greg, Joey, Aisha, Rosa and Peter representing the whole cast of thirty-one. There was no reason why either fewer of them should have gone – for David Lomax had all their measurements in his pocket – or why Mr Howard and Jem couldn't have travelled with them, but no one thought to question the decision to take two vehicles. No one thought much either of Jem's being ushered into the sports car, although Joey had whispered to Peter,

'Sucker-upper. That's what you get for being a crawler.'

He had said it without rancour, however, and, after all, the journey over to Lower Manhattan wasn't a long one. Miss Carrbridge had not been released from lessons in the end, on the grounds that she didn't drive and had three sophomore sets to cover.

Mr Howard had been slightly surprised by Louise's demeanour that morning. After the fitting of Jem with the dress with the slit up the leg the previous day, she had seemed her usual demure, slightly depressing self. Mr Howard had wished her a pleasant evening and she had confided that she was going to a party with her flat-mate.

'Nice party last night?' Mr Howard had asked.

'Oh, no – we didn't go in the end. But thanks for asking,' Louise had replied.

'Ah, a jolly evening at home?' Mr Howard had smiled.

Louise had smiled back, with a bursting smile like an expanded sunflower.

'Oh, very jolly,' she had said, her eyes looking inward for a moment.

Mr Howard had hoped that her absence from the trip over to Stacey's would not depress her; she was costume-mistress, after all, but she took it with what was, for her, a rollicking laugh.

'Oh heavens! It was my fault for not telling Harry earlier. In any case, you don't need me. David can drive. You have the vision of what we need. Jem's main costume is sorted out, and Aisha and Rosa know what to look for. They're perfectly capable of finding hats, shoes, jewels and other accessories. It's those boys who need to go, and you've got the range of sizes.'

No drooping and no resigned sigh. Amazing.

Keeping an eye on the bus behind in his wing mirror, Mon Howard, ridiculously unable to keep a holiday jauntiness out of his voice, cried,

'Are you enjoying being in the play, Jem?'

'Oh, yes, Sir. It's great,' replied Jem. Mon watched to see how the wind of their passage in the open auto lifted Jem's dark-brown hair. He liked the way it lay with definiteness against Jem's pale skin wherever its sculptured shape led it to. There were no untidy straggles, no small hairs and then smaller ones blurring the divide. There was hair, and there was skin – and that seemed attractive to Mon Howard, who hated untidiness in others.

He looked sidelong at his youthful passenger, pondering what degree of disgust Jem would feel if they were ever to find themselves together and unclothed. The excitement of the thought made him give a sharp intake of breath, so that the boy looked fully at him.

'I mean, it's fun being with the others in the play, but hard work too,' continued Jem – feeling that he should have expanded his reply.

They had gone south of St John's University campus and joined the 25, Queens Boulevard, at Hillside Avenue. The roar of wind and other traffic on the highway made it necessary for them to shout at each other.

'Got enough room?'

'Yes, Sir, Mr Howard. It's much better than going in the bus. Do you particularly like British sports cars?'

Mon Howard nodded, smiling in the roar.

Oh, phooey, I am being a boring *goob*, thought Jem. Why am I saying such kiddish things? Do you like sports cars? Oh no, Clarke, I specially bought it as a penance for my sins because what I *really* like driving is a garbage disposal truck. People think teachers have a boring life, mused Jem, but Mr Howard doesn't seem to; he's out as soon as he can go, except when doing the play. He looks smart and cool, he's got this car. He does love rehearsing us, I can see that. It's the coming-together of his vision of us, I suppose. Getting guys through exams must be like that too, I guess. Jem had not thought for more than a few minutes about teaching as a career, but – unlike most of his friends – he had mused about it now and then. He stole a full look at Mr Howard's face. With dark shades on, the profile was unbending and keen. For a moment, Jem *was* Mr Howard, with his wit, his easy discipline, his trips abroad to Europe, his wide reading and his Morgan – and he wanted to stay being him. God, how different he was from Dad – worrying and worrying about business and money and then running off with his secretary. Mr Howard's perfect *completeness* had no shred of squalid selfishness in it, no sad dependence on an interior agenda of need. Yes, Mr Howard could afford, in his life, in his job, to be himself. Beyond his slight sense of inadequacy sitting in close proximity to his English teacher was a moment's enlightening hero-worship, and Jem felt changed by it.

I do really, really like him, thought Jem.

'You know, Jem, I can't think of anyone I've met recently,' said Mr Howard, 'whom I like as much as you. You've got talent, you're reliable, quick, full of understanding and always cheerful. I don't think I've ever seen you unable to smile – except when being thoughtful; and it's fair enough not to smile then.'

Wicked. Uncanny. He knew what I was thinking about *him,* mused Jem. But how nice to be liked by Mr Howard. Jem basked in his teacher's approval. Although Joey had characterised him as a crawler, Jem wasn't a toady. What he valued, more than most things these days, was to feel in sympathy with those he admired. Jem had not been fiercely ticked off, shouted at or criticised in earnest since his early teens. His mother's weary little strictures were nothing like his absent father's violent rages. His rare combination of charm, intimacy, dependability and humour made every adult he had come across, outside his close family, take to him. He and Mr Howard smiled happily at each other.

'As for what you were asking, dear boy, I DO like European sports cars – even though you can't cram much into them. The storage space is all behind the seats in this one. Makes it awkward,' he went on, catching Jem's eye, 'if one has, say, a quadriplegic with one as a passenger and one suddenly needs a spanner.'

Jem spluttered in mirth and Mr Howard joined him. They were united by a sense of the ridiculous. And Mon was to do it again a little later. A huge truck drew alongside with 'Dunlop' on its tyres. The traffic was slowing as they approached the Queensboro' Bridge. 'See that tyre?' said Mon – and he quoted solemnly: *'John, with his new Dunlop tyre, ran o'er the head of sweet Maria. When she died in frightful pain, he had to blow it up again.'*

Mon caught Jem's twinkling eye and they both collapsed in splutters. The truck moved on in its lane. 'Harry Graham,' said Mon, 'like this one: *Making toast by the fireside, nurse fell in the fire and died; and what made it even worse, all the toast was burnt with nurse.*' His eyes bright, Mr Howard snicked into a lower gear. Jem, the delight of giggles still rippling his solar plexus, lay back in the Morgan's seat, not quite conscious of the mutual bonding of a shared humour.

Jem had never been across the bridge in an open auto; indeed he had seldom gone into Manhattan at all, and not often by car, and as he gazed up at the stupendous girders of the great structure, Mr Howard suddenly asked,

'Is your full name Jeremy?'

Jem, who had been wondering how long it took to paint the bridge from end to end, replied,

'Yes, Sir. After Jeremy Finch in *To Kill a Mockingbird*. It is my mother's favourite book. And that's why I'm Jem, of course.'

'Miles better than Jerry. I thought it was something like that. It's a nice name and it suits you.'

I am getting a few compliments today, thought Jem: talented, witty, understanding, cheerful, nice name. For just a second, Jem felt a stab of suspicion – a needle-touch of mistrust – of his smooth teacher. He took a sidelong look at the calm profile, the shades, the distinguished, slightly greying hair, the competent hands on the top of the wheel-rim, as Mr Howard slowed to get south onto 2nd Avenue. And as he was looking, Mr Howard turned to face him and, meeting Jem's completely serious expression, smiled easily.

'Nearly there now,' he said. 'Just off 55th Street, before FDR Drive. An amazing old warehouse.'

Does it *mean* anything that I'm in the car, rather than in the bus? Jem couldn't quite remember how he had ended up in the Morgan: he hadn't expected to travel any differently from the others, so he knew he hadn't hinted at it. One minute he was waiting to clamber into the bus with Greg and Joey – intent on grabbing a seat next to Aisha if possible – and the next he was in the sports car and he and Mr Howard were moving off. He could see Aisha and Rosa sitting together confidentially, so that would have been that; besides Aisha had given no sign of singling him out. Mr Howard, on the other hand, had. If anyone might have been expected to go in the Morgan it would have been Greg, a Senior and on Mr Howard's Literature Honours Program. But Mr Howard had taken no special interest in Greg's mode of travel to Stacey's. Had he, then, wanted Jem and no one else to sit with him in the car? And why? A portfolio of the aggregated comments Mr Howard had made to him since *The Duchess of Malfi* had started flickered through Jem's mind. Surely it couldn't *mean* anything?

The game that Jem had played, as Julia, of basking in the mist of desire that came to him, as he fancied, in waves from Aisha and Rick, was suddenly less of a game. In the car, now, he was just Jem Clarke, not quite seventeen, a boy at High School, on his way to help try out costumes for his school play. And that's another thing; why am I needed today? I've got my costume. One of the others would have done just as well as a clothes-hanger – most of them are my size.

I'm not Julia – I'm a boy playing a girl in a high school end-of-semester drama.

And then, just as quickly as the faint, glancing blow of outrage buffeted him one way, Jem found himself lurching in the other direction. All right, suppose Mr Howard has grown fond of me? He can't mean anything odd – he's far too old for all that. But he said he really liked me. Well, that's good, surely? Jem had a few moments, as the Morgan drew alongside a red-brick wall punctuated with high windows, to analyse what he felt about that liking. Suppose it *was* a sort of love – a romantic thing, like those older and younger warriors in Ancient Sparta? He was mildly amazed to discover that the idea of being one half of a special, loving platonic relationship with Mr Howard was not off-putting, not disturbing – as it would have been with any of the other teachers at St Matthew's High. Part of his mind registered it as one of the most enthralling things that had happened this year – this remarkable year of the play and his part of Julia.

No more could be digested; the minibus drew up with a squeal of brakes and the selected costume-triers tumbled out, laughing and shouting. Jem saw that only back at home in his room would he find time and peace to play these ideas over in his head, like someone snicking back to their favourite track.

Mr Howard opened the door for him and he pulled himself up. He had time to feel (before they all went into Stacey's, and as he looked at Rosa, Aisha, Greg, Joey and Peter, so seemingly carefree and full of youthful happiness) a sudden strange longing for the uncomplicated times before *The Duchess of Malfi*; for the mild affection he felt for his yellow and chrome chopper, his reading of well-known novels recommended by his mother, for his tolerant averaging of basketball scores with Jan, the anticipation of his getting his own compact hi-fi. But in the poise of his body was his almost-knowledge that, whatever he might desire, those dear, dead days would never return.

Mr Howard busied himself with introductions.

'Yes. It's us again, Mrs Dandridge.'

'Not wanting a camel this time?'

'What a memory you've got! Ha, ha, no. But a Cardinal's outfit would be useful.'

'Cardinals are easy. It's the bigger desert quadruped outfits that pose problems. So what's the show this year?'

'*The Duchess of Malfi.*'

'Well I never. That's a challenge for the kids. It can still be quite chilling, can't it?'

'And we've got the usual biggish cast that old Webster specified. Thirty-one in all.'

'Right. Seventeenth century Shakespeare style. That starts in Row 12 down there.'

'No – it's not seventeenth century at all. I'm going for modern-ish dress, but stylised, outlandish, you know. Black leather outfit for Bosola, Victorian coats for villains, Nazi soldiers' uniforms – that sorta thing.'

'Oh, very with-it. I hope the parents will approve.'

'Most of them are *not* theatre aficionados,' smiled Mr Howard. 'We could dress them all in *Snow White* outfits and their parents wouldn't jib.'

'Well, well. Tell them to come in and NOT to forget to put things back on hangers when they've tried them on. You can use these shelves for your collection.'

'Thanks, Mrs Dandridge. And you've been well this year?'

Leaving Mr Howard making a few more remarks to Mrs Dandridge, the selected cast trooped through into the Late-19th and 20th century aisles, their high windows overlooking the subway lines.

'Shall I take the 1930s and see what I can find, Mon?' asked David Lomax.

'Uhuh. And if Aisha and Rosa go with you they can try out girls' stuff for themselves. I'll try for Greg's old woman and I'm going to look for Riccardo and, perhaps, Joey.'

'But I'm here, Sir' said Joey.

'Oh, right. So you are, brave warrior….'

'How unimportant can you get?' murmured Joey to Peter.

'You're not blue-eyed Jem Clarke, are you?' Peter whispered back. Teenage boys miss very little.

'Well, you guys try on some smart, dark-coloured suits for courtiers; perhaps a coupla tuxedos. The effect should be classy but intimidating. Show me when you've found what fits. OK?'

He strode off between the racks; rack on rack up to the neon lights strung out down the length of the old warehouse. 'We need virtually a pantomime dame outfit for you, Greg. You're so good as a drag part that I think we need to make you a little outrageous. Mad, huge, fanciful hat, perhaps? And a real fox fur, and a coat which goes back to Queen Mary.'

'What does that look like, Sir?'

'Don't worry. I'll show you. It's a bit before your time.'

'But not before your time, eh, Sir?'

'Tee, hee, hee to you, McManus.'

'What about me, Sir?' asked Jem. 'I've got my costume back on campus, haven't I?'

'Hm, you have and you haven't. Just as Greg has got to be obviously a drag part, you have to fool them right up to curtain call and beyond. Cleo Jakemar, remember. I like Miss Carrbridge's dress on you, but you could try others if you fancy them, and we might improve on her wig, and it's vital you have a really zappy coat too. You've gotta look twenty million dollars' worth of glam, you know. As believable a conniving sex-bomb as you would look if you were a *real* girl. Remember you have no lines at all in that first scene. We've gotta capture what you are by looks alone.'

His smile enwrapped Jem between the draperies. Jem began to feel shy about the next stage. How was he going to try on these dresses? There didn't seem to be any changing-rooms nearby. Was he expected to slip them on in these narrow gangways in front of the others? And why? His dress at school was ideal, he thought.

Greg's voice came muffled from the next row.

'I've found an amazing flouncy thing with sort of gems on the front. Shall I try it on?'

With a start, Jem realised that he and Mr Howard were on their own with dangling dead animals perfuming them in a warm cocktail of aged scent and mothballs. Mr Howard reached up to a high rail and hooked off a thick, inky-black coat of pure gloss.

'Try this, Jem,' he said. 'It's just what I had in mind for when you first appear. Slip it on.' Jem reached for the coat. 'Allow me, madam,' said Mr Howard, and stepping behind Jem he slipped the coat over his shoulders. 'Pop your arms in – that's right.'

'Oh!' gasped Jem as the astonishing smell of the coat came up to his nose. The luxuriant softness of the fur brushed his cheeks. He wrapped the body of the coat round himself – snuggling into it. It was, he felt, the most glamorous garment he had ever handled.

'Yes, *that's* more like it!' cried Mr Howard. 'Might have been made for you. And it'll go perfectly with your dress.'

'It must have been real expensive,' gasped Jem.

'Oh, yes. That's pure dark musquash.' (Mon didn't quite know whether it was musquash or not, but he never admitted that he didn't know something to his students – it was what secured his reputation for omniscience) 'Wear that in the street now and you'd get a tin of red paint tossed over you.'

'By an animal welfare nut, you mean?' Jem stroked the gloss. 'I suppose it is cruel to kill them to make one of these, but....'

'....but you can see why people do it?'

'Yes. It's the softest thing I've ever felt.'

'Right. One coat for Julia, then. Can you get it back on the hanger and take it to our shelf?'

Jem, aware that he was doing so reluctantly, peeled off the lovely, heavy coat. As it left his shoulders, he felt ordinary and dull again. He took it over to the shelf, imagining the coat's impact with his cream evening dress. Rick would go bananas! He lingered by the shelf, not just because he was absurdly reluctant to leave his coat there, but because he wanted a moment to digest his almost certain impression that Mr Howard had let a finger stroke his cheek as he had helped him on with it.

Meanwhile, the choosing went on, and one by one the clothes-horses returned to the shelf bearing their finds.

'Have I got to drape this mangy, malevolent-looking mongrel round my neck, Sir?' asked Rosa, coming up with a fox stole. 'Greg thinks it would suit Coriola when she's arrested by Bosola. She tries to appear dignified before his executioners throttle her, but…'

'….but you don't think that thing's very dignified?'

'Its eyes are accusing us, Sir.' Said Aisha.

'Watch it, Rosa, I'm sure I saw it move! It's trying to bite you!' cried Joey.

'Eeeeeh!'

Protests notwithstanding, the fox (later christened Freddie and destined to a popular, if very dead, play mascot) joined the other bits and pieces.

'Long cigarette holders?' asked Mrs Dandridge.

'Yup.'

'Lorgnette for the old lady?'

'Got it.'

With three boxes of accessories and thirty hangers of variegated costumes to haul out, it took some time to load up the bus, but eventually they were ready to leave.

'Could we get an ice-cream before we go back, Sir?' asked Aisha. 'I'm so hot.'

'Fine,' said Mr Lomax. 'I'll just pull in and you can jump out. You'll have to wait 'til I see a suitable place – but it'll be before the bridge. Okay?'

Mon Howard was about to open the Morgan's passenger door for Jem – ridiculously like a man attentive to the comforts of a woman, he reflected –

when Jem's clear voice said,

'As there's still a seat or two empty, I could go in the bus with the others, if you like, Sir.' And before Mr Howard could say anything, he climbed into the minibus, took up a box of bits and sat next to it on a double seat at the rear. Mon, turning his door-opening gesture into a flicking of his finger along some dust on the windscreen, made no comment. He didn't offer the vacant seat in the Morgan to anyone else but got in and started up.

'See you back at St M's', called David Lomax.

Mr Howard nodded curtly, put the car into gear and headed off back towards 2nd Avenue.

'Right,' said Mr Lomax, 'all aboard.'

The others scrambled in.

'Didn't you like your drive up here in the Morgan, then?' asked Greg.

'You felt car-sick, didn't you?' scoffed Joey.

'I thought I'd get in on the ice-cream bit,' said Jem, outwardly calm. 'Old Howard might not have wanted to stop.'

But inside he was oddly furious with himself. Why did I do that? he kept asking. How un-classy, how abrupt, perverse and – and *young* of me! And then he thought how strange it was that he should feel sorry for Mr Howard and critical of himself for hurting Mr Howard's feelings. Why should a man of the world in his British sports car want the company of a sixteen-year-old boy, anyway? Probably he was relieved because he didn't have to make conversation to a pupil all the way back to Queens again. No doubt he was glad that he had his car to himself and could speed along un-pestered by requests to stop for ice-cream. Jem felt that none of this was true. With his usual perception he realised he had done something uncaring. He *knew* that Old Howard was disappointed that he wasn't going back with him. And knowing that – almost for a certainty – set him off worrying again about whether he wanted Mr Howard to have special feelings about him. Surely the teacher was behaving oddly if he did care, passionately, for snatched moments of the society of one of his boys? So back Jem came to the very strangeness of all this and the ambivalence of his own emotions. He cared that Mr Howard cared for him, and he wished it were not so.

Should he ask anyone's advice?

But whose?

And what about, exactly?

Everything was such a mess – and tomorrow there would be another *Duchess* rehearsal.

In the rushing Morgan, Mon's brain was pulsing with two linked thoughts. Jem cut me. If Jem deliberately cut me, he's knows there's something between us. Each of these thoughts carried its own wounding drip of acid; possibly the latter having the sharpest sting. If the boy, under eighteen, speaks to another adult about such a thing, I am in deep trouble. But, oh, it was so unexpectedly painful that Jem chose the bus over the car; as painful as being stood up at a teenage dance. But if his reasons are what I think they are, then I've shown my hand too obviously. He is embarrassed, frightened, repulsed, no doubt – and who can blame him? Why, why, should I assume he has gay leanings, just because he looks lovely in a dress? Ah, but he looks lovely when NOT in a dress, doesn't he? Stop! Stop *right there*!

Swiftly, Mon ran over everything he had said and done with Jem, and nothing incriminated him. In no way, even in words, had he betrayed his intense secret desire. The boy, if he suspected, had nothing to go on. *Nothing!*

Oh, I've got to be so careful – so very, very careful, thought Mon. From tomorrow's rehearsal, he decided he would be, to Jem, no more, nor less, than the tolerant, ironic producer he was to the others.

Mon gave a sudden jump at the wheel.

Suppose Jem doesn't *come* to the rehearsal?

Suppose I've risked the success of the play?

Suppose Jem pulls out of Julia's part? And barely three weeks to find someone else!

There are no more girls, but there must be another boy who......

But who could be Julia as Jem was Julia......? Oh God, God! What a mess it all is! cried his inner voice – echoing Jem's exact feelings at the same moment.

The Morgan, its passenger seat unoccupied, roared on down the 25 and all Mon could think of were Jem's lips smeared with ice-cream.

June : **THE GARDEN OF EARTHLY DELIGHT**

When David Lomax had parked the minibus – and its passengers, after carrying costumes and boxes of bits into the rear stage area, had gone home – he went upstairs to the Faculty room.

Louise was still there, photocopying. She looked up.

'Hi. You're back late.'

'Yes. A long afternoon fondling dress material with the Luvvies. Is Mon around?'

'No. I haven't seen him since you set out.'

David's forehead wrinkled, perplexed.

'How odd,' he said, as Louise began making some tea for them both. 'I mean, old Mon vamoosed without a word from Stacey's. I really had expected to find him here at base.'

'Oh, I expect he assumed I'd still be here and we'd get the stuff out anyway,' replied Louise. 'You had the bring the bus and the kids back anyway, so he thought he might as well just skip off home.'

'Well, I still think it peculiar he didn't tell us he was going to do that. Normally he's last off the sinking ship.'

'I think we're last on the Titanic tonight. Even Khalil's car's gone. Like a bit of chocolate?'

Louise produced a Hershey bar from her school bag.

'Oh genius. Just what I'm gagging for. We stopped for me to get ice creams for the drama queens, but I didn't fancy one.'

'You're very generous, buying lollipops for all.'

'Screw that. I've got the receipt. It's coming out of takings. I'm not subsidising Greg McManus' waistband.'

Louise smiled – a pleasant, open smile, less apologetic than her normal attempts. David Lomax, reaching out automatically for a second chunk of chocolate bar, and receiving it with a tolerant grin from Louise, felt aware for the very first time that Miss Carrbridge was a girl, not merely a colleague. He'd known her since the beginning of the academic year, of course, and for ten months he had pigeon-holed her in his mind as "a typical WT". WTs – women teachers – in his book were invariably neurotic, had a history of emotional problems, got tearful in the Faculty leisure room about classroom skirmishes, took marking home, joined the American Association for Teaching English, wrote out long lesson plans before teaching them, were often absent with mysterious headache-related ailments, got bitchy and defensive at meetings and eventually had breakdowns and left un-mourned by those who thought women had little to offer boys' high schools anyway. One of David's favourite arguments was that the drop in interest of boys reading in their teens was because they were too often taught by WTs. 'Boys need *men* to tell them that *Far From The Madding Crowd* is a damn fine novel, otherwise they put info like that in the same bracket as their moms nagging them about keeping bedrooms tidy,' he would say.

Somehow, this evening, Louise had transcended her WT status and, David realised, was being good company and easy to talk to. He hadn't looked forward to being trapped in the bus with a gaggle of pupils and Miss Carrbridge, especially after Mon's weird decision to take his own auto, and had been relieved she hadn't been given leave to go. Now, he felt himself re-appraising her.

Of Mon's equally odd decision to give the spare seat to one of his boys, David had not given much thought. If anything, he would have expected Mon to take one of the two older 12th grade pupils: Aisha Keating and Greg McManus. It then occurred to him that Mon had been wise not to take Aisha. He thought that she and Rosa had rather a "thing" for their director and they would quarrel afterwards, and if Aisha had gone she would behave like a little tart. David privately believed that all Senior Grade girls were tarts; being nearer in age than Mon to his 12th grade pupils he heard more of what went on. But still it was strange for Mon to have gone with Clarke – and also strange that he hadn't brought him back.

'Last square, Dave?' asked Louise.

'Eh? Oh, yeah, thanks Louise. I'll add it to my list of things I owe you. Twenty cups of tea, at least, a pack of exercise paper from your supply and now nearly a whole Hershey bar.'

Louise gave that engaging smile again and David, over the rim of his mug, measured her up in the light of his new-found approval. He liked her flinty-grey eyes, with their intelligent, wary, private dots of pupils. She reminded him of someone coming permanently out of a darkened building into the sun. He liked the long curly lashes which surrounded those eyes and the hint of dark smudge under them. He liked the firm, Celtic skin of her face, whitish with veins of roses, and appreciated the framing effect of her hair. Even without being conscious of them, he had admired her upright figure and largish bust. As she always wore long skirts to St Matthew's every day, he couldn't be sure about her legs, but they looked all right now with the material hugging them. In fact, now he could give attention to it, he wondered why he had passed her over for the last ten months.

'Are you happy, then, with the costumes?' she asked. 'I thought it was worth your going over there, even if we have to find another eight hundred dollars.'

'Yeah, it's another eighty or so bums on seats. Let's hope we get the support. I'm not entirely sure about the old lady outfit for Greg. He looks like a turkey in drag.'

'It's such a tiny part. He'll get a laugh, perhaps. Gosh, do you realise we've only got three weeks left to sell the play in? The cast have booked over a hundred and fifty, and the girls say a lot of their friends are coming from St Philomena's. But Mon was pointing out yesterday that the seniors are in graduation mode, almost mentally no longer here, and only a few stalwarts from last year will come back, the Junior High kids won't turn up at all, and that leaves just 11th grade, most of which have booked to see their pals. That's a sales base of only two year groups to fill two hundred and fifty seats on three nights.'

'I thought Mon was being a bit ambitious with this one. Perhaps we should have just used the Drama studio with a few bits of furniture. The costumes would just about be covered. After all, there's no copyright to pay, for a change.'

'I – I was thinking, while you were all over there, that is, of a way to increase sales a bit. Are – are you dashing off, or have I time to tell you my idea?' said Louise with more than a little of her usual apologetic manner.

'Er, no. Well, that is – yes – I've nothing specially on. Why don't we discuss it over, say, a Chinese? After all, I've got to eat and I'd be happy to have your company.'

Davis surprised himself considerably with this offer and, as soon as it was made, regretted it. He had half-promised to look in at the St Matthew's Alumni Sports Club, and, while a Chinese would probably have featured eventually, it would have done so later in the evening, soaking up a lot more than one of Louise's cups of tea. However, having offered, he couldn't very well back out. 'What about the Pekin Garden? Then I can run you to the subway, or – er – home afterwards.' David remembered that Louise didn't drive and that she lived somewhere over towards Manhattan.

Louise too was in some difficulty about how to regard this invitation. It would be nice, even necessary, to talk over this business of ticket sales, which Mon Howard, with his superb disregard for non-literary detail, had passed over to her. But she had never yet lingered late in Queens and – more to the point – she was anxious to speak to CoCo after what had passed between them the previous evening.

CoCo had been still asleep when Louise had crept out to get her train, so they had said nothing to each other since the strange, wonderful, disturbing night they had spent together. At the memory of what had occurred, Louise felt an unfamiliar warmth in the centre of her body and a sudden leap of her heart. She now knew how to recognise desire: a hunger and restlessness in the nerves, like being surprised in the middle of a gasp.

There was no doubt that she had discovered something with CoCo. She feared, however, that what had passed between them would make it impossible any longer for her to share CoCo's apartment, but as she hadn't had time to talk about it, she had no idea what CoCo's thoughts were on the subject.

When CoCo had sat up on her double bed, waiting for Louise to appear in her loose night-robe, she had worried that she might be about to light a fuse which would ignite an explosion, the aftermath of which luck, rather than judgement, would determine. In her belief that it would be helpful to teach the ex-nun a little about the joys of her own nervous system, she had not erred. Louise, in nightmarish embarrassment at first, and with growing confidence by the end, had been encouraged to act freely. They had lain together naked, leg to leg, CoCo telling Louise what she did to herself, trying to explain its delight to her friend. Louise felt like a person in a movie, outside herself, a looker-on, so strange was this weird occasion. They spoke for some time, CoCo questioning and encouraging, Louise tentative and guiltily curious. Then they agreed to touch and explore each other, and Louise had seen and felt CoCo reach orgasm. She had not done so herself, although she had felt great pleasure, but, a little later, following CoCo's tips, she had come to her own first ever moment of climax, with a huge sense of surprise.

'My God!' Louise had gasped, clinging to her friend, 'So that's it. That's what it's like.'

She had fumbled to pull her robe over her legs and breasts and, shamefacedly, had drawn her knees together. But CoCo had whispered,

'Don't be ashamed, Lou. It's nature, it's ordinary. It's not shaming.'

Before she had gone back to her room, while CoCo lay languorous near her, Louise had returned to an earlier question,

'What is this like with men?'

'Hm. It definitely depends on the man.'

'To be honest, it's men's *bodies* I'm quite frightened of.'

'They're much the same as us really. Just with a bit stuck on in front, more hair and no boobs. They can be inhibited too. Don't be fooled by the movies. They may say they want to get you to bed, but when the crunch comes they can be real fumbly and self-conscious. It's all part of the relationship thing; they're human too and bring their baggage with them.'

'There aren't many men I like at St Matthew's,' Louise had said, following her own train of thought.

'What about the interesting older man – your Faculty Head? You've talked enough about him these last few months.'

'Oh, Mon. He's a sweetie, but I know he's not interested in me. He once started training to be a priest. I'm sure I've told you that. He's really stuck into his work and he's very – how can I put it? – very self-sufficient. He's really witty, but under it, I think he's rather pure and contained. I know he appointed me because of my Catholic background and my time in training for the religious life: *A fellow feeling makes us wondrous fond* and all that. But I've never thought he had the faintest interest in me as me. He simply lives for his job. You've no idea how much he takes on.'

'Hm. As I've said before, I must meet this paragon. Anyone else, apart from that gorgeous sixteen-year-old of yours in the drag part?'

'If you count him, there's David Lomax. He's young, but definitely not my sort. He's very sporty and likes cars and baseball and that sort of thing.'

'Could be worse. What does he look like?'

'Oh, I don't know really,' and Louise had been surprised to discover that she couldn't describe David Lomax at all. 'Big. Ordinary. Fair-haired. Quite a friendly face, with some freckles. Bluff and, even though he teaches Eng Lit, not at all high-cultured. He's pally enough, I guess, but we've only seen more of each other since *The Duchess*. He doesn't teach in the Junior high at all and generally hangs out with the sports staff. He teaches Games or Sport Science, I guess you'd call it, as well as English, you see.'

'I see. I don't mind the sound of him at all.' CoCo had mused. 'Maybe he's more my type than yours.'

'No man is my type,' Louise had stated firmly. 'Not yet, at any rate.'

'But dear one, that's just what I want to change. That's why I wanted to edge the topic round to sex. You do need to feel more comfy about that side of things; then you'll start to see men differently.'

'But CoCo,' Louise had muttered, 'I'm still a virgin. And stimulating oneself for the hell of it isn't what the Church thinks is right; it isn't about procreation.'

'It is if it's about helping you to find the daddy of your offspring and knowing how to keep him happy to bring them up with you. Besides, the Church has a poor argument there. You don't need lemon meringue pie to stay alive – a handful of grass and a dead rat would have as much sustenance. It's about taking pleasure in existence.'

'Well, I guess I don't know....,' had murmured Louise.

'You just go out and find the nice guy who's waiting for you. You'll have no problems. You know why?' Louise shook her head. 'Because you are loving and gentle and serious and pure....'

'I don't feel so pure anymore, talking about all this, and after what I've done with you,' had grinned Louise ruefully in the gloom.

'Of course you are. Any man would worship you. You've got all the right things in all the right places and you're unspoilt by life. The perfect combo.'

'What are you thinking about?' asked David.

He had cleared up their mugs (by putting them in the sink for a woman cleaner to wash up tomorrow) and was waiting for a response to his invitation to have a Chinese with him.

Louise, with a jump, came back to the St Mat's
Faculty leisure room from CoCo's bedroom.

'Oh. Yes, yes, I'd like to,' she twittered. 'I'll just
need to ring home first. The girl I share with was
expecting me in soon.'

She moved away to the payphone in the passage to
speak to CoCo. While she did so, David fished the
bursar's summary of what was left in the play budget
account from Mon's pigeon-hole. Jeez, only $76.50.
The slips of paper were flimsy in his large hands.

David, as an ex-St Matthew's student, was a real
"company man". Now thirty, he had gone into 7th
grade the year Mon Howard had reached his tenth
anniversary at the school. Mon had taught him as a
sophomore and throughout his 11th and 12th grade. He
had gone on to read English at the University of
North Carolina at Wilmington, distinguished himself
in the Seahawks baseball and track teams, had
obtained his modest degree (and the trace of a
southern accent) and, after a post-grad teaching
qualification at New York State University, he had
come back to his old high school, where he had had
the luck to do most of his work-placement practice.
Mon had appointed him gratefully. He knew David to
be loyal, solid in basic reading, good on discipline
and interested in lighting and all things electrical and
mechanical for his plays. In the eight years David had
taught in the English Faculty and the four that he'd

been Mon's sidekick, he had equipped the Drama studio with lights, installed a PA system in the auditorium and managed to buy an aluminium scaffolding tower for lights positioning and focusing paid for by ticket sales. His rise to second in the Faculty had not been the result of a career plan, but the moves of his immediate predecessors – one to the priesthood, the other to California.

His social horizons were not wide. The St Matthew's Alumni Clubhouse in Turner Avenue, the Star of India and the Pekin Garden, the bars along Jewel Avenue, his parents' home near Kissena Park, his apartment south of the expressway, and the Faculty leisure room comprised most of his world. He never failed to go on school ski and baseball trips, considered himself a good Catholic – although he preferred golf to Mass on many Sundays – drove a Volvo, not in its first youth, dreamed of one day buying a Harley-Davidson Electra-Glide, lived for the results of the World Series, tennis from Wimbledon, American football, the US Open and, when all else on TV failed, US/Canadian ice hockey. His English teaching was sound because he kept effortlessly good discipline, but he tended to limit it to those texts he had himself mastered at school and college. Taking his cue from Mon, he professed to have no time for the latest educational ideas ('boloney'), talk of replacements for honours programmes for all four high school grade levels ('horse-shit') and recent suggestions that he should go on training courses for his career development ('get a life'). He didn't plan ahead or think about applying for chair of faculty posts elsewhere because he never seriously contemplated leaving St Mat's – although, of course, he constantly threatened to do so ('this place isn't what it was/the new principal's a dick-brain/we're on a knife edge, discipline-wise'). Part of his thinking embraced the notion that, in the fullness of time, he would step into Mon's shoes.

David, unsentimentally and unselfconsciously, worshipped Mon, and his own finer parts – sensitivity, a measure of interest in culture, desire to help young people grow – had their provenance in Mon's way of doing things. In his last year as a pupil at St Matthew's he had toyed, quite seriously, as some Catholic boys do, with the idea of the priesthood. Had he been of Mon's generation, he might well have gone through a seminary and ended up as a fine parish priest, but he had collided with the collapse of interest in vocational religion after the '70s, so his largely inchoate desire to serve had transmuted into a yen for teaching.

He had had two emotional affairs, one at university, and one four years ago. Neither had yielded much happiness, especially the last. Sylvia had been older than himself, a divorcee with a small boy, and she had thrown herself at him during her short time teaching History at St Matthew's. They had slept together for eight months – mainly at her apartment while the child slumbered in the next room. David had been proud of the fact that he had a lover, and as most of his colleagues knew about it and considered Sylvia attractive, if unsuitable for him, he had been able to feel a man of the world and a playboy – although unable to escape a strong feeling of sin and guilt. At times he considered marrying Sylvia, but too often he found her prickly and difficult to deal with on day-to-day matters. She hated sport, didn't get on with his friends, loathed Mon, whom she considered an intellectual snob, was allergic to most foodstuffs – especially Indian and Chinese – and was desperately homesick for St Louis. She begrudged David any time she spent out of her company. Jeez, he would think, imprisoned in her bed, no wonder her husband hauled his ass. That shamed sense of wrong-doing prevented him from taking Holy Communion at Mass at this time too, so that when it all blew over – in a surprisingly low-key way – and Sylvia returned to St Louis, he felt a great wave of relief. Lacking the moral courage to bring the affair to an end himself, he was stupendously glad that it had ended in something like friendship. He had not attempted to get in touch again, and had heard nothing from her, so for a whole academic year had breathed the delightful ozone of freedom.

In his own way, therefore, David was as unsure about asking Louise to have a meal with him as she was about accepting. Suppose she turned out to be another Sylvia?

'What's the big idea, then?' he asked, when they were settled in the Pekin Garden, and had exhausted chit-chat about TV shows, movies and the English Faculty.

'Oh, *The Duchess* – yes. Yes, it's – er – it's about trying to sell more tickets.'

'I've advertised it in the parish rag,' said David. 'We did that with *Kiss Me, Kate* and it brought in quite a few of the old biddies. And the parents have had it puffed back in the Principal's mid-semester letter home, and I've spoken to assemblies in Junior high and to the sophomores so far.'

'I've heard about those. How you actually burn a ten-dollar bill in front of the boys to ram home how cheap the seats are.'

'It works every time – provided they haven't seen it before. I pay myself back out of receipts. Mon says it's against the law to destroy bank notes, so I'm thinking of just making photocopies in future; no one will spot them. Oh, and I've got Lizzie in Art and Design beavering away on some large-scale ads for it; silk-screens, I think she said. And, of course, the big push in all English lessons from Monday.'

'So you're doing what you and Mon usually do?'

'What *I* usually do, in any case.'

'But I thought that there was a problem this year, isn't there?'

134

'Oh yeah. The play's got a smaller cast than usual and the fact that it's a 17th century oldie is only going to generate about forty customers. A cast of thousands in a popular musical brings in the grannies. We had ninety Luvvies in *Oliver!* not counting the orchestra, and cast groupies filled two of the three nights on their own.'

'My ideas are probably silly,' said Louise – quite like her old self now and wondering if her sales notions *were* all that clever after all.

The waiter arrived with dishes. David seized a spoon.

'Egg fried rice? Chicken? No – go on. I could do with a few ideas. Dim Sum?'

I was thinking of a couple of periodicals....'

'....and another beer, please,' said David to the waiter, just as if he hadn't heard her. For a moment it occurred to her that he might resent her muscling in on his well-tried selling plans. 'Periodicals, you say?'

'You see, CoCo – that's the girl I share with – and I were browsing over the magazines for sale at the Met, and I came across two which gave me the idea. One was *The Senecan*. I'd never heard of it. Have you?' David shook his head, his mouth full of mixed vegetables in soy. 'It's called that in honour of Lucius Seneca, the ancient Roman who invented the five-act play and the Revenge Tragedy....'

'....as in the style adopted by Webster, Middleton, Kyd, Shakespeare and company?'

'….and the periodical also deals with the *Moral Essays* and research done on his work….'

'….Seneca. Nero's tutor, murdered by him in old age, had almost none of his plays performed? Yup, Mon told us about him in 12th grade, I'm sure.'

'….and it has advert space.'

'Adverts? What? For things about Seneca?'

'About what Seneca inspired. Writings. Readings. And so does the other periodical, *Jacobean Explorer*. That has reams of info about plays written in the early 17th century – and pages about who really wrote Shakespeare, you know, Earl of Oxford, Bacon, and all that.'

'So you think – what? That we should *advertise* our play in them?'

'I rang the editorial offices of each. One's based in on the Harvard campus, the other's right here in New York. If we get ads in *The Senecan* by Monday they'll make the next issue, which comes out about ten days before our play. And an ad in *Jacobean Explorer* gives a week before we're off, and they go one better. They have a fortnightly news-sheet; next one due at the end of next week.'

'*Duchess of M* advertised nation-wide, eh?' David spooned some beef chow mein. 'Well, well. Who'd have thought of that? Clever old you.'

With relief, Louise realised that he wasn't offended at her suggestion of a new way of doing things. 'But would people,' he went on, 'read the ads in time to make a difference? And they wouldn't be all that interested if they didn't live round New York, surely?'

'It's probably a bit too late to take full advantage of the idea, but I did find out some interesting figures yesterday.'

'What?'

Louise fished out a folded slip of paper from her pocket and smoothed it out on the tablecloth.

'Guess how many people bought *The Senecan* – according to their circulation figures.'

'God. I don't know. Two hundred?'

'Fourteen thousand and sixty-seven.'

'You're joking! Who'd have thought it?'

'And *Jacobean Explorer*? Twenty-one thousand, seven hundred and twenty-one across the USA, Europe and Australia.'

Louise folded her bit of paper again. David's amazement amused her, and she smiled openly at him in the low light. 'I take it you never thought of reading one of them?'

'No, never. I hadn't known they existed. And it's a bit weird and elderly, don't you think? All that mania about who wrote what nearly four hundred years ago. It's really a load….'

'….of horse-shit. I know,' grinned Louise.

'Well….'

'Anyway, I haven't told you my *other* idea – not really.'

'Which is....?'

'We send out a decent photo of the cast on set and in costume and a few details to the Jacobean Association which publishes the *Explorer* and they circulate it all. I told you that they have a newsletter coming out in a few days, for libraries, university departments, and that sort of thing, and I rang them and they'll put in our pic and ad for nothing.'

David stared in admiration at Louise's flat-bottomed colleen's eyes, sparkling and unselfconscious in her eagerness.

'Brilliant!' he cried.

'And,' she went on, 'do you know how many people belong to the Jacobean Association?'

'Eleven million?'

'Oh, you! It's actually over seven thousand.'

'Jeez, Louise. Talk about needing a life.'

'Maybe, but some of those seven thousand must live within a ten mile radius of New York City and would like to see a spirited performance of the seldom staged *Duchess of Malfi*. We don't want all seven thousand – but fifty or sixty extra people might help.'

'So, you've convinced me, already! If we could get, say, fifty asses on seats at $10 each, that would be fine. But what's it gonna cost us?'

'That's the beauty of it. Next to nothing. *The Senecan* charges only forty dollars for a half-page ad – so that would break even if we got four ticket sales from them. But then, when I was ringing this guy, Joe Pinfield, at the Association, he said they'll do it for free, because we're a high school. AND he'll send a reviewer down. He always needs material and news items, I gather. And at his suggestion I got in touch with this other great old gent in Nova Scotia and did a quid pro quo.'

'Nova Scotia, Canada?'

'Apparently, Halifax, Nova Scotia, is a haunt of Webster fanatics. His two great tragedies, *Duchess* and *The White Devil*, were first performed on the North American continent at a theatre in Halifax and there's a museum about him. I think, from what he said, there's an ancestral connection.'

'And the quid pro quo?'

'We advertise the museum in the St Mat's mag, in our programme, and at the play, and he gives us a slot in this month's Webster Museum newsletter. A very long shot, but….'

Well, zowie! thought David. She's got more balls than the All-Stars. Who would have thought of, and done, all that? Not that nut-jobs are likely to come to Queens from Canada!

'Clever old you,' he beamed. 'And Mon?'

'We started to talk about it before he set out to get the costumes today, but I had to rush to a class, and he seemed a bit preoccupied about something, and them Jem Clarke jumped into his car and I didn't get the chance to tell him anything more. And of course I haven't seen him since.'

'Mon'll be real happy, you'll see. Louise, old colleague of mine, we'll do it together and I hope you won't think I'm a sexist bastard if I say that I had no idea you'd come up with something so bright.'

'Not bad, then? For a girl.'

They both sensed the satisfying warmth that working on a shared cause brings. It enveloped them and they grinned happily in the near-empty gloom of the Pekin Garden before splitting the bill – to faint but relieved protest from David – and getting back to his car.

It was not yet dark. Louise asked him to drop her over at her usual subway stop and not bother to drive her to Jackson Heights. He was grateful for this – it gave plenty of time for a drink or two at the St Mat's Alumni clubhouse – and he chalked it up as another point in Louise's favour.

As the train rattled her home, Louise found her thoughts divided between her reluctant and simultaneously eager desire to talk to CoCo again and her new-found approval of David Lomax. Not a bad person, really, she thought – for a man.

June : **ON HIS OWN – AS USUAL**

Repent, and sin no more. The words of absolution whispered in Mon's head. How? *How* repent? How is it possible to *repent* of love? Loving Jem isn't a sin. The *sin* of love can't exist. God is love. All love is pure. I don't need to confess my love as something filthy, do I?

Trying to keep an unreasoning bitterness of disappointment and a hurtful tang of rejection from joining his sense of injustice and overwhelming him, Mon drove away from Stacey's in a rush, forgetful of David Lomax, the minibus, the play, of everything but the loss of Jem.

Why had Jem chosen to go back in the bus? Oh God, God, if this is the beginning of a complete withdrawal by him from me, what on earth am I going to do?

An empty picture of grinding for three more weeks on the play without Jem in it scattered itself across his brain. Then he steadied his thoughts. Ridiculous! Jem would never give up Julia now – not on the eve of performance. Besides, I haven't given him a reason. Oh, how did those lines of Lucius' go? *The boy disdains me. He leaves me, scorns me. Briefly die their joys that place them on the truth of girls – and boys.* The lines danced in Mon's inner ear as the splintered sun flickered through trees onto him.

It shocked him to realise how intoxicating had been the pleasure of Jem's company on the drive into Manhattan, and how desolate he felt without it now.

And, following from an imagined play production without Jem in it (and suppose he asked to leave my Eng Lit class too?) came a bleak, bleak picture of life at St Matthew's without Jem there. Oh, it's going to happen, sighed Mon. Miserably, Mon tortured himself with the reflection that even if everything went right: Jem stayed in his teaching group next semester, stayed in the play AND even decided to be in *next* year's play, he'd still be gone after all that – forever.

I can't believe, thought Mon, that I've become so – so unbalanced about a boy of sixteen. How can something like this happen to me?

Because it's happened before. Three times. *The child is father to the man.* Right as usual, Wordsworth. It's just unfinished business going back to bobby-sox. That's all.

Mon then started thinking of the nearby, terrifying grief – Jem-less – of the summer vacation, and by turns he came back to the essential mutability of love based on youth.

Even when he has left St Mat's, he'll be only eighteen, and how old will I be?

This reflection led Mon to see the impossibility of actually living with someone so many, many years younger – and of the same gender too! He horrified himself by realising how little *that* meant to him. It was as if such love was taken for granted. Well, it was, in the increasingly liberal present – but not for someone in Mon's position. He felt quite emptied by the reminder that no one would understand. Jem's mother – oh, imagine her anguish! David, Doctor Bennett, Harry Doyle, his friends, no one – just no one – would be on his side, on love's side, if his feelings slipped into day and became action. And what action? Kidnap Jem? Flee to Mexico?

Finally, unbidden, came the cruellest thought of all. Later, aged thirty or forty, Jem wouldn't *be* Jem, but a grown-up stranger with five o'clock shadow and a man's paunchy, ungainly body. The Jem Clarke of Julia fame was an evanescent mirage – a creature born only of *The Duchess of Malfi* – created by Mon himself – inspiring this agonising love before disintegrating into the commonplace: becoming just another ordinary, dull American suburban guy.

What a comedy it all is!

I made Julia and I made her – he – it – to last for as long as it takes the applause to fade. Might as well think of making a pet of a butterfly.

Gradually, by such musings, Mon grew calmer and reason crept back.

Okay, so I can't have what I want?

Which of us can?

Yet the precise reason for Jem's desertion....yup, give it its true name....continued to nag at Mon even late that evening, especially after he had taken a disturbing, empty, solitary comfort in an action he had been trained to think of as sinful and had almost (guiltily) been able to imagine Jem in his arms, their faces close together.

February 2020: *CREDO IN UNUM DEUM*

After he had stood up, then sat down, then stood up once more – those by now re-familiarised motions of the service of the Mass – Janek began to feel a sense of regret that he had so definitively lapsed from his religion. He stole a glance at Lindy. She had bobbed up, bobbed down, knelt and crossed herself in imitation of him. *Man sees God in the face; woman through him* popped into his mind. What did she know? What help could she be now?

It was after Francis' death; that was when it just wasn't possible to have faith any longer. My dearest little son – cruelly despatched from life. The pain is too recent, too raw for me to believe in a God of love, I guess. But at school I had faith. I was happy. No doubts there, until......

As the service for the dead Benedictine brother had wound on, Janek felt his thoughts finger at the stiff wrappings of the past. Mr Howard, now; there *was* a teacher. Bet there aren't any left like that. Janek wondered why the news of the old boy's death had been so upsetting. Yes, it was that play – *The Duchess of Malfi* – which had made the impact so many years ago. Before that summer I knew nothing, thought Janek, absolutely nothing. Such a clear picture formed in Janek's mind of the two teenagers sitting together in class, that he gave a low gulp of emotion.

Those lost boys! Lindy looked round and up in surprise, but she didn't notice the moisture in her husband's eyes. It was all she could do to suppress a great yawn of boredom.

It has to be faced, ran Janek's thoughts, I am unhappy, unfulfilled, bitter. I don't like what I do, and I'm tired of Lindy. She's sick of me, I'm sure. *Why couldn't Francis have lived?* With a convulsion of the mind, Janek saw with clarity that he had only been utterly happy at St Matthew's. I wouldn't have said I was, if I'd been asked then, but I was, wasn't I?

When did the unhappiness start?

It was long before his marriage, his promotion, the birth of his son. All those had given him satisfaction – once. But those teenage feelings of transcendent joy, personal worth and power, freedom, love of living – when did they fade and wither?

I really think it was – it must have been – when Jem left.....

The thick, distinctly flavoured emotions Janek always savoured when Jem's disappearance came back to him, blurred the sounds from the altar. Why had he not seen what was coming? Had he not discovered that terrible thing on the second night of the play? Why hadn't he gone to old Howard and said something? Why hadn't he been firm with Jem? If he had, would they still be seeing each other?

A highly unlikely image came to his mind of himself and Jem in a bar in Greenwich Village, drinking peaceably, each in contented middle-age, each, perhaps, with sons at the old high school, visiting each other's houses…. Just as if *The Duchess of Malfi* had never existed and the corrupt Riccardo had never done what he had done. For surely it must have been that bastard who started it; surely it hadn't been Jem himself?

Could I have been *jealous*? In that way?

Surely not?

Janek was quite surprised at the fierce pain that came back again – quite as poignant as it had been in that far-off summer. He heard the shrieks as Julia's face was eaten away, saw Jem's cheeks flushed at night, and his dark-shadowed eyes at morning, those long, awful months after the school was sued, Mr Howard left St Matthew's and Jem vanished forever….

28 YEARS EARLIER
July: BOSOLA GETS REALLY INVOLVED

'I don' know why you got yourself so involved,' said Cian Walsh, Riccardo's friend.

'Oh, it's a laugh,' yawned Rick.

They were in the room reserved for senior 12th graders in the Avery Building, Riccardo perched on the corner of a table, swinging his legs, Cian earnestly looking up at him from his chair.

'Yeah, but look, if you go to this dress rehearsal – all day, for God's sake – you're going to miss Felicity's picnic party completely and you won't want to come on to The Pipe Factory afterwards.'

'Yes, I will. Give me a ring at home about a quarter after six when you're coming back from the picnic. I'll join you by seven. Howard never rehearses after five-thirty.'

'It's a pity about the picnic, though. Are you sure you can't get away mid-afternoon? Felicity said she was specially expecting you.'

'Cian, I can't. How many times, man? You know what old Howard's like – or rather you don't; but take it from me he'll go ballistic if I just walk out halfway through. I've got the main part. I am Bosola.'

'But....'

'This play is his pet project. He freaks out if a guy is two, three minutes late for rehearsal. And,' added Riccardo, 'I don't really blame him, you know. He

148

insists on quality, and he won't get it unless he has reliability.' Riccardo found himself quoting Mr Howard's words: 'Bring me your poor, your huddled paraplegics and I'll turn them into actors. Talent is merely an option – quality is built on attendance.'

'What are you talking about, Rick?'

'Only quoting the Maestro.'

'Well shove it up your ass.'

The first performance of *The Duchess of Malfi* was now only three days away, and Louise, David and Mon had forced out of their minds the fact that they were, according to their contracts, full-time teachers. End of semester tests for the junior high boys, plans for the summer vacation, Athletics Day, text orders, class lists, timetabling, moving of pupils up and down sets, completion of the Faculty's paperwork relating to audits, targets and forward plans (which Mon referred to as "my finest works of pure fiction") were all forgotten as Webster's drama metamorphosed from an amusing, private, self-indulgent hobby into a public showcase of St Matthew's abilities.

David had hired an extra sound system with 12-way mixer, a 200 watt PA amplifier and two column speakers on stands, and had borrowed his father's reliable old Revox tape-recorder on which to record background music and sound effects. For the last few days he had been trying to recruit Pharhad, the prompter – now no longer needed – to become sound man on the backstage team, but Pharhad, who knew nothing about sound equipment, had refused. He would rather be stage manager and continue to be on hand for prompts, he said, because they might still be needed. There was sense in this, so David was still looking out for an operator when, carting the system into the auditorium from the back of his Volvo with Riccardo and Greg's help, Riccardo called over,

'Hey, Jem. That big, fair-haired guy you hang with – didn't you say he was a hi-fi whizz -kid?'

'Jan Franitza? Yes, he's hi-fi mad. Knows it all.'

'How about, Mr Lomax, this Jan – Jem's pal – coming on board to work the stuff?'

So – at a light word, Janek joined the stage team. When the system for incidental music and effects was up, Riccardo surprised himself (because he was, by nature, not much of an involver) by making another suggestion. Although the auditorium was not enormous, sound from the stage did get rather lost and Janek had given his opinion that when the seats were full the absorption would have a further negative effect on audibility.

'What about mikes?' Rick had asked.

'We can hardly have radio mikes for a cast of thirty,' grunted Mon, 'besides there's nothing more off-putting than some actors having mikes, and some not. It sounds very odd.'

'I wasn't thinking of radio mikes,' explained Rick. 'I had a picture of those microphones which run along the stage front and pick up everybody.'

'Brilliant! *Rifle* mikes,' cried Janek, catching the drift. 'I know just what's needed, Mr Howard. Shure rifle mikes with condensers, and I know where they can be hired here in Queens – if there's dough left.'

'Seems a good idea,' admitted Mon. 'Too many of the cast sound like elderly librarians whispering among the reference shelves. How many do we need?'

'Three would be fine, Sir. Stage left, stage right and stage centre. We can snick one in on a little stand between the moveable steps down front, and the others on the stage lip.'

'Gimme the details and I'll go call your outfit now, Janek, and hope they have them, that I can pick them up tomorrow, and that they work. Putting trust in you, big boy.'

'It'll be great, Sir. Jan knows,' said Jem, grinning with pleasure at Jan's decisive interjection. He had smiled at Riccardo too, and the older pupil, catching his sparkling eyes, found himself re-assessing Jem in the scale of things yet again, and admiring him as a team player. I guess, he thought to himself, that I'd be happier if I had a friend like him.

'Felicity will be pee'd off,' persisted Cian.

Rick came back from his thoughts about rehearsals – and Jem.

'Oh, I don't know,' he murmured. Really, this

conversation was becoming a bore.

'After last month? She's thought of nothing else. That's what you get when you screw a girl at a party. What did you expect?'

'Don't go on about it. It was an accident, really.'

'You're so keen on putting it about, aren't you?' said his friend. 'You're a bastard sometimes. And the least you can do is turn up for her birthday picnic.'

'I've told you, you cretinous craphead, that it's an all-day rehearsal. Perhaps I shouldn'ta gotten involved, but I did.'

'Yeah, only you would try to be in a play, in a big part, in your last semester. You're right, you shouldn't have gone to those auditions.'

'It seemed a long way off back then, and how was I to predict that Felicity was going to get the hots for me? I didn't even know her then.'

'You didn't know her in the biblical sense. True.'

'Oh, ha, ha. I'm not able to come to the picnic. Sorry. If you think I've behaved badly to Felicity, I'm not going to cap it by behaving badly to old Howard and the cast as well.'

'But....'

'And it's not just Howard – it's the rest of them. We're a sort of team now, Cian.'

Rick's regular Mediterranean face went into frowns as he tried to define his inexplicable commitment to what was, after all, only the high school play. 'It's hard to explain to someone else, but they all depend on me. Or rather, each of us depends on the other. When one of us is absent the whole thing just doesn't work. It's because only *we* know what we're supposed to do, and when, and how. See? Oh, it's difficult to.......'

He tailed off. Cian, not an involver and not a team player, any more than Riccardo had been last year, clearly didn't understand. His eyebrows lifted.

'I see all right. You're after one of those two St Phil's babes in the cast, aren't you? Bye, bye, Felicity.' He narrowed his eyes and drew his mouth down into what he felt was a knowing, wise expression. 'You know what? It's being kept away from girls most of the year, man. Jeez, I wish we went to a co-ed high. An' I wish we weren't Catholics, with all our hang-ups about girls and sin. And then you wouldn't go crazy because you get to spout Olde Englishe to a coupla visiting drama-queens.'

Rick smiled. Across his inner eye came a picture of Rosa and Aisha – laughing, always laughing, with their different little come-on ways and their amusingly serious Theatre Studies student approach to their parts. They included him and Greg, the two seniors, in their approbation, he knew. Their attitude to younger boys playing character parts was subtly different. They were straight and friendly with those others, but they flirted with him – more so than with Greg, he realised. Yet of late Rick had noticed a change in the cast chemistry; yes, of late, Aisha, in particular, had seemed to switch an invisible ray from him to Jem Clarke. Without being in the least able to analyse the complex feelings that went with this knowledge, Rick knew himself to be jealous, and puzzled to discover that he was jealous, not so much of Jem, as of Aisha herself. He half-discerned that not only did he see her as a rival, but, with a pleasing squirm of degeneracy, that since he had seen Jem dressed as Julia, he desired Julia for himself.

These thoughts made it hard for him to respond crisply to Cian Walsh. He could hardly confide to his friend that an 11th grade boy was beginning to occupy his thoughts more often than Felicity whom he had once slept with. Still, one thing was certain.

'I can't, repeat can't, come to the picnic, repeat picnic,' he said. 'And that's that. *You* get off with Felicity; you'll find she's a good little go-er.'

'I've got the point. And the disco? The Pipe Factory? Can you come on to that?'

'I expect so. Keep a rum and coke warm for me.'

Cian, who had come in specially to appeal to his friend, grunted, stood up and went back into the sunshine. Riccardo dropped into the chair he had left and sat staring ahead of him.

It was exciting to think that he could be, might be, on a chase.

He shrugged Felicity's thin, possessive image off.

Julia – or rather Jem – in a long dress with a slit, replaced it.

You have a pretty way. Come I'll disarm you, and arm you thus.... Yes, during that scene, he had taken to holding Julia's head in his lap and caressing her hair and face. What did Jem Clarke think of that? Later, he planned to do as Webster's stage direction indicated, if Old Howard let him get away with it: *Bosola kisses her.* What would Jem think of *that*?

Rick Parisi had had a fairly successful time as a student at St Matthew's. Single-minded, clever, selfish, charming, he had got help when it was needed and shown that he could handle several disciplines for study in his junior year: English Literature, American History, Art and Italian – and excel at them. He was athletic, but not interested in teamwork. Swimming and running had been his areas at 9th and 10th grade. He played acoustic guitar well and had appeared as a soloist at two school concerts.

In all these pursuits he had run alone; his decision, in his last year, to audition for *The Duchess of Malfi* could not be explained by anyone.

His parents had been horrified.

'Ricco, why you wanna risk your grades? Is not sensible,' his dad had groaned.

A baker from Stresa in the Alpinia, his father had settled in America over twenty years ago. He loved New York and boasted about his success when he went home to Italy.

'Nowhere else in the worl' to be,' he would say.

'Theatre, concerts, art galleries, *ristoranti*, and much, much money.' He seldom, if ever, went to the first three, but he would rub finger and thumb together to indicate how crafty he had been in getting rich. His "Alpinia" patisserie products were sold in cafes and supermarkets all over the city. His big new Mercedes was a sign of that. He did not want his only child to follow him into the bakery business, nor did his pretty, financially astute American wife. Whatever Rick might feel about the matter, his parents had already mentally established him in the Law, perhaps eventually in politics. It was why they had selected St Matthew's. Rick's studies were of unarguable importance, and his taking the part of Bosola seemed to his parents an act of wilful perversity.

Rick himself, not knowing what demon had led him into becoming a St Mat's thespian, was, however, glad that it had. His times at rehearsal had become some of the happiest of his school days, perhaps because they had begun to change him. He had a lot of his father's drive and his mother's acuity, but in him they had hardened into selfishness, because he was spoilt, and into a heartless self-pleasing, because he had no siblings. 'You'll just have to accept that I'm a bit of a bastard,' he used to tell friends whom he had upset.

Now he had turned nineteen, his selfishness had broadened into a man's pursuits. With girls in particular, he did what he wanted. His father, a devout

Catholic, who had also favoured St Matthew's for its ethos and moral teachings, became aware of his son's activities with mixed emotions. Part of him gave a Mediterranean welcome to signs of virility and a romantic disposition. *'Ah, sempre i giovanotti,'* he would murmur, fondly – but erringly – recalling that he too had been a ladies' man before being ensnared by his sharp-featured little brunette New Yorker. Signor Parisi turned his eyes from his son's precociousness at home, but when, back in Stresa, he had asked his older brother, Claudio, what he thought, that wise man said, 'Just make sure he uses protection,' raising his eyebrows and privately congratulating himself that he had not brought up his own children in America.

Riccardo had discovered sex later than many boys, some way through his fourteenth year, and had not endowed it with any warm fantasies about relationships with others but had been almost peremptory and efficient in satisfying a bare requirement, rather as he might have gulped a can of coke to slake thirst.

He had made love to three 11th and 12th grade girls, two of them from St Philomena's, Felicity being the last of the line. She had put his choice of her down to an accident of perfect compatibility, but he, having got what seemed at the time an urgent need, had now lost interest in her.

As he continued to sit in the empty communal

room, it came to him that he had no real interest in the other girls in *The Duchess* either. Aisha was appealing in her African, bronze way, Rosa was a doll, of course, and Suzie nicely submissive, but if there was one conquest Rick wanted to make it was of Julia. Imagining, a little shamefacedly, variants of himself in Bosola's black leather with Julia in his arms, he now felt a new hot-faced excitement each time his thoughts dwelt on it. He had had a shock when he first realised that he had got used to thinking of Julia as a desirable girl, submerging the undeniable fact that Julia was a boy. Yet it gave him a tang, a stomach-tightening thrill, which made his girl conquests seem naïve and ordinary. Seducing Jem, now….that would be *something*! *That's* what I like about being in the play, he thought. He had no clear idea exactly what male lovers did with each other, so, for a change, he felt fluttery and inexperienced all over again. What would Jem be like, naked, and as excited as himself? Rick felt like someone about to step out of light onto the dark side of the moon. The challenge was there! The reward unknowable! A homo-erotic affair! It was all so extraordinary and unforeseen.

Riccardo was unjust to himself to believe that his commitment to the play was entirely romantic and lustful. It might seem to him that forging a relationship with Julia in the little time left was his main purpose, but since early June his better side, that which appreciated a job well done, rose to a difficult challenge of memory, discovered the satisfaction of working in a team, of the facing of mutual challenges, of respect of his director and co-actors, of the sublimation of self for the greater good, had dominated. For several weeks those who knew him (with the exceptions of Cian and Felicity) had thought better of him.

July 1992: SOME OF THE TEAM ARE DISTRACTED BY ROMANCE

By dint of concentrating on the job in hand, Mr Howard had reached a state of equilibrium about his one-way romance. Sometimes he felt like a being with a limb cut off when not in Jem's presence; sometimes when in that presence, his love was so intense that he was sure others could see the flame-like arc, travelling in one direction, between them. But generally Mon stabilised himself by reflecting that the play would run until the end of the week, Jem would be Julia and all would be well. He refused to consider days beyond that, like a patient destined to have a distressing operation in the near future who manages to lessen the dread by concentrating with fierce, if nightmarish, enjoyment upon the present. In between the day-long rehearsals he had secured for the cast, he imagined happy scenarios – like getting Jem to accompany him on an educational trip to Europe in the summer vacation – which became more natural and easy to bring off the longer he dwelt on them.

David Lomax had painted the scuffed stage-top and completed the lighting script for Janek and his little brother, Francis, and the CD of music and effects. He and Louise fussed over the return of costumes to hangers marked with an actor's card and hunted for the many little props needed to give eye-interest to the plot. He threw himself into these things recklessly, abandoning correction of work and even a compulsory training session on the value of coursework ('load of pointless horse-shit') which earned him a tart note from Dr Bennett, the Principal. And all the while he kept an eye on Louise.

She had become David's shadow. For her, as for him, the play had become everything. The ordering of the set, props and costumes came close, in her mind, to the beautifying of a home – and she infused an aura of devotion into their joint labours. As the first night came ever closer, Louise recalled with pleasure what she had done in the Faculty leisure-room after school the week before. Such a tiny action, but it seemed to her to have changed everything. David had been making a list of some props they still had to procure, balancing a pad on his left leg. In order to make a point, she had found herself placing her hand directly on his knee, and he, dropping the pen, had taken her hand and held it. As their gaze met and he smiled, she realised she did not find the touch off-putting; rather it electrified her. David, on his side inexplicably pleased by her delicate fingers, the gesture of which he had interpreted as a caress, had found a churning of desire for her. His rapidly developed fondness for Louise had not, until that precise second, contained any component of sexual interest. Now he thought that he did want to get to know her intimately, and so their work on the play was invested with a sweet urgency it had not possessed before.

Riccardo looked down with emotions of barely understood wonder and protectiveness on Julia's closed eyelashes, perfect complexion and delicate neck. Upon his lap, her weight lay easily, belonging there. Her slightly damp fingers were clutched in his.

'I will arm you thus,' he said, for the twentieth time. He felt the expiration of her breath on the hairs of his forearm. Part of her dress had fallen open and a finely shaped leg stretched out. Rick could hardly catch his breath. Should he actually kiss her on the lips now? He had still to put this direction into action and felt he could hardly leave it until the actual first night. Time seemed to stand still for an instant, and then he heard Old Howard's voice,

'Have you guys died? Next line, Julia! *Now am I a wanton* – and, by the way, Jem, you should have made some attempt to kiss Bosola. You're supposed to be seducing him. A quick peck on the cheek'll do.'

Jem had not again felt Aisha's sherberty kiss, although he had hoped it might happen once more. A smaller part of him was drawn to the anticipation of this, however, than to the disturbing presence of Francis Franitza's golden-haired head in the stage-right wing near the glass windows of the control room on smoke machine and furniture-moving duties.. Although he had got the boy into the team, nothing had come of it. Jem still had what seemed to him shameful yearnings but had no idea what move to make.

Julia had taken possession of him so completely that it was as her he found himself flirting, outrageously, so it seemed to that detached, sensible part of his mind, with those from whom certain waves seemed to emanate. Francis was not one of these, Jem had to admit. Rick, by contrast, was. Jem had divined for some time that the older boy had an interest in him – just as he had an interest in return. He liked to lie, breathlessly, in Rick's arms in *that* scene. He liked to see, close-up, the hairs on Rick's arms and the dark eyes above him. Once, thrillingly, he had felt, lying across Rick's legs, hard evidence of the older boy's excitement.

None of this meant that Jem had the faintest idea what to do next. Neither he nor Rick had clothed their thoughts in words; each seemed to be suspended in an eternal present, entwined in Webster's verse, but each knowing that it would all be ending in a few days. Then what?

Jem's awareness of Mr Howard remained a powerful force too. Had he the opportunity to think up a fitting metaphor, he might have described Mon as a high priest presiding over an infinitely delicious and perturbing rite of bonding – but as no such fancy occurred to him, he simply sensed the requirement for his director to be there, another flame in the sensual conflagration of *The Duchess of Malfi.*

On the Sunday before the week of the play, Mon had gone to Mass as usual in Manhattan. This week, however, he had not gone to the Jesuit church. His priestly training and his belief that if you join a club you should stick to its rules, had ensured that at some time within the permitted 24 hours: Saturday evening from 6.00 to the end of Sunday, he would be at Mass in a large church. Mon liked his religious buildings dark and big, preferably ornate, in baroque style. The previous Saturday he had gone to the 6.00 Mass (because Sunday was given over to endless rehearsal) and had been annoyed by a sermon from one of the Jesuit priests he usually liked. Its theme had been on the dangers of too great an adherence to liberal values, and had touched on the gay movement, which encouraged perversions with no smack of salvation in them. Mon had known, of course, that, as far as orthodox moral theology was concerned, homo-eroticism was a deviation from a God-ordained natural path of human relationships. But Mon had also known for years that he was homosexual – not, he believed, as a result of conscious choice – but as an accident of DNA or chemical make-up. He also knew he was decent, cultured, often inspirational, kind, clever, temperate, honest, reliable and caring of others. It did not follow, he would say to himself, that he should be chucked into Hell with Adolf Hitler.

Besides, he didn't cast his love out for *all* men, or for *all* boys. In his whole life he had deeply loved only four people, but – and it was an unfortunate but – they had all been male.

So it irked him to feel himself sermonised against by the Jesuits into a deviant pervert, kicking his heels at salvation. They could take a running jump! He'd go elsewhere for a bit.

Mon's choice for Mass the Sunday before the play was St James' on the East Side – also dark, Victorian, large, with a whiff of incense in the air. There Mon buried himself in a far corner beyond the pools of devotional candlelight and earnestly prayed for resolution.

He wasn't so idealising not to give full weight to the powerful sexual feelings he had for Jem – as well as the tenderest of loves – and he wanted to know what God thought about that. Who else but God had given him his desires? He prayed in a wax-scented penumbra and longed for an insight, a sign for the path he should now take.

The reason for such prayer was that he had, of late, believed (wrongly, as it happened) that his love was beginning to be returned.

And – if it was – why *should* it be resisted?

The State of New York was not likely to approve of gay relationships between teachers and their pupils. Any expression of his love for Jem, however willingly entered into by the boy, would criminalise him. Although he told himself he could retire when Jem left St Matthew's and leave teaching, to be free to live with the young man, he recognised the idea as the moonshine it was. As he had reflected before, Jem at nineteen might not be *that* Jem who was the centre of his life at sixteen.

Mon longed to have been alive in Ancient Greece where men and their boy lovers were honoured.

It had been by dint of very close observation that Mon had formed his impression that his own fascination was, in part, returned. What about that recent PE lesson? What about Founder's Day?

Mon and David had needed a dark-wood bench for the scene of the madmen. On it, later in Act V, Julia would lie in Bosola's arms. Right up to the last week the cast had been using three foyer chairs pushed together, because Mon knew there would be no trouble finding a bench in the Athletics faculty.

He had gone there the day before dress rehearsals began to speak to Alan Furniss, the faculty head. The gym had been full of boys when he had poked his head round the door. Mon had last looked into the gym a full ten years earlier, so Al sauntered towards him, saying,

'Rare bird, eh, Mon? Come for a bit of body-building?' and Mon had framed a suitably facetious reply when ....BAM! He had realised Jem was there – there! – across the gym, leaning back on the parallel bars, like the male figure in Leonardo's cartoon, arms stretched out, legs apart and dressed in a blue singlet and white shorts.

Mon had about thirty seconds in which to make his ironic riposte to Al, ask if he could borrow a nine-foot bench, and absorb every detail of Jem's figure in a state of earthquake shock – all of which he had done without a change of expression. But Jem had seen him come in, had whipped his head up, and their eyes had met and held. Mon knew his appearance had made a difference.

He had never seen Jem out of full clothing before, even when as Julia accoutred for the role in her long dress, so he had not appreciated Jem's naked arms, shoulders and legs. In the few seconds that had been allowed, Mon had noticed everything, and (although Jem's chest and shoulders were not yet filled out) it had seemed to him beautiful. The light on Jem's rounded biceps, the veins in them, the delicate hair under his arms, his tallish figure's proportions about the waist and hips, the long legs, the white socks at the ankles, those calves which looked so feminine in tights, the mysteriously alluring smile on his lips, the way the blue singlet set off the pale skin and definite shape of Jem's chestnut hair – all these careered one after another into Mon's consciousness.

Jem's skin was so white! No – not white; white suggested unhealthy pallor. In keeping with that perfect face, Jem's arms and legs were magnolia, vanilla. The roundness of his limbs seemed just....so miraculous to Mon. He knew that Jem was no sportsman – he had made it his business to find out everything about Jem: his interests, his associates, his timetable. Oddly, he had not remembered that Jem had compulsory physical education at that time. Yes, he was no sportsman, no rough out-of-doors tumbler with scratches and wounds from the baseball ground. Instead, here was this marbled cream, set off by shorts and vest. Mon ached to see Jem unclothed. All his life, he had, unconsciously, admired young men with dark hair and fair skin. He knew yet again that he would never be moved by anything other than this creaminess of unblemished flesh, warmly energised by the living blood.

But what mattered to him afterwards as, shakily, he had retraced his steps to the English faculty – mattered as much as the intense aesthetic jolt his visit to the gym had given him – was a feeling that Jem had *wanted* him to gaze on his outspread figure; had, after the first startled realisation that Mon was in the gym, welcomed that opportunity to connect with him again; had – as Mon was aware without needing to turn around – followed his director's figure with his eyes until it had left the room.

This tiny, but, to the obsessed Mon, enormously significant occasion had been preceded by another earlier one.

Founder's Day services, some weeks before the

play, were always made to coincide with the Catholic Church's moveable June Feast of Corpus Christi. There were two repeat Masses, 7th to 9th grade in the morning and 10th to 12th grade in the afternoon, held in the Catholic Church on Warwick Plaza which was just big enough to take half of the whole school of 800 boys. Unable to get a seat in the pews at the afternoon service, Mon had gone up to the choir loft – a useful dodge guaranteeing a bit of comfort in the crowded building. With a wink to Tony Randells, the Music faculty head, who sat at his organ watching the altar through a mirror for his cues, Mon had perched near the edge of the loft, able to lean on its curved balustrade.

Immediately, he had begun to sweep the pupils' heads for Jem. He knew where Jem's class was, and he could see Zac Anstruther, Jem's tutor, so it was just a case of patiently running his gaze along the backs of heads until….

Strange, this obliviousness to all those other heads.

Four hundred of them, and every one irrelevant.

Where *was* Jem? Behind that pillar? No.

Mon felt a sudden, ridiculous panic. Had Jem skipped Founder's Day service? Why? Had he gone home ill? Mon had started to edge across to the other side of the choir loft to begin further scanning when – *there* he was!

How did I miss him? Mon thought. Only one boy's hair was so – so definite in outline, only one had that curve of cheek and detailing of nose and lips, only one had that heft about him – a sturdy elegance, not exactly delicate, but....

Oh God Almighty! Mon had thought, this is like one of those prurient queer French novels: *Les Amours des Jacques et Roger*, about tortured priests and boys with soft wavy hair and an abiding interest in altar serving and virgin martyrdom. How despicably adolescent I have become!

Then, as if mimicking an episode from just such a book, Jem, who was wearing his occasional reading spectacles, had seemed to sense the laser of Mon's eyes on his clear-framed neck and had turned slowly, looking up from the order of service in his hand, and held Mon's eyes.

To Mon that look was of startled....awareness. It was a shot of pure ravishment and confirmation of what he hardly dared to admit. Oh yes – Jem was interested in him! Of the innumerable teachers at St Mat's *he* stood out. Without knowing he was in the loft, Jem had looked up. Was he alive to many possibilities? This infinitesimal second had made Founder's Day utterly memorable to poor Mon.

The last days of *Duchess* rehearsals drew to an end, and Mon entered a nightmarish period of agonising private physical activity more fevered than anything he had known since adolescence, sometimes on four occasions each day: at home, in the faculty toilets, in the English book cupboard and once (about which he was ashamed) in his car in a side road. No longer of the age at which such feats are effortless, he could not always manage to achieve release, but the struggles seemed part of the painful excitement. All were propelled by a fevered picture of Jem in singlet and shorts in the gymnasium.

Mon knew that the next step (if there was going to *be* a next step beyond the play, and whatever that step might be) was now up to him.

'David?'

'Yup?'

'Busy?'

David Lomax was squatting down and peering into the back of the sound console, trying to fit a five-pin DIN plug in the right way round. Louise had come up behind him.

'You know the mag ads we put out?'

'Hm, yeah.'

'….about the play?'

'Yeah, yeah. Oh, damn!'

'I mean the ones with the cast photo. For the Webster Museum and the *Jacobean Explorer* news sheet?'

'Yes, yes. I know, Louise. The ones for the Loony Society. What about them?'

With a click the plug went home and a needle flickered on the mixing desk. 'Ah, that damn mike's working at last. Darned thing. It wasn't a loose connection at the stand plug after all.'

'Oh well done, David. But look, I wanted to tell you about this weird letter I've had.'

'Letter?'

David stood up, pleased at his electronic success. Louise smiled at his tousled hair and flushed face. He is such a poppet, she thought. She had lost her awe of his strength and, true to the nature of womanhood, had begun to see the eager little weaknesses of the boy within.

'Let's see the thing then,' he said.

Louise fished it out of a folder she was carrying marked: '*DUCHESS of MALFI* SALES and BOOKINGS' in her clear, privately educated girl's print. It ran;

Dear Miss Carrbridge and the St Matthew's Dramatists,

We are delighted to see that you are putting on Webster's 'The Duchess of Malfi' – his best work, we think. None of us on this committee has seen the play in performance for several years.

Your cast certainly look the part upon that very professional set, and how interesting to see your choice of modern costume for them - most effective.

Can you put five tickets aside for us on Friday 17th? We'll pay on the door, if we may.

With good wishes for your opening night,

Yours sincerely,
Alan Clemmy,
(Chairman: Webster Heritage Trust, Trevanaunce
Summer School, Merivale.)

'Oh, brilliant!' said David when he had read it. 'Five Fridays. That's another fifty dollars. That scam of yours was a stroke of genius. Quite a bunch of the bookings are from people not connected with the school, so they must have read your ads. It's gonna put us up another few dozen seats, you know.'

'Thanks, David. But that's not the point I'm making. Have you seen who has *sent* this letter?'

'Er, well, yes – Alan Clemmy, whoever he is. An old play fancier type, I suppose. What's so odd about that? Oh,' David paused. 'Oh, I see. You mean, why should a member of the Great American Public, however besotted with all things Jacobean, want to see Greg and Jem in drag and Joey and Co horsing around in a school play?'

'I did partly mean that. But that isn't the oddest bit. See this?' Louise's shapely fingernail tapped on the information after Alan Clemmy's name. 'Webster Heritage Trust, Trevanaunce. The funny thing is where it is based. I've looked up Merivale in the Faculty room.'

'In the good old 1963 *Highways of North America* map book, left on the telephone table by Archie Hugonin RIP?'

'That's the one. Do you *know* where Merivale is?'

'No. Sounds like a Gilbert and Sullivan village.'

'It's on the Atlantic coast – in Canada.'

Louise gave David a significant stare. Her eyebrows were raised and she stuck out her lower lip, as if to query: what do you think of *that*?

David was slow to catch on.

'Is it? So what?'

'So why should Alan Clemmy and his chums want to come *eight-hundred miles* to see a kids' play?'

David gazed at her. After a moment's thought, he said,

'You're right. It's odd. I never thought an ad in the Halifax guys' mag would get results.'

'Very weird.'

'Hm. But no harm in it. If they've been dying to see it for ages....'

'Oh, come on! It must have been on someplace in eastern Canada itself, or in Maine over the past few years.'

'Yup, yup. I get the point, Louise. But they *know* about our version, don't they? Thanks to you.'

'Oh, you mean because....?'

'Because clever you stuck the ad in their newsletter or mag. It might jolly well have been put on, to hysterical demands from lonely light-house keepers and Webster-reading foresters, ten years ago by the Alternative Shakespeare Co of New Brunswick, just a quick speed-boat trip from Prince Edward Island or wherever, but alas only ten cod fishermen and a dolphin knew about it. So, Alan Wotsits and his merry nut-jobs couldn't go along and wonder at it. They only *read* about it nine months later in the Nova Scotia Chronicle's Theatre and Society page and thought: Oh my GOD, we've gone an' missed it AGAIN!'

'So it's not that weird?' said Louise, having waited patiently for David's hammer-blow humour to expend itself.

'Nope.'

'Okay. Thought I'd tell you anyway.'

'Oh God. I can't eat anything, Mom.'

Jem pushed his breakfast away. His sister said,

'I wasn't nervous when I played a fairy, was I, Mommy?'

'Jem,' said Mrs Clarke. 'Promise me you'll have something solid for lunch today. How much pocket-money have you got left?'

'Oh, I'm fine. About fifteen dollars. I'm fine, Mom, really I am. I'll go grab a Big Mac before make-up begins. Quite a few of us are planning to do that.'

Doors opened at 7.30. Curtain-up was at 8.00. Cast make-up and costuming began at 6.30. For many of them it wasn't worth going home at the end of school. Jem could have walked to 172nd St, eaten and walked back again with time to spare, but he knew he would be unable to leave the aura of the play for as long as that. The cast needed to be together, clustering like the hunted in a protective pack. They felt that they could just about tear themselves away from the contemplation of the set, lights, recorder, amps, mixers, and – most unnerving of all – the empty raked arena of expectant seats, to pay a quick visit to Macdonald's at the end of Civic Boulevard.

'We can go over our lines while we eat,' said Joey. Joey was still not quite word-perfect. Mon Howard had ceased to make his usual torrent of sarcastic comments and had left it to the boy's sense of occasion and adrenalin to carry him through.

Jem had left home that morning in a state bordering on hysteria. His mother and sister would not be coming that night but intended to be there on Thursday and again on Friday, this time in company with Jem's and Betsy's Aunt Rene and his grandmother. Jem was glad that no one from his family would see him on the first night. He wanted to concentrate on the play, on being Julia in it, on his relationship with Rick as Bosola, with Francis Franitza (there in the wings with the 'Mini-mist' smoke machine), and with Mr Howard. He wanted to give himself up to the sensual, mystical experience of his (admittedly) smallish part. He was glad that he had definitive appearances on both sides of the interval, each in spectacular costume, and he felt the need to immerse himself in all of it, untrammelled by the embarrassments and endearments of childhood and home.

He had awoken early in the grip of an extraordinary, vivid dream in which he was in a hospital ward with Mr Howard. The room had high white walls and china light shades, like the sort of hospital one sees in a black and white movie, and Mr Howard was in a tight black suit with a high white collar. Jem sat opposite him unclothed, except for Julia's wig. 'You really ought to keep your legs together, Julia,' Mr Howard was saying, just as he often said at rehearsal. This dream had chased itself up and down his mind all day and he looked forward to seeing Mr Howard at costuming to see if he was somehow different, changed, because of it.

Rick seldom wondered nowadays why he had been insane enough to volunteer to take a central part in a play while working for exams; a play which took him into St Matthew's most days while his contemporaries were in a bar or, as semester ended, pulling money at vacation jobs.

Everything had changed recently, as he explained to Cian. He looked forward to rehearsals eagerly, he knew his lines, and Mon had altered his opinion of the young man and congratulated himself on the ameliorating influence the school play always had on the boys. Now, on the afternoon before curtain-up, Rick wondered if he might suggest that Jem and he have a snack together before make-up. He even calculated that he could ask Jem to come home with him and spend an hour in his attic room after eating. He had framed what he was going to say in that room: Jem – I'm going to be honest with you. I think there's something between us – an attraction. Do you feel it? I'm not queer, Jem; nor are you, but don't you think we could go a little further? Interference from his parents was not a problem – his father stayed at the Alpinia Bakery until the evening and his room was in a roof conversion at the top of the large house. No, the problem was what Jem would say in return. Would he say: Yes, I find you attractive too. Shall we start by jerking off together? Or would he stare, horrified, embarrassed, shocked? What then? No, no, surely he wouldn't react like that. Surely he has realised something of what I am feeling about him? Jeez, they had come within an inch of kissing on the mouth in the last rehearsal! Right. I'll take him home tonight. There's plenty of time. He felt very stimulated at the thought of it, with an excitement totally new.

He caught Jem with Greg McManus, Joey, Liam, Dominik, Aisha, Rosa and some of the other older cast members in the auditorium at four o'clock. They were standing in a line up on set gazing over the empty seats ahead. He heard Liam say, 'I just know I'm going to faint,' and Joey reply, 'At least you know your lines.'

'Hi,' he said, walking on stage among them.

They clustered round, smiling. He might be a Senior in 12th grade, several months older even than Greg and two years older than most of them, but he was *of* them, a member of the Inner Circle, a Master of the Mystery.

'It's awful seeing all those seats, isn't it?' said Jem, smiling directly at him.

'Awful,' echoed Rick, not knowing quite how to frame his invitation. In the dim auditorium Jem, in white T-shirt and dark, tight trousers made his heart turn over.

'I….,' began Rick.

'We're all going down to McDonald's,' said Joey. 'Like to come with us?'

Rick gazed at him.

'McDonald's?' he repeated.

'Yes, the well-known populist purveyor of animal slurry and calorie-drenched fries to the uneducated of America,' smiled Joey. 'You've heard of them, surely, even in 12th grade?'

'Oh – I….Yes, of course. No, no thanks, I – I won't. I'll see you later….at….make-up/'

Rick made his way back to the foyer doors.

'Gawd, he's more nervous than the rest of us,' laughed Joey.

'He's got more lines than you have,' smiled Aisha. 'Mind you, at least he knows them.'

Jem looked after him. Strange. He thought he had

seen something other than nervousness in Rick's face. Sadness? Disappointment? Rejection? Desperation? Surely not? But Rick's expression stayed with him during their walk down to Civic Boulevard.

Rick himself, alone and thwarted in a bar by the park, couldn't understand why he hadn't gone with them; nor could he believe the strength of the jealous pain inside him.

July : THE FIRST NIGHT

There was a roar of excited voices in the blacked-out rooms off the stage. Heavy opaque plastic, gaffer-taped to the window frames, let in no light, and no one passing the end of the building could see what was going on inside. The auditorium was also in black-out condition and, because the July night was very warm, resonated to the sound of ceiling fans drawing out as much hot air as possible before the performance began.

Make-up was going on, with Louise Carrbridge, Susie and two other 11th grade volunteers from St Philomena's Theatre Studies dividing the cast between them. The simple characters, whose faces needed almost nothing, had been done. Mon loathed the 'pierrot-on-heat' style favoured by Joyce Gilcrest, who had offered her services at every play for many years until her retirement the previous summer. With Louise, Mon now took a minimalist approach. 'Nothing's gonna disguise the fact that they're kids, so why bother? Unless it's a character part, let's keep it simple.' In came greaseless foundation, the lightest of eye-shadow and all of it water-soluble. 'Put your face under the faucet when you get home,' said Mon.

For *The Duchess* only the brothers, the Cardinal and Ferdinand, needed to look middle-aged and Jem and Greg had to be feminised. All attention in the make-up room was focussed on these four. Susie and Louise stood each side of Jem. The delicately painted eyebrows, the twirl of mascara on upper and lower lashes, the slight hollowing of nose and cheeks, the rich red of lipstick, the sheen of flawless foundation – all were in place, and Julia was re-born.

'Okay, Jem. Head back a little, and on goes the wig. Susie, keep the curls off Jem's lips.'

The lustrous bronze locks fell on each side of Jem's face, framing it.

'That's it, I think, Miss Carrbridge,' said Susie.

'Shaved your legs, Jem?' grinned Liam.

'Smooth as a baby's wotsit,' smiled Jem. He was going to show Liam, but he felt shy about letting the others stare at him. Joey tweaked the slit dress open, however.

'Woo-haaah!' went the two boys.

'Amazing,' said Louise. 'Your mother wouldn't recognise you.'

'Yes, it's a pity, really, that I told her and Betsy that I was doing this part – especially as I'm on the prog as Cleo Jakemar. But surely they'd know anyway....'

'Jem, *I* hardly know, and I made you up. Next!'

Greg came forward for the virtuous Delio. He did not need to change to his Old Woman role until Act II, scene 2. His straight, prim mouth and high forehead, and half-moon tortoiseshells framing his sharp little eyes, helped him effortlessly to assume the censorious and fussy manner of a stage old lady, to the admiration of the cast. They had grinned delightedly when, during dress rehearsal's application of his spinster make-up, he had tapped Louise on the arm with his umbrella handle and cackled, 'Well done, my young girl.'

'Next!' cried Louise and Susie.

Mon's head appeared round the door.

'Are you decent?' he asked, before venturing in further. 'Keep it down a bit. The punters are in.'

'Oh, can I just take a peek and see if my parents got the reserved seats I asked Mr Lomax to keep for them?' asked Rosa.

'Dear girl, no!' cried Mon. 'You've got costume on. It's the depths of kids' school amateurism to have members of the cast appearing in costume front-of-house. You should know that, a stage luvvie like you.'

'Okay. Sorry, Sir,' sighed Rosa.

Mon smiled at her.

'They're there,' he said. 'I've just heard from Mr Lomax, so keep your knickers on.'

'Oh, thanks, sir,' gasped Rosa, beaming.

'How many in tonight, Sir?' asked Riccardo.

'I'd say about a hundred and forty, but there's still twenty minutes to go, and they're rolling in. The Principal's giving drinks to about thirty guests in his study.'

A millwheel seemed to turn in Jem's stomach.

Over a hundred and forty! And more to come! Only now did it hit him that he was going to play Julia to an audience. Others – strangers – were going to see Julia's voluptuousness and allure. What a comfort it was that they were going to peer at the programme and see 'Cleo Jakemar', not Jem Clarke, in the role.

'I'm feeling frightfully nervous, Sir,' he said. His voice had the quality of a little boy's and Mon's heart melted for him. He put an arm across Jem's shoulder.

'You are going to be a *sensation*, old son,' he said.

'But can I really do it – and be convincing?'

'Of course. And have fun. Just pretend it's one of our ordinary Tuesday rehearsals.'

Jem gulped and tried to smile bravely. Ridiculous, he thought, this weaving of snakes beneath the shimmering dress. Mon looked at the sinuous figure in make-up and fur. He wondered what more he could say, and found it difficult to speak. Jem's loveliness was nothing short of breath-taking. 'I believe in you, dear young friend,' he said at last. Then he thought: that sounds odd *and* corny. But Jem was smiling sunnily again and he knew he'd said the right thing.

'Lord, why did we do Jem up so early? He's not on at the start. How long before curtain-up?' cried Louise.

'You've got more than fifteen minutes. The Principal's dead-head high-ups won't be on time. But I agree that tomorrow and Friday it would be better to do Bosola, the brothers and Delio before Jem.'

Mon then left the make-up area to check with David Lomax that the lights and sound were ready. He found David presiding over the Revox reel-to-reel deck, which he had wound to the Baroque music, ready for the dimming of the lights.

'Pure vintage, Beatles-era, eh?' smiled David. 'Right up your alley, Mon.'

'Just remember, callow youth, that there was a time when I had to tell you what a Studebaker was. Don't mock the ancestors. But,' Mon added, peering into the ventilation slots, 'are you sure this antique's not gonna let us down?'

'Positive, Captain. I've oiled the bearings and that's about it. It feeds into the modern amp here. See?'

Mon gazed at the cat's cradle of wiring and shuddered.

'Oh well, there's always Pharhad, Janek and me to sing madrigals in the wings, I suppose.'

He took a look through the glass panel into the auditorium. 'Not bad for a first night – given it's not *Guys and Dolls* or *Oliver!* Congrats, m'boy.'

'Largely Louise. She had the idea of advertising more widely.'

'Hope we don't have an inspector in,' added Mon gloomily. 'I forgot to fire-proof the set.'

Janek Franitza appeared in the make-up room, stolid and unexcited as usual.

'Where's Jem?' he asked.

'Over there with Tony,' said Joey. 'What are you doing back here?'

Janek looked at him for a moment.

'Come to wish you all luck, especially Jem. Where did you say he was? Oh God! Is – is that Jem?'

'Ah, you haven't seen him in drag, have you? Sexipoo, eh?'

'Hi,' smiled Jem, floating towards his friend, the silk of his long dress swishing, his stockinged leg showing at each stride, and his high heels clicking. 'Come to check up on your little bruv?'

'No – well, that is, yes. But I mainly came to wish you all the best, Jem. You've got a demanding part.'

'Well it's not all demanding. I don't think you've seen the whole thing yet, coming on board at the last min, but Julia's death takes a bit of dexterity.'

'Yeah, it seemed difficult when I read it.'

'Read it?'

'Yup. I bought a copy of the play last month and read through it to see how you fitted in.'

Jem was, for a moment, astounded. Janek's predictable stolidity seldom surprised him, but he was surprised now. Not being involved until the last minute, he was the friend left behind, Jem realised. And yet his interest had been deep enough for him to seek out the difficult old text and peruse it. Jem appreciated the depth of friendship that underlay this and he was very touched. He placed a hand, brilliant with nail varnish, on his friend's arm caressingly.

'Thanks, Jan.' He squeezed Jan's arm. 'Thanks.'

Janek looked at the nails and at Jem's provocative lips with an evident mixture of interest and distaste. He pulled his arm away from Jem's grasp.

'See you at the end? I've got to take Francis home then.'

'Yeah, sure,' said Jem, and, keying himself in to Janek's perception of things, added, 'Just give me a few minutes to get all this drag and crap off.'

Jan nodded, with one last look at the eye-shadow, bra, wig and lipstick, and went back to the light box. He didn't bother to seek out his little brother.

Jem stood, after Janek had gone, in a state of mingled amusement and annoyance. He disapproves of me! Then, with his customary fair-mindedness and perception, he realised that Jan was disturbed by seeing his pal in such outrageous drag. No, thought Jem, not disturbed, but in a mysterious way *hurt*; he feels as if he's lost something or been turned away. Jem, who for so long had accepted Julia as his *doppelganger* and who had, chameleon-like, adapted to fit her persona, had become capricious, demanding, overtly voluptuous, now saw for a moment through his undemonstrative friend's eyes the – the unhealthiness of his absorption.

Rick came up behind him, dressed in his black leather outfit and coat – the epitome of pitiless evil.

'Whew!' he whistled. 'Just look at you!'

Jem, turning his thoughts from Janek, studied Rick's face. What he saw there was frank friendliness and admiration. Rick was not disturbed by Jem as Julia. The sense of cold water sloshing on him, which Jan's short visit had given, ebbed away. Jem Clarke, ordinary school kid, student of Geography, English and History, gave place again to seducer and adulteress, doomed by lust to perish.

'Right. Ready, everyone?' hissed David. 'Mon? Mon! Are the cast in position?'

'All ready,' replied Mon from the doorway of the cubicle.

'The enemy in place?' For David the 'enemy' was all parents, any guest of the Principal and each of the high school governors.

'All lackies accounted for. Give them one quick flash.'

David reached for the dimmers for the Front of House lights.

'They should be so lucky, ducky,' he muttered – a quip he had made whenever Mon spoke of the House flash for the past eight years. The orangey glow in the auditorium ebbed, then rose again. A couple of late-comers tumbled into their seats.

'Good luck in here,' murmured Mon.

David and his team: Jonathan and Mark, equipment-mad devotees who loved David, Mon and the St Mat's productions, although they had never dreamt of auditioning for parts themselves, crouched over their lighting sliders. Janek, next to them, was on the sound desk.

'Tape on,' whispered David. 'House lights fade. Stage left up.' Music began playing through the big speakers. 'Mikes up, Centres up to six,' whispered David. Delio and Antonio entered.

Backstage, taking his cue from the centres rising, Francis pressed the red button on the remote smoke machine control. 'Fresnels at stage centre up to eight. A and B par-cans to four,' mouthed David. In a wisp of smoke, Bosola entered, pausing with mouth drawn down.

David hardly needed to utter the moment-by-moment cues. Jonathan and Mark, veterans of several shows, knew exactly what to do and had all their cues encoded in a specially prepared script; but they didn't mind the hissing – it meant that Mr Lomax was with them, interested in them. It was all part of a precious routine. The techies instinctively looked to Mon as the officer in charge but prided themselves – as 'other ranks' have always done – on knowing more than he did.

The St Matthew's High School July production got into its stride.

Mon, in the wings, returned to an interior monologue which had run up and down his brain for more than a week. He and Jem were sometimes in his sitting-room, sometimes at Jem's house on 172nd St (which Mon often drove past at night, absurdly, as he knew, like the young lover in *My Fair Lady* singing *On the Street Where You Live*) and more often in an impersonal hotel suite. They sat at right angles to each other, Jem on the sofa, Mon in an armchair. The gap between us is huge, Jem, and I'm not just talking about the years of experience I had before you were born, but I don't think any of it matters. And it doesn't matter to me that we are of the same gender, Jem, because if I love I love.

Perhaps my love for you started when you became Julia. Either way, it's a love for another human being for whom I have such a tender longing, such respect and desire to look after, that it over-rides everything else. It's essentially loving where love is, irrespective of the petty restrictions of age and gender between us. And so, bearing in mind that should you want anything, anything, Jem, you only have to ask for it, whether it's money or a car or just having someone to talk to about your own feelings.....

Jem and Dominik sat in the larger stage right wing on the gym bench. Although not due to appear until Act II scene 4, Jem simply couldn't wait calmly in the green-room, out of the sound of the play. It mattered to all of them that the enemy was receiving the show well. Riccardo came to join them,

'It's going well, don't you think?' whispered Jem.

'Aisha and Mat sound great. It just flows. She's got a lovely voice,' agreed Dominik.

'I still feel nervous,' admitted Jem, pushing a wisp of tumbling wig from his eyes.

Rick had a longing to put his arm round Jem's shoulders and draw him close, but with Dom sitting the other side of him, this was hardly possible.

'I hope it'll carry on okay when we appear,' whispered Dominik. 'It's ironic that, being impotent Castruchio, my you-know-what rate has gone up about eighty-five per cent this week.'

'Your what?' asked Rick, although he had heard. His heart hammered suddenly.

'I've hardly stopped,' whispered Dominik. 'I guess it's been the waiting and not sleeping at night. How about you, Jem?'

Rick breathlessly watched in the slip of light to see what reply Jem would make. Jem, often tormented by his physical desires, did not feel comfortable with these personal conversations, so he made an indefinite sound and muttered,

'I know what you mean.'

His fingers plucked at the hem of his dress. Rick followed the curve of light along his thigh and up to Jem's face. He knew, from the blush beneath the make-up and the drooping eyelashes, that Jem could have expatiated further. He longed to penetrate beyond the link he had with Jem as Bosola and to find that place, if it existed, where he could be himself,

Jem not be Julia, and where they could speak secretly about their experiences.

Black-out! A spatter of applause!

At last Jem's scene rushed up. Jem waited near Francis at the smoke machine. His entrance on the arm of the Cardinal, was a good one. Lights blazed up on his glamorous costume. Hs eyes flashed and his clear, light voice brought out the shades of Julia's pretences at love and constancy. His nervousness had vanished. The actor took over and he became the seductress. Like many quiet people – in every-day modest, self-deprecating and controlled – when on stage and in total disguise, Jem found a level of escape from the ordinary which was convincing.

Janek was hardly able to believe that this was the same kid who sat beside him taking down Geography, Eng Lit and History notes.

Aisha, herself enormously impressive in her role as the Duchess, thought: he is really good. What a dear he is!

Francis muttered, 'What a ham!'

Several in the audience peered down at their programmes in the gloom, wondering who Cleo Jakemar was.

During the interval, which Mon had established at the end of Act III, partly because it marked the Duchess' imprisonment, and partly because it made the second half shorter than the first – always a good idea in Mon's book – the cast assembled in the green room and were brought orange drink and Coke from the auditorium. Eyes sparkled, cheeks glowed, everyone clapped everyone else on the back, hugged, chattered excitedly, old private animosities forgotten. The applause, quite long, had gone to their heads like a cocktail. It had all been worth it! Several had doubted anyone would come to see the play, others had secretly expected a disaster, some had actively disliked it, deeming it obscure and morbid. But now....well! Those annoying days when dusk fell at four o'clock and old Howard kept his cast grinding and they had to crawl home on over-crowded buses and trains; those sunny Spring afternoons of May and June when others skipped off into the light to go to the pool or the parks and it seemed unbearable to slave at 17th C lines in the dusky auditorium while sunlight poured in from the foyer; the nerves, the clashes, the jealousies were all forgotten in that most perfect of frenzies an acting troupe experiences when the applause is warm and sustained.

'Terrific, man!'

'Oh, well done!'

'You were brilliant!'

'It's a hit, isn't it?'

'Wow! Did you hear that clapping?'

'Good old Howard. He had it right!'

Voices trilled off the green room walls.

Behind the glass panel, at the sound and lighting

desks, David and Louise were hosting a few colleagues and friends. Jonathan, Mark and Janek had gone to join the cast back-stage.

'Fantastic sound,' said Tunny Linehan, 'It's like bloody *Star Wars.*'

'Mon's choice of music.'

'You've done a great job on costumes, Louise,' said Bruno Zampa. 'All very trendy, but so dead right for the parts – especially that Bosola.'

'David,' said Jeff Tork, a young teacher new to the school that year, 'who's that amazing girl – the one who came on for a scene in Act II?'

David and Louise caught each other's eyes for a second, each raising an eyebrow by a fraction.

'Oh, erm, Julia, d'you mean? The Cardinal's mistress?'

'Yes, that's the one. Cleo Jakemar, or however you pronounce it.'

'You – um – liked her performance, then?' asked David.

'Well, yes. She's not like your Aisha Keating, of course; that one's quite an actress, but your Cleo is a cracker. Stage presence, and all the right things in….'

'….in all the right places. Yes indeed,' smiled David. 'Great complexion.'

'Terrific legs!'

'Lovely eyes.'

'Beautiful hair.'

'She's a nice person too.'

Louise was twinkling with glee behind Jeff, who went on,

'She's in the 12th grade at St Philomena's, I suppose?'

'Yup. Her name is pronounced Jak-ay-mar, and her full name is Cleopatra, but we just call her Cleo. She does Theatre Studies. Isn't that right, Louise?'

'Oh, oh, yes,' twittered Louise, playing up, 'she's a very nice girl; frightfully talented. Wait 'til you see her death scene.'

'Oh, gee. She dies? Well, I must tell her how good she was afterwards,' said Jeff. 'Can I go back-stage?'

'Of course. The cast'll be thrilled to have groupies at the costume-room door. I'll meet you there at the end.'

Jeff Tork and the others left the lighting cubicle, Jeff evidently smitten by Cleo Jakemar.

Louise and David collapsed, shrieking.

'Oh Lord! He *can't* think Jem's a real chick! He must need glasses!'

'Jem's pretty convincing, David.'

'Ten outa ten for your make-up and costume, Louise. Well, his face'll be a picture after the costumes are off. I can't wait!'

Jem pricked up his ears, as one does when one hears one's name. He had left the crowd to put on a bit more lipstick at the make-up table, and he heard Francis Franitza's shrill voice outside the door.

'Oh, I got Clarke to get me into this play. He's all hotsy-totsy with my brother. He fancies me a lot, the big fairy.'

Jem froze, lipstick in the air.

'You little shit,' came another voice, which Jem recognised as Joey's, 'Jem's not a queer-boy and even if he was, he's not *that* desperate.'

'That's all you think,' said Francis loudly, 'Well, I've done things for him, if you must know, at our house. He pays me to. He's told me he loves me. I can tell you he's circumcised, if you want proof.'

Jem sat as if turned to concrete. The little bastard!

And it was made all the worse because Jem had, after all, exercised so many fantasies this semester about the younger boy – *and* he had suggested that he join the back-stage team. But to come out with….with….!

Jem whisked out into the corridor and came up against Mat, Joey and Greg. Oh, Jistus, if Greg believes what Francis has said, it'll be all over 11th and 12th grade.

Jem grabbed Francis by the collar.

'Ow! What? Who?' gasped Francis, spinning round. 'Oh! Oh, it's you, Jem. I – I – you didn't hear what I was saying just now…?

'I did. And you're a lying little brat.' Jem raised his hand to smack Francis' head. The child squealed.

'Go easy, man,' said Joey.

'You heard what he said,' cried Jem, 'and it's

lies….'

'Is it?' yawned Greg, with the lofty tolerance of a senior student's knowledge of the world.

There was a step along the corridor.

'Tell them, Francis,' hissed Jem. 'Tell them it's all lies.'

'Lies?' said a voice behind him.

Jem turned to see Janek gazing at his young brother with his hands on his hips. Jem let go of Francis' collar as if it was red-hot.

'Oh, Jan. Look, I….'

'What's the little asshole been up to *now*?' asked Janek.

Francis wriggled away from Jem.

'You saw what he did, Jan. He grabbed me! He was gonna hit me!'

'I expect he had a good reason. What have you been saying?'

Greg raised an amused eyebrow.

'Your charming brother has been recounting the sexual favours he gives Clarke in return for money.'

There was a dreadful silence. The expression on Jan's face was grimmer than Jem had ever seen it. Before he could speak, Jan's voice came harshly,

I'm going to tell Mom and Paw you've done this,' said Janek. 'Don't you realise, you stupid little idiot, the harm that malicious gossip like that can do?'

Francis stood in dismay.

'You – you wouldn't tell Dad….?' he gasped.

'I'm telling him tonight.'

Greg butted in.

'So are we to assume that your dear little brother has made it all up after all?'

'Tell them, you lying little creep,' snapped Jan.

'Yes! Yes. All right! It's lies. I – I don't know why I made it up, why I said it!'

'I do,' said Janek. 'It's because you've got a filthy mind now you've gone an' discovered sex, you're desperate to be noticed all the time, you'll do anything to make out you're important and special, you take advantage of anyone who's kind to you, and you can't tell fact from your imagination. You'll end up in a penitentiary.'

Francis' eyes filled with tears and he blundered away from them.

'Jan!' cried Jem. 'Don't let him leave! He's needed to work the smoke machine!'

'I'll sort him out, and if necessary Jonathan and I can run a remote cable and control to the wing. Don't worry,' said Jan. 'Look, I just came back-stage to grab a coke and to say that you were – were wonderful, Jem.'

With a nod, he ambled calmly back to the control cubicle.

'Hell of a good guy, that mate of yours,' said Joey.

Jem nodded, unable to speak. Jan was a diamond. Jem ran over in his mind the vague sense he had had recently that Jan was upset about something, and wondered if Jan thought he had been neglecting him. No, that wasn't quite right. Had he been taking him too much for granted, perhaps?

'Oh, God, God,' he breathed, plucking a wisp of wig from his eyes. It was all getting difficult. Really it was. He remembered one of Mon's quips from *King Lear: Sharper than a serpent's tooth it is, to have an ungrateful child*, and shamefacedly erased Francis' image from his little gallery of fanciable people before getting into position for his wait until Act V.

July : JANEK FRANITZA'S MISERIES

The rumbling adult voice went on and on. Sometimes a shriek or a high, mocking laugh interrupted it, but usually it was the bass accompaniment to Janek's descent into slumber. He had not, as far as he was aware, known a single day when his parents had not quarrelled. What they quarrelled about, he did not understand. His mother sometimes implied that they disagreed about him – about his schooling, his future, his fondness for his grandfather. Francis – already disturbed, as Janek was to realise when they were both much older – was very frightened of their father. He seemed to spend his childhood hunting for the sympathies and approval of older boys and men, a tendency that was to scar much of his early adult life. Not until he left America to work in various overseas cities did Francis begin to sort himself out.

The boys' father, Ladislaw Franitza, was a motorcycle engineer of considerable talent. His draughtsmanship and understanding of metallurgy had taken him from Czechoslovakia and the under-funded resources of Jawa to Britain and the dying days of Norton-Villiers-Triumph. The Polish girl who had been his lover had accompanied him and they married, in a Catholic ceremony, in Andover, Hampshire, and went to live in a stark new house not far from the green-field NVT factory. Janek had been born there. Soon afterwards, Ladislaw had realised that the end was in sight for his firm; but not before they had sent him as chief workshop engineer to one of their last big dealerships in America on the West Coast. From there, after the collapse of the UK motorcycle industry, he applied for, and got, the job of sales manager of a large Honda dealership in New York. His days of self-respect and happiness were over, however. To work in a shop! After the glory years of engineering! He now had another little boy to look after, more school fees to pay, his wife's father living with them and the prospect of selling nothing but Jap motorcycles until he was sixty-five.

Halina Franitza began to regret her decision to live in England when she found herself abandoned in the house in Andover with a small child; but there had been comfort in the reflection that Ladislaw was a respected engineer – none when he became a salesman in America, although at least Los Angeles had been warm. She had hated the damp, scabrous tenement they first moved to in New York.

'Look what you have brought us to!' she would scream. 'You are such a failure!'

Eventually Ladislaw mortgaged himself heavily to move near to St Matthew's High in Queens, so that the boys could have the Catholic education Halina insisted upon. His dream of retirement was slipping away, but he began to believe his chances of being retained at Honda were growing slimmer.

'A Catch 22 zituation,' he was fond of saying. And Janek heard this phrase many, many times in his boyhood without having any idea what it meant.

Perhaps because of tensions at home, perhaps because he had come young to the notion that life was awkward, Janek grew up into a reticent, outwardly stolid, self-contained youth. He seldom risked a rebuff by exhibiting his feelings or expressing a point of view at variance with his parents' (and that depended on which parent he was with at the time), so that his school contemporaries thought him cold, or dull, or snooty. Francis, by contrast, was like Halina: wilful, capricious, noisy, manipulative – so the brothers hadn't much in common.

For a few people Jan had the deepest and most loyal of attachments. Chief of these at school was Jem Clarke. Not finding it at all easy to express demonstrativeness (he saw too much of that from his mother) and unwilling to demand too much (his father's expectations and disappointments had made his life one long complaint), Jan was content to watch carefully over those he loved. It was always with a sense of quietude that he slid into his seat next to Jem each day in term-time. They nodded at one another, briefly smiled, and left each other to his own thoughts.

This made it painful when Janek suspected – knew – that Jem was growing away from him. *The Duchess of Malfi* was the culprit, of course. Ever since auditions, Jem had seemed to change. There were times, like that irritating evening when Jem and Francis had been so thick with each other in Francis' bedroom, while Janek had sat in the window-seat, glumly staring on – when he felt almost ashamed of Jem. To show silly, vain Francis that level of vivacity! To conspire with him to lock Jan out into an arctic landscape! Jem had never seemed capable of mindless cruelty – until that day. Then, coming on just as quickly, Jan's fairmindedness reminded him that Jem was just full of life and fun – and why should he not be? He made every effort to see existence as he imagined Jem saw it: a rainbow of interesting new experiences. When Jem lightened his voice to practise his falsetto for Julia, Jan smiled indulgently – but he never really found it funny. He told himself that he must not be envious of Jem and his talents, and it was easy, after all, to admire and cherish him and his priceless friendship.

He had not told Jem how achingly beautiful he used to find him – back two years earlier when they were just fifteen. Janek admired Jem's sweetness of temperament and ready, mysterious smile more than any attribute of any human being he had known. He sometimes rocked to and fro in his room, on the edge of his bed, in an agony of misery because *he* was not Jem. To have Jem's looks! To be so admired by girls – and other boys! Jan's antennae had picked up both

Aisha's and Riccardo's rays later on in that semester, even though he had not then been connected directly with the play.

As winter changed to spring, Jan – against all his own expectations of himself – composed a poem to Jem. He was never to let Jem see it, but the writing of it gave him an incoherent satisfaction he hadn't believed possible; and, indeed, he remembered it, word for word, across time, nearly thirty years later. It was called *Being Your Friend.*

I lie in my pain underground
My features are lost in the mud
I try and I try to rise and to fly –
And when crushed by hatred and misunderstanding
I call out your name in the flood

You are bright as an angel of fire
I have nothing – but you are my own
When you are beside me I'm happy
I try not to feel jealous that everyone loves you
I whisper your name all alone

I wish we could sometimes change places
Yet I'd always be me, never you
I live in a crypt far from beauty and light
But you take me upstairs on a peach-flavoured skate-board
You do it – that's just what you do

The poem seemed to take on a talismanic significance beyond the dreadful events of that August after the play; in fact, Jan attributed his ready memory of it to a lifetime's insecurity, loss and sadness. It had been forged in the heat of teenage longing, at a time when so much had seemed possible, and all that was needed was his closeness to Jem to help make it happen.

When his belief grew that Jem was changing, Jan tried to go down that strange bisexual roadway which Jem seemed to be travelling. He went once into his mother's room and dressed himself entirely in her clothing, forcing his large hips into her fragile panties and grappling with her one of bras. In the mirror he tried to like what he had done, to see how Jem felt as, daily, he became Julia in the play. He failed. Without one shred of erotic tremor he regarded his image – unmistakeably stolid, middle-European, fair-haired and male in the absurd dress, underwear and tights – and had a dreary moment of inner knowledge that he would probably never inspire longing in another.

It worried him a little that he was seventeen and still a virgin. Naturally, part of his mind accepted his church's teaching that sex outside marriage was a sin, but the other twentieth-century, liberal, New York part lashed him for his lack of knowledge. He had once felt sure that Jem had had a girl – wrong assumption though that was – for unconscious awareness of his desirability seemed so at home on Jem. It was in his beguiling smile, on his breath, in the movements of his limbs and eyelids. Jan never spoke to Jem about this. In the oddest way, their friendship was too special for that. Sometimes Jan felt he daren't dip his finger in currents that roared underground beneath them.

Janek prayed night after night, with strong, unforced sincerity for his parents to be happy with each other, for his own life to be fulfilled (he knew not how) and for Jem to remain his friend.

July: THE SECOND NIGHT – ACT I

Riccardo woke late with a jolt. He knew he had been in the throes of a happy and life-enhancing dream, but he could remember nothing of it except a sense of standing in a vast atrium with storey after storey of balcony rising above him to a starry sky, and in front of him the down-slope of a stage. Someone's hand was in his, and the building was full of a lemony scent.

He sat up in bed, the sheet falling from his naked chest. Light streamed in under his thick curtains. He felt extraordinarily elevated and then remembered why. He was going to be in *The Duchess* again tonight, with Jem. He lay back against the bed-head and relived once again the pleasure of last night's applause, of taking a bow on his own to rousing cheers, of that scene where Julia had lain in his arms, warm and heavy, and he had kissed her.

Jem was in a lesson as usual with Janek quietly by his side. With only a few days of the summer semester to go, compulsory Religious Education was in progress, and the importance of a detailed knowledge of the synoptic gospels was being pointed out. The compulsory paper which all 12th graders sat at St Matthew's was still a year away, but, as Mr Bianchalloff was saying, the trick was to embed the material now.

'The last thing you'll want to find is that another academic year has started, the syllabus has moved on, and you are having to dredge up unfamiliar material on top of the new. That's why this semester's essays have been so important.'

As he nodded compliantly, Aisha's and Bosola's lines chased themselves up and down Jem's mind, providing a distracting counterpoint to Mr Bianchalloff's sage advice.

'And,' continued the RE teacher, 'In this last homework, try to connect the gospels' interpretation of Christ's ideas with the social theme you have selected. Remember that your overall point has got to make clear the impact of Christian teaching in the world today......'

Mr Bianchalloff's earnest rumble receded into the background....

Wasn't it so *funny* when Mr Tork had come to the green-room door with Mr Lomax and asked to meet me?

Jem put his arms round himself in an ecstasy of satisfaction when he recalled Mr Tork's face at the door, and his congratulations. Every word of that conversation came back to him.

'I couldn't believe it when Mr Lomax told me you were one of our boys in 11th grade. I was completely fooled. Mr Lomax here shot the bull about you being a Theatre Studies St Philomena's girl....'

'I wanted to make your experience of the evening more fun for you, Jeff.'

'Anyway, you took my breath away, Mr Clarke. Don't know how you did it.'

'You should definitely go on the stage, you young ham,' Mr Lomax had smiled. 'Oh, and Mr Tork said he thought you had a great figure, so get you, ducky!'

'See, I was completely fooled.'

'Oh, well – it was Mr Howard's direction, really,' Jem had said, blushing. And he heard Mr Tork say, as the two teachers went off down the passage together, 'What a nice, modest lad he seems too,' and Mr Lomax reply, 'One of the nicest.'

As a result of Jeff Tork's little mistake, Mon Howard thought it would be a bit of fun if Jem were to remove his wig at the curtain call after the second and third nights' performances and reveal that he was, in fact, a youth, not a girl – and Jem readily agreed, by now rather keen that everyone knew just who Julia really was. He recalled how people had surged round the cast as they had gone into the auditorium after hanging up their costumes. It had been a blurring succession of claps on the back and gratifying smiles.

Then there had been the walk back towards 172nd St with Aisha, Rosa and Janek in the warm July night. Only last night! – and Jem's thoughts recreated that special occasion....

The four had come out together, Jem gazing round.

'Where's Francis?' he had asked, rather guiltily.

'He's gone straight home,' had replied Janek.

'I feel a bit bad about....'' Jem had begun.

'Well don't,' Jan had interrupted. 'If you want to know, I've come to an arrangement with old Howard. I'm going to work smoke from the lights box, and Francis is dropping out of the show. I've agreed to say nothing at home.'

'I'm not sorry,' Aisha had said, 'He makes awful comments to us girls sometimes.'

'I would apologise for him,' Jan had muttered. 'But one can't help one's relatives.'

Jem had thought: yes, that's true. Look what a little bitch Betsy can be sometimes. But one's friends – that's a different matter. He had felt a strong wave of affection for Jan and had been about to put his arm across Jan's shoulder, when Aisha had taken Jem's hand and pulled him in towards her.

'I've got to turn off at the end here,' she had murmured, 'but I just wanted to say that it's been really great being in the St Mat's play with you, Jem.' She had lifted her head, pulled him to a halt and had kissed him near the lips. Out of the corner of his eye, he'd seen that Rosa had gripped Jan's arm, and that he had casually put his hand down and entwined his fingers in hers. Jeez! Fancy old Jan doing that!

Without knowing how they'd got there, Jem found himself with Aisha in the shadowy doorway of Wheatley's Furniture Mart. The bright orange-yellow words "Sizzling Summer Sales Start Saturday" seemed to burn into his eyes. He was leaning against her, breathing heavily. His mouth had met hers and, with a faint remnant of stage make-up tanging his tongue, he had licked her full lips. As she had once done to him, he had inserted his tongue into her soft mouth. They had clung together, exploring each other. Jem's left hand had cupped her breast (he'd never felt a girl's breast before) and his right had passed from her back to her bottom. Part of his consciousness had noted that he was kneading her rump like a chef expelling air from pastry; another part was embarrassed by the erection he was sure she could feel through his jeans. He didn't want absurdity to creep in and was relieved that she had responded vividly to his kiss and had enfolded his bulge in her right hand. Several minutes passed. Jem had been aware that they had been gasping for breath and that there was a curious echo of it which he understood came from Jan and Rosa, next to them in the doorway. He had a stab of astonishment – Jan, with his hands all over a chick! – before he sensed that his hand was manipulating Aisha's groin and her breathings were as quick as his own.

Suddenly a light came on from above the depot frontage.

It was still only just after eleven and traffic was passing. Aisha was brought back to a sense of place. Jem was not, regardless of all but his urgent lust.

'Jem. Jem,' she had whispered. 'It's time to say

goodnight.'

'Who's down there?' a sharp voice had called from above. 'Is that kids? Get outa that doorway or I'll call the cops.'

Aisha pushed Jem away from her, angling her knee to disengage his legs, noting the boyish intentness of his glowing face in the streetlamps. 'I'd ask you back to my place, only it's so late, and my Mon and step-dad…' She had tailed off, smoothing her blouse down. Jem dropped from an urgency which had left him dizzy to become aware of Rosa kissing Jan goodnight, holding his face in both her hands, like people do in movies.

'See you tomorrow, boys,' carolled the girls, as they turned up Garrett Boulevard, leaving Jem and Jan gazing after them. They went out onto the sidewalk and gazed at each other.

'Phew!'

'They're go-ers, aren't they?' said Jan.

The boys continued to regard each other shyly – each aware that the other was aroused, but embarrassed that the other should know it. They had never, in three years of friendship, spoken of emotions, sex, love, girls or relationships. They had confined themselves to games, TV, bikes, cars, hi-fi, movies, books and the personalities of the St Mat's teachers.

'Aren't they just?' Jem had echoed, as casually as he could.

Both were inexperienced, but neither could have admitted it to the other. Jem had felt, however, that he had had an insight into his pal. Jan was as flushed as he was. A swift glance downwards had shown him that Jan was as excited as he was. Probably Jan, in the privacy of his bedroom, does what I do in mine. This reflection made him feel the comforting kinship of humanity, and then the sobering realisation that he himself was, very likely, a rather ordinary person doing very ordinary things – just like ordinary, everyday Jan, in fact.

He now stole a sidelong look at Jan's impassive features as the RE lesson on the Synoptic Gospels moved towards its end. Their eyes met. Yes, last night had been amazing, hadn't it?

It was six-thirty again and Louise and Susie, this time assisted by Aisha and Rosa, were making up the cast, ready for the second night. Once again the group of student friends had strolled down to McDonald's, and once again Mon, David and Louise had had an early snack and a couple of glasses of red wine at Rosy Q's by the park.

Aisha had given herself the task of applying Jem's pancake foundation. Her competent fingers dabbed and smoothed while she chattered away.

'Oh, I said, if you're gonna quote Third World countries at me you're really gonna spoil the whole afternoon. There was this piece we were doing in a class about how Lacoste makes a T-shirt in Cambodia or somewhere and it only costs eighteen cents and they charge twenty-five dollars for in Macey's, an' she was really going on about how immoral it was....Up a bit, Jem....and then we read about this firm that makes knickers – you know, panties, in New Jersey and they cut them out, like, in triangles, then a container takes the triangles by ship to the Philippines and they sew them together for a cent a dozen and a ship brings them all back again, and it's *still* worth doing because American workers want such high wages, and the union bosses are so....Oh, I've dripped a bitty-bit on your boobs, Jem. Pass the towel....So I said to her, Look, Miss, if you stop buying the things they make, they'll all starve in Cambodia and the Philippines, so where's the harm in shopping? Well, she couldn't answer that....'

Aisha's voice went on while Jem metamorphosed into Julia. He had started the make-up session with a thumping heart. Aisha was going to run her fingers over his face and shoulders! But funnily enough, now he felt totally impersonal about her, like someone at a hairdresser's. Aisha, on her part, seemed to have inspanned Jem to a circle of chat-chums and treated him as someone with whom she could feel at ease and gossip. This was so much at odds with the passion of the previous evening that Jem was unable to find the right way to get back to those moments of delirious caressing. There seemed no path through the torrent of words, so he kept an urbane, fixed smile on his face, wondering if she would ever say again what he remembered so vividly: 'I'd ask you back to my place, only it's so late.'

After getting home, Jem had pondered the implications of this for some time before dropping into exhausted sleep. Did it mean she would ask him back earlier in the day, perhaps when her parents were at work? What was "her" place? Did she mean her bedroom? And ask him back for *what,* exactly? Vague instructions about condoms floated into Jem's mind. She was over a year older than he was; had she asked boys back before? And if she had, what did that say about her? And would it matter that she was a black girl? Suppose they began to see a lot of each other, what would his mother say? What would her parents say? In fact the thought of what Aisha evidently (probably? definitely?) expected him to do at "her place" was oddly un-erotic.

And now she chattered on like a parrot, screwing up her eyes to peer impersonally at Jem's mascara. It was as if he were a customer at a beauty salon. How odd.

Mon Howard was the subject of a ton of congratulations and an ounce or two of criticism in the big teachers' leisure room when he ambled in at lunch. The criticisms came from those staff who had noticed a steady fall-off in the work rate of the actors in the play, had slightly resented the three days the cast had taken off lessons for dress rehearsals, and disapproved of cases of absenteeism put down to exhaustion.

'They were up late, you know,' Mon had explained. 'I expect they'll be in soon.'

'Typical luvvies,' chuckled David. 'They've got their public to please again tonight, the duckies!'

'Besides, it's surely a question of character. I notice that some of the boys with the biggest parts are in. They're the sort who can take on a challenge and see it through,' put in Louise.

The three producers were practically backed up defensively against the EVABOYL machine by the proponents of homework on tectonic plates, synoptic gospels and suchlike ephemera.

'Still,' said Jeff Tork, 'the play was real good.' He turned to his colleagues. 'If you haven't got tickets, go tonight.'

'Tickets!' cried Louise. 'I must go down and sell a few more during lunch.'

She dashed off for the tin of change, the account book and the ticket books.

'I'll help,' said David, following her.

Mon was left to splash some hot water onto his Lipton's.

'I guess that's post first night third-degree over for today,' he drawled. 'I'll have a word to the cast about attendance tomorrow when I see them later. But cheer up. Only two more performances.'

'Well, good luck again. Break a leg,' came from most. A few were silent. What with thirty-two boys out of lessons and off sports training, the auditorium out of action, Mon's, David's and Louise's classes needing cover and too many 10th to 12th grade students given over to thespianism, the less artistic teachers felt disobliging – and they didn't always hide it.

Mack Sweeney, Faculty head of Sports and Economics teacher, had complained to David a day or two ago in the bar at the St Mat's Alumni's sports ground.

'I can't think why Howard needs five goddam months to put on a two-hour play. If I was in charge, I'd say: Look, there's the goddam text, learn it by next week or you're detained until you dam well do. Then I'd get them onto that goddam stage and say: Right, say the dam lines, speak up and don't fidget and ponce around. And that would be goddam that. Done and dusted in a fortnight.'

David had replied, grinning,

'Hm, there's a bit more to it than that, Mack old son. You know, in some ways, it's harder work than coaching the baseball team.'

Mack had spluttered into his Carlsberg.

'Horse-shit, Lomax. You're getting as big a Luvvie poof as Howard.'

The excitement of performance evenings was not, nowadays, felt strongly by Mon Howard. He had produced over twenty shows, one after the other, sometimes twice a year, for sixteen years. He preferred the jollying along of an eager cast on a typical, damp March afternoon, when he should have been at a Faculty meeting, to the late bedtimes, long hours and uncertainties of show nights. This year he felt differently. The rapidly dwindling time that Jem would be in his orbit gave him a feverish need to make the most of it all. Rather than leaving the setting-up of the auditorium and foyer to Pete and Leroy, he carolled cast members, including Jem, of course, to help the site staff with extra seats, ticket tables and "reserved" notices. He came to costuming and make-up, something he hadn't done for years, and was in the wings during the show, encouraging with smiles and thumbs-up signs, instead of sitting up at the back or in the lighting cubicle. David noticed this and was amused.

'The old guy's taking this one real seriously,' he said to Louise.

'Doesn't he usually?' she asked.

'Oh, yes – at rehearsal stage. But he never normally fusses round at make-up and in the wings.'

'He likes this cast.'

'Hm, they're generally likeable, I suppose, aren't they?'

'They're all adorable!' cried Louise, quite forgetful

of her hesitancy and reserve in her enthusiasm for all things *Duchess*. 'I really will miss everything when it's all over,' she added. Gosh, I mean it too, she told herself. This has been the best year of my life. What a reflection on the rest of it! I am part of all this. I belong. Everyone likes me – and I like them. Her face lit up. David put out his hand and squeezed her arm. They smiled and nodded at each other, happy in complicity.

Make-up was over, the "enemy" in place, the Principal was bringing his new load of guests across, sound and lights had been checked and Mon, standing on a chair, was giving his second-night pep talk.

'We've got a nice big audience tonight. About two-fifty so far, I'd say....' (Jem and several others experienced a familiar, queasy, interior jump) '....and that's because everyone's heard how good you were last night. Mr Lomax has sold two hundred dollars' worth on the door. This means you've gotta be as *good* as last night, or better. Joey, Mat and Rosa – you need to speak up a bit. The mikes are getting you, but not always clearly. Rick, you need to slow down, especially in those soliloquies. Tony, I've said it before, and I'll say it again, don't shuffle your feet while speaking. Keep still. Aisha, you were wonderful....' (the cast gave a brief spatter of applause) '....but you were late on stage for Act IV, scene two. You come on, alarmed, *as* the madmen howl, not after they've finished. Now, I know you're pretty tired, but I guess that cuts no ice. You must concentrate at all times. The mob out there has paid good money to see you. A family of four will have forty dollars tied up in you tonight.'

Mon paused to let this sink in, gazing down at the young, serious faces.

'I confidently expect tonight's performance to be the best of the three,' he went on. 'Last night you were nervous and there were a coupla little fluffs; tomorrow you're going to be more tired *and* over-confident – a bad combo. Tonight is the one to remember. And that's why…,' Mon paused, realising he had gone on a tad too long and that fidgeting was starting, '….that's why we've got the local papers in and it's being photographed by Mr Fraser and Mr Ormond. They'll be copies of snaps and the article for you and for the archives and the magazine. God bless and good luck.'

He clambered down and a buzz started.

'Wow! The papers!'

'That old rag!'

'I've been in *The Flushing Gazette* twice now.'

'I wish we could make, like, a film of it.'

Louise clapped her hands.

'Quiet now, please. We're on in two minutes. Get into positions.'

'Jem. Jem!'

Rick's voice came in a sharp whisper.

220

'Yes?'

Jem was sitting in the stage left wing, listening to Act III, scene 3. For some minutes Rick had been watching him watching the play. He was strangely touched by what he saw. Jem was leaning forward, elbows on his knees, his cupped hands cradling his chin, his forehead catching the glow, his face framed by Julia's wig, and his eyes bright and intelligent. His mouth was silently moving, reciting each line as his fellow actors said them. He knows the whole play, thought Rick – and this appealed tremendously to him. How sparkling, how *involved* Jem always is.

Rick was led by his observation into the reflection that here was what seemed to be a perfect human being. Jem, to all appearances, had no faults. He was predictable and mature, he never seemed to lose his temper, (Rick had not been present at Jem's exasperation with Francis), he was modest, generous, loved humour, was generally either thoughtful or smiling, was extremely intelligent, was….oh, just perfect. Rick felt an astonishing protectiveness of the younger boy and a deep sense of satisfaction at being with him. He was actually proud to find he loved him, not disturbed, not even questioning of it – even of his increasing erotic need of Jem.

Not as pleasant a person as he wished others to think him, Rick was not blinded as to his true nature. He had been brought up to put himself first. He had, in a male-dominated house, pleased himself since infancy. He always had plenty of pocket-money and, latterly, an allowance which his father thought proper to a young man of nineteen. He had the use of a pre-owned car and knew that the rich baker would give him a new one of his own when he left high school. If he had been pressed to define himself honestly, he would have said that he was canny, cynical, pleasure-seeking, occasionally brutal, and apt to use others. He prided himself on being Italian, but he worshipped the ethos of *The Godfather* more reverently than that of the Pope. Yet, suddenly, there was this strange, different, Jem-factor.

Pushed by a moralist, Rick would not have condemned homosexuality outright. His father would certainly have done so, but he was old-fashioned and not at all liberal. When fourteen, Rick had adopted the prevailing 10th grade code of sneering at gays, but as he didn't actually know any homosexuals, it had been rather academic. Now, at nineteen, he took the view that whatever turned you on was acceptable enough. People were people, male or female – a handsome boy or beautiful girl could alike be objects of desire. This was late 20th century New York, for Crissakes!

He couldn't, however, remember ever finding another boy attractive to him, except that one time, long ago in Stresa, when he and Luca Andreotti had experimented with kissing each other on the mouth, and he had thought Luca beautiful. His predominant feeling, therefore, about Jem's effect on him, was one of deep surprise. Equally surprising was the difference he felt about Jem from his ordinary conquests. Predatory by nature, he had never expected to fail in his pursuit of girls – right up to Felicity, whose party he had cut for rehearsal. It didn't matter what *they* thought of him, but it mattered terribly what Jem's ideas about him were, he found. It mattered too that Jem's interests be put first – and this coloured the yearnings which Jem, even when not being Julia, aroused in him. With Jem he felt less of a conquistador than a suitor. Not long after his nineteenth birthday, then, with his schooldays as good as over, he had, he supposed, fallen in love for the first time.

Sometimes a voice whispered that he was going soft – and pervie with it. Loving a youth of seventeen – not even seventeen until the 18th of August! Rick even felt a sense of shame at having looked up Jem's date of birth in the office records, on the pretext of wanting to get him a present. How soft could you get? Yet how was he to resist the enormous tug on his feelings? He couldn't spend half a day away from Jem without itching to be in his company. Like Mr Howard, he was unable to contemplate the ending of *The Duchess* without something very like fear. When it was all over – then what?

'Jem?' he whispered again.

'Oh, sorry, Rick. I was just thinking how good the

kids are as pilgrims tonight. It's going real well again, isn't it?'

Ah, *and* he's generous with praise, *and* he's a marvellous team player, thought Riccardo.

'Yeah, they're doing great. Listen, come the interval, can you pop outside?'

'Outside?'

'Yes, just….outside. It's so hot in here. We've got more than twenty minutes before the re-start. I thought we could just sit on the wall by the labs, or something.'

'Well, okay,' replied Jem, hesitantly. He didn't like to leave the play's close radius. 'Just for a while.' Then he realised that there was something unusual in this. All his interest in Rick flared up, replacing his concentration on the play. What on earth does he want to talk to me about? Jem's modesty and his sense of place in the scheme of things led him not to expect much from the mutual drawing-together which he knew happened when, as Julia, he lay in Bosola's arms. Jem liked those arms, the strong body and dark eyes of the 12th grade Senior, but he worried secretly about those likings, finding it a relief to pigeon-hole them as belonging to his "Julia" periods, and not to the essential Jem Clarke.

They sat together for a few more moments until Rick was due on stage again.

'Have you got the letter?' whispered Jem. Rick nodded, patting the pocket in which the lying letter to the Duchess was folded.

After the Duchess' arrest and her brave monologue: *I am armed against misery,* there was a loud clapping and part one was over. Rick came back to Jem's side. Jem stood, smoothing the slit dress over his thighs, unconsciously provocative. He had got into the habit of twirling the necklace he now wore and now, also unconsciously, his hand went to his bosom and fluttered there among the diamante gleams.

My God, he is the loveliest thing I've ever come across, breathed Rick to himself. The dangerous flare of lust came over him as his eyes travelled along Jem's arms to his bare rounded shoulders (for Jem only wore the hot fur coat when on stage). He saw himself pulling Jem down upon a bed, pressing his mouth to Jem's quizzically amused lips and helping him take off Julia's clothing until all of Jem was revealed. All that came between them was a diaphanous dress, the Faculty bra, Julia's sheened tights and an undergarment – but such barriers still!

Hoping that Jem could read his thoughts, and then, just as fervently, hoping he couldn't, Rick led the way out through the back-stage area to the fire door at the end of the passage, which was propped open by a chair to let a little draught find its way up to the stage. It was still light, but cloud cover was beginning to dim the summer evening. It was all Rick could do not to take Jem's hand.

July : MORE OF THE SECOND NIGHT

'Where are they?' hissed Mon Howard.

Pharhad looked up from his script which he was readying for Part Two.

'Where's who, Sir?'

'Where's Jem? Where's Riccardo? They haven't wandered off, have they? I wanted a word with the whole cast during the interval.'

Pharhad left his stool and dimly shaded light.

'I'll go and see, Sir.'

He went off into the stage-right wing, behind the set, down the passage and into the green room, passed Janek coming along and went round to the stage-left wing. Two wooden chairs were there, empty, next to a fire extinguisher. He padded back again.

'Well? Any luck?'

'They're not on set, or in the green room, Sir.'

'Well, bless you for hunting, Pharhad. Go and take a thoroughly deserved break.'

Mon had only thought for a second of scurrying round for the missing two himself. It was too absurdly Mother Hen-ish to go fussing round as if he didn't trust his boys. Ridiculous! But not knowing what Jem was doing had grown painful. With Jem in view across the set, dressed as Julia, bathed in the spill of light, Mon had achieved a Nirvana-like happiness. *The Duchess* was going to last forever, Jem would always be Julia – young and desirable – and Mon would always be in charge: controlled and controlling. Yet now, with Jem no longer visible, and Riccardo missing, Mon felt uneasy. Too ridiculous of me! They had probably just gone to the john. He went into the green room to speak to the rest of the cast.

'Now fades the glimmering landscape on the sight,' quoted Jem.

'Uh?'

'And all the air a solemn stillness holds.'

'Where's that from?'

'Gray's *Elegy*. I don't know why I remember it, but I seem to have a good memory for bits of poetry.'

'Even if it's not particularly relevant, given that it's still light and the glimmering suburbs of Queens aren't exactly fading,' smiled Riccardo.

'True – but then I couldn't think of a bunch of lines which would fit.'

'I'm pretty impressed you can think of any.'

Jem and Rick sat on a low wall which bordered the car park and faced a strip of lawn. Behind them, the warm hoods of cars clicked. Jem dangled his legs from the wall.

'Must be careful not to rip my tights,' he said.

'I hope you don't think it peculiar of me to ask you out here with me,' commenced Rick, 'but I wanted to ask you something.'

Jem looked sideways at him from under Julia's

curls.

'Ask away,' he smiled.

'I – er – I've really enjoyed doing this play with you, you know,' said Rick.

'You've told me that. Thanks,' replied Jem.

'Well, my point is, what's going to happen when it's all over?'

'What do you mean?'

'I mean that – if it doesn't seem weird to say it – that I'd like to go on seeing you; when it's over.'

'Oh.'

Jem couldn't think of an adequate reply. He analysed again what he thought of Rick. He liked him. No – he didn't exactly *like* him, as he liked Janek, but he experienced a sort of interior excitement when he contemplated Rick's image. He wasn't sure it was anything to do with ordinary liking.

'What do you think?' persisted Rick.

'Think? Um, I - I'd like to keep up with you very much….but surely….?'

'….but I'm leaving St Mat's for College and you're only in 11th grade, so there are practical difficulties?'

'I suppose I did partly mean that, but Rick….?'

'Where's the practical difficulty? It's the beginning of the vacation. I don't know what you've got planned, but I'm flexible until the results come up. You're not going to summer camp, are you?' Jem shook his head. 'My dad is giving me an allowance,' went on the spoilt Riccardo, 'so I haven't got to get a job or anything. So – so we could meet. That is, if you're around.'

'I think there's an idea about my sister and me going to Florida to see my father. My mother isn't keen on going – they're separated, you see – but Betsy and I might be…. I just don't know yet.'

'Couldn't you say you'd been asked to spend a bit of the vacation with a school friend? I mean, we could go to Italy. I've got relatives there, in Stresa.' Rick, who had only just thought of this idea, warmed to the theme, 'My grandmother lives there. She's got a really nice villa with more than one spare room. What about going over to Europe and staying with her?'

Jem, who had not spent a moment's holiday time without the constraining company of his mother and the infuriating company of his sister, was taken aback by this suggestion. What on *earth* would his mother say? How could she afford the air fare to Europe? What would he and Rick do in a country where, presumably, Rick spoke the language, but Jem not a single word? After all, he didn't know Riccardo that well. He had, it is true, fantasised about getting to know him better, as the Rs in his diary testified, but his fantasy had always taken the shape of Rick coming to his bedroom on 172nd St, in a house conveniently emptied of his family. There, without words, an enactment of the Bosola/Julia scene would take place – but going much further, of course. In these imagined scenes, Jem had seen himself as the dominant partner, and Rick, a languorous admirer, driven mad by desire.

'Well, what do you think?' Rick's voice, low-pitched and in earnest, sliced through his vapourings.

'Gee, I don't know. I....'

Jem tailed off.

Rick, like Jem, had fantasised with equal lack of connection with reality. Sometimes, lately, he had formed a half-glimpsed plan of taking Jem away with him – to the West Coast, perhaps. When the fog had parted, however, he had seen the inevitable presence of Jem's parents (he hadn't known they were separated), the continuance of Jem's education, his own father's brutally jovial face, his own college plans, Jem's age, the problem of money....a multitude of objections and difficulties. What he hadn't envisaged was hesitation and puzzlement on Jem's part, although he really might have. He too had seen himself as the dominant lover; in his own cut-and-dried arrangements, Jem was always waiting, eager shiny lips apart, for him to resolve difficulties. More than once Rick (who had trouble imagining Jem without his Julia costume on) had thought that they could go a hotel as a couple (Jem clinging to his arm in the foyer) and stay in a wide, firm double bed.

It occurred to him now, sitting as close as seemed natural to him on the wall, that Jem wasn't at all clinging, helpless or feminine. Perhaps that was part of his strong appeal – not that he was effeminately un-boyish, but that he wasn't. Rick abandoned ideas of Jem in drag in the lobby of a Los Angeles hotel, his high heels ringing on the marble.

'Well, I suppose it's a bit sudden for me to come out with this. I realise that, but – and I've got to say this, Jem – I don't like the idea of us saying goodbye forever at the cast party tomorrow. I guess I thought you'd feel the same.'

Jem was stung into making a reply.

'Oh, I do. I – I want to see you again. It's just that I don't know how, over the long term. It depends where you go to college. We could meet up in vacation for a – a pizza or something and swop news.'

Even as he said it, Jem realised that there was something ludicrous in this picture; something miles away from the complex hard-to-define emotions which this conversation was engendering in him.

There was a silence. Neither knew what to say.

Rick clenched his left fist and then opened it.

'I don't want to swop news about what syllabuses we are studying while eating a pizza,' he said. 'I can't believe you don't see what I'm driving at – at what I *do* want.'

Jem, who did see, said nothing. Once again his hand fluttered to his bosom to twiddle Julia's string of glittering jewellery.

Rick looked round quickly. Chrome twinkled in the empty car park. To anyone who saw them, as they passed the high school, they would just be a boy and a girl sitting on a wall. Rick put his hand on Jem's leg and let his fingers grip the thigh muscle. For both it was a moment of significance. They had not touched each other outside their roles as Bosola and Julia. Rick's fingers felt the diaphanous material of the dress ride with it as he ran his hand up the younger boy's leg. Jem gave a gasp.

'Rick – really.... I....'

'To be honest with you, Jem, I want to go the whole way with you.'

'Whole way?'

'Yes. Everything that we both like doing. I want to do it with you. It. You dig?'

Part of him couldn't believe he had uttered the words.

'Oh. Yes,' murmured Jem, his eyelashes dropping.

'I want,' continued Rick, enjoying the impact his directness was having on his young companion, 'to lie *naked* with you in a *bed*. Not eat pizza. Do you understand me now?'

Jem could not respond. For about three seconds he felt angrily affronted, with the alarm of the seduced, but immediately following this he felt so amazingly happy that he wanted to leap up and cry aloud. Now this was something! This was close to his inarticulate fancies – those dreams he sometimes carried from

rehearsal into the private haven of his room on 172nd
St. Then he felt appalled again. He had been – what
was the word? – propositioned! An older boy, a
young man, had actually suggested that….that….

His conflicting feelings must have shown in his
face, for Rick asked, with a quizzical smile,

'Are you shocked?'

Jem struggled to think of the best combination of
words to express both the joy and the perturbation,
and couldn't. 'Oh, come on, Jem. I just don't believe
you're shocked – not really. I've seen you look at me
in rehearsal. You've known that I had a hard-on last
week when you were in my arms – and I've known
you knew it.'

'Well, yes. I….yes, but this is – is so….'

'You're nearly seventeen. You know about sex.
How long since you started playing with yourself?'

It was back again; that fear Jem had of discussing
such topics – as though clothing what had been
glorious fantasies in words made them concrete and
less magical, somehow crude, faintly comic and
depressingly banal.. But Riccardo pressed him, taking
Jem's hand in his – not without another quick look
over his shoulder. 'Come on. How long?'

'Since I was twelve – just before my thirteenth
birthday.'

'Yeah, well that was four years ago, and I'm sure
you've been busy since.'

And Jem, only too conscious of enthralling and

lust-mad days when he had had four or more pleasurings, could only nod. 'You're no different from me, Jem. Although I didn't start until I was fourteen – and since then I've slept with a few girls. Have you?'

Jem, who wished he could give an answer other than the true one, whispered,

'No – none. Not yet.'

Rick smiled, slightly grimly.

'They're a lot of trouble, you know. Nothing's ever for one night and they talk about you; at least the kids I've slept with do. Being absolutely honest with you, I prefer doing it to myself when I feel I need to. You can concentrate on your own feelings and sensations then. In fact, I'm not sure the old Red Indians didn't have it right in what they said.'

'What? What did they say?'

'Young woman for business; young man for pleasure – or something on those lines.'

'Oh, honestly, Rick.'

'But wouldn't it be great? I mean, exploring those sorts of things? I've never wanted to....never even considered doing it with another....'

'....another guy?'

'Another guy, yes, until....'

'Until you met me, you were going to say?'

'Exactly. Until I met you.' Rick felt much better now. It seemed as if, by being brutally plain and direct, he had taken control again – a control he felt he had lost somewhere during the articulation of his unrealistic holiday plans in Stresa. 'And since I've been in this play, I've thought of nothing else. Jem, I really do think it's a – a type of love.'

'Oh, Rick, surely....'

'Yes, I do, in the usual way of the word, believe that I am in *love* with you. That's why I don't want just to wave goodbye in twenty-four hours' time. I couldn't. I can't do that.'

Jem put his hand over Riccardo's. It now seemed an easy thing to do.

'I guess I wouldn't want that, either.'

Rick pulled Jem to his feet.

'Come on. Let's go inside. I've said what I wanted to. We'll be missed.'

They went back into the building, Rick pulling Jem by the hand. At the end of the empty corridor there came a hum from the auditorium foyer. Rick pushed Jem into the stage-right wing, took him by the shoulders and brought their mouths together. For a very little second, Jem sought to squirm away in panic, but Rick held him steadily and as their lips met Jem felt a bolt of lightning racket through his nerves. His left arm instinctively went round Rick's waist; his right came down between them. Rick dropped one hand through the slit in Julia's dress, lifted the undergarment and forced their groins together. Jem's tongue explored Rick's even teeth. He had one coherent thought: he tastes slightly peppery. Rick felt the caress of Julia's wig on his face. Jem's mouth was soft, and Rick feasted on the gloss lipstick, fighting a gasp as Jem's hand, of its own volition, pressed tightly on the bulge of his leather trousers.

There was a step.

Neither noticed it until a change in the air made them come to themselves. They jumped apart. Janek stood in the opening, his eyes on Jem.

'Old Howard's going bananas,' he said. 'He wanted to have a word with the cast and no one knew where you were. And now the interval is over.'

The play!

Incredible – but Rick realised he had forgotten all about it. The interval was over, and he was due on stage as Bosola!

'Christ! I'm – I'm coming,' he said. The twin shocks of overwhelming passion and the appearance of Janek had robbed the usually glib Riccardo of speech. 'I – I'm ready.'

The three went swiftly down the passage. The rest of the cast were coming along from the green room. Jem's brain, nerves and body were in turmoil. He knew his lipstick was blurred, his eyes glazed, and his wig tousled. He felt Rick grab his wrist.

'Will he say anything?' said Rick, shakily.

'What, Jan? No. No.' Jem's voice was also tremulous with passion and shock.

Mon came up to them, having calmed himself, and not seeming particularly alarmed, Jem was relieved to note.

'Talk about last minute,' he grunted. 'Get ready, Mr Parisi.'

Jem's performance was convincing, as usual; perhaps a little more so. True, he fumbled a line, as his thoughts kept slotting back to the kiss in the wings, but something of his emotions and intensity of anticipation found their way into his acting. Bosola was now, somehow, Rick – so the seduction had a vibrancy which was new. When he came on to take his bow, the applause was prodigious, given the relative smallness of Julia's part in the overall plot.

At the end of the play, when Jem was back in his T-shirt and jeans, his mother, with a soft bloom of tears in her eyes, embraced him fondly and proudly. Even Betsy, not known for her praise of others, said,

'You were better than the one who was the duchess, Jem. You were brilliant, even though it was weird seeing you as a girl.' And she kissed him.

Jem refused a lift back with his mother in the car. He didn't think he could bear being encased in his family's normality just yet.

'I'll walk back, Mom,' he said. 'I've still got traces of make-up to get off. I guess I'm real hot, and I'd like the air.'

'Don't be too late, darling,' said Mrs Clarke, and she and Betsy juddered off in a whiff of exhaust.

I must see Rick, thought Jem. I must talk to him. The wall where they had sat was now in darkness.

Inside the auditorium, Mr Lomax and Jonathan were rewinding the music effects tape on the old Revox machine and Jem could hear its quiet squealing through the loudspeakers. Mr Howard was picking up discarded programmes from the seats. He seemed about to say something to Jem but gave him instead an unfathomable look. Jem realised he had to make an apology.

'I'm really sorry you were worried about Rick and me, Sir. We just slipped out to get cooled off.'

Mr Howard seemed, for a moment, to be about to say something stronger than his mild comment.

'Without telling anyone you were doing so. Never mind, you were both terrific when you got back. Better stay in the theatre, though.'

'Thank you, Sir.'

Jem was grateful to Mr Howard. Many teachers would have cut up rough about missing a cast pep talk. He knew how important it was to Mr Howard for his boys to be team-players. The team was what mattered. As Mon often said, quoting Mr Spock, *The needs of the many outweigh the needs of the one.*

'Jem, you are okay, aren't you?'

Jem wondered for a ghastly moment if Mr Howard somehow knew about that kiss, and he was sure he could read something else in addition to friendly concern.

'I'm fine, Sir.'

'Well, that's great. You've got more than a hint of

eye-shadow left on, you know.'

'Oh, yes. I'm just going in to get it off.'

Mon watched Jem go out to the green room corridor and then resumed collecting programmes. Darling boy, he was thinking: even lovelier as Jem than Julia. Oh, God, God.

Mon had spoken to the enthusiastic, pretty and slightly fluttery Mrs Clarke and to the pert little sister of Jem's. It had been forcibly driven home to him again that his infatuation was cruelly hopeless. That pretty woman was probably some years younger than he was. He saw in a second of hideous clarity her hurt face when she learned that her teenage son had been seduced by his middle-aged homosexual English teacher, and in a further second he saw a courtroom weighing her defenceless motherliness against his perverted desires. The end of this evening had almost brought the clanging of prison doors to Mon's ears. The lonely pain of it! And tomorrow the play would be over. Was there no hope at all?

Jem hurried from one back-stage area to another. Where was Rick? Then from the car park he heard his voice and ran out towards him. Rick was sitting on the hood of a car in conversation with a dark-haired youth and two girls.

'Oh, hi, Jem,' he said as Jem came up. He turned to his companions. 'May I present Julia, alias Cleo Jakemar, alias Jem Clarke. I've been listening to raves about all of us. This,' he went on, 'is my cousin Giovanni, my cousin Mirella – on my aunt's side of the family – and Giovanni's friend, Sara.'

Jem nodded smilingly at each of them in turn. The dark-haired boy he recognised as a 10th grade pupil. He hadn't known that Rick had a relative at St Matthew's. The girls smirked at him. One of them, Giovanni's sister Mirella, said,

'You look a little shorter than you seemed on stage.'

'I was wearing high heels,' replied Jem.

Rick stood up and went round to the front door of the auto.

'In you get,' he said to his companions. 'I'll be out in a minute. I've just got to get something from the green room. Give me a hand looking for it, Jem.'

As they went in, he pulled Jem close. 'I've gotta go now,' he said. 'We'll talk tomorrow. Remember, it's not *if*, it's now *where* and *when,* isn't it?'

Jem nodded. Rick held him close, enwrapping him, and kissed him again on the mouth. 'Be careful going home. You're precious to me.' He stepped back and was gone.

Jem picked up his ruck-sack and took out his jumper. The night suddenly felt chilly. He heard voices in the passage. Janek, Jonathan and Mark were coming from the lighting cubicle.

'Oh, hello, Jem. I'll walk back with you.' Jan turned to the techies. 'See you guys tomorrow.'

Jem walked down to the end of the road and turned towards 172nd St with Jan by his side. They had done this walk a thousand times, but now a heavy silence enwrapped them. Janek was the first to break it.

'What you're doing is wrong, Jem,' he said.

Jem made no reply. He ached to feel Rick's arms round his body. Of course it wasn't *wrong*, he thought irritably. How can anything that feels so right be wrong? 'I probably have no call to say anything,' went on Jan, 'but I'm your friend and you're on a dangerous course. What you are doing is a sin. Surely you can see that? How far has it gone?'

Jem stopped and faced him.

'Look, we are friends, Jan. But this is different, and it's just not your business. I'm sorry you came into the wing when you did – but there it is.'

'I feel it is my business.'

'It *isn't* your business, Janek.'

A shroud of disappointment seemed to hang between them. Jan was judgemental, was he? Disgusted? Jem felt extraordinarily irritated by his friend's lack of understanding. 'I can't help myself, Jan,' he went on, trying to explain. 'And I don't think Riccardo can.'

'Don't tell me you're gonna say "this thing's bigger than both of us" like someone in an old movie. Only yesterday we were smooching the girls. What about that?'

'That wasn't the same. What I felt with Aisha was

just nothing to what I feel with Riccardo. It's more like – like pain, but it's the only thing that's important to me right now.'

'I defended you from my brother's dirty little tongue, too.'

'Oh, that's completely different!'

'Is it? It doesn't seem so to me,' muttered Jan.

There was another long silence. They had reached the point where Jan branched off.

'Look. Don't let it change things,' mumbled Jem.

Jan peered at him under the streetlights. Jem thought he could read something in his eyes other than moral judgement. He wondered if it was jealousy. You couldn't tell with Jan. What if he were hurt by all this?

'I still think it's fundamentally wrong,' said Jan firmly.

'All right, leave it at that. See you tomorrow?'

'Of course,' said Jan, turning his steps into Sachs Boulevard.

Jem gazed after his pal's solid figure. He knew Jan meant well, and he liked him as much as ever. But oh, sex changes everything. Where had he heard that line? It *is* changing everything.

Much later, in his attic bedroom, Rick lay naked on his bed, his legs apart. He was fondling himself, close to climax. In his mind he replayed Jem's kiss, its saliva, softness and that Christmassy taste of lipstick.

He felt again the weight of him, leaning close – and he pictured that time when they would be able to explore every little detail of each other. He had done some surreptitious reading in the library and had clearer ideas about how two men might make love. The excitement of anticipating such things with Jem made him feel almost dizzy.

Not IF anymore, just WHERE and WHEN. The words drummed insistently in his brain.

Jem's figure seemed almost to be with him in bed, lying next to him? No – kneeling astride him! Yes, that's perfect! …. Where….and when….

He looked along his chest at himself; his fondling changing to a swift grasp, he drew his legs up and arched his back and his tremors began.

'Jem!' he cried, his voice explosive in the silence.

July : A MOST PECULIAR INVITATION

The Duchess of Malfi was on its third night. The tired cast had been made up for the last time – or so they believed; for the last time the mixers, the lanterns, the audio, the smoke and the props had been checked. Louise had sold no more tickets during that day. She and David feared that they had oversold already. Each of the cast had relatives and friends booked, some for the second or third time. Mrs Clarke was to be there again, helping other parents with interval refreshments. CoCo D'Souza, with a new boyfriend, was coming. David's mother and his oldest school friend would be there. The mysterious Alan Clemmy and the Webster Museum Trust were due to mingle with the Principal's own guests. When David had explained that they had come all the way from Canada and were probably staying in a hotel in Manhattan, it was the least Dr Bennett felt he could do. To the more than the mild amazement of Mon, the St Matthew's staff and the cast themselves, the old 17th century tragedy had – quite against prophecy – become a popular success, easily as well attended as *Guys and Dolls* and *The Boyfriend* had been in previous years.

Louise sat with David in the lighting cubicle, just behind Jonathan and Mark. Janek perched on a stool ready to operate the Revox and the remote smoke control, trying not to generate such dense clouds that the audience could barely see the actors. Louise had expected to go home each evening after make-up but had surprised herself by not wanting to do so. It was no joke getting back to the apartment at nearly midnight and then dragging up again at a quarter after six – not for three days running. Yet she could not have walked away from the play without leaving something of herself behind. The concentrated camaraderie of the tech team, the frantic scurrying backstage, the nervous excitement of the young cast, Mon and David being everywhere at once, the 'enemy' out there in the dark, watching – well, it was all rather wonderful.

'God, you look a wreck,' CoCo had kindly told her that morning. CoCo had been, for once, up early herself. There was some kind of flap on at the lab.

'I *am* a wreck,' had muttered Louise, trying to disguise the dark smudges under her eyes.

'You need witch-hazel for those shopping-bags,' had grinned CoCo, 'but it's too late this morning, anyway.'

'Only once more *bound upon a wheel of fire*, then the long glories of the weekend,' Louise had said. 'See you at St Mat's at a quarter after seven?'

'Definitely. After all this I wouldn't miss out for anything. I'm dying to see Lomax, of course, and *Uber-direktor* Howard too, remember.'

Now, her face softly lit by the shaded desk lights

and the glow from the dials, Louise breathed gently by David's shoulder. The fair curls of hair on his forearms were sleek, his heavily made hands precise with script pages and sliders. Louise, like Rick and Mon, was dreading the end of it all. She had considered it *de rigeur*, like whinging about working conditions, for a teacher to express an extra-curricular activity to cease – but what would happen when it did? She and David, for instance – would they work on another play? And that wouldn't be until the far end of the next semester at the earliest. There was the great unbridgeable gulf of the summer vacation. What would she do during that? She had a depressing picture of the hot, dusty August streets of New York, and herself eking out the days in pretended interest in the latest exhibition at the Guggenheim. CoCo, she knew, was heading for Goa to visit relations, probably with her new guy too, back-packing and hilarious. Oh, what would be nice would be a break somewhere like – like up in the Appalachians with, well, with someone like David. She felt a gush of fond feeling as she sat behind him, studying his inverted, unconscious face in the refection of the glass panel.

Loud voices came from the stage.

'Stand by,' hissed David.

'Yes, Mr Lomax, Sir,' whispered Jonathan back – although he was perfectly aware that a major lighting cue was upon them.

At the interval, Susie came in and approached

David as he was preparing to leave the box.

'Scuse me, Sir, Miss Carrbridge, but I've got a message from the Principal for you.'

'Message? What message? I bet it's about too much smoke.'

'No, Sir. He's asked if you and Miss Carrbridge would join him to meet his guests.'

'Oh, thanks, Susie.' He stood, tucking his shirt in. 'Damn. I bet that means we're gonna get patronised by some self-important governor, some pig-ignorant local Catenian or stuffy old trout who hasn't understood a word of the play.'

'If I have to grovel, I'd like a drink first,' grinned Louise.

David turned to Jonathan, Mark and Jan, who had been listening with amusement.

'See you later, kids. Don't bring any girls in here for an orgy during the interval, or, if you do, don't get their bra-straps entangled in the sliders. I don't wanna have to re-set levels.'

The three boys tittered dutifully.

Dr Bennett's study was crowded. Loud voices were raised in appreciation of the play and 'the evident enjoyment' of the young cast. Mon Howard was there, looking distinguished and actor-ish in his black polo-neck and greying hair. The Principal had, in fact, been pleased at Mon's choice of a demanding classical tragedy, rather than a common-or-garden popular musical. He felt it gave St Matthew's a bit of class, just what a rich kids' private high school should have – although he would, perhaps, have preferred a Shakespeare history, like *Henry V*.

'Ah, David and Miss – um – Carrbridge!' cried Dr Bennett, making a superhuman effort to remember Louise's name. 'Just the people. I want to introduce you to Sir Alan here. He's from the Webster Museum Trust at Merivale, Nova Scotia, and he has very much liked what he has seen.'

'How do you do?' said a shrimp-like, very well-dressed, balding man in glasses, with a strong upper-class British accent. 'I do appreciate your reserving the seats I requested. This,' he added, turning to a group clustered behind him, 'is my committee. Ron Portray, Zach Hall, Edward Leaven – he wrote the book about the links between Webster, King James' Court and the early American settlers, you know – and Roger Gollop, our treasurer.'

Clutching their wine glasses, the group of five moved closer round Louise and David, grinning encouragingly. Neither David nor Louise had found their voices yet, being very much surprised to hear Alan Clemmy introduced as 'Sir Alan'.

'Thoroughly enjoying every moment,' came the rumbling voice of Roger Gollop. 'The music and lights particularly. Your department, I gather?'

'It's a thousand pities we can't stay for the second half,' went on Sir Alan, 'particularly as the cast are doing such a good job. But we will meet again. Your Principal has the details.'

'Can't stay?' repeated David.

'Yes, such a pity. But our flight leaves at eleven-fifty, and it's now nine-thirty. Dr Bennett tells me you don't finish until well after ten-thirty – so it would be cutting it too fine.'

'Oh, so you're not staying in New York,' stammered Louise, 'I thought I heard that – that is, I was sure you were at a hotel….'

'No, no. Flew in this afternoon. Back overnight. Our plane arrives at Halifax at two a.m., and then we drive down to Merivale.'

'Gee whiz, you will have had a long day and night,' said David. 'I hope it was worth it.'

'It was worth it. Very, very much worth it. Well, I think we really must say thank you again and goodbye.'

'Goodbye,' rumbled Roger Gollop, looking round for a place to put his glass.

'*Au revoir* would be more appropriate,' smiled the author of 'the book', Edward Leaven.

'Oh, so you're coming back?' asked David, more puzzled than ever. 'You know this is the play's last night?'

'It is, and it isn't,' twinkled Sir Alan. 'Your Principal and Mr Howard have all the details. So nice to have met you both. My congratulations to your children.'

With a professional, toothy British grin, Sir Alan turned from them and made for Dr Bennett. David and Louise saw the two of them exchange a few remarks and then the whole posse from the Webster Museum Trust made for the door and vanished.

'Well! Who woulda believed it!' gasped David.

'How very, very odd,' murmured Louise.

'Bunch of absolute weirdos,' snorted David.

'Mad as hatters.'

Mon came up.

'Hello, you two. Time to get the show on the road again. Had an interesting chat with the Websterites?'

'What the hell was it all about? Did you know they've hauled ass before the play's second half, even though they came down from Halifax to see it?'

'And,' put in Louise, 'they're on a night flight and will barely get home before breakfast.'

'All to see our paraplegics hamming it! That's Canadians for you!'

'One of them is a crazy Brit, isn't he?'

'Look,' said Mon, breaking in on the chorus, 'they've made an almost incredible request. I'll have to tell you later; the interval's gone on for twenty minutes as it is. Just this – this *isn't* the last night of *The Duchess*.'

'What!' cried David and Louise.

'It's not the end. I'll speak to the cast when it's over. Come along to the green room during costume removal. I'll tell all then.'

'But, hey, Mon…'

'Mon, please!'

'No! Back to work, guys! Chop, chop. One minute, then flash house lights; then two minutes, and on to the second half. I'll tell the cast they've got three minutes.'

Mon hurried off. David and Louise looked at each other. Uppermost in Louise's mind had been her regret at the play coming to an end – and now, according to Mon, it wasn't going to.

'Not ending tonight? What does that mean?'

'Beats me,' muttered David. 'Total lunatic asylum, this place. We'll find out soon, anyhow.'

He stumped back to the control cubicle and Louise followed him, feeling very happy. Now this was fun! This was unexpected, therefore welcome!

'Quiet! QUIET, per-lease, ladies and gentlemen!' roared Mon. There was a tremendous chattering and cackling in the green room. All thirty-one of the cast were screaming to each other at once, clapping each other on the back, kissing and making wide, theatrical gestures. Waiting parents and friends were forgotten in the oxygen of release from strain.

Mon mounted a chair with a sheaf of papers under his arm.

'Three cheers for Mr Howard!' cried someone, and a burst of applause drowned out Mon's voice. He smiled indulgently. They had already dragged him onto the stage with a stolid David Lomax and blushing Louise and he had got his bottle of whisky from the cast. Greg and Liam had found a Scotch whisky called 'Teachers' and believed themselves wittily original in choosing this particular brand for their favoured pedant. He had received, as had David and Louise, a signed programme in a frame, and been warmly thanked by Dr Bennett.

He gazed now at the glowing faces surrounding his chair. These dear boys and girls – how they would remember this night, this last night of *their* play, in performance of which they had found something in themselves that might have been forever hidden. How diffident they had been six months ago: Joey and Liam awkward and silly, Rosa and Aisha distant and defensive, Riccardo supercilious, Jem self-effacing and quiet, and look at them now, buoyant on the wings of their success (his success, not that they entirely knew it) and drunk on unexpected applause and self-knowledge. Mon's fond smile ebbed for an instant into sadness. How many times had he reflected on this and had had these hilarious scenes enacted before him? And all the young, eager faces of the past grown old.

'Dry up, everyone!' came David's bluff boom, and, eddying in irrepressible whispers, the racket became silence.

'Ladies and Gentlemen of *The Duchess of Malfi*,' said Mon. 'I have astonishing news and a request to make to you all. I do not want nor need the answer to this request until 3.45 on Monday, when I would be obliged if you would all briefly call in here at the auditorium on your way home.'

There was an immediate hum.

'Monday?'

'Did he say Monday?'

'Is it another photo, do you think?'

'Is the Doc throwing a party for us?'

'Heck – we're going to transfer to Broadway!'

'Ha, ha, ha!'

'Oh, it'll be about costumes. I've split my jacket at a seam.'

Mon called for silence once more.

'During tonight's magnificent performance….'

Laughter and some clapping.

'….during the performance we had some guests from a Museum Trust based in Nova Scotia, Canada. Their chairman, Sir Alan Clemmy, has specially asked us if we could bring our play, in its entirety, to Nova Scotia and give one further performance for an Arts Festival in early August. Doctor Bennett has given his permission, but I would need your agreement, and that of your parents. We would be leaving on the Wednesday before the performance to give us two days to rehearse on a new stage. That's why you've only got until Monday to let me know because we need to act quick.'

He paused, amused by their rapt faces.

'Now, during the second half of tonight's performance, Mrs Monks ran off these explanatory letters with dates and details ready for you to take home. So take one each. Jonathan, Mark, Janek, Pharhad, Susie – you guys too.'

Gibbering began again. Realising he had spoken for long enough, Mon finished.

'Enjoy your party tonight – you deserve it. You're going to Greg's, isn't that so?'

'That's right, Mr Howard, Sir. All at my place. You're very welcome too, Sir.'

Cheers from the cast.

'Thank you, Greg. Most kind. I might look in. Your parents deserve a congressional medal for bravery. Anyway, enjoy it, and remember, if it is your wish – as it is mine – *The Duchess* will have one more airing in Canada.'

He stepped down, passing the sheaf of letters to Riccardo for distribution. The roar resumed at a higher level. David and Louise went to each side of Mon and hustled him from the green room.

'What on *earth*'s it all about, Mon?' cried David.

'I wondered if Sir Alan had asked something of the sort,' said Louise.

'I mean,' went on David, 'our guys and girls have done a good job, a very good job, but are they really up to taking the play on a foreign tour?'

The three teachers plumped down on the front seats in the empty auditorium.

'All I know is this,' said Mon. 'Sir Alan told the Doc that up at Merivale there is a sort of summer school foundation – you know, arts and crafts, local history, poetry readings and all that. Apparently, they've got a decent little theatre with lighting and audio. All you need bring are the sound tapes, Dave. I told him they were on reel-to-reel mono, but he said they've got all sorts there, so just bring tapes and costumes.' Mon smote his forehead. 'Costumes! Jeez, I'll have to give old Ma Dandridge at Stacey's a call on Monday and ask if we can hire them again in a fortnight. God knows how we're gonna get them up there.'

'Do you think they can let us have them?' asked Louise.

'Oh yeah. You saw how many costumes they've got. Anyway, I must tell you about Sir Alan's one stipulation.'

'You mean there's a catch?'

'Not really. Just an odd request – and he was real insistent about it. We must make NO changes to the cast. Everyone in tonight's show must come to Canada. *Everyone.* I thought that was a bit peculiar, as he's asking kids who might be off away on vacation.'

'It is peculiar.'

'Not that we could make last minute changes to the cast, surely?'

'Well, quite. That apart, however, we're on.'

'How much….?' began David and Louise together. They stopped, grinning at each other.

'How much are we getting? Well, brace yourselves: all expenses, all flights, all accommodation, all extra hire charges, all teacher costs for our time, and five hundred US dollars for the Drama fund. So who could say no?'

'The Doc couldn't.'

'Precisely. And, after all, it's the vacation. You two don't mind getting involved, do you? I couldn't manage the sound and light stuff, Dave, So what do you both think?'

'Oh, yes!' cried Louise. 'That is, no, I don't mind. It sounds marvellous. I was feeling quite let down at the thought of the play coming to an end.'

'I'm on, I guess,' said David immediately. There was the fun of the thing, of course, and the interest of seeing Nova Scotia, but there was being with Louise on a jaunt, and that interested him most of all, he was surprised to find.

'Bennett wants us to report to him here when we get back. No objections to popping in during the holiday? I thought we'd have some sorting out of costumes anyway.'

'Bung-ho, squadron-leader, as Sir Alan might say,' laughed David. 'But I still think it's odd that they wanna pay so much for a kids' school play. Odd, with a capital O.'

Back in the green room, Mon's news had had an

electrifying effect. Still high from their success, their relief at having pulled it off and the intoxication of audience approval – the wave of love that pours over the stage lip – the cast had no doubts. Of course they could do it again! They could do it a hundred times! Only Joey looked doubtful.

'Oh shiteroo!' he muttered. 'I'm supposed to be going on the French Exchange at the end of July and we've paid already.'

'You'd better tell Sir,' said Mat. 'Mind you,' he added, 'The Cardinal isn't a really huge role. Pharhad could probably mug up your lines in a week.'

'Screw that!' cried Joey. 'I never wanted to go over to Froggie-land. It's because my Dad thinks I should, because we had that kid Norbert with us.'

'Well, good luck getting out of it.'

Jem dabbed a big piece of cottonwool in removal cream and scrubbed at his foundation and lipstick, frowning into the mirror.

'Gently, Jem,' came Louise's voice. She stood behind him and deftly took over. 'With delicate skin like yours, you've got to be careful.'

'He's got beautiful skin, hasn't he?' said Riccardo, who, having changed into cream shorts and a sweatshirt, was hovering near Jem while he was getting ready to leave for Greg's. He winked over Louise's head at Jem over the mirror. Louise saw it.

'Well, he has, Riccardo. No need to joke about it,'

she went on, not realising that Riccardo wasn't joking, but meant it. 'He's lucky. So he shouldn't scrub and rub at it too hard. A lot of girls would kill for his complexion.'

'I'm just rushing to get out and tell my mother that I'm going on to Greg's,' mumbled Jem, as Louise wiped away the foundation. 'Are you coming to Nova Scotia, Miss Carrbridge?' he added.

'Of course. I can't leave you to fend for yourselves without your wardrobe mistress.'

'Where are we staying when we're there?'

'I don't know, Jem. I don't, in fact, know much more about it all than you do. I think Mr Howard is going to call Sir Alan Clemmy over the weekend. Until then we don't know details.'

'It is strange, isn't it, Miss?' said Riccardo.' I mean suddenly asking us up there, don't you think?'

'I think we all find it strange.'

'It must be to do with the play being an old English classic, mustn't it? – if it's an Arts Festival and a Museum.'

'I imagine so, but as I've said, Jem, I *just don't know* – yet!'

The cast went along 54th Avenue towards Greg's house declaiming lines from the play. David and Louise in his car, and Mon in the Morgan, had gone on ahead to thank the McManus family for hosting the party and to put in their brief appearances. David and Mon knew that it was *noblesse oblige* to turn up to these cast parties, but equally *de rigeur* not to stay too long.

'Are the McManuses remaining in the house?' asked Louise, as David's car went through Pickering Plaza.

'I would if it were my joint,' said David.

'Why? Do they get out of hand? Surely not?'

'Well, not really. The sort of kids who are in the play are usually good sorts, but when the strain's over and they've managed to get some drinks down, and when there are a few girls there, it's best to have the parents on the spot. There's no such thing as a totally civilised teenager. And it's often gate-crashers that are the problem, as you probably know.'

'Not really, David. Remember I've had a sheltered life. In fact,' added Louise in a burst of confidence, 'I've never been to a party like this one. Not even when I was a girl.'

'Good God!' said David. And then he added, 'Oh well, I don't suppose you've missed much. Boys drinking and a bit of heavy petting ain't everyone's idea of a spectator sport.'

Louise tried to envisage what he was describing.

'Will Rosa, Aisha, Susie and those friends of theirs be okay?' she asked.

'Better to ask whether the boys'll still be boys by morning. "He went into her arms a mere lad an' he came out a man!" You've got some serious go-ers there.'

Like CoCo, thought Louise. What a lot I seem to have missed out on.

Greg's parents were totally unlike their camp, extrovert son. Mrs McManus was fair and faded with the beginnings of bad arthritis, Mr McManus tall and rather grimly jovial in a censorious Irish way. Louise felt, with relief, that libertinism would be unlikely under his eye.

Mon was already present, sipping a whisky on the sofa. Not long after David and Louise had been given their drinks, there was a whooping and cackle of chatter from the road outside the house.

'They're here,' smiled Mon.

July: GREG'S PARTY

Music blared from the big back room in which the McManuses had laid out snacks and drinks. A mild version of Buck's Fizz was available, a fruit punch, and some chilled lagers for the older pupils. Slices of warm pizza, crisps and nuts and squares of fruit granola were being attacked. Conversation skirled shrilly. David was embroiled in a hi-fi product name-swap-fest with Jan and Mark, Louise was the subject of confidences about some of the teachers at St Philomena's from Rosa and Susie, and Mon was lying back on a long sofa with Jem on one side and Greg on the other. Rick, perched next to Jem on the sofa arm, waited patiently. Jem was very conscious of the nearness of his bare legs. Mon was amusing them by telling yarns from previous shows and the things which had gone wrong in them.

'Yeah,' he was saying, 'I guess I've gotta bad streak as far as severed fingers go – that's three I've had to deal with in less than twenty years. But gee-whiz, the time we had to scrabble round in bits of pig's blubber to find Mungo's finger was the darnedest!'

The boys liked Mon in raconteur mode. Rick smiled urbanely, privately wondering how long it would be before he could suggest that he and Jem went home. Jem had drunk two glasses of lager, then had sipped from a vodka bottle being secretly passed round by Liam. He did this in order not to seem unfamiliar with vodka in front of Aisha but hadn't liked it much. The result was that he found Mr Howard frightfully amusing. His eyes sparkled and glimmered and he fixed them on Mon's drawling mouth admiringly. At times like these he felt that Mon was just the sort of person he wanted to be. He was unaware of Mon's knee touching his, but Mon wasn't. Greg, uplifted beyond himself by the execution of yet another – but sadly his last – dramatic role, shrieked exaggeratedly at Mon's sallies, reaching over him to slap Jem's thigh or arm.

'Oh yeah, and the sound of that machete going through the top knuckle and Mungo's voice saying so calmly: "Sir, I think the meat-axe has slipped"! – they'll stay with me forever!' drawled Mon, basking under his distinguished greying hair between his boy admirers.

'Ha, ha, ha, ha!' screamed Jem and Greg.

In the passage between the front and rear rooms, David said to Louise,

'What did your friend Chantal think of the play?'

'CoCo? Oh, she loved it, she said. She doesn't know Jacobean tragedy and found it quite disturbing. What did you think of *her*, David?'

'A very striking type,' said David guardedly. He had an instinct that it would be unwise to lavish too much praise on CoCo. 'Looks a bit bossy.'

'Oh yes, she is. She bosses me around, but she's terribly kind.' It pleased Louise very much that a wedge had not been driven between her old friend and herself by what they had done together on the night of Barnaby's party. On the contrary, it was just a further tie of experience and fondness, thankfully uncomplicated, like a holiday they might have spent in each other's company.

'She's got her man-friend under her thumb, I thought,' said David, who, in spite of finding her attractive, hadn't really liked CoCo.

'CoCo was so funny about Mon,' said Louise. 'You know what she said about him?'

'No, I don't think I was listening in to that,' replied David.

'She said: "He's lovely and impressive, but I just *knew* he would be gay".'

'What!' cried David, 'Mon *gay*? How ridiculous.'

David let the notion turn over in his brain, compared it with his long friendship with the older man, took a swig of beer from his can, and dismissed it. 'Horseshit. Your friend CoCo's on the wrong track there. Why, Mon's married – or was.'

'So I gathered. Still, it was funny her coming out with it, just like that.'

Mr and Mrs McManus were in their book and record lined study upstairs. All the books belonged to her; her husband was an Irish song fanatic and his LPs helped him cope with exile in America.

'It's a bit noisy down there, Eamonn,' she said.

'Oh Jeez, its only eleven-thirty yet. Give them another half hour to let off steam and then I'll go and start winding it down.'

'Cheerio, you guys,' announced David. 'I'm off. And as I'm giving Miss Carrbridge a ride home, she's off too.'

'I wonder what *other* kind of ride he'll give her,' whispered Rosa to Susie.

'Goodbye, Mr Lomax, Sir. Thanks again,' chorused some of the boys.

Jem stood up unsteadily, his hand reaching out to Mon's for support, before he could stop it, and came over to Louise.

'Thank you so much, Miss Carrbridge, for all the help you've given me with make-up and things for Julia. I really appreciated it.'

'Jem, dear,' (Louise surprised herself by adding this word), 'I've loved helping you all. And we'll bring Julia to life one more time in Canada, won't we?'

'Oh yes, Miss. I hope so.'

His speech made, Jem stepped back to let others say their piece. What a great kid he is, thought David. Kind, perceptive, solid gold. He noticed that one or two of them were ignoring Louise, but not Jem. Yup, terrific boy.

'Mon,' called Louise over to the sofa, 'we're just going.'

Mon stood up, tall and dark in the shaded lights. He knew he should be leaving with them. He had done as he usually did – spoken a congratulatory word to every boy and girl, been screamingly funny for quarter of an hour and impressed Greg's parents by his suavity and obvious grip. Now was the time to go. But he couldn't. Ridiculous though it was, he was unable to pull himself out of his orbit around Jem. That clutching hand had spoken unintended volumes to him. Far from appearing young and absurd in his slightly tipsy state, Jem appealed to him more than ever. He burned to be alone with him – although he hadn't the faintest idea how that was to be accomplished. The sensible thing, he knew, was to leave, thanking God for Alan Clemmy and Co., under whose auspices he was to work with Jem into August. But sense didn't come into it; only a strange, desperate, lonely passion.

'Oh, you go on,' he said, 'I guess I'll have a few words with the Macs and one more drink. See you Monday.'

David shrugged and he and Louise, relaying their thanks to his parents via Greg, passed out into the night.

Jem felt a hand on his shoulder.

'Follow me,' said Rick. Through Jem's fuddled senses shot a dart of wide-awake fear and lust. He knew what Rick wanted him to follow for. With a hand on the passage wall, he went through to the kitchen. Rick opened a door, ushered Jem past him into the garden, and carefully closed the door again.

'Look what I've found,' he whispered. He led Jem, taking his hand, round to a bench with a flower-covered arch, like a miniature summer-house. 'Here, take this.' In his hand was a little rolled cigarette. He produced matches from his sweat-shirt pocket. 'Have a puff.'

'What is it?'

'It's only a joint – just a little one.'

'A joint! I don't want to take anything, Rick.'

'Oh, c'mon. It's nothing. It'll help.'

'Help what?'

'Sex.'

'Oh!' Again that cold thrust of passion more like terror, which gave him immediate stiffening. Riccardo took the joint, lit it and took a long drag.

'I sometimes – only sometimes, mind, as my father would go right off the dock if he knew – smoke a bit to loosen up. To let the libido roll.'

'Oh!' gasped Jem again.

With his conscious mind telling him not to do it, but with his instincts and nerves flaring, Jem took several sweet, vegetable-tasting puffs, inhaling as Rick had done.

'Christ, I do love you, Jem,' murmured Rick. 'This evening has gone on forever.'

Jem leaned towards him, clutching him first with both arms, then letting one hand fall to Rick's bare leg. They brought their mouths together with a bruising jar, then Rick's stubbly jaw grated on Jem's smooth skin as he put his lips to Jem's ear.

'Just open up. Don't pull any clothes down. You never know.'

Jem's hand dropped to his zip, found Rick's hand there before him, and together they got ready for mutual stimulation. With gasping kisses, they stood up unsteadily, each fumbling and panting with lust. They jammed themselves against each other, pushing in with their hips. Each was grasping the other's erection, thrilled by the intimacy. The mixture of drink and the joint's instant high made Jem feel he had entered a new body – one which felt and savoured things differently from the old one. The familiar tension rose and rose in him, he rubbed Rick as though he were coming in Rick's body; he felt Rick's left hand under his T-shirt, slipping down into his jeans and feeling down to his inner thigh. The other hand, exploring Jem's circumcision, set off cymbal-like crashes in Jem's abdomen, as he moaned in ecstasy.

'Wait. Wait. Look,' Rick, gasping, produced what felt like a towel. 'I picked it up in the kitchen.' He placed it over Jem just in time. Pulling away for a moment, then clinging tighter than ever, Jem came with electric stabbings he hadn't had before – his whole frame had managed to convulse in climax. The usual stickiness was on his hand as he continued to stimulate Rick. Rick's hand joined his and, with Jem's mouth pressed to his groans, he came to his own climax a minute later. For a moment they clung together upright, then, still kissing, they dropped to the bench.

Jem was shaking. He folded up the damp kitchen towel and tucked himself back inside his jeans. Rick lay back, one leg crooked, the other stretched out languorously ahead of him, still partially undressed and exposed.

'Oh, oh God,' he said. 'That was incredible.'

Jem laid his head on Rick's shoulder.

'I feel real dizzy,' he murmured. Rick put an arm round him.

'I hadn't meant it all to be as sudden as this. I'm sorry.'

'Oh. No. it was fine,' replied Jem, as though he were speaking about a slice of apple pie. 'I liked it.'

Yes, his nerves and flesh told him that he had liked it! It had been the fiercest sexual experience of his short life. But he did feel so light-headed and jumpy, yet lethargic at the same time; also frighteningly thirsty.

'Rick, I must get a drink.'

'Stay here for a minute. I'll fetch you one.'

Rick pushed himself back into his shorts, buttoned up and, disappearing round the edge of the little arbour, went off towards the house. Jem lay back, both hands resting in his lap. The night seemed hot and dry and it spun round him. He felt salt on his tongue and realised that his lower lip was bleeding. Other than these sensations and a tremor deep in the centre of his frame, he felt nothing – as though time had stopped, or he had died. So, this was the end of *The Duchess of Malfi*, was it? It seemed to him as if the whole of the last months dressing as Julia had been leading to this one chaotic orgasm. He laughed quietly, pressing back against the flowers. He was shaky, he felt sick, was hot, jumpy and faint, but he had never been happier. It wasn't, perhaps, a normal happiness, like waking up to the scent of frying ham and eggs or remembering that he was going to get a present. These were items of low-intensity joy from childhood. Now he had the elation felt by a mountaineer on his peak, or a man on the moon – the thrill of a life-changing task accomplished.

Rick came back with a tumbler of water.

'Drink,' he said. Jem seized the glass in both hands and gulped savagely at it. 'Hey. slower, Jem. Otherwise you'll throw up.' Sitting attentively by him, Rick wiped Jem's face. Jem gasped when he saw the towel. 'Oh, don't worry. It's not the other one. I chucked that in the pedal bin. I've snaffled another.'

'Won't Mrs McManus miss them?' was all Jem could say. He felt the damp hair being smoothed off his forehead.

'It's the liquor you took before the joint. I'd forgotten you'd gotten a bit woozy. Sorry,' said Rick.

'I'm being pathetic,' muttered Jem. 'It – it all happened so quickly.'

'I know. It was like a dam breaking. Jem, I've been wanting to do that with you for more than a month, day and night. Sometimes I thought I was going insane. But look, I'm really, really sorry that you haven't liked it after all.'

'But I did!' cried Jem. 'It was – was absolutely wonderful.'

Riccardo peered into Jem's face in the gloom.

'It *was* wonderful,' he repeated. Then he added, 'Can we start again?'

'How do you mean?'

'I mean more civilised, more gently. Less like a couple of dogs going at it – if you know what I mean.'

'You mean….now?'

Rick, who had drunk nothing but Coke, was still feeling the high of the joint. He could have had sex again. Jem's intimate presence was an aphrodisiac, but he realised his young friend had had enough.

'No, not now. Of course not now. You just sit and sip this water. Then I'll get you some more.'

The music stopped in the house. Jem and Rick continued to occupy the flowery bench and, by degrees, Jem felt much better.

'Hey! Hiya!' came a yodelling call from the

kitchen door. 'Hey, Rick? Jem? Are you guys out there?'

It was Greg's voice. It was followed by Mr McManus' rumble.

'Will you hold it down a bit, you eedjit. You'll wake the street.'

'Sorry, Pop.'

Rick got up from the bench and appeared dimly on the lawn.

'Yeah, Greg, we're here,' he said to the silhouette figures. 'Hello, Mr McManus. Jem Clarke and I just came out for some air and we got talking about the play. I'm sorry if we've done the wrong thing.'

'No, no. You're welcome. At least you two are quiet. Greg just wondered if you'd gone home.'

Jem came out of the dark to Rick's side.

'Hello, Mr McManus, Sir. We're just coming back to the house. It's been lovely out here.'

Rick chucked the second kitchen-towel into a bush.

In the bright light of the party room, Jan gave the flushed Jem a very meaning look, but Jem smiled blandly at him.

Half an hour later, Rick had dropped Jem at the house on 172nd St and Jem had found refuge in his silent bed where, at last, he could go back over what had happened and determine what he really, *really* thought about it.

Streetlamps lit and re-lit Louise's face in the car as

she sat next to David.

'Oh, no. Honestly. It's too far. Really it is.'

Louise hated the sound of her voice irresolutely protesting as David drove further and further into the city.

'No prob, Louise, I've said,' he replied, then, changing the subject, 'Mon wasn't running true to form clinging on with the kids tonight. I thought he might come out for a late Chinese with us or something.'

'It's amazing the way those boys hang on his every word, isn't it?' smiled Louise.

'He's a good story-teller. I loved his bullshit tales when I was their age.'

'He's got a repertoire, then?'

'Oh God, yes. I've heard some of his yarns about fifty times.'

Louise stretched back in her seat. David's eyes flickered over to her for a moment, appraisingly.

'I'm just so pleased that *The Duchess* carries on for a bit longer, aren't you?' she asked.

'Yeah, I s'pose so. But usually the spectre of a five day school trip with the St Mat's paraplegics doesn't turn me on....'

'Oh you hypocrite! You went skiing at Christmas and I've heard you talking about the Athletics tour to Virginia.'

'Sport's different. I don't usually volunteer for things like *Romeo and Juliet* with the RSC on

Broadway, unless Mon hints very heavily and sings auld lang syne.'

'Anyone would think you weren't a cultured man, David, to hear you speak. In fact I wrongly thought you were a real philistine until I got to working with you.'

'I'm not particularly cultured,' muttered David, almost as shamefacedly as if he were pointing out that his syphilis wasn't at the contagious stage. She flung up her hands.

'I thought that argument we had with Mon about Keats the other day showed that you knew a lot more than you admit.'

'Poetry's different. Besides, that was about work.'

'Go on, admit that you don't like people – other guys – to think of you as bookish.'

'I'm not bookish!'

'You are a bit.'

'No. I'm not.'

'You are underneath.'

'I'm NOT!'

'Yes, you are, so.'

'I am not.'

'You are.'

'Look, Louise,' cried David, grinning (because he liked talking with her about himself), but exasperated, 'can you damn well bury this line of conversation? I'm a sportsman, period. You think what you think, but I know what I know.'

Louise, not at all abashed, twinkled at him.

'I think you're very nice, and sensitive. And you don't know how nice.'

She was astonished with herself for saying something so CoCo-ish, but pleased because he looked pleased. There was a silence in the car. David grappled with unfamiliar emotions. So, Louise thinks I'm nice, eh? Well, she's pretty damn nice too.

'I'm looking forward to being in Nova Scotia with you,' he said, feeling his cheeks burning.

'And me with you,' said Louise simply.

'With the mad men of the Webster Trust.'

'Exactly.'

'I tell you, I think it's so bizarre that they took one look at the Malfi Luvvies tonight and asked the whole gang up to give a show. Why Mon and the Doc don't think it odd, I'll never know. I suppose they consider anything St Mat's does is so slam-bang fantastic that naturally the whole world wants a part of it.'

'They did a wonderful job, though.'

'But *that* wonderful?'

The Hudson River came in sight.

'Hang a right, then a left, and I'm there,' said Louise. 'Honestly, this is noble of you. I feel I've dragged you miles out of your way.'

'Only about seven, I should think,' smiled David. 'And, say, seven back, don't forget. But hey, I'm just that sort of guy.'

'And then on the left. This is it.'

'God, you must start at about six in the morning to get over to Queens by school start. Why didn't you get a job at a closer place?'

'There wasn't one going. And think what I'd have missed. Besides, once I'm on the subway I'm okay. It was worse in the winter, but I haven't minded it since Easter. At least I get a bit of a walk before the station.'

'Have you thought of moving nearer?'

'Oh, several times. But there's CoCo, you know, and I'm used to being more in the city and all...'

'Yeah, I know. St Mat's *is* out in the bush.'

'Precisely. I'm surprised they don't ask for visas.'

'Which one?' asked David, peering down a long vista of steeply stepped brownstones.

'1442. Just another couple. There. Look, there's a space behind that pick-up.' David pulled in. 'I – er – know it's rather late,' Louise went on, 'but do please come on in and have a drink and a snack, won't you?'

Already having planned to accept if Louise made such a suggestion, and prepared to hint if she didn't, David jumped at her offer, nipping round the car to open her door and casting an eye round to make sure all the windows were closed.

Louise opened up and led the way in.

'We're on the first floor,' she said quietly. David allowed his eyes to measure up her firmly-turned calves and good ankles as she went ahead of him. He liked the momentary twinkle of light on the ankle-bone and the strong-looking ligaments hollowing out her lower leg as they took her weight. At the turn in the stair, he gazed up at her bottom as it whisked up the last three or four steps. For a moment he wondered, fearfully, but with anticipation, if he might be expected to make love to her when they got inside. Memories of his feisty, neurotic widow came back. God, Louise wasn't in the same ball-park at all. Making love to her…. tonight? Did he want to do it? He felt very self-conscious at the thought. Were his socks really clean? He knew his shirt was rumpled and that it had been hot in the cramped lighting booth. He was by no means fresh from the freezer. How much would that matter? Would he be able to take a shower first? But *she* wouldn't be fresh, either. Would she take a shower first? Would she like them to shower together? He decided that all these things did matter and that he was not ready for the intimacies of even the partially clothed body, when it occurred to him that Louise shared her apartment. Of course! CoCo would be there. That was all right. He wanted, he told himself, to get to know Louise a lot better, but tonight was not the night.

Louise said, loudly, as he came in after her,

'It seems we've got the place to ourselves. CoCo's out.'

Had David not been thinking of socks and crumpled shirt, he might have picked up the tremor in her voice. She, like him, had rather counted on CoCo being in – if not up, at least in bed reading or watching TV. Louise had a stab of misgiving at having invited David to an empty apartment. She too wondered, agonisingly, if she was meant to be 'nice' to him – whatever that entailed – and how she was to begin and how far to go. Suppose she didn't want to go all that far, and he did? She knew she wasn't ready for that sort of thing. She had never seen a man's nakedness, except in art galleries; and most of those were of the Michelangelo type where the organs are reassuringly small – or hidden.

David shut the door and came (blinking, for Louise had turned up the living-room dimmer to fullest glare) into the room behind her.

'Oh, sorry,' gasped Louise, turning the glare down again.

'Thanks,' said David. 'A bit Yankee Stadium there for a moment. Still, there's plenty of community care for the blind.'

'What would you like? To eat or drink, that is. I mean: tea? Coffee? Some wine?' asked Louise, trying to inject a practical, hospitable tone into her voice.

'Um, whatever.'

'I don't think we've got any beer.'

'Oh, I don' want anything like that, thanks,' said David. 'I've had a few drinks tonight already and there's always the pigs to watch out for. On my way home. It's the time they check.' David was proud of the way he had managed to insert the info that he did expect to go home sooner rather than later and was not expecting to stay the night.

'Oh, of course.'

'Tea would be fine, or coffee. No, make it tea – if you've got some.'

Shoot, he thought, now I'm sounding like a Goob from Goobsville. Indecision. Saying the obvious. Of course she's got tea or she wouldn't have offered it.

Oh dear, thought Louise. This sounds so stilted. Why can't I just be normal, put water on to boil and be the little woman? After all we've been through with the play – this heavy-handed politeness is so...so...

David heard himself starting to say: 'Nice place you've got here' (astonishing himself with his clichéd banality), when Louise dead-heated with him to suggest that he take a seat while she made tea. The two comments banged together in the air.

'Sorry.'

'No, sorry. You were saying....'

'Sorry. No, you were asking me....'

They gazed at each other.

'Suppose I sit down,' said David, 'while you make tea.'

They both laughed and the upsetting, unexpected strain ebbed away.

'Just what I was going to suggest, actually.'

'Oh, you were, ack-cher-lie, were you?'

'Yes, I jolly well was.'

'Well jolly well pop on with it and I'll see what books you and CoCo like reading.'

When they were sipping from mugs, David in the armchair and Louise curled up at one end of the sofa, they fell to discussing *The Duchess* once again.

'What do you suppose is behind Clemmy's insistence that there be no changes to the cast?' asked Louise.

'Mon said he thought it a bit odd, especially when, apparently, that shambling orang-utan, Gollop, weighed in even more agitatedly than Clemmy. What's it to them if you took the part of Coriola, or I became Castruchio?'

'Not that anyone would be likely to change roles, anyway.'

'We might have to make changes if some of them can't go next month.'

'Surely they'll want to go?'

'Oh yeah, I think that's safe enough. After a success the cast always feel they can put on dozens of extra performances and fascinate hundreds more people. They can't because they peak on night three. But they'll be keen on the trip, I bet.'

'It's in vacation though. Someone may be off to summer camp, or holiday. And there's a French exchange, isn't there?'

'There you are then. Watch this space.'

'How, by the way, are the costumes getting there? They'll need two big hampers.'

'I could take one of the minibuses,' said David. 'But it's a long drive. It'll need an overnight stop, maybe two.'

'David,' said Louise – surprising herself again – 'if you end up driving up there, can I come with you?

David put his mug down by the side of his chair, got up and stood by the sofa next to her.

He looked rather pointedly at the space next to her and raised his eyebrows interrogatively.

'May I?'

'Oh, yes. Yes, of course.'

Louise moved up, uncurling her legs to make room for him. He sat down. Not sure which she would appreciate least, he decided to take one of her hands, rather than drape his arm round her shoulder.

'Let's suggest it to Mon. It would cost the Webster lunatics a fortune to ship them by plane. I'd really like your company on the journey too.'

Louise smiled broadly at him. Again, not knowing how she would take this, he raised her fingers to his lips and kissed them. She gave a little gasp but didn't withdraw them. Encouraged, he leaned slowly towards her and brushed gentle lips on her cheek. Close to, he liked her skin and those dark-fringed goblin eyes. So he kissed her again. She turned a little and pursed her lips, so he placed his own upon them, once, savouring their lovely softness. She gave a sigh.

'What's wrong?' he whispered.

'Nothing. You're the first man I've ever kissed,

you know.'

He could say nothing to that, but did, this time, let his arm encircle her shoulder. She leant against him, re-curling her legs. He could trace her thighs from the appealing angle of her knees to her tight-skirted bottom. The pricking of desire he began to feel was something he knew he must not reveal until much later in their relationship. But he was going to have that relationship! So they sat, embracing, quietly talking – partly about him and his teaching career, partly about her time in the convent – until CoCo's key was heard in the lock at about one o'clock.

David drove home not long after that, finding that he was repeating: 'Oh, yes! Oh, *yes*!' over and over again. Life was sweet!

Nearly dawn, and the squeaking of the first birds littered the air. Jem lay awake, thinking of his father. Three years is a big percentage of a sixteen-year-old's life, and Jem had long since ceased to mourn his father's departure, or to find the house on 172nd St strange without him. Yet tonight he rotated his father's personality in his mind and wondered what his father would think of him and his recent behaviour. He pondered his own character too, trying to calculate how much of himself had been formed by the missing man.

The glow from the streetlamps made its familiar line under the curtains, and Jem watched the line become pink as the sun strengthened. The vivid events of the previous evening: the last performance of the play, the aching nakedness of feeling in Greg's garden, pirouetted through Jem's mind – first one thing, then the other; the roar of applause for the play, the hot frantic sex. What *would* his father think of that? Letting himself be touched, stroked, kissed, stimulated….by another boy! Is that what Dad would have expected me to end up doing? With his certainty of his father's horror – and the certainty seemed more stark than his worry about his mother finding out; he'd gotten used to leading a hidden, parallel existence to hers – came the thought that perhaps he was LIKE his father.

Jem had never considered his father's departure in the light of a violent passion – but that's why he left, of course. He had fallen in love with Catherine, had, presumably, needed her love more than he needed his wife's or children's and had abandoned his familiar world to be with her. Wasn't Jem himself making those circumstances in which he too might have to leave home, high school and family, and be wherever Rick was? Home wasn't enough. Only the dramatic savagery of irresistible passion mattered – and he was only at the beginning; a vista of wild and uninhibited love-making opened up. Rick had promised that it was only a beginning. And what was going to happen next week, next month, next year, in the grip of this raging fever?

Watching the brightening glow, Jem made himself face the question: did he, dared he, go on with this….this thing with Rick? They both knew, with the strongest of instincts, that what they had done that night was not a culmination, but a start. Where would it end?

Several times already, as he had lain awake, he had vowed that he would do nothing like it again. It was wrong, as Jan had told him. It was perverted, unnatural – it could only lead to misery, the destruction of his education and his relationships with family and friends. It was insanity. It had only come out of the play, out of dressing as Julia, for heaven's sake! Yet he knew that if Rick's voice were to come up, siren-like, through the curtains with the bird calls, now – even now – he would rise and go down to him.

Would his father disapprove so much? Hadn't he bequeathed his character to his son? Riccardo, Catherine – was there such a difference? That is why I'm like I am – full of passionate and secret feeling. I'm what Grandpaw Clarke used to call me: a chip off the old block, whatever that means.

It was the strangest of things: to see his father in this light – a confused creature, aching with yearning, prepared to abandon his world to satisfy it. Jem fantasised a scene in Florida with the girl he had run away with – Aisha, say – and his father clapping him on the back. You young dog! Like father, like son! And Catherine and Aisha smiling in the background, united in pride of what their passionate lovers had done.

But Rick wasn't a girl. It wasn't the same.

The imagined scene under the palm trees couldn't work if Jem substituted Rick for Aisha.

Yet I am so *sure* I love him! Jem nodded. He thought, as he lay with beating heart, about Rick's body, his black and gold eyes and knowing smile, the regularity of his tanned face, his hard muscles, and the undiscovered universe of tantalising intimate possibilities he promised. It must be love!

He mentally reviewed his emotional growth since the age of fourteen, then going into fifteen – after his father had walked away. Perhaps I'm the typical child of a failed marriage, hunting for a father figure. Well, of course! That is it! I am making substitutes.

He felt so excited by this new discovery, this explanation, that he almost lifted himself to one elbow; but he was too tired, too much on the cusp of exhausted sleep to move.

Rick, Mr Howard, Jan, even silly little Francis: all part of my search for what is lost. For a few moments, it seemed to Jem entirely logical that the horrifying and compelling pull towards homosexual love which seemed steadily to have characterised his growth in the last year, could be explained by his father's defection. Yes. In Francis I saw *myself* at fourteen – in Rick I see *him*.

Jem gave a deep yawn and the orange and pink line spangled as his eyes watered. No. No, Rick is a crystallisation of something different, surely? Nothing to do with parenthood! Nothing to do with the child of the father. Jem felt again the vivid kisses, the hot limbs, the completeness of coming in Rick's arms, and Rick coming in his. It was all part of the now, the new, what he had become on the edge of seventeen. He could not, in truth, cry out: Oh, Dad! What have you made of me? He had made himself.

He had a last longing in the dawn. He longed to be twelve again, still unknowing, still interested in toys, still to meet Mr Howard, still to dress as Julia, still seeing his father's tall frame lying across the green velvet armchair and matching stool, watching TV. He tongue nearly said a word that was shaped like 'Daddy' as he slept at last.

February 2020: SANABITUR ANIMA MEA

Janek Franitza had been surprised by the number of monks who had filed in at the beginning of the Requiem Mass and who now stood in two lines on each side of the dead man's coffin on its catafalque.

The celebrant had just turned and, facing the mourners, had intoned the prayer of humility before communion: 'Lord, I am not worthy that you should enter under my roof, but say the word and my soul shall be healed.' The congregation began to break the pattern of their places and head for the sacrament at the altar rail. *Sanabitur anima mea*....my soul shall be healed, mused Jan. Would it be right to take communion? It's been so long.

'Are you going to communion?' Lindy hissed.

'I don't know if I ought,' Jan whispered back. Then he said to himself: Why not? I've suffered. I've been cleansed. I lapsed, but I've gone on believing some of it. What have been my sins? No murder, no defrauding the poor of their wages, no worship of false idols. If dear little Francis had....had lived....we – I – would have brought him up as a Catholic. It wasn't my fault that the zing went out of life – and out of faith too. My soul shall be healed.

Lindy pulled her legs back so that others could pass her. Jan was already in the aisle. His face was composed, but he felt the impact of what he was about to do – its enormity and its triviality; the Real Presence in the consecrated bread, the gutless slice of rice-paper, like the underneath of a nougat bar. He hadn't taken communion since Francis had been admitted to hospital. He was conscious of the unknown lovely woman. She had left her pew just after he had left his. She was now just one person behind him in the queue. That knowledge seemed of greater significance than his return to the sacrament.

A server opened a hinged bar in the altar rail, and the priest stepped out with communion for the imposing Italian in the top pew. Its occupant put his tongue out in the European manner to receive the Host. Jan instantly knew – as he should have known from the beginning – who the Italian was. Riccardo. The crutch should have been enough, for God's sake! More than twenty-five years; no, nearer thirty! The youth of nineteen whom Jan had so distrusted must be in his mid-to-late forties now, but a lot of his energy and arrogance remained to him – crippled as he was. Why should *he* have come to the funeral? But, of course, he had played Bosola. Was he, in his way, still loyal to the man who had changed all of them?

Well, well. Riccardo, that bastard. What *was* his other name? Short syllables flitted in Jan's mind, but made no shape that clicked.

He was in front of the priest. He put out his palms, left hand uppermost, and took the Host, lifting it with finger and thumb to his mouth. The cool, salt-less crack of the wafer was instantly familiar. As in childhood, he wondered how seriously he ought to take those words: '*He that eateth and drinketh unworthily, eateth and drinketh damnation to himself*'. I am not worthy. Jan had confirmation of this as soon as he turned to go back to his place. His eyes sought the eyes and lips of the lovely woman as the wafer began to dissolve in his saliva.

Before he left the sanctuary's orbit, he bent his gaze once more on the still Italian. Would he be recognised, as he had recognised? No. Riccardo prayed, his hands clasped. Near him, his young companion watched him. Neither had eyes for Janek.

That terrible summer, after the play cast had got back from Nova Scotia! All back, except the wretched Riccardo. That must have been the last time I saw him – before he was taken to hospital in Halifax. Oh, Jem, you went to the hospital, of course. And I saw you only once more, the day before Mrs Clarke and your little sister (Jan found he couldn't now remember Betsy's name) took you to Florida.

Suppose Jem too is dead?

Janek felt a pricking of tears at the thought.

Jem had mattered so much to him, and they had been so long apart....

Lindy, who had moved to the outer end of the pew, sighed and shifted her legs grudgingly as he squeezed past them. Engaged in trying not to trip over his wife's handbag, he did not catch the startled gleam in the handsome woman's eyes as she, in her turn, passed his pew and seemed to pause, irresolute, as if confirming a hunch. He had no idea, either, of the courage she had shown in staying in the same building as the Italian with the crutch. He had no eyes for anything but the past.

28 YEARS EARLIER
August: NOVA SCOTIA

The plane bumped down after its short flight and the myriad pine-trees of Nova Scotia strode away from the airport to the horizon. Sir Alan and Dr Bennett had, with remarkable speed and efficiency, ensured that the cast, crew and teachers had their passports (or, in the case of quite a few of the students, their certificates of US citizenship) to hand for the five-day visit. Joey, after all, had managed to arrange his French exchange later in August, but two very minor characters had to go off with their families, so the capering madmen and a couple of courtiers would need to double up. Mon hoped, in the face of Sir Alan's strange insistence, the disappearance of two such tiny parts out of a cast of thirty-one would pass unnoticed.

As for David's and Louise's half-formed plan to drive up the costumes and props in a school minibus, Sir Alan arranged for a haulage firm to collect everything on the Tuesday before they left, so all would be ready for Thursday's first rehearsal. Mon ceased to marvel at or question exactly why they were all doing this and turned his mind to a less pleasing topic. In the coach to the airport he had, he fancied, detected an air of intimacy between Jem and Riccardo. Before they sat together on the plane – not, noted Mon, Jem sitting with Janek, his friend – he could see Jem shooting fascinated glances at Riccardo, and Riccardo smiling into Jem's face, with what, in a less tough individual, could almost be defined as sloppiness. Mon just *knew* there was something going on between them, and it dated from that party on the last night of the play.

He had not been pleased to discover that Riccardo and Jem had left the McManus' house at midnight. He had hung pathetically on and on until nearly one, unaware of this, and hoping to have a few more moments with Jem. He knew it was unreasonable to feel angry and hurt, but he did. He had tried to get a grip on his dangerous obsession in the last week of July but had failed. The responsible teacher in him wanted to get Jem away from Riccardo before anything corrupting occurred between them; the homosexual in him approved of signs of love between boys and was protective of it; the lover in him was furiously affronted and jealous. Caught between extremes of pastor and devotee, it was little wonder that Mon had more to think about on the flight to Canada than Sir Alan's eccentric stipulations.

The party had been met by Roger Gollop and ushered out to a fifty-seat motor coach.

'Just a short drive – little more than two hours,' boomed their jovial host.

The coach had headed south to Mahone Bay, through Lunenberg and Bridgewater and took a turn towards the ocean, following signs for Merivale.

'Y'know,' said Mon to David and Louise, 'I oughta feel a sense of home-coming as a guy who was Canadian-born, but it's really so different here. People expect Nova Scotia to be like New England, but it's not.'

'Perhaps it really *is* like Scotland,' said Louise.

They pulled in between stone gateposts and ran up a drive to a Scots baronial style house overlooking the sea. As gravel crunched under their wheels, a pointed-arch porch door opened and Sir Alan Clemmy came out, beaming, and stood on the steps. The cast of the play trooped out, staring round them.

Sir Alan ran his gaze benignly over the boys and girls, and they smiled sheepishly, or cheekily, back. His eyes then darted past Mon, David and Louise to the coach.

'Welcome to you all,' he said. He seemed to wait for someone else to clamber out of the coach, and when no one did, he peered sharply at the cast clustering around their teachers. The gimlet eyes played round them – 'like a laser', Jonathan said afterwards.

'Look,' said Sir Alan, 'please go into the hall. Edward Leaven is there. He and Roger will show you where to freshen up and get refreshments. Please. Please.' He gestured fussily to the steps. David, Louise and the cast began to make their way into the building. 'Just a minute,' he said to Mon, detaining him by the arm.

Mon stopped politely.

'Yes, Sir Alan?'

'What's all this?'

'What's what, Sir Alan?' asked Mon.

'The cast are not all here.'

'Oh,' murmured Mon. 'You've noticed.'

'Of course I've noticed. I specifically begged you....'

'Hang on,' interrupted Mon. 'I really had no choice in the matter. I assured you that I had intended no change of personnel in the play, and I hadn't – not when we last spoke. But since then I discovered that two of the boys had made arrangements to go on vacation with their families in early August, and I....'

'Boys! What boys?' barked Sir Alan testily.

'Boys called Christian O'Malley and Milos Taviarian. They were in the group of madmen and courtiers – but we're just doubling up. It won't make a difference and....'

'Stop! Stop! I'm not talking about boys playing courtiers. Damn them! I don't care how many madmen and courtiers you've got. I'm talking about the girl.'

'What girl?'

'The girl, damn it! THE girl. You haven't brought all of the girls.'

'I have. In fact I've brought all three girls connected with the play – one of them helps with make-up and costumes.'

'I couldn't see the girl.'

'Well, come and meet them. I assure you, Christian and Milos apart, they're all present and correct.'

'Right.'

Sir Alan whisked back into the porch, forgetful of ushering his guest before him. He was extraordinarily agitated. Mon, following, shook his head and hoped that the next few days were not going to be annoying. Sir Alan was evidently eccentric. But then you had to be eccentric to drag a high school play across the border on little more than an expensive whim. Oh well, thought Mon, I guess it'll be an experience for the kids.

The hall, constructed in Victorian neo-Gothic revivalist style, leapt up to a hammer-beam roof. A minstrel's gallery ran along the end opposite the porch. Tall windows gave a view of the Atlantic. In the centre was a heavy table loaded with chilled Coke and snacks. Four huge bowls of crisps, taco chips and peanuts ran down the middle. Smiling with hospitable friendliness, the bookish Edward Leaven and the untidy Roger Gollop were urging their young guests to drink and munch. David and Louise had been offered, and had accepted, glasses of red wine.

Mon and Alan Clemmy approached the table and sharp eyes ran in and out of the little groups standing with cans and popping crisps into their mouths.

'She's not here,' said Sir Alan. 'Roger! Edward!

Come over here a second.'

The helpers disengaged themselves.

'Yes, Clem?'

'I've been telling Mr Howard here that there's no sign of the girl.'

'God, Clem. I thought I couldn't see her,' said Edward Leaven. 'I assumed she was out there with you.'

'She isn't here at all!'

Mon stared with astonishment at the open-mouthed dismay of his hosts. Only too clearly they were deeply disturbed. He caught David's eye and crooked a finger. David and Louise drifted over to join him.

'Thanks for the welcome, Sir Alan,' said David. 'It's very nice of you to provide all this.'

'Yes. Never mind all that,' snapped Sir Alan rudely. 'I've been asking your Mr Howard here where the girl is and he flatly refuses to admit she hasn't come.'

'What girl?' asked David and Louise together, echoing Mon's earlier question.

'THE GIRL!' hooted Sir Alan. 'God's teeth! How many times do I have to say it? Your wonderful girl – Cleo Jakemar – the one who played Julia so memorably.'

'Oh, my Lordy!' cried Mon. He and David shook their heads and laughed. Their cackles went up into the dim beams.

'I must say….' began Edward.

'No honestly, Mr Leaven, Sir Alan. Julia's here all right. But she was played by – by – a boy.'

Roger, Sir Alan and Edward gasped.

'A b-b-b-boy?' stuttered Roger Gollop.

'Yup. His name's Jem Clarke. There he is,' said Mon, pointing to Jem standing in a group demolishing tacos at the far end of the table.

Sir Alan, Roger and Edward looked at each other and gaped disbelievingly over at Jem.

'Oh, bugger. That does it,' said Sir Alan.

Mon took the little man's elbow.

'Why don't you tell us what's going on?' he said. 'There's something more to this than meets the eye, isn't there?'

The three members of The Webster Trust nodded.

'Okay,' said Edward Leaven, 'we'll come clean. We would have to have done by Friday evening in any case. Don't you think so, Clem?'

Sir Alan nodded.

'Yes, but not now,' he replied. 'There's supper for your children at the Trevanaunce Summer School. After it I suggest we show them to their quarters and then sit down and we'll explain everything. The children – they're old enough to be left, aren't they?' he added anxiously. David and Mon smiled, thinking of Riccardo, Jonathan, Mark, Aisha, Rosa, Greg, Dominik – all between seventeen and nineteen – and their lives of shopping, part-time jobs and partying in New York.

'Oh yes,' said David. 'They can be left. The three youngest of them are fourteen.'

'Just before we go I want to show you something in my study,' said Sir Alan. 'It won't make sense without an explanation, but we'll go into the full story after supper. Just come over the corridor a minute.'

They followed him into a pleasant, ordinarily decorated room with a TV set, hi-fi and many shelves of books and papers. One wall was covered with old pictures of steam locomotives. Above the chimney breast were two photographs.

'Over here,' said Sir Alan.

The four of them clustered round the photos and Louise gave a little shriek.

'Exactly,' said Sir Alan.

In the larger of the photos several people, caught in the act of clapping, were standing round a sapling which was being planted by a pretty dark-haired woman wielding a spade.

'It – it's Jem!' gasped Louise.

Jem's face, or rather Jem done up as Julia, smiled over the little mound of earth – an intimate, attractive smile familiar to the three visitors from New York.

'Well, I'll be…..' began David. 'What are you doing with Jem Clarke's photograph?'

Sir Alan directed their attention to the smaller photo. This had been taken indoors. Again a group was clustered, this time behind a sofa. On the sofa sat a heavy-looking, red-faced man in his late forties. He was holding the hand of – Jem Clarke. Jem was sitting, his well-known shapely legs crossed, his head leaning on the plump man's shoulder. Again, most noticeable, was Jem's mysterious and lovely smile.

'Who is she?' asked Mon, the first of the three to realise the obvious. 'By heavens, she looks so like him though. I wouldn't have believed it possible. So, who is she?'

'Ah, that's just it. Not "is she" but "*was* she". A terrible thing happened to her and she's dead.' Sir Alan coughed. 'Explanations later. I do want to meet your clever young man and congratulate him on his convincing performance. Not by the mantelpiece though; by the windows. I don't want him to see these photographs. Not yet.'

'I'll go fetch him,' said Louise.

Mo gazed at the girl in the photo. As he did so, an ache swept through him, an immense regret. Look at me, so lovely and so dead, the image seemed to whisper – and you never knew me. If only whatever ridiculous God administered the affairs of the world had done the obvious, good and life-enhancing thing, and brought her and me together! Just a few years earlier – not so many as would alter human history, I should not have made a disastrous marriage, I should not be a frustrated, moonstruck gay in love with a teenage boy, and this wonderful girl would be alive and adored – by me! Just a cruel twitch of geography, some uncaring tweaks of time and gender – and two of us are ruined! So much for a glorious Creator and His great plan of compassion! Mon put a hand up, furtively, while David and Sir Alan conversed across the room, and touched what seemed to be Jem's face.

There were steps in the passage and Jem came to the door with Louise. After the flight and the drive, he did not, perhaps, look his very best, his T-shirt being rumpled and his hair fluffed up, but Jem always managed to seem a little fresher and more blooming than others.

Anyone who had spent a lot of dough to bring, for whatever arcane purpose, an actress over 800 miles across the border, and then discovered he had got a sixteen-year-old youth instead, might be excused some irritation. Sir Alan darted a fierce look at him as Jem stepped into the study. His glance went from the girl in the photos to Jem and back again, at first in disbelief, then with understanding. He nodded several times, his creased little face relaxing. He was a fair man, and it wasn't the youth's fault. He was such a handsome boy too, and he had acted Julia's part so well. Clearing his throat, and remembering suddenly his own far-off days at his British boarding school when beautiful boys acted female roles in school plays, and how they were esteemed, he came towards Jem with a certain tenderness.

'My dear boy – Jem, isn't it? You played Julia in the play?'

'Yes, Sir,' said Jem, looking from Sir Alan to Mon

and back again.

'I wanted to meet you and tell you that I thought your performance was most remarkable.'

Jem's face brightened with delight.

'Thanks very much, Sir,' he smiled. 'It's not a real big part, but I liked playing Julia somehow. It sort of took me out of myself. I hope I'll be okay when we perform here.'

'Of course you will. I'll look forward to some more talk with you, Jem. Pop back to your friends and tell them we're moving on to supper in a few minutes.'

'Yes, Sir. And thank you for the drinks and crisps. We were all very thirsty.'

Jem left, with Sir Alan's eyes following him.

'What a nice boy.'

'He is indeed,' said Mon, feeling very proud of his pupil.

'Can you see the similarity?' asked David.

'Oh God, yes. He's very good-looking. Obviously in make-up and wig and everything, he'd be quite different, quite feminine, as I recall. It's the eyes and nose that are quite like hers, but mainly that smile. It's uncanny.'

'Just a couple of questions,' asked Mon. 'How come you didn't know that Julia was played by a boy? One of the bits of fun at our curtain call was Jem pulling off his wig and revealing that he isn't a girl.'

'Oh blimey!' cried Sir Alan. 'You forget, we didn't see the end. We left at the interval.'

Mon, David and Louise looked at each other.

'So you did,' said Mon. 'And you went away thinking Julia had been played by a girl.'

'Of course. And,' said Sir Alan severely, 'her name – his name – on the programme was Cleo Jakemar.'

'Anagram of Jem's name,' put in David. 'And only doing what Webster would have done. No girls in Jacobean drama.'

'I've got a question as well,' said Louise. 'You obviously only came to our production because there was a girl with an amazing resemblance to your young woman. What I can't understand is how you *knew* we had a Julia who looked like her.'

'Blame whoever put out the ad and cast photo in *The Jacobean Explorer* and our newsletter,' replied Sir Alan. 'I take that publication every month and I couldn't believe my eyes when I saw that snap of your Julia sitting at the front on the stage steps.'

'We know who's responsible for all this, don't we?' said David.

'Yes. It was me,' gasped Louise. 'I thought we'd sell a few more tickets.'

'I hope you'll come to realise that you can accomplish a lot more than that, if young Jem is as good an actor as he seems, and if you and he are willing to help me....'

'Us,' put in Roger.

'Us, of course. But let's get the young 'uns over to their quarters. Then we'll talk.'

August 1992 JULIA'S DOUBLE

Supper was provided from the Summer School kitchens. It was good: a *chilli con carne* with rice and warm French bread, fluffy mushroom quiches, tomato salad, bean salad and ice-cream to follow. The cast gobbled enthusiastically, talking at the tops of their voices. Mon, Roger, Edward, David and Louise sat among them discussing the play, their parts, the flight, their holiday plans. Sir Alan had disappeared to 'collect some bits and pieces we need', as he put it.

Edward Leaven stood up and banged a spoon on the side of an empty dish until there was silence.

'Ladies and Gentlemen of *The Duchess of Malfi...*,' he started. There was a ragged cheer. David frowned down the table. 'Welcome to Trevanaunce and to two days of rehearsal on your new set – which, by the way, very much resembles your old one, although it's a bit smaller. We are happy to have you as our guests and I know that are going to be surprised by your accommodation. When you're ready, I'd like you to collect your bits of luggage and follow Roger Gollop and myself out of the door to the end of a concrete path which starts at the corner of this building. It's lit all the way, but stick to it because you'll be waking through part of a railway freight yard. Okay?'

Five minutes later, the cast, with overnight

rucksacks, were stepping out in the cool Canadian dusk. Around them huge oblong shapes glinted. Edward led; Roger boomed out explanations.

'The Canadian rail system terminates at Halifax, but back in the 1890s there was a plan to build a line through here to Liverpool and round to Yarmouth on the Bay of Fundy. Nothing came of it, but some miles of track still exist between Lunenberg and here. There's quite a lot of enthusiasm for restoring it for summer tourism. Alan has put money into it, so has the Canadian tourist board. We've acquired rolling-stock and two locomotives, one diesel and one steam. The steam one is a 1930s 4-6-2 Pacific which should draw the crowds, eh?'

The cast gazed round in the gloom. Most of them had never been on a train, other than the New York subway.

'This is one weird place, man,' murmured Pharhad to no one in particular.

'Here we are,' said Roger. 'The sleeping-cars; where you will be our guests for the next few nights.'

'Great! Cool! Sharp! Way out!' came from the cast as they gazed up at the long flanks of huge ex-Canadian Pacific sleepers in the glimmer of yard lights. These stood on a spur of track which crossed the road by which they had entered the complex. Empty rails ran parallel to it. A gate was drawn over the line. Beyond the road, the track dipped slightly on a gentle gradient. On this slope was a rocking-handle operated inspection trolley with locked brakes.

'There are steps at the end of each coach,' said Edward Leaven. 'Now, Miss Carrbridge, you have the last compartment in the first car, and you girls have the next three. Mr Howard, Mr Lomax, you have the remaining ones. The end compartment has kettle, cookies, mugs, and all that. The rest-rooms at both ends are plumbed up, but if any of you wants a bath or shower, you'll have to come back up the path to the school bath-house. You can see it to the right of the door we came out of.' He pointed back down the concrete path. The cast squinted at a clerestory roof close to the main summer school wing. 'Now,' continued Edward, 'the other cars are for you boys. Most of you will need to share compartments; first-class has gone to staff and the young ladies. Each one has two berths, one up and one down. You guys will share the wash-rooms and the end of each coach. All clear?'

'Sounds good,' smiled Mon. 'Makes a change.'

'Finally, don't feel you've got to bed yet. It's only just dark, after all. There's table-tennis, snooker and a TV back in the summer school. But I'll just say that we generally expect everyone to be in their berths by eleven because the school is closed up for the night at that time. Breakfast is where you had supper, and it starts at eight-thirty and finishes at nine-thirty. Any questions?'

He looked round at the boys and girls. They raised

eyebrows at each other.

'Trains don't run on these lines, do they, Sir?' asked Liam, peering at the gleaming parallel stretch of rail alongside the one on which the sleeping-cars stood. 'I mean, during the night.'

'No,' smiled Edward. 'Your cars are permanently braked and wired up. The other line goes on after a switch beyond the gate towards Lunenberg, but nothing runs on it. That trolley can move, and we use it for inspection, but it's braked, and the gate is always left closed over the tracks.'

No one else had any questions. 'Settle in as you please. Mr Howard, Miss Carrbridge, Mr Lomax, perhaps you would join Alan, Roger and me back over in the school when you've seen everyone's happy here.'

He nodded at Mon and made his way back to the building. Roger hovered near David.

'Not really all Canadian Pacific,' he said in his low rumble. 'We got this one from the route to the west from Chicago to L A. Built in the U S of A. The second one is a 'fifties design from the Burlington run – so not strictly right for Eastern Canada. But the first-class one where you are is. I think it's better laid out than some of the American versions – Pullman-inspired, y'know.'

'Oh, Yup. Right. Excellent,' said David.

'Well, see you in a while.'

'Yes. And thanks, Mr Gollop.'

'Call me Roger.'

'See you in about ten minutes then, Roger.'

There was a general movement to the steps of the sleeping-cars. Riccardo was among the first to get into one of the boys' cars. He flung open the door of the second twin-berth along, chucked his stuff in and went back to the steps.

'Hey, Jem!' he called urgently, as Jem came up to door level. 'In here. C'mon.'

Greg was looking in at Riccardo's carry-all on the lower bunk.

'Wanna pal in here?' he asked.

'Thanks Greg, but Jem Clarke's got the upper bed,' said Rick.

'Hey, okay,' murmured Greg, passing on. 'As long as I don' have to share with Jonathan or Mark and talk about hi-fi or lighting all night.'

'No way. They'll be in together, you bet.'

Rick put his arm across the corridor which ran along the length of the car until Jem was next to him. 'In you go,' he said, and Jem threw his over-night bag through the door. He caught Jan's expectant eye further along and knew perfectly well that Jan had expected to share with him. He smiled along at Jan, but got only a frown in return. Then he saw Jan go in with Tony. Oh dear, he thought.

'This is a miracle!' laughed Rick. 'Isn't it great?'

Jem felt again that odd mixture of sudden desire and fear he had experienced when Rick had said,

'Follow me' in the McManus's garden. For a second he hung back, well aware that if he entered he would be committing himself to a deepening sexual relationship, and would alienate Jan, who would guess what was going on. He had enough belief in the instinct of his peers to guess that they too might sense something.

He looked up at Rick's happy eyes; his gaze followed Rick's strong brown arms to his hands; he bathed in the desire Rick gave off. Hadn't he fantasised about something like this in his room on 172nd St? All doubts left him as currents of arousal began. He longed to feel Rick's hard flesh in his hands again, as at the party, and the crushing pressure of the older boy's mouth on his own. What could be wrong with something so violently needed?

Jem came forward into the little compartment, right up to the window. Rick closed the door and clicked the bolt shut. Jem's hands relaxed their hold on his bag and, dropping it, he stepped towards his friend – his lover. With careful gentleness they clasped each other, feeling for each other's mouths. Oh yes! Nothing wrong with this!

Mon Howard, in a moment of absurd fancy as Edward was explaining things, had harboured thoughts of sharing a compartment with Jem. He had felt faint at the joy of it. But, as reason supervened, and Edward Leaven had apportioned places out, his brief hope had expired. The last thing he saw was Jem going up the steps of the boys' car after Rick. Jem and Rick. *Was* anything going on there? He thought of the time he had been too inhibited and frightened to express the love of his own far-off schooldays. The flame which had scorched him then touched him now for an instant, so that Jem's image was overlaid by those of his first unforgotten love. He felt again the helplessness of youth and savoured it in wonderment. I haven't grown up at all, he thought. With a nod to David and Louise, he followed Edward up the path. He felt he needed a drink.

David grinned at Louise.

'You do the dolls; I'll do the guys.'

Louise clambered up to her single-berth cabin, panelled in dark wood with black-and-white photographs of far west canyons above the bed. She was delighted with it, and very relieved that the washroom was next door. She had not fancied appearing among her pupils in night attire.

'You two okay?' she asked Rosa and Aisha, who were perched on Aisha's bed, staring round.

'Yes, Miss Carrbridge. But it is real small, isn't it?'

'Cosy, though.'

'Yes, it is cosy. I never knew you could sleep on trains. Can you still?'

'Oh, I – I think so,' replied Louise, not sure, but dredging her memory for information about cross-continent rail journeys. 'I'm pretty sure you can still go from New York to Los Angeles nowadays, but it's expensive, and across Siberia from Moscow.'

'Wow! I wish we were going somewhere in the night, don't you?' sighed Aisha.

'I don't know how much sleep we'd get if the train was actually moving. Perhaps it's got good sound insulation.'

David marched noisily through the other coach.

'Sorted, guys? All got slotted in somewhere?' he boomed. From open doors came a hum of talk. Everyone had picked someone to share with.

Hearing the cheery voice outside, Rick disengaged himself from Jem, slid back the bolt and opened the door.

'We'll have to wait 'til later,' whispered Rick. 'Sit down,' he smiled, looking at Jem's obvious arousal.

Jem sat shakily, drawing his arm across his lips.

'You know you don't have to squat here until eleven,' said David, peering round the door at them. 'Mr Leaven said the summer school's open.'

'Yes, Sir,' gasped Jem. 'Thanks, Sir.'

David passed on.

'I think we should go up to the school,' said Riccardo. 'No one's going to go to bed yet, so it would seem odd if we did. It's only just dark. Might as well watch TV.'

'Or – or we could play table-tennis – as there's a table,' muttered Jem. 'But first…..' He wondered how he was going to live without release through the next hour. 'First I'm just going to pop to the…..'

'What? To the john?' Rick raised his eyebrows. 'Jem,' he said, 'I know what you mean.'

'I'll meet you up at the school.'

'No, you won't. I know you want to go and jerk yourself off, don't you? I can see you're ready for it. I am too. But, Jem, half the fun is waiting. It's what I said at the party – about not rushing and shooting off.'

'But I'll be able to do it again later,' moaned Jem. 'Honest, Rick. I must do it now.'

'You're missing out. We will do it more than once tonight, but you've got to stay interested, and you won't if you sneak off to the washroom and come there on your own. Some of the drive will have gone, obviously. So let's keep high.'

It was a struggle against his nerves, but Jem nodded. Then the thought of the joy when they came back poured over him. Rick was right. He stood up, glancing down at his zip, and patted his friend's face.

'*I am a wanton*', he said, quoting Julia, 'Let's go, big boy, before I change my mind.'

'Happy in your little nest?' asked David, leaning on the door frame and smiling in at Louise.

'It's lovely,' said Louise. 'The girls were just telling me that they didn't know you could sleep on trains. I did, but I hadn't realised it was all so like a dear little room in miniature. I thought it would be drab and uncomfortable, like camping in a mini-bus.'

'This is first-class, remember,' grinned David. 'From a time when first-class *was* first-class.'

'Look,' cried Louise, 'at these little drawers and this fold-away table and those tiny sockets for razors and things. Yours must be the same.'

'I haven't done more than chuck my stuff in. I went to see if the guys had got sorted.'

'Which they have?'

'Yup. Now, when you're ready, it's time to mosey across for that pow-wow with the mad men and find out why they *really* wanted us here.'

'And that apparently it's to do with Jem. I hope I haven't started anything too annoying.'

'Wouldn't you rather be in Nova Scotia than going in to St Mat's to help count the stock of text books?'

'Oh yes! Of course I would!'

David handed Louise down the steps from the car. They made their way to the summer school. Roger Gollop was in the room where they'd had supper, munching an apple.

'Ah! The last of the clan! Right.' He heaved his bulk up. 'Follow me.'

Up a staircase they went and came to a brown varnished door marked: *Please Knock*. Without doing so, Roger shoved it open and David and Louise found themselves in a small, crowded room with a table by the far wall and as many chairs as could cram into it. On the table were maps and photographs – including another of the one of Jem's double, the lovely dead girl, on the settee with the red-faced man.

'Take a seat,' said Sir Alan. 'You've met everyone here, including Ron Portray and Zach Hall who came to the play in New York.'

Ron and Zach beamed encouragingly.

'We enjoyed it very much – what we saw of it,' said Zach.

'We five are the executive members of the Webster Museum Trust,' announced Sir Alan. 'I'm sure you know that Nova Scotia was founded as Acadia in 1665 by the French at Port Royal. Then, after William's War, 1688 to 1697, and Anne's War, 1702 to 1713, the Treaty of Utrecht recognised the British conquest of Acadia. Port Royal changed its name to Annapolis Royal, after Queen Anne, of course, and in 1749 the capital moved to Halifax, established by Edward Cornwallis. The fact that he set out to exterminate the original Mikmaq Indians who were the true owners of Acadia, we will pass over. By 1755 most of the French were expelled and the seventy-five-year-old war between the tribes and the Brits ended with the famous Burial of the Hatchet in 1761.'

'Al, can I just nudge in and tell our guests that nowadays less than one per cent of the population speak the old Mikmaq tongue,' interjected Edward Leaven. 'Most Nova Scotians are of English, Irish, French or Scots descent.'

'Well, we Europeans did not behave well over the

Mikmaq – but one can same the same about Cherokees, Sioux or Aussie Aboriginals, I suppose,' said Sir Alan.

'Go on, Al. Sorry I butted in.'

'Okay. Now to my point. The Queen's Playhouse, Halifax's earliest and only theatre, put on its first play in the mid-1780s – and you now can guess which one and by whom.'

'*The Duchess of Malfi*, of course,' said Mon.

'Of course. And it was from the fact that Webster the playwright was first played in the whole continent of North America right bang here in Nova Scotia that the Museum Trust was established in the 1870s, at the time of a great revival of interest in Jacobean theatre. The Trust is now associated with the Dalhousie Arts Centre and Nova Scotia Community College. We go in and give talks about the writers of the late-Elizabethan and Jacobean period and their work to students of all ages.'

'Are you going to tell us about the girl who looks like our Jem Clarke?' asked Louise – and she blushed, for it occurred to her that she had rather rudely changed the topic.

'I'm coming to that,' said Sir Alan, catching the eyes of the Trust members. 'Now, you see here, on the map, my house at Merivale?'

'Yes.'

'If you follow the line of the early twentieth century railway down from Lunenberg to where we are now, the Trevanaunce summer school, you will see it ends in a yard of sidings. You and your children are sleeping in cars on one of them. At the moment, this is the terminus, right? About, er, six miles up what used to be the line towards Lunenberg, just here, look, is a break at Oskquat.' He stabbed at a dot on the paper.

Mon, David and Louise peered down at the strongly-marked rail line and then at a faint thread for about an inch on the map after its snipped-off section at Oskquat.

'Um, why is the line so much fainter just after Oskquat?' asked David.

'Because it's just a footpath at present. The track-bed is there, but there are no rails laid beyond the break. We have them; they are piled up ready not far on from here. And we have concrete sleepers and dumpers full of ballast. The entire line is restored from Lunenberg to Trevanaunce apart from that little section. But Lunenberg is where the tourists are. We are left high and dry with the line cut in two. We intended to base a large arts centre here.'

'But we arrived by road all right,' said Mon.

'Yes, yes. But the whole point of a heritage rail line is that people can pay to go from one centre of entertainment and interest to another. There's nothing at Oskquat.'

'And are we able to complete the link-up?' said Roger. 'No, we damn well can't because of Mister bloody-minded Althorne. Less than a mile to do, and we're stymied.'

'Who's he?' asked Louise.

The three visitors from New York were beginning to feel their heads spinning. What had all this got to do with the play, with Jem and Julia?

'He's the big guy on the sofa in that photo and he owns the land at Oskquat where the track-bed lies.'

'Ah, the one with the famous girl.'

'That's it.'

'And she…..?' prompted Mon. Really, the Trust members seemed almost to assume that their guests knew the back-story of all this, so large did it loom in their own lives.

'She is – was – his second wife, Celia,' resumed Sir Alan, 'Killed, oh, two years ago now in a car smash near Halifax. She'd been coming back from a party with, er, well, with her closest friend and they hit a truck.'

Mon, David and Louise looked sombrely at the photo. Somehow the girl's close resemblance to Jem made her death more poignant, as if it had been Jem who had died.

'So, what are you saying?' asked Mon. 'You mean this Althorne is stopping you from closing the gap and completing the railroad?'

'Why? What's he got to gain?' said David.

Sir Alan seemed to pinch up as if an invisible nutcracker were compressing him.

'For a start,' he muttered, 'his wife's best friend was my daughter, and she was driving. She had had a driving ban, but I lent her my car; quiet roads round here, little traffic, no traffic cops, you know. So there was a real stink after the crash. And, worse from Tom Althorne's point of view, my daughter survived. She did eighteen months in jail, but that wasn't enough. Tom was one of us, y' know. His family goes back to the early days of Halifax. His great-great grandfather rebuilt the theatre. He loved the Jacobean Society. And now..... ever since Celia's death, he's been drinking, brooding.......it's been awful.'

Mon, David and Louise felt constrained from doing anything other than making mumbling noises of consolation. This was becoming embarrassing.

Edward Leaven stood and reached for a file.

'What is so very extraordinary, and what took us to New York, and you all up here, is this.' He flipped the file open. Play programmes and stage photos were revealed. 'Since the early 1980s we've had summer music and drama here at Trevanaunce. Locals like it, and it draws some tourists. The small theatre in which your cast will be performing at the weekend was paid for by Tom Althorne, and we suggested to Zora Franklin, who was drama lynch-pin at the summer school back then, that the first plays put on should be specific to the Webster Museum Trust and to our work generally.'

'Don't say you put on *The Duchess of Malfi*!'

gasped Mon.

'And *The White Devil* – on alternate nights. Tom had another reason for getting so involved. Celia was a fine actress. She had worked in Toronto and Montreal in classical theatre. Tom wanted to name the arts centre after her, when it got built.'

Edward stopped, tidied the play programmes and photos back in the file – without having shown them to his guests.

'And there's more to tell us, Mr Leaven, isn't there?' came Louise's clear voice.

'I was going to tell you about the strangest of strange coincidences,' said Edward.

'You can guess, can't you?' said Sir Alan, taking up the tale again. 'Celia Althorne, who kept her professional stage name of Celia Montclair, played Vittoria in *The White Devil* with crackling brilliance, while an actress from Halifax, Dorothy Stride, took the Duchess in the other play. But Celia played....'

'Julia!' cried Louise and Mon simultaneously.

'Exactly.'

'Oh, gimme a break!' gasped David.

'Yes, Celia played Julia – giving her a rest from the large part of Vittoria in the other play. Celia, who so resembles your Jem that they could have been brother and sister. Celia, who was killed by my banned daughter. Now do you see why we wanted your high school show down here? We thought that if Tom could see the play and Julia in it, it might remind him of his original intention, might help him start cooperating again on restoring the railroad and naming the Arts Centre after his wife. A gamble maybe, but we had to try it.'

'That,' put in Roger, 'is why it was such a shock to find that your Julia is a boy.'

Mon, David and Louise then heard that Tom Althorne had built a shrine to his dead wife in neo-classical style in a circle of grass in a dip between two hills. This shrine was right where the railroad tracks would be laid. He would hear no talk of moving it.

David couldn't help catching Louise's eye as if to say: told you it wasn't because the St Mat's Luvvies are such brilliant actors, so brilliantly directed, that they deserved an international engagement.

Sir Alan took off his glasses and pressed his fingers into his eye sockets.

'I couldn't tell your Principal all that. I just said we'd appreciate a performance of the play as an opener of the vacation season.'

Edward Leaven broke in,

'We will have to abandon the Tom Althorne plan, seeing as we have no girl.'

Mon looked round at their disappointed faces. It would have been wiser of him not to gainsay this opinion in view of the tragedy that was to come, but something made him want to convince them that all was not lost.

'I don't know,' he began. 'Jem is unusually bright

and sensitive. His Julia will convince Mr Althorne. It did you. And if Mr Althorne wants to meet the actress – well, if they weren't together too long, or alone, I reckon it could work.'

'Come off it, Mon!' said David. 'Being on a stage in role is one thing. No one's gonna be fooled by a teenage boy in drag right up close.'

'Tom *will* want to meet Julia,' said Sir Alan. 'It's the resemblance. How could he not?'

Mon surprised himself by his eagerness to help the Trevanaunce summer school. What did it matter to him whether an antique steam railroad was completed or not? Something in him was stimulated by the idea of Jem almost becoming a young woman; as he had been moved by the notion that he too would have loved Celia had he known her.

'That young Clarke of yours doesn't look in the least like a woman,' said Roger flatly. 'He might pass muster in stage costume; but in this room? In jeans and a T-shirt? No way.'

'Not in casuals,' said Mon. 'No. But in a dress, with a full wig and make-up. He could do it.'

'Come on, Rog,' said Sir Alan, 'You were convinced in New York. But the important thing is, surely, will your Jem *want* to get involved in this? If he won't play ball, it's no use. And, even if he does agree, will he carry it off? Would he prepared to be genned up about the project and say the right things? It's a hell of a lot to ask of a kid.'

'Jem's got what it takes,' said Mon stubbornly.

'He's got to agree first, Mon,' put in Louise.

'Of course.'

'He'll agree. He is a remarkably cooperative boy. *And* he'll make it work.'

There was a silence as the Trust members looked round at each other.

'We'll go ahead,' said Sir Alan.

August: **THAT STUPID PLAY**

A quizzical dog's face looked up at his master. Receiving no answering look or pat, the retriever whined.

'Shut up, Bill,' grunted Tom Althorne.

There was silence. Tom Althorne ran his finger along the trace of butter on his plate and licked it. He poured a slug of Scotch into the glass by the plate. For the sixth or seventh time that morning, he took up the invitation he had been sent.

A performance of that damned play!

Why had Al asked him? Some sort of olive branch?

He drained the whisky in a single gulp.

Bill whined again.

'All right,' muttered Tom. He took the last piece of toast, spread it thickly with butter, cut it in half, took a bite out of his half and stuck the other down under the table. Immediately Bill wolfed it, slurping. 'And don't gulp it like that', added Tom.

An invitation to *The Duchess of Malfi,* performed by American students.......

He poured another small measure into his glass – just a capful. A small one.

........That awful play: long, tedious, meaningless, full of sour memory, and yet......

The sunlight had fired her hair as she had stamped her foot on the soil round the newly planted tree.

Clap, clap, clap had come the applause. And so the start of the line from Lunenberg had been commemorated with smiles and kisses. First the railroad – then the Arts Centre and theatre. His money, but her idea. He wanted it all for her. She had done it all so well. From being an actress of national standing to becoming his wife, she had effortlessly managed everything. She had been elegant, poised, kind – with just that touch of real dignity and care about others which had prevented any bitching about her. She had been careful with the Althorne fortune too. Nothing had gone to her head. She had made fast friends with the staff and the estate workers. The members of the Jacobean Society and Webster Trust adored her. He had dreaded catching snide remarks about the difference in their ages, how she had ensnared him after the Drama Awards in Halifax – but there had been none. She had turned her charms, her shrewd mind and actress's skills to her new role and had triumphed.

Yes, she had been a triumph!

And then she'd got pally with that little bitch Stephanie Clemmy; and then she got pulled into performing in those two plays. Everyone knew Al had no control over Stephanie. Banned from driving, and then.....

Tom poured one – just one – tot and chucked it back to stop himself thinking again about that awful crash, and that black, black night of hell....

Bill gave a tentative bark.

'Yes, yes.' Tom heaved his bulk to his feet. Time to visit the shrine. To be with *her*.

That stupid play. Well, he'd have to see. Have to think about it. Might go, might not. A great deal depended on how he felt on Friday night. Last Friday he had hardly been able to climb the stairs to bed.

August: IN THE SLEEPING-CARS

No one forgot their time at Trevanaunce that August, but six of the visitors from New York had special reasons for remembering their three nights in the sleeping-cars. The other thirty-one found the first night quaint, very silent – apart, in the boys' car, from the unaccustomed breathing and movement of those with whom they had to share – and hard to adjust to. By the second night they had grown used to the narrow beds and close confines, but many had difficulty sleeping because of nerves about the coming day's performance. On the third night, all but three got to bed very late with either relieved or sorrowful reflections that *The Duchess of Malfi* was, at last over, and with minds buzzing with the drama of what had happened to Rick and Jem. By Saturday afternoon all but three were winging back to New York to start delayed vacations.

Jan Franitza, occupying the bottom bunk while Tony turned creakingly in the top one, lay with a sense of anger at Jem, not unmixed with concern. Jan liked Tony well enough but didn't really know him. He had expected to be in the same two-berth compartment as Jem, as Jem had known he did – so there was a sense that he had been the victim of disloyalty. Jem Clarke is *my* personal friend, isn't he?

That should mean something.

Worse was his knowledge that Jem and Riccardo were engaging in certain games in their compartment. How could one boy love another boy – in that way? Yet, as he lay in his bunk, his mind fleshing out lascivious imagined details, he also felt disturbingly aroused. Just think what *they* were doing only five compartments away! Whereas he…… Why couldn't Jem have done that with *him*, if he had to do it? He had grasped himself and was rubbing himself almost absent-mindedly as he struggled to analyse his reactions. Would he have done it with Jem, if Jem had asked him? If they had been sharing a compartment, sleeping together, would it have seemed natural? He astonished himself with the reflection that, yes, it might have seemed natural – here in the sleeping-cars, far from home. And he might have done it with Jem in the darkness – yes, if asked. He saw Jem's long eyelashes over closed eyes, as his hand moved. He followed the probable actions of his friend, although he had no idea what was possible between two males beyond manipulation of each other. With Rosa though…..yes, with her……

Suddenly, he was aware of two things; one, that he had been making a certain amount of rustling noise – inescapable in such a small space – and two, that he was nearly at climax. All he had to hand was a sock, and he came silently into it, stifling his fast breaths, and lay in an agony of embarrassment lest Tony had heard him. But Tony's breathing continued undisturbed and Jan fell asleep with a resolution made. The next night he would visit Rosa.

Rosa was, as David had told Louise, a "go-er". She had allowed several youths to make love to her in her 11th grade year so far, and she had felt little interest in any of them beyond the fun of intercourse. She despised boys who were shy, eager, clumsy and grateful. Janek came firmly into this category. While big and muscular for his age – just seventeen – he was not striking in any way, certainly not unusually good-looking; he had little conversation and was evidently inexperienced.

Even she, however, was intrigued when, with the barest knock, Janek appeared inside her compartment on the second night.

How he had got up courage to go there, Jan could not have said, but he had studied Jem closely on the morning following the Wednesday night and had fancied he had seen signs in his face of Jem's depravities. Jem certainly seemed tired at rehearsal. Jan couldn't bear another frantic night under Tony, with forbidden, awful, yet stimulating images flitting through his brain, followed by the soaking of another sock. If Jem was travelling his road, why, he would set out upon one of his own.

Tony was snoring annoyingly, having just fallen asleep, when Jan got from his berth. He stood a time in the dark, his face a foot from Tony's, then slipped his jeans on and went into the corridor. He had clutched up a copy of *Hi-fi World* in order to colour his appearance with the excuse of visiting the john, and went through the connecting gangway into the car beyond, where the girls and staff slept. What he would say if Mr Howard came out and saw him, he didn't know. Absurd excuses, culled from sleep-walking scenes in movies, came to him. But there was no sound, and he slipped along to the third compartment from the end, which, by casual questioning of Aisha, he had found out was Rosa's, opened the door and shut it gently behind him. Rosa was in her bed, propped up on one elbow, reading a magazine under a dim lamp. She gasped, her eyes snapping,

'Janek! What are you doing here?' and then stopped as, agonised, Jan put his finger to his lips. 'What's up? Is there a joke on or something?'

Jan shook his head and said simply,

'I just wanted to be with you.'

It was the best thing he could have come up with. Rosa took in his flustered, puppy-like appearance: his ruffled hair, alarmed eyes and blushing skin. She examined fondly his heavy, young-looking chest and arms, and she wasn't put off by them. Woman-like, she felt a brief need to be severe.

'You've got a nerve, barging in like this.'

'I know. I know. I'm sorry.' Jan couldn't have felt

less like a devil-may-care seeker after sensual delight.
'I – I'll go now.'

'No, you won't. Come and sit on the edge of the
bed. Let's talk for a bit, anyway.' She patted the
berth. 'Have you locked the door?'

'Oh! No.'

'Well, just pull the bolt over, can you? I wouldn't
want Aisha or Susie popping round for a chat, or Miss
Carrbridge poking her nose in.'

Jan quietly shot the bolt and turned to face her.

'Now, why do you want to see me?' asked Rosa,
getting a little excited by the nearness of Jan's half-
naked body, and because she didn't need to ask the
question.

'I couldn't sleep. I've been going over in my mind
about us. I really liked kissing you, Rosa.'

'*Did* you?' she said archly. 'And you'd like me to
kiss you again, I suppose?' He nodded, and then gave
a gasp as she put her hand to his jean's belt. 'Why
don't you slip out of those and get into bed with me?
He froze with mixed terror and excitement. 'Oh,
c'mon!' she laughed, pulling the zip down. 'Hm,' she
added, as she appraised his nakedness, 'I'm game, I
suppose, but only if we don't rush it. I want my
climax too; and only if you wear protection.'

'Protection?' echoed Jan. 'Oh, shit! I didn't – I
didn't think….. I haven't……'

'Typical,' she sighed. 'Lucky for you I'm prepared.
Pass me that bag. No, not that one. The square one.'

Jan gave her a small black vanity case. She fished inside and produced a condom. 'Get that on you and we're in business.'

Jan took the packet, desperately trying to recall the sex-ed lessons he and Jem had sat through the previous year with carefully studied expressions of bored knowledgeability. He had had this very thing demonstrated by a grand-motherly, grey-haired nurse using a piece of sawn-off broom-handle. Now, alas, his mind was a blank.

'You haven't used one of these before, have you?' Rosa asked. He shook his head humbly. 'Well, never mind. Luckily I know. Stand by the bed. Get your jeans and pants right off. And don't go soft on me.'

He stood by the berth while she flipped open the packet. He could feel his excitement ebbing away. With a flick of her eyebrows at his flushed face, she took hold of him and rubbed with one hand, while stroking the inside of his legs with the other. Then she slipped the rubber over the hard flesh and rolled it down. Jan recalled that this was what one was supposed to do – roll it down. Funny how he had blanked, just when it mattered.

He could hardly believe this was happening to him. He both disapproved and was thrilled. Rosa removed her T-shirt and he gaped at her breasts with their big, brown nipples.

'Get in, Janek,' she murmured. Instinctively he put his head between her breasts and began lifting himself to mount her. 'No! Not yet,' she said. 'I hate it when you boys rush it. Here, give me your hand.' She guided his hand and he gently explored the curls, and the complex soft flesh. She continued to rub him slowly but stopped every now and then. 'Don't you dare come yet,' she whispered in his ear. 'Make it last. If you feel you're coming, think of something unsexy, like nuns, or rice pudding.'

In the dim light of her reading lamp he looked down her body. She had kicked away the bedclothes. He was amazed by her beauty. How could Jem desire anything other than this? He did not consider his own firm, young limbs beautiful, nor the gentle glow of his fair skin and eager, honest face.

When she was ready for him, Rosa showed Jan how to enter her. Although she liked the reverence with which boys of her age or younger approached her body, Rosa wished Jan was a bit less respectful.

'Thrust harder,' she gasped. He did as he was bid and very soon was rewarded by a wonderful orgasm of a strength and complexity he hadn't known before. Then came the difficult bit: Rosa wanted him to go on moving inside her, so he struggled to think of all the sexiest things he could, while she encouraged his hand to help her. His brain flamed with half-suppressed images of Jem and Riccardo, then of himself, naked with them, then of himself with this girl. Fortunately for her nerves and for his dignity, he managed to remain firmly in her while she came to her own climax and was stimulated by the pulsing grip he felt as she fluttered to an end.

'Wow! Oh, gosh! Oh! That was really nice, Janek,' she said, pushing him off her.

'Oh, yes! It was! Thanks, Rosa,' he gasped.

He stood at the wash-basin, sorting out the stickiness and mess of the condom, but not caring. His heart was singing inside him: "I am no longer a virgin! I am no longer a virgin!" and his self-respect soared higher and higher, so that he felt a love of all his fellows – especially Jem. Yes, especially him. Would he have done this amazing thing with this girl if Jem had not brought him into the play?

'I'm sleepy,' said Rosa.

Jan, in his jeans again, kissed her cheek. His knowledge that she had found pleasure in sex with him gave the kiss an air of authority and maturity. He had been going to thank her again but stopped and instead simply bade her goodnight. As he went back down the narrow corridor he was suddenly struck by the fact that he had committed a grave sin. He couldn't quite accept that his immortal soul was now, according to his church's teachings, in danger of damnation. Vague promises to go to confession as soon as he was home again fluttered in his head. Sex before marriage? Yesterday he would have said it was very wrong. Now he felt he just didn't care.

When he got back to his own shared cabin, he realised he'd left *Hi-fi World* in Rosa's compartment, and he saw that as somehow symbolising an immense change in himself..

David Lomax, like his young charge Janek, had lain awake for much of the early part of the first night. He seemed to see, in the dark, Louise's bright eyes. He realised that, in spite of her quiet manner and her diffidence, she was perceptive, clever and alert. He admired her figure in the summery dresses or well-cut, cropped trousers she wore on vacation. He liked her humour, her concern for the boys and girls, her devotion to Mon and to St Matthew's. David loved his old high school with a depth of feeling that didn't need words; indeed no one would have guessed it if relying entirely on his put-downs and cynical asides. It was a bit like loving New York, or America – a guy just *did,* so had the right to whinge about them now and again. That Louise relished her job appealed to an unarticulated part of him. In short, he knew no better woman. He had *never* known a better woman.

It was sometime during that first night that David decided to ask Louise to become engaged to him. He knew that marriage would require something better than his untidy rented apartment. He knew he could raise a mortgage two and a half times his income – but what would that buy? For a home worthy of the name, he and his wife's incomes would need to blend and be calculated as one. But suppose she ended up pregnant? Suppose she got tired of him? David supposed all day. By the end of it he had thought: Screw it! She's got to agree first, *then*'ll be the time to talk about money. But the calculations continued to rotate in his head. Fond of teaching Hardy's *Far From the Madding Crowd*, he had imagined himself a Sergeant Troy: fascinating, capricious, cruel, sensual. Self-knowledge, however, forced him to re-assess himself as Gabriel Oak: dependable, thoughtful, thrifty, loyal. He was just at the age when the latter figure seems preferable to the former, so his sensible calculations lasted until he decided he *could* afford to marry. Now came the asking.

Had not Louise told him that he was the only man she had ever kissed? How wonderful and rare if it were really true. And why shouldn't it be true? David nodded emphatically in the dark. Yes, it *was* true. Louise was unspoiled, a good Catholic girl, made by God for him alone. He regretted his own few experiences, but not whole-heartedly. It was different for a man. A man had to have had a little practice so as to be sure of making his wife – Louise – happy.

Yes! He would ask her on Thursday night.

On that night, David and Louise shared a romantic happiness which they never forgot. The *Duchess* rehearsals were over; only the Friday performance lay ahead; that which had brought them together was about to slip away into the past. The future awaited. With happy sentimentality, on the Friday morning,

David bought, in the summer school gift shop, an HO gauge model of a Canadian Pacific sleeping-car. He intended it as a little souvenir he and Louise would keep forever.

Louise was lying in her berth, her light on, thinking what a nice week this had been, when she heard a tap on the door. Her heart leapt, although she had been hoping for such a tap. Somehow, being in the sleeping-car was not like being in a house; normal parameters faded away. Louise felt like some romantic heroine on The Orient Express. She popped her legs over the side of the berth, unlocked her door and let it open slightly. As she had hoped, and half-expected, David stood there.

'Oh! Come in,' she twittered. 'I'm glad to see you......'

'You don't mind, Louise? I wanted to speak with you.'

'What – what about?'

She took in his figure, the brilliant white vest, the boxer shorts in a dark striped material. She had never seen his naked arms and legs. David, realising this was an occasion for firmness, and in order not to lose the advantage of surprise, came to sit next to her on the bed. Their bare legs were touching. He took one of her hands and, grasping it to give himself courage, said steadily,

'I'd like us to become engaged, Louise. I have fallen in love with you and I want you to think about becoming my wife.'

He was tempted, like Gabriel Oak in the novel, to add a business touch and inform her that he had calculated they could afford to purchase a house between them, but a lingering shred of sanity stopped him. Louise was a romantic, he sensed, and would not give thought to anything outside her feelings.

There was a silence.

So, it had come! Two years after leaving the convent a man had proposed and it was open to her to join the ranks of normal womanhood. Louise's moral training would never have allowed her to live with a partner outside marriage. In the midst of her joy, she coolly understood how lucky she was to have met and grown fond of another practising Catholic.

No time for hesitation then. He had honoured her.

'David! Of course I will – will think about marrying you. I'd love to become engaged to you.' She paused, seeing the light from her reading-lamp glisten the hair on his legs. 'Oh, this is marvellous!'

It might not have been the best-phrased of acceptances, but it was the one David wanted to hear.

'Can we lie together and talk about it?' he whispered.

She nodded, unexpectedly, he thought, and they slipped into her berth. She turned off the light and they lay in the darkness in the narrow bed, feeling the miracle of each other's bodies. As it was only an inch from his own, he gently kissed her mouth. She then responded. He caressed her back and legs.

Thanks to Coco's encouragement she knew how to interpret her rising desire and he helped her. Wondering if it would spoil things, but unable to prevent himself, he slipped the boxer shorts down, and she explored him. The feel of him astonished her. Somehow, in her ignorance, she had expected a man's penis to be wet and cold, like a piece of damp garden hose. Now she felt a spurt of maternal liking for its soft-skinned, eager warmth. With her fist gripping it and his hand buried between her legs, they gently caressed each other. David, whispering, asked if she had a towel to hand. He was anxious not to dampen her bed and, worse, alarm or disgust her when he came. With a hand-towel nearby in his left hand, they continued kissing and caressing until, with rare luck, they reached their climaxes at the same time, clinging to each other with delight and release.

She had never believed that she would have sex before marriage. He valued the ideal of a stainless girl. Yet they were happy with their compromise. They had avoided going too far, had left plenty for their wedding night and yet had proved their compatibility. David stayed a long time with Louise wrapped in his arms. To prove that lightning can strike twice in the same place, they had an identical experience on the first night they got back to New York in David's bed – although their coming together was a reaction to the sad events of the last night of the play, and came out of the need for mutual comfort, after hours of regretting the way in which the Canadian adventure had ended.

By the time the new semester began, they had advanced their marriage plans to the following June, good sense continuing to walk hand-in-hand with passion.

Jem and Rick had not, after all, played table-tennis on that first night at Trevanaunce. They had, desultorily, watched TV until the summer school closed, each pre-occupied with their unsatisfied lust.

'You're an intellectual, aren't you?' Jem had asked.

'Why?'

'You seem to like documentaries or history programmes.'

'I've never liked moronic crap,' Rick had smiled. 'But then you don't either, do you?'

'No,' Jem had admitted. 'I don't know why. Betsy and Mom do.'

'You shy away from what's vulgar. I like that. I guess it's why we're both involved in a demanding seventeenth century play.'

'I always want to define myself in the – the light of what someone has done or said in the past. I think it helps me to work out who I am.'

'You know who you are more than I know who I am,' muttered Rick.

'Oh, no. You're older,'

'Older means more confused.'

'Does it?'

At eleven they had returned to their compartment and locked it.

Jem had felt inexplicably shy. His muscles ached for release, but here he was, alone for the night in this tiny space with Rick Parisi, who had never seen him without clothes on. Their feverish love-making at Greg's party had, after all, been in the dark and fully dressed. Jem had never liked removing his clothing in front of others for swimming or showers. He didn't have much confidence in the attractiveness of his body, although his self-esteem had, of late, been boosted by the admiration of Mr Howard, Aisha and Rick himself. But that, he reminded himself, was admiration of Julia, not of Jem.

He sat on the edge of the lower berth.

'I feel sort of shy, Rick,' he said, coming clean.

Riccardo was unzipping his jeans but stopped.

'How do you mean?'

'I'd be happier if the light was off, I think,' murmured Jem.

'Don't you want to do it?' asked Rick directly.

'Oh, yes! I do,' said Jem, hanging his head. He was yearning to make love again.

'Hm,' said Rick. He knelt and took Jem's chin in his hand. He was struck by the vulnerability of the beautiful oval face. Pity and love vied with lust in his heart. 'I tell you what,' he went on, 'let's just get used to each other. You're worried about stripping off in front of me, aren't you?' Jem nodded. 'You think you don't look too good?'

'Well, no, not exactly. I'm not the hunch-back of Notre Dame, Rick, but…..'

'I really like it when you make that sort of comment,' laughed Rick. 'If it's any comfort, I'm not too pleased with the way I look, either.'

'You? You look great,' said Jem, and stopped, feeling that his warmth sounded soppy and clinging.

'Hey, tanks fer de endorsement, man.'

He stood again, his waist on the level of Jem's eyes. He stroked the highlights of Jem's hair and re-positioned himself to sit next to the younger boy.

Jem's eyes – vulnerable now, sought his.

'Let's just talk,' said Rick. 'As we're doing so, let's remove bits of clothing as well. Like a slow strip-tease. You'll feel miles better.'

'Okay. But talk about what?'

'Well – sex, of course.'

Jem blushed hotly. Now it was coming. Could he manage to answer and question calmly without crippling inhibition?

'I'll start,' said Rick, laying his hand on Jem's leg. 'Now, let's see. Remind me when you first started doing it to yourself?'

Jem took a swallow.

'I told you I had my first when I was twelve.'

'Ah. So you *approved giddy and wild things in yourself* quite early on?' said Rick, quoting from the play. 'Where did you first do it?'

'Oh God. Well, you know that café up at Kissena Park? It has washrooms out back. It was there.'

'Jeez. In a public place. You took a risk.'

'Not really. There was this other boy – he kept look-out. His name was Marc Harbeth. He lived two houses down from us, but he's moved to Chicago since. He said he'd discovered this thing you do to yourself and that it felt real nice. We were just talking, watching a little volley-ball game, near the café. He said he wanted to do it, and would I keep watch, and then I could do it while he looked-out. So we went to the john, and there was no one there, so..... We didn't realise it was sex. His theory was that it was like a dredging out of sediment in the bladder – that's what the white stuff was.'

'Weird! An argument for sex education at an even younger age. And after that?'

'We did it whenever we could. We shared a cubicle at the swimming-baths most Saturdays. One of us always kept watch. You know, I hardly ever saw him come, and he seldom saw me. At the crucial moment one of us was usually looking towards the doorway. Although we heard each other, of course. Funny really.'

'Did you keep up with him?'

'No, I haven't heard of him for nearly four years.'

'Interesting. Your first experience being with another boy, I mean. Although I don't suppose it's unusual.'

'What about you?' asked Jem, anxious to move on from Marc Harbeth.

'Me? I was just fourteen and I think I discovered it in bed. Other guys whispered about it, but I hadn't felt anything until then. You've got more than a year's experience on me, Jem.'

When it was put like that, Jem felt less childish and shy. He felt even better when he discovered he did it more often than Rick. Rick had bluntly asked him how many times a week he came to orgasm.

'I make a mark in my diary every time,' Jem admitted. 'I've been doing that since Easter last year. Now I put a letter. It's when I do it while thinking of someone I fancy – like you, Rick. I put an R in the margin.'

'What a great idea! Oh, Jem, I do really love you! You're so original!'

'I suppose when you add them all up it comes to quite a lot, and I guess I've been doing it at the same rate for the last two years at least. I – I did it less when my dad was around, but since he left I guess I've become more private, more on my own at home, you know.'

'Oh, Jem, I didn't know about your dad leaving home.'

'Well, it's been a while. But I think that's when I

got a bit more obsessed. Perhaps it was a comfort – like a drug – I don't know.'

'Poor Jem,' whispered Rick. 'Do you want to go on talking and undressing?'

'Of course. I'm glad you know about me,' said Jem. His face was flushed.

'Let's remove our tops,' said Rick, slipping off his T-shirt. Jem stared at Rick's dark nipples and saw that that the hair on his chest went down his stomach and below his waistband. He wrenched off his own top, conscious of the pale boyishness of his chest and arms.

'Tell me about the rate you do it nowadays,' prompted Rick, opening his legs as he lounged back next to Jem.

'I can tell you the tally for the last eight months, if you like,' said Jem. 'I'll just get my diary.' He rose from the berth, his arousal uncomfortable in his tight jeans. Rick reached out and took the swelling in his hand.

'Phew! You *are* ready, aren't you?'

'I just don't want to come in my clothes,' said Jem.

'Get your diary, and let's remove something else. Jeans next.'

They took their jeans off and stood, their underpants straining. Jem fished his diary out of his bag. His voice was husky.

'Here,' he said. 'I started marking on January the first. So, from then to now it's thirty-one weeks, so

I'll count from there.' There was a long pause while he did so. Rick ran his hand up and down the back of Jem's leg. 'Er, that's 248, not including today.'

'Jesus! What's that divided by the weeks?'

'Um, it's – let's see – so, it's 248, and I'll add three, say…..'

'Why? Because you expect to do it three more times before Friday?'

'I hope so, Rick. So that's 31 into 251, um, that's just over eight a week.'

'God! Every day – more than every day!'

'Yes. Is that a lot?'

'And there must have been days when you weren't at it – like when you've had 'flu, or it was Christmas day…..'

'Why Christmas Day?' interrupted Jem.

'Oh, well, it is a sin, isn't it? That's what we've been taught – although it's a sin I like so much that I don't think I can give it up yet.'

'I'm not sure about all that,' said Jem. 'I'm pretty convinced it's natural, and therefore God-given. But I can't remember about the first three Christmasses. And I hadn't started marking then.'

'Anyway, I think eight or nine times a week is a lot. I wonder if you're a kind of sex addict, Jem?'

'Oh, come on! How many do you have?'

'Not being obsessive about it, I don't calculate exactly, but a lot less than you. More since I started feeling for you as I do,' added Rick. 'But a lot less before then. Quality above quantity, you know.'

'I usually get quality too,' smiled Jem, archly.

'So, Jem dear,' said Rick, 'if we assume that you're doing it on average nearly four hundred and twenty times a year, and you've been at it for four years, you've already had nearly one thousand seven hundred orgasms! And you're not seventeen yet!'

Jem's face was hot and his breath coming shallowly.

'And I need another, Rick.'

'Are you happier about being nearly naked in front of me?'

'Oh!' Jem gasped, having been so stimulated by their calculations that he had forgotten he was only in his underpants.

'You say you want to do it now. Well, I want to look at you while you do it,' said Rick. 'I just want to watch, if that doesn't seem weird. I don't want to miss things about you.'

'How do you mean?'

'The expression in your eyes, the movement of your muscles. Come on, you're worth looking at.' Rick knelt again in the confined space by the lower berth. 'Let's be completely naked now,' he breathed. He and Jem pulled off their undergarments and drank in each other. 'You are so attractive,' Rick went on, putting his hands on Jem's knees and pushing them wide apart. 'Look at that.' He pointed to a long delicate vein running up the inside of Jem's thigh just under the white skin. 'That's what I want to see – the detail.' He knelt back on his heels, his thighs spread, pre-ejaculate dripping from him. 'See? I'm nearly there, but I can wait. I like waiting. Go on, relieve yourself, Jem. You've been holding back since ten.'

'Yes, I've been wet for ages too,' gasped Jem.

Feeling more aroused than he had thought possible under Rick's gaze, Jem began to rub himself. With Rick caressing his knees and thighs, Jem's fingers coaxed his body to climax in less than two minutes. He then lay back with glazed eyes.

'My turn,' Rick gasped. 'I loved the expression on your face as you came. Your pupils suddenly got wide and your lips pouted. You looked younger, but there was a force in you too. *Your bright eyes carry a quiver of darts*, as my alter-ego Bosola puts it to Julia.'

He knelt close to Jem, rubbing quickly. He put one arm round Jem's bare calf and came almost immediately, his open mouth kissing Jem's knee. Jem dropped to a crouching position and they clung damply together. 'Another R for your diary,' murmured Rick.

Rick was right in his earlier prophecy that they would have sex again that first night. They both seemed to wake together in the dawn, as light was pushing through the blinds of the compartment.

'Rick?' whispered Jem from the upper berth.

'I'm awake,' replied Rick from below.

'I loved what we did.'

'When I was kneeling there with you on a level with my eyes, and, Jem, you looked – you were everything I wanted, and your legs were pale with those veins, like marble......' He tailed off incoherently. 'Can I climb up and be with you?'

'Of course,' said Jem. He snipped on his reading light, peeled back the bedclothes and lay naked, naturally excited again. Rick, standing by the berths, ran his hands down Jem's body from his shoulder to his ankles, leant forward and took Jem's erection into his mouth. The electric shock crashed through to Jem's spine and down his legs. Rick let go again.

'Hm. Tastes interesting, if you know what I mean.'

'God, Rick! If you do that again, let me wash first,' cried Jem. He hoped Rick would not be put off doing it again.

'Don't let's bother about washing. Let's do it again now. But look, I want to hold you this time. Like this.' He ascended to the top berth and lay by Jem looking into his face. The narrowness of the little bed forced their bodies together. 'And Jem, I'd like you to try one of these as you climax.' He reached down to the shelf by his pillow and produced a couple of small amphules.

'What are they?'

'They're called "poppers", amyl nitrite. You pop one in your fingers and inhale just before coming. I've saved these for our second go. They'll make it

346

amazing. You'll see. And let's go a lot slower, shall
we? We've done it together twice, and each time
we've come in about a second and a half.'

'I can't help it,' breathed Jem. 'Once it starts, it just
takes over. I always want to make it last, or delay it
and prolong it, but…..' He reached out for his popper
and stuck it under his pillow.

Rick raised his arms and turned Jem's face so he
could lick it. Jem smelt the tang of sweat from both of
them and the underlying chalky layer of dried semen.

'Have you……,' asked Rick, cupping Jem's ear in
his lips and tracing with them the vein on the outside
of Jem's neck, '……have you tried to get to orgasm
without touching yourself? Just using concentration
and thoughts?'

'Funny you should ask that. It's been an ambition
of mine,' whispered Jem. 'Have you managed it?'

'No, not yet,' admitted Rick. 'But stopping every
now and then is the secret of making it last and
making it more intense when it comes. Just as not
doing it at all when you're crying out for it is one of
the best games in the world.'

And so they made their next love-making last, each
stopping just before climax, panting, struggling and
grappling each other, arms and legs entwined, with
crushed lips and burning faces, gasping and groaning
on the crest of delight.

Lust was like a winding punch in mid-chest, like
the pouring of a molten stream of shiny tin under the

skin and over the eyeballs; the universe of taste, smell and the sparking nakedness of the body so focussed that Jem thought he was about to watch a grenade explode in front of him. Then, at the end of endurance, he knew it was time to inhale his popper. He cracked it and breathed it in. At once, he had no back, other than the tight knitting of his muscles, no body beyond the explosion in his groin; the world was in front of him and, yes, it was all exploding, all cracking apart. His mouth open, full of Rick's hair, he came in his friend's fist. Rick had had to clamp his other hand on Jem's mouth – his gasp had been more like a scream. A moment later, Rick had roughly turned Jem round, with the intention of taking him from behind; an act of selfish violence that shocked him when he thought about it afterwards. Jem squirmed fiercely away.

'No, Rick, I don't want that,' he had gasped.

Although frantic with lust, Rick had heard him, pushed against his lower back instead, cracked his popper and came.

Not having made love in a bed with another boy before, Rick had been amazed by Jem's physical strength. By day, in ordinary circumstances, Jem was a shy, gentle, pleasant youth; by night, with straining muscles and surrender to gasping pleasure, he seemed a completely different being.

Exhausted and sticky, they fell apart. The compartment was stiflingly hot. They studied each other's nakedness in the steadily brightening dawn light, with a sort of astonishment at what they had done together.

'Sorry, Rick,' said Jem. 'About that…..'

'Okay. I guess I shouldn't have tried it; I was sorta beside myself….'

'It's just that I've always hated the idea of that somehow. It does seem unnatural.'

'Whereas this, of course, is what all your average well-bred youths do when holidaying at summer school?'

Jem smiled at him and he smiled back.

'What a mess,' murmured Jem, shaking his head and beginning to dab himself dry with an end of the sheet.

'Ah, well. That's enough for now, yeah? Shall we try to get a couple of hours' sleep?'

Jem nodded.

'I didn't mind one thing….I mean tonight – what you did with your mouth….I'd like to try…..'

'Mouths? Yes, so would I. I've never done it. Have you heard of *soixante-neuf*?

'No.'

'You have me in your mouth while I have you in mine. Sixty-nine, see? It'll work because we're the same height. We'll do it tonight, narrow bunk or not.'

Jem's blood pounded in his ears. The idea of it! Of *that*! Tonight! Tonight seemed infinitely far off.

'Rick….Suppose?'

'Oh no,' smiled Rick. 'let's leave it until we've showered tomorrow. Remember, it's more fun when you've waited for it.' He jumped down from Jem's berth. 'Nightie-night. And thanks, Jem.'

Jem fell backwards on his damp sheet. He felt spent, but unfulfilled – an odd mixture. As he drifted into sleep, he rotated the natural way in which he had seemed to become the passive partner. Rick had the ideas, supplied the poppers, called the tune. Was it because he was the older? Jem, who didn't think of himself as effeminate, thought he minded. Then he saw the whole picture, as if lit by fresnel spots on stage. HE was Julia. Of *course* he was. And Rick was tough, effective Bosola. '*You have put love-powder into my drink,*' he murmured in Julia's voice. He was beautiful Julia; Rick was the wicked assassin, unable to resist her. Oh, then it's all right, after all…….

On Thursday's rehearsal Jem abandoned any last shreds of male-hood. The shyness about his body he often felt vanished, and his libido rocketed into space. He set out to make love to the Cardinal, then to Bosola, on stage through his femininity, his airs, and clutchings. He hardly seemed to have been a boy at all. Edward Leaven and Roger Gollop, who came to afternoon rehearsals, began to wonder if Alan Clemmy's melodramatic (and, to their mind, hopeless) plan might not work after all.

August: ON THE EDGE

At 10.45 on the second night, a quarter of an hour before the summer school closed, Mon decided that he would go to Jem and explain the circumstances of the Webster Museum Trust's decision to bring the play to Nova Scotia. He had asked Sir Alan for one of the photographs from the study at Trevanaunce House and had it in his compartment to show Jem. Mon, having thought about it, was by no means convinced that Jem should actually meet Tom Althorne in drag; he felt that Julia on a stage at a distance was very different from Jem close up, without the lines to shelter behind. However, he had promised the Trust group that he would ask him.

As he went through the connecting gangway, Mon saw a movement at the far end of the nearest boys' car. Jem's compartment door had opened and Riccardo had emerged, bare-chested, and gone to the washroom at the far end. He waited a minute or two then made his way down the corridor, and, with a perfunctory tap, opened the door. Straight ahead of him, leaning back on the little table beneath the window, was Jem.

'Oh, Rick! Come ON! Let's start! I'm *so* ready…..'

Mon froze in the doorway. Jem was naked, legs apart, one hand resting on the top berth. When he saw that it was Mon Howard who had come in, he jerked his legs together, his hands flashing to his groin, his face flaming with confusion.

Mon's mind was a relay of contrasting responses. He was sure Jem wasn't just out of his clothes preparatory to donning pyjamas – that stance, and his words, meant something very different. Mon knew what they were going to start as well as if they'd told him. He knew he should be outraged, censorious; he could see how aroused Jem was before his pupil's hands had whisked defensively into position. He was amazed at Jem's carelessness, but envious of the self-absorption and abandonment of inhibition that had led to such lack of care. His predominant feeling, however, was pity for the boy's confusion.

'Sorry, Jem,' he said, as easily as he could manage. 'I didn't know you were undressing for bed. When you're ready, can I have word, through in my quarters in the next car?'

He retreated to the corridor, conscious that he had been staring at Jem's naked body for what seemed like hours. He had gorged on every detail.

Oh, Almighty Saviour! Help me! Mon almost pressed his fingers into his skull to erase those images which, he knew, would agonise him for days to come. And he had played that little game! Hey, oops, sorry! I didn't know you were *getting ready for bed!* Mon had never wanted anything in his life so much as to hurl himself back into the room and force Jem's mouth to his, to feel the hot flesh in his arms.

The washroom door clicked again. Riccardo came swinging into the corridor. The hatred Mon felt for him! This wop school kid with his glossy mane! That Jem could be his – was waiting for him! He ought to be in prison! He's over eighteen and Jem's still just sixteen! This goes beyond a bit of schoolboy experiment – we're talking seduction of a child here! And what they are doing – in the eyes of the church – is a grave sin, worthy of damnation if not confessed and repented! Yes! But Mon's hypocritical censoriousness wilted as soon as it flowered. Riccardo was a pleasant, clever youth, hard-working, harmless and doing a fine job in the demanding role of Bosola. No criminal! He had evidently reached a part of Jem that no one else had. They were both young, both possessed of strong feelings, each yearning to discover a universe of passion new to both of them. He then recollected that, at nearly seventeen, Jem was over the age of consent. And, when all was said and done, the sins of the young were not so very serious – hardly the stuff of bombing in war, slavery, mass killings, terrorism, huge financial fraud. By the time he'd got this far, and Riccardo had reached his compartment, Mon almost sentimentalised himself to tears. They were just two poor boys! Jeez, and so little happiness, or time for happiness, in the world!

So, instead of practically putting into train a citizen's arrest on Rick, Mon simply nodded at the young man.

'Evening, Mr Howard, Sir. Want to speak to us?'

'Yes, yes, Riccardo. I just wanted to see Jem for a moment. I want to talk to him about Sir Alan's plans for tomorrow. I gather he's not in bed yet. Send him along, can you?'

'Yes, right, Sir. Goodnight.'

'Nightie-night,' said Mon – in unconscious imitation of Rick's words to Jem the night before – 'Last show tomorrow.'

'Yes, Sir.'

Mon went off back to his car, the debonair school-teacher, friendly, but with a dash of easy, off-hand authority. Oh, but what an empty, lonely game!

A few minutes later there came a tentative tap on Mon's door. Mon smiled, rather grimly.

'Come in,' he called.

The door opened and Jem, looking very young, appeared in the compartment, clad in blue jeans and a white shirt. For some reason he had put on the glasses which Mon knew he needed for reading, and these gave him a strangely virginal look – as if a boy saint, like Stanislaus Kostka, had appeared on earth.

'Just trickle in, Jem,' said Mon (the affable play director). 'I hope you weren't on the verge of getting into bed – to sleep.' (Mon couldn't stop this barb.)

'No – no, Sir. I – um – was getting ready, sort of – for bed, Sir, as – as you know, when you – you came

354

to the…….'

'But you can spare *me* a minute?'

Really, thought Mon, I must stop this sarcastic intonation, otherwise the game's blown. Jem, on his side, couldn't be certain what his teacher had seen, or divined, and prayed that Mr Howard had noticed nothing special – apart from someone getting ready to retire for the night. In the pause, Mon thought that perhaps he ought to warn his pupil against adolescent homo-erotic games in case they had a lasting and damaging effect, but he didn't know how to begin. He also suspected that Jem and Riccardo were too involved for the word "games" to have a convincing ring. So, he kept up the pretence that nothing amiss had been occurring or had been noticed, and, with a creditable face for one so young, so did Jem; and what Mon had seen and what he was fairly sure Jem knew he had seen when the door opened, was not mentioned between them.

'We've got a problem – a challenge, I should say, about *The Duchess*,' began Mon. 'I expect all of you must have wondered why the Webster Museum Trust up here was so keen to invite us?'

'A few of us did, a bit, Sir.'

'There is a reason, Jem – and it concerns you.'

'Me?'

'You as Julia, anyway.'

'Oh.'

'Yup. You see, the publicity photograph Miss

Carrbridge sent out to their magazine, trying to drum up ticket sales, made Sir Alan and his friends jump out of their skins, because you were in it.'

Jem's clear forehead wrinkled.

'Me?'

'Have a look at this,' continued Mon, producing the photo of the young woman on the sofa. Jem took it and jumped.

'It – it's not me!' he gasped.

'No, of course not, but don't you think it's *like* you as Julia?'

Jem peered at it more closely.

'I – I suppose it is. Who is she? It is a she?'

'Oh yeah – it surely ain't another sixteen-year-old boy in drag. There's only one Cleo Jakemar. It's a young woman who was killed in a car crash here in Nova Scotia. She was the wife of this guy on the sofa.'

Jem transferred his gaze to the red-faced man beside his double.

'That man is called Tom Althorne, and he's never gotten over her death. He owns all the land between here and where the Trust wants to push through the old railroad track from Lunenberg to the summer school centre here to attract tourists. He won't let them do it because he's built a shrine to his wife where the track runs, and because Sir Alan's daughter was driving the car in which Mrs Althorne died.'

'What was her name?' Jem asked. 'Her other

name?'

'Celia.'

'How frightful that she's dead. And what's the problem you talked about, Sir? You mean, we can't put the play on after all?'

'No, no. On the contrary. Not only does it go on, but, Jem, dear old boy, you have got to do something to the best of your ability. Tom Althorne's coming to the play, he's going to see you in your part, and he's gonna want to meet you afterwards......'

'Oh, no! I couldn't. I wouldn't know what to say!'

'......because, Jem, Mrs Althorne – Celia – was the last woman round here to play the part of......'

'Not Julia! Surely not?'

'Yup. Not only are you nearly identical, but you were both Julia. She was an actress and took the part of Vittoria in Webster's *White Devil* too. Both plays celebrated two hundred years since Webster's first performance in the Americas up here in Halifax,' explained Mon, teacher-like in not wishing to leave information undelivered to the young. 'Anyway, I know this sounds completely crazy, but Sir Alan and the other guys think that Tom Althorne will be softened by seeing the old play again and you in it, and will relent about the use of his land.'

'But.....'

'In know, Jem. It's probably a stupid idea, but Sir Alan's dragged us up here for this one thing and I thought that if you felt you could play ball....'

'Oh, Sir, I don't know. I – I just don't know. Am I *that* convincing?'

'Of late, Jem, you have *been* Julia. I don't know how, but you've convinced everyone.'

Jem flushed, hugging the secret of being able to be Julia, particularly with Bosola.

'But afterwards? Actually *talking* to him, Celia's husband? Surely when he sees me up close, he'll see that I'm not a girl?'

'I don't think he'll twig, in a dim light. You're modest, Jem, which is nice, but you've no idea how beautiful you look in make-up. You have such a very lovely face to start with.' (Here Mon stopped abruptly, realising that Jem was staring at him.) 'Look, you keep your glad rags on,' he resumed, 'while the others are getting changed. Miss Carrbridge will tart up your lipstick, eye shadow, mascara, etcetera, before you meet him. We'll keep it dark and brief, but don't say too much. Use the Julia voice and behave in a shy way. The less you speak, the better. Now – don't you think you could do it?'

Jem's brow was still wrinkled. Somehow he felt he was being asked to do something wrong and unfair.

He picked up the photograph again and angled it into the light. He found it hard to judge ages in adults, but he thought Celia Althorne looked about Miss Carrbridge's age – miles younger than her husband. The habit of obedience was strong in Jem. Just as he had smoked Rick's joint when told to, and had popped the popper; just as he had first agreed to be Julia at Mon's insistence, so he felt he could not refuse to pretend to be a young woman for this red-faced, heavily built widower. But to do such a thing! Surely Mr Howard was wrong to ask him to practise such a deception? Wouldn't it be more likely to bring back pain and grief than to soften Mr Althorne's heart? Jem knew nothing about death, but he felt the loss of his father. How would he feel if a man looking like his dad walked into the compartment? Then he thought it was stupid to make that comparison because, of course, it *might* be his father, whereas Celia could hardly be brought back from the dead. Would Mr Althorne feel that Jem was making fun of his sadness? Wouldn't he know that old Sir Alan had come to New York to see *The Duchess?* Perhaps he didn't know and it would be all right. Yet it was the element of cold planning that unsettled Jem's conscience.

He tried to put some of these misgivings into words. Mon, having his own doubts, was sympathetic and agreed it was all rather a gamble.

'But worth a shot, Jem, don't you think? I mean, if it brings the guys up here back together, and if you're not too put out by doing it?'

'I'm not thinking of me, Sir,' said Jem austerely. But even as he said it, he knew he was thinking of himself. There was more than enough of a child left in Jem to feel that he was being asked to do a thing that a schoolboy shouldn't be asked to do – and he couldn't help resenting Mr Howard for jockeying him into that position. Jem sought for a compromise, while Mon watched his face.

'Couldn't I just avoid having to *meet* Mr Althorne after the play, Sir? I don't mind being Julia on stage as normal. It's the bit afterwards I don't feel happy about. It doesn't seem a – a – *good* thing to do. Suppose it makes him unhappy?'

Mon took in the wrinkle of anxious thought on Jem's forehead, the doubtful shyness of his eyes behind those saintly spectacles, the youthful curves of his face in the shaded glow of the compartment's light.

I'll never love anyone again as I love this boy, thought Mon. You're no saint, Jem, went on Mon's interior voice, not about certain things, I'm sure of that – but you're on the side of the saints.

'It *is* a shitty thing to do, isn't it?' he said, surprising Jem by his choice of adjective. 'And you're quite, quite right. I'll tell these jokers so. No meetings with Tom Althorne. Just the play – just good old beautiful Julia one last time. I'm sorry I even considered the other idea.'

'Oh thanks, Sir! Thanks very much! I'll do my best to keep Julia one hundred per cent feminine for one last time.'

All resentment gone, Jem beamed at Mon with a return of the fresh, open trust which Mon hadn't glimpsed since he and Jem had motored together in the Morgan up to Stacey's.

'And not a word to the others,' added Mon.

It was the moment for Jem to go back to his sleeping-car. Their interview was over.

Mon knew that this was it; on no further occasion would Jem be so naturally in a bedroom with him. The priapic madness which had possessed him for so long seemed to roar to a surface just below their feet – as if a shark were about to tear through the car floor under their foot-soles.

Like a hyper-realist painting of a youth, Jem was – in all parts – all in focus at once. Mon could almost taste the softness of his eyelids, sense the tickle of his wave of hair. He saw, in a comprehending sweep, the tiny, chromed screws that held Jem's glasses together, a thread on the button of his shirt, the veins on his bare neck and on his wrists, the tight stitching on the creases of his jeans. Up, down, across, all in focus at once, was everything on Earth that Mon desired. He could hear his own breathing, and he could feel his hand rising up to take Jem's face and cup its cheek and jaw. That was how he was going to do it – to bring those lips, with their aching curves, towards his own with a compelling grip.

He reached out a finger and touched Jem's mouth. It was such a soft touch Jem didn't move. Even the twinkle of the tiny screws of his glasses was still.

Mon felt electrocuted, sick, in pain – and a long,

long time seemed to hang between them: between the man who had travelled over forty years to unite in cauterising love with – with...... and – and.........

'Do you need me for anything else, Sir?' asked Jem, his innocent lips moving silently against the roaring in Mon's ears. He had thought that Mon had put a finger to his lips as a sign that no one else should be told about Tom and Celia. Already his own thoughts were careering forward to his own berth and the naked pleasure that he and Rick had promised each other that night.

Mon shook his head, and Jem left the compartment.

During the night, all that was sensible, rational, honourable, clear-headed and good in Mon rose to the surface. He resolutely pushed all his fervid pictures of Jem clothed, Jem naked, Jem as Julia, to the deserts of his brain and confronted the violent demons of his infatuation with a resolution born out of a renewed sense of what could and could not be done.

Of *course* Jem could not act out a sick pantomime after the play with Tom Althorne; of *course* Mon could not have Jem as a partner in love. Certain things *were not, could not*, be done.

Mon had constructed his own darkness – at first out of little splinters of wood: a glance here, a catching of the eye there – then from great, thick-limbed timbers, until he was in solitary confinement behind his own fortress wall. What he had laboured to build, he could labour to unpick, in the same lonely silence wherein he had first worshipped.

That night Mon became the sixth person to have a change in life direction in the sleeping-cars of Trevanaunce. He decided to go back to the religious life and try again. I'll resign in October, he thought. I'll leave St Matthew's at Christmas. I'll get into a monastery, not as a priest, of course, with an estranged wife, but as a simple lay brother. I should go where I won't be tempted, won't be tortured. I'll try and make it work again and do what good I can.

Instead of lying with lascivious, hopeless fantasies burning his mind, Mon prayed for the best for all that he loved: his colleagues, his pupils, the church, the boy.

By the end of the night he found, to his surprise, that he was happier than he had been for months.

August: GHOSTS

The cast had rehearsed on their new set for the last time and were having an early supper before the play began. The new summer festival director of the foundation, Josie Innis, had informed them that the take-up of tickets had been most encouraging and that there were barely a handful of seats unoccupied. The draw of students from New York had been a factor.

'Mai deah,' she had cooed at Mon, 'Half of them could go on to dwama school and no questions asked. When Edward told me a school play was coming, I thought, Oh, phooey, and nearly emigwated. Keep my name *orf* the pwogwamme, sweets, I said to him, wight, *wight* orf. But now I just want *all* the cwedit!'

'You don't know how near I came to excising *my* name from the programme back at St Mat's,' retorted Mon, twinkling at Josie, whom he liked a great deal.

Greg, Aisha, Rosa, Jem, Liam and Co. were very nervous, excited in a different way from the performances at school. Something about their treatment at Trevanaunce made them feel like visiting celebs and they determined to show the backwoods folk of Nova Scotia a thing or two.

It was a shock to step from the hot dry sunshine into the velvet black of the theatre. Narrower than the auditorium at St Matthew's, it was purpose-built: a sealed, windowless box with a conventional

proscenium and galleries of tiered seating. Right at
the top was the lighting cubicle with the faces of
Jonathan, Mark and David behind the panel.

'Oh God! I wish it was over!' said Joey. 'I just
know I'm going to screw up tonight.'

'Just do as we've rehearsed,' said Mon quietly,
coming up behind. 'Stay coooool, man,' he intoned,
in an exaggerated West Coast drawl. The cast
grinned. Good old Howard.

Louise had gone up to the control room. Her hand
rested on David's shoulder. She smiled contentedly at
her little group of men: David with his broad,
protective back and exact fingers resting on the
recorder's buttons, the chestnut-shiny boys' heads
wagging as Jonathan and Mark perched at their
sliders, making wry jokes and predicting imminent
electronic disaster.

Sir Alan Clemmy came whisking backstage.

'Break a leg, everyone,' he clicked. 'Stop 'em
dead.' To Jem he said nothing special but squeezed
the boy's arm. 'Tom's out there in the second row, at
the centre gangway,' he whispered to Mon.

'You weren't sure if he'd turn up?' asked Mon.

'Roger said he wouldn't. I wasn't so sure. It's been
a couple of years, but he *is* a patron of this place. Also
I suppose he's curious to see the play again.'

'I hope it doesn't prove a mistake, stirring up
memories better left undisturbed.'

'An absolute gamble, I grant you, old man. But if

he enjoys the kids' performance and is intrigued by young Clarke, it might just do the trick. *Faint heart never won....*'

'*....fair lady,*' finished Mon. 'Yes, quite, Let's hope you're right.'

Sir Alan twinkled off down the passage and into the theatre. Mon was left with his pupils.

'*May The Force Be With You,*' he intoned solemnly. 'Enjoy yourselves.' Suddenly – idiotically – he felt that they should say a short prayer. Then the moment passed; Mon disliked cheapening God's help by invoking it for trivial things.

The faces round him, lovely in their youth and make-up, touched many strings. Ah, the children of *The Duchess of Malfi* – my last play; they'll flit from me, but I shall remember them.

He gazed fondly at his charges, then seemed to crispen up, to be the familiar Mon Howard. He winked at Aisha, patted Liam on the head, touched Greg's and Rosa's arms, gripped Jem's elbow, smiled a comradely smile at Rick and went into the wing to sit, as ever, near his prompter, Pharhad. As he passed Jan he whispered,

'Give 'em plenty of eerie mist tonight, big boy.'

Jan, who had fitted two unused canisters to his machines, gave the thumbs up.

A roar of music came from the PA, house lights dimmed and *The Duchess* went into its last ever performance.

'I say,' came Sir Alan's clipped voice. He had left his seat at the end of the first row and had made his way round to the wing. 'I say, I thought I'd just slip out and tell you that Tom seems to be enjoying it so far. No worries.'

'He hasn't seen Julia yet.'

'True. Anyway, come and meet him in the interval.'

Sir Alan flitted away again and on stage the Cardinal and Julia disposed themselves in black-out in the wing, ready for Act II, scene 4. Jem's nerves were jumping, as he stood waiting for his entrance. He felt terribly tired. During the afternoon, in a break in rehearsal, he and Rick had slipped into the woods above the school to have sex. Jem had been dressed as Julia, and, partly stripping out of costume, but leaving Julia's wig, stockings and bra in place, had then knelt, sitting back on his heels with legs apart, on the forest floor in front of Rick. Rick had removed his top, but simply pulled his leather trousers to his ankles and left his boots on, and this part nakedness in the open air and sunlight had brought them both to a frenzy of arousal. Nor had they slept much the previous night, although their surrenders to pleasure had been wonderful. The promised intimacy of *soixante-neuf* had featured, and then frantic stimulation with a Polaroid camera, with which they had taken shots of each other in different poses.

Mon touched Jem encouragingly on the shoulder.

The black fur coat felt, to Mon's fingers, sumptuous but vulnerable; Jem frail and diminished inside it.

Even as he took those first hard, heel-clicking steps down the slope of the stage on the arm of the Cardinal, he heard gasps from several places ahead of him in the dark beyond the lights. He forced his brain to concentrate on the script, but it wavered dangerously between his nerves – still zinging from the recent discoveries he had made with Rick in the sleeping-car: those exhausting two nights of experiments in the orangey light, the stifled cries and astonished, unbelieving sensations of mouth, muscles and skin – and his intellect: disapproving of the deliberate bringing back to life one of the dead.

As he came to a halt in the concentrated glare, and the Cardinal asked him *'What trick did you invent to come to Rome without your husband?'* no reply came from the open red bow of his mouth. The dark shadows under his eyes gave intensity to his unwinking stare. He thought he heard a sound more like a sob than a sigh. His red-painted nails fluttered to his bosom. He felt the tightness of the dress against his legs, except where the slit let their curves break out. The fur coat enwrapped him in its pelt-scent. The tension in and beyond him in the theatre grew and grew.

Before Pharhad could spoil the moment with a prompt, Jem heard his voice – voluptuous, husky, slightly hysterical and unmistakably feminine –

saying: *Why, my lord, I told him I came to visit an old anchorite for devotion.* And the Cardinal took Julia's hand and, kissing it, smilingly chuckled: *You are a witty, false one!* After that the scene whizzed on its accustomed way.

At the interval good manners supervened, and Tom Althorne suffered himself to be led quietly away by Sir Alan and Edward to the summer school, where drinks were to be served. But once out of earshot of the public, he burst out with,

'How DARE you ask me to this!'

Sir Alan and Edward exchanged glances.

'Tom, old lad....,' Sir Alan began.

'Did you think I'd be pleased by it, for Christ's sake?' shouted Tom. 'I don't know why you did it, but I'm going to find out how!'

'But, Tom, we thought.....'

'Fuck what you thought! Fuck it! Fuck the lot of you!'

Spittle edged Tom's mouth with angry bubbles.

It was most uncomfortable for Mon, David and Louise, who had put their heads round the door, Josie Innis having shepherded them along to meet the red-faced patron.

'I guess I'm sorry if we're barging in,' murmured Mon.

'Not at all. Not at all,' gasped Sir Alan, clearly relieved to see them. 'Please, please, do come in. I want to introduce you to Tom Althorne. Tom, these are the producers of the play from St Matthew's, New York, and they are acquainted with the story of Celia's death.'

Louise came up and shook Mr Althorne's hand. Once again, manners preserved equilibrium and the angry widower calmed himself to greet the three producers.

'A – a very well-acted show,' he muttered. 'Congratulate your cast.'

'Tom was surprised by your Julia,' put in Sir Alan.

'I don't mind telling you that I was *more* than surprised. I was telling Alan here that I was damned angry when she first appeared. You heard the gasps of astonishment in the theatre. Everyone was thinking what I was thinking. I can't understand, if you *knew* about the resemblance between your girl and my poor Celia, why you invited me. And as for you, Alan, you must have damned well known how I would feel, sitting there....'

'It was an unfortunate coincidence,' put in Mon, catching Sir Alan's and Edward's eyes, 'We were thunderstruck by the resemblance of your late wife to our – our Cleo, but we've only been here two days and it would have been impossible to make changes.'

'So *you* didn't know about this, Alan?'

'Only from Wednesday, of course. But actually I thought the resemblance purely superficial.'

'Nonsense!' snorted Tom.

'I can only apologise and repeat that we couldn't

do a thing about it that wouldn't ruin the play,' said Mon.

'I'm not blaming you, of course,' rumbled Tom. 'It's not your fault, obviously, but it gave me a hell of a jolt out there. Did these fellows tell you that my poor wife actually played Julia in the same play?'

There was a pause.

Mon thought he caught the tiniest oscillation of Sir Alan's head.

'My God! No! Of course not. We – we knew of her tragic accident and her resemblance to Cleo Jakemar, but, no, I guess I'm amazed by that coincidence.'

'To think she had been in the same part!' cried Louise, catching on. 'Astonishing! What a freak of fate.'

'Extraordinary,' put in David gamely.

'No wonder….,' added Louise, although she had no idea what she might add to that expression.

Mon felt that they had not coped very well so far. He strove to minimise things further.

'So you were shirty, I guess, at being asked along to this. You, um, felt it was a little insensitive, all things considered?'

'A little! Hellish insensitive is what I was saying when you came in. Are you a Canadian?' he added, changing tack and seeming to regard Mon for the first time.

'Yes, by birth and in childhood. Sharp of you to detect it. I've lived in the US for many years.'

There was a pause.

'Well, let's have a drink, anyway,' suggested Edward, lifting a bottle of wine.

'Make mine a whisky. I need it after what you jokers have done,' grunted Tom.

Mon, Sir Alan, David and Louise caught each other's glances yet again. It seemed that the patron and landowner was calming down. They watched him sidelong as he gulped three large whiskies, clutching the bottle that Sir Alan had found in the summer school common room entertainment cupboard.

After the interval, Edward and Sir Alan observed him narrowly from their seats as, bottle and glass in his lap, Tom took nip after nip, with unwinking eyes on Julia whenever she appeared.

At the end of the performance, with perspiration pouring from them, the company took their last bow. Tom Althorne stood up, came forward unsteadily to the stage edge and, clapping loudly, looked up at Jem. He took in the fine legs, the sheen of the dress, the sumptuous fur, the perfect complexion under its tumbling wig.

'Bravo! Bravo!' he cried and, to Jem's horror, reached up, obviously to bring Julia forward. He flipped his fingers, but Jem, missing a bow with the rest of the cast, stood still in confusion, looking, to Tom, more like the dead Celia than ever. 'Miss Jakemar! Come forward!' he boomed.

Mon heard the boom and realised that someone

should intervene but felt he couldn't himself appear on stage from the wing. It would look too much as if he intended to make a speech. He hoped the cast would lead off, but all were peering down at Tom.

Sir Alan left his seat, came up behind Tom and grabbed his elbow.

'Leave it now, Tom. You can see she's confused.'

Tom wrenched his arm away.

'She should take a bow on her own; the other main parts have,' he said. 'She was wonderful. You were wonderful, Miss Jakemar!'

The audience clapping was continuing, but a confused note was creeping into it and Mon knew from experience that it was about to die. The cast, thrown by Tom Althorne's irruption, had to be got off right now. Mon sidled to the edge of the wing.

'Greg!' he hissed. 'Greg! Lead them OFF! Off now! Take Rosa's hand and lead her off!'

Greg, quick on the uptake, nodded. He reached for Rosa's arm, caught Joey's eye across the stage, then Tony's and Aisha's. He pulled Rosa into the wing.

'Hey, whatya doing?' she snapped. 'We've got another bow.'

'No, you haven't. Everybody off,' said Mon grimly. One by one the actors left the stage. Seeing them go, David signalled Jonathan and Mark to begin fading. He had a vague feeling that he'd missed a beat somewhere, but dispersal was the cue for the start of a slow dropping of the lights.

'Tape on,' he muttered. 'Slow fade, guys. Wait 'til the last man's out for total black-out.'

Music warbled, the lanterns dimmed, and Jem, aware that he and Rick were the last to leave, took a final curtsey – he remembered to do this – and they left the set together. Immediately David hissed, 'House lights' and the clapping stopped and the audience stood up, chattering. Tom was left in the aisle looking at the set with Sir Alan by his side.

'Silly lil' girl,' muttered Tom. 'Did you see that, Alan? She got shy. What a lil' darling! And God, Alan, so like poor Celia! I thought once or twice that I was losing my fucking mind, you know. Her voice is deeper, huskier than Cee's, but what a lovely voice – lovelier than Cee's really. You remember her lisp?'

Tom was excited, enthusiastic, mellowed by drink. Perhaps, thought Sir Alan, the plan has worked. We're talking like friends again.

'Come and have another drink with Howard, Lomax and Miss Carrbridge,' he said.

'Screw them,' grunted Tom stoutly. 'I want to meet Miss Cleo Jakemar, of course.'

'Oh, well, Tom, she's only a student. I'd give it a miss. She – she's pretty ordinary off stage.'

'Don't be stupid, Alan. You think I don' want to meet Celia's double? C'mon, man, let's get round back-stage.' Wasting no more words, Tom blundered off, his movements made clumsy by the near whole bottle of whisky he had drunk.

Mon was among his charges, aware that Tom was not far behind.

'Jem! Jem. Don't change yet. I fear that what you didn't want to happen is going to happen. Now, leave all the talking to me.' Jem, thoroughly startled, bundled back into the hot fur coat. Louise appeared between them. 'Quick, take Jem into the ladies' room, Louise, and do something about his make-up. Just touch it up and make sure he looks one hundred per cent female.'

Louise pushed Jem into the ladies' washroom.

'I – I can't meet that man,' cried Jem, feeling almost close to tears. 'Not in real life. I told Mr Howard. I….'

'Sit down, Jem,' said Louise gently. 'And let's do first things first. Let me just check your complexion and, Jem, pull up your left stocking – it's sagging.'

Jem bent down to twitch up his hosiery and he realised, suddenly, that he was in a ladies' washroom with Miss Carrbridge. He saw his own face in the hard light. It was a young woman's face. He stared at his red lips as if they were someone else's.

'Oh, Miss Carrbridge, I can't….'

'Just sit quietly for a second, Jem dear,' said Louise. 'He can't come in here, can he?'

She put her hand on his shoulder and he was comforted.

The cast had gone through to the summer school's cafeteria for a post-performance party. The theatre was empty. Sir Alan, Tom Althorne and Mon were left at the doorway leading to the stage-rear area.

'Where *ish* she?' slurred Tom's loud voice, reaching Jem and Louise in the washroom back-stage. 'I wanner meet her. Has she gone to the party?'

'I expect so. Let's go and see,' said Sir Alan.

'I didn't notice her going past. I saw the others go past. I didn't see her go. Don't pull at my arm, Alan, you old bastard. Don' pull at it, for Christ's sake.'

Mon and Sir Alan looked at each other over Tom's head. Surely he wasn't going to make a scene?

'Well, I'm going over to the cafeteria,' said Sir Alan crisply. 'Come on, Howard. If you don't want to meet the cast, Tom, you don't.'

He whisked away to the door in the foyer. Tom, undecided, called out,

'Hey! A'right, man! Wait for me!' and lumbered after him.

Mon went quietly along to the washroom and opened the door.

'Well done, Jem. You can come out now. Let things settle a bit. You look absolutely convincing, if the worst happens and you have to meet him.'

'Mon, Jem really doesn't want to see him, and I must say…..'

'I know you don't, Jem,' said Mon, interrupting Louise, 'but I haven't thought of an explanation why you can't, yet. If you had to have just a word, as Julia, in the car-park, say, and in the dark, just to shut him up as he's leaving, do you think….?'

Jem, reassured by the presence of his teachers, nodded.

'I can manage a few seconds,' he said.

Crash!

The heavy swing-door between the auditorium and the back-stage area was shoved right back against the wall. Jem, Louise and Mon jumped, spinning round.

Tom Althorne had not, as it happened, followed Sir Alan into the school, but had blundered back into the theatre. His eye immediately fastened on Jem.

'Why, *there* she is!' he cried. 'I *thought* she hadn't got past us.' He came forward beaming, his forehead shiny under the passage bulbs. 'My *dear* young lady,' he began, taking Jem's hand and holding it, 'I wanted to congratulate you on your short but wunnerful performance.' He smiled into Jem's face. 'Ah, so thassa wig, is it?' he continued. 'I wondered if a modern girl would natcherlie have such tumbling locks. It's a bit 'sixties now, isn't it? Miss Carr-wotsit, couldn't I take this young lady, after the cast party, to look at some photographs? Of a woman I loved who played Julia once, y'know' he added, smiling fully and closely into Jem's face. 'I think you may be innerested in the sad lil' story I can tell you about a girl *so* ve'y, ve'y like you who p-played Julia once, long, uurgh, long ago.'

Under the stimulus of his words, he couldn't help a little sob catching his voice at the end of the sentence.

In his befuddled state, they seemed to him the most beautiful words he had ever uttered.

Jem, knowing the story, could think of nothing to say. It seemed safest to smile mysteriously, which he did.

'Your smile is so familiar to me,' murmured Tom, taking Jem's hand again. To Jem's confusion, Tom began raising it to his lips. Mon intervened.

'Right, Let Cleo here change, Mr Althorne. She's the last one in costume and we want to pack everything up.' By now, Mon realised that, through whatever agency, he *must* get Jem away from the building. It was clear to him that Jem, without Julia's lines to sustain him, was not going to be able to cope with close scrutiny. So: get Jem away safely to the sleeping-cars on the pretext of changing, and then find the excuse for Cleo's complete disappearance.

'Oh, no. No, no, no. Do' go an' change yet. Spoil everything. Stay as Julia a little longer. You'll disappoint me if you go off an' come back in Doc Martens an' jeans. That's such a beau'ful dress. Here, lemme escort you, Miss Jakemar. Take my arm.'

Jem, as if in a dream, put his hand through Tom's burly elbow and allowed himself to be walked out into the foyer. Mon and Louise hurried behind, like scampering, undignified bridesmaids.

The big man kept up an affectionate pressure on Jem, whose high heels struggled to balance the lumbering strides. Alcoholic breath fanned his face.

Tom's eyes twisted into his, solicitously rough and – perhaps unintentionally – leering.

'Wish you'd be my guest,' he muttered. 'At my house, y'see. Old enough to be your pop, I know – but you'd gi' me great pleasure if you'd come an' stay…. Why stuff it in a sleeping-car? I'd like to show you Celia's house…..Celia's shrine….. Interest you because you're so, so….' The grunting monologue accompanied the weighty footsteps until they were out in the carpark. Mon pulled Louise close to him.

'Go into the school and ask Sir Alan if we can use that little room near the common-room – where we first heard about Celia,' he whispered. 'We can't risk someone in the cast giving Jem away. They don't know about this, remember.'

'Okay, Mon. Keep it all low-key, you mean?'

'Yes. And, Louise, dimly light. Tell him that.'

A dark blue Cadillac sedan was parked near the theatre entrance. While Mon was whispering to Louise, Tom had swung open its door and made to hand Jem into it. Not sure what the plan was, and losing eye contact with Mon, Jem had confusedly sat upon the squab, his legs drawn up, his high-heels on the sill.

'Wai' there, Miss Jakemar. I wanna explain to Howard. He'll tell them. Who wants to go to a party? Howard! Hey, look, I'm….' Tom clambered into the driver's seat, started the engine, and let the window down. The steering-wheel rested on his big stomach. 'Howard,' he called. 'Thank Alan for me. I'm going home now. Miss Jakemar is – is desirous of seeing Celia's shrine.'

Desirous? Shrine? Mon came up behind the car quickly. What's he talking about?

The Cadillac began to move. Jem had left it too late to get out. The door closed on him as the car jerked away. Mon realised that his pupil was being borne away into the night in an auto driven by a man very much the worse for drink.

'Sir! Mr Althorne! Please! I don't want to....! Please stop the car. Look, stop!' cried Jem in real alarm. He had abandoned Julia's light, breathy tones and had spoken in his own voice – youthfully male. Tom didn't seem to have noticed. Breathing heavily, he fumbled the car's lights on.

Jem wrenched the door open and put one leg partly out. He didn't dare to jump yet as the car was now jerking fast round the complex towards the Lunenberg road. He shouted twice, feeling slightly foolish, as if he were in a movie,

'Help! Help!'

Tom's right hand fell on his thigh and wrenched his leg back. The door clicked partly shut again as they took a corner at speed.

Sir Alan, who had come out after getting Louise's message, joined Mon, who was gazing bemusedly after the Cadillac. Behind them, drawn more by a sixth sense that a drama was in progress than by the shouts they had heard, several of the cast appeared from the building.

'What's up?'

'What's happened?'

'It's Jem!'

'That guy's got Jem!'

'There – in that car!'

'God, he's putting it on, isn't he?'

'Jem!' cried Rick.

'You, boy,' snapped Sir Alan, gripping Rick's shoulder, 'cut across the tracks – over there – and get to the level crossing gates. Pull them across. Get the pins out. Go ON! He's got to drive round the engine sheds and get over the cattle grid. You'll get there first!'

Grasping at once what he had to do, Rick streaked across the dim yard towards the gates, which were about a hundred yards beyond the end of the sleeping-cars. He stumbled and fell to one knee agonisingly, but bounced up, bleeding, and ran on. Mon, Sir Alan and David set off after him.

Rick dashed past the inspection trolley and reached the level-crossing gate just before the Cadillac slewed into sight. He ripped the retaining chain's pin from its socket and began heaving the gate across the tarmac. The Cadillac clattered over the cattle-grid and headed for Rick. Its headlights were on full beam. Rick, blinded, pushed harder, then, conscious that Jem was a passenger in the car, hesitated and let the gate swing back on him a little. He feared he might cause a fatal pile-up if the heavy beams completely obstructed the car's progress. Its left wing caught the gate a heavy blow. Rick was thrown to the ground. Jem was jerked forward and sideways across Tom's lap. The car ran onto the railroad track, barging the inspection trolley with its right flank. Tom shouted,

'Fuck it! Fuck it! Fuck it!'

Jem clawed again at the door, but this time it wouldn't open. Tom swung off the ballast and back onto tarmac. With lights cutting into his retinas, Rick did not perceive the inspection trolley's braking-lever drop, the retaining bracket having sheared off on impact, and the shoes slacken their grip on the wheels. He couldn't see that it was trundling down the gentle slope in the dark, but lay, his senses spinning, with his right leg across the track.

The damaged Cadillac roared off into the night.

The weighty trolley rolled lazily (almost imperceptibly to Mon, David and Sir Alan as they raced up) over Rick's lower right calf, its first wheel crushing the bone and muscle, causing his shattered leg to contract, so that the second wheel partially severed his right foot.

382

August: HER SHRINE

It was not much more than an hour later, but the world had changed for those at the Trevanaunce summer school.

An ambulance had run over from Lunenberg, Rick's unconscious form had been transferred from the life-saving skills of David Lomax to those of paramedics. 'Darned good tourniquet, friend. Needed strength to get it that tight.'

Rick's father was to take the morning flight to Halifax and had already threatened an action in law.

The shocked cast of *The Duchess* were huddled in corners of their sleeping-cars or out on the track being comforted by Louise and Aisha.

Mon and David were in Sir Alan's car, heading north towards Tom Althorne's house.

When the Cadillac had bounced back onto the tarmac and speeded out into the road, Jem had completely lost his composure. He had clenched his fists and rained blows on the red-faced man as they bucketed onwards.

'Stop it! Stop it, you silly girl!' Tom had yelled, using one hand to drive and the other to capture one of Jem's flailing arms. 'I'm not going to harm you, for Chris' sake! Calm down!'

'Stop! Stop the car!' screamed Jem. He had seen Rick hurled back by the level-crossing gate. So great was the pain of witnessing that, it was as if his own body had lain crumpled. He knew instinctively that Rick had been injured. He had not yet had time to worry about himself; that was only now surfacing on the turbulent waters of his mind – like the awful bursting of magma to the ocean's surface. This old man was insane; was dangerous, a destroyer. Jem cursed and shrieked, thudding blows onto the fat arms and chest. Tom was podgy, but he was strong, and he had to be. His arm only just held Jem back in his seat.

'You little fool! Stop struggling! Do you want to kill us both?' he gasped. He was amazed by the physical strength of this lovely girl and intrigued by the firm leg muscles and hard arms he had felt. He knew he was very drunk, that he had done a stupid thing, that he had damaged his car, that he had frightened this extraordinary Celia lookalike. Of what had befallen Rick, he knew nothing. But he wasn't going to stop now. As a sort of talisman, Celia's shrine kept insinuating itself between his eyes and the glowing dashboard dials. If he could just get *there* – get home – and show this wonderful Cleo Jakemar his *memento mori*, the compilation of souvenirs of his dead wife, well, everything would be all right. Why shouldn't he put this Cleo up for the night, in the lavender-coloured spare room? Why shouldn't he have the honour of showing this remarkable girl how like his own wife she was? Dimly he remembered an occasion after a New Year's ball when Celia had fought and cursed him in a car – just like this. Jem's fury was almost a return to his fiery marriage. God, I'm not far from the airport, he thought. Have her there in time to catch the New York flight. And now it was all being spoilt. Those bastards have done it again! Why had someone tried to close the gate? Why had Cleo started to scream in panic? What is *wrong* with everyone?

The disaster that had overtaken his cast had shaken Mon deeply. The teacher in charge, under whose supervision one pupil had sustained dreadful, life-changing injuries, and another had been kidnapped! What could be said? And be done?

Now, with nausea catching at his throat, Mon watched the trees chicane past Sir Alan's car.

'I hope he's all right!' cried Mon. 'Put it on!'

'I'm going as fast as I dare,' retorted Sir Alan. 'Don't worry. I know where he's going. Only a few miles now.'

In a long stretch of Scotch firs, the car slowed. 'It's just off this bit,' said Sir Alan. Bright gates leapt out of the dark and David clung on in the back as the car swung through them. 'The old railroad line should run on just up here. We go over it on a bridge, down the hill, and then we're at Tom's house.'

He stopped outside a dark building and switched off. The low glow from the tiny township behind them barely irradiated the base of the void. Sir Alan opened his door. 'Follow me,' he mouthed. Mon and David emerged, taking in the unmistakeable table of a railroad embankment some distance away, not high, but solid and man-made, running down from the north. David tapped Sir Alan's shoulder.

'Is that the track from Lunenberg?' he whispered.

'That's it. The house is dark.'

'It doesn't look as if anyone's here,' said Mon. 'And there's no sign of the car.'

'Can you see a light?'

'No.'

'Are you sure he brought Jem here?'

'Where else? This is where he lives.'

'They couldn't be sitting with the lights off.'

'It's a big house. Perhaps they're at the back.'

'Does he live alone?'

'Tom? Yes. Who'd live with him, poor bastard? People come in to look after him, and there's the estate workers, but they wouldn't be here now after midnight.'

'Shall we just knock?'

'What? Bang on the door?'

'Why not? And why are we whispering? Either they're here, which we want, or they're not. So, let's bang.'

They pounded with a hinged iron dolphin on the heavy panels.

Jem felt as if he had passed from hopelessly

ignorant childhood to an adult weariness too
burdensome to be borne – all within a couple of
weeks. Two Fridays back had seen the last of his
triumphs as Julia at St Matthew's, his strange, drink-
fuelled, drug-hazed love-making in Greg's garden;
the intervening days had drawn him into his bizarre
role as a dead girl's double, had opened his flesh and
his mind in the sleeping-car to intimacies only
fantasised about, had cemented his long-suppressed
conviction that he was gay, had seen him fall
desperately in love, and know that he was loved in
return, had featured a further dramatic coup as Julia,
and now had plunged him into a dangerous journey in
a foreign country with a drunken madman.

Somewhere, in the shadow of these adventures,
was Jeremy Clarke of 172nd St, possessor of an unsold
chopper bicycle, brother of Betsy, schoolboy enquirer
into tectonic plates, the gospels, the Restoration, and
the poetry of Keats, and not seventeen for another ten
days. But that ancestor individual had surely become
lost – as distant as Neanderthal man.

He lay on a hard stone shelf in a locked building.
Velvet black sprigged his vision with tiny meteors.
Julia's wig tickled his cheeks, Julia's dress felt
insubstantial, so that he wished he had trousers on,
and Julia's fur coat was across his chest like a
blanket.

Nothing was audible except grunts from the floor.

There, he knew, Tom Althorne dozed with laboured, drunken breathing. Jem had gingerly felt his way round the small chamber and his fingers had closed upon a handle. He depressed it, but there was no movement.

When the Cadillac had shot through gates on a tree-lined road, had climbed a track and stopped before a slab of embankment which blocked out the lower part of the sky, Tom had fumbled the engine off, had gripped Jem's wrist and had sat breathing heavily and deliberately. Jem had not dared to speak. He remembered that he had shouted in his own voice earlier.

'Celia.....I mean...,' Tom had muttered, 'I – I wanted you to.... That is, after I saw you tonight, I – I wanted to get away, get you away from all those....all those....' He had stopped and turned to Jem in the car. Jem could see nothing but his glittering eyes. 'You're not Celia, of course,' Tom had said, and then, which seemed horrible to Jem, he had added in a bewildered, pleading voice, 'Are you?' Jem had mutely shaken his head. Tom had sighed. 'She was good to me. Good *for* me. I am....was....much older. That makes a difference. She didn't love me as much as I ....' He had stopped and transferred his grasp to Jem's left hand. 'It's been a long time since she died. People think I – I should have got over it. You unnerstand, don't you? When....when I saw you....'

Jem had nodded again, and had managed to whisper,

'Yes. I understand.'

Suddenly he had been unable to stop shivering. A tremor had run from his ankles to the wig, and his teeth had clattered together.

'You're cold,' Tom had murmured. 'I'm sorry. Let me show you the shrine I made for her.'

He had put his arm across Jem's shoulder in order the draw the fur coat round him more snugly. 'Come, come. Up you get, you poor dear. I shouldn't have…. Just adjusting your coat. Come in for a moment. See her portrait. Then I'll take you back….back to….'

Jem had found the big man's arm propelling him into the dim box between the car and the end of the embankment, or whatever it was. Tom had jammed the key into the lock (it was on the same ring as his car keys) and had pushed open the metal door. He'd clicked a switch and the shrine had been dimly lit by a bulb above their heads. 'Oh, it's not very bright. The battery needs changing….' Tom had murmured. The light had grown feebler as Jem had looked at it.

They were in a simple stone oblong. The door was on one side, a small metal-grilled window faced the door, and on another side was a stone bench. Opposite the bench was a large portrait of Celia, executed in oils, and under this an altar-like table with dried flowers and pieces of jewellery on it.

'I often come here – just to think,' sighed Tom.

Jem had stood gazing at his likeness. The atmosphere was dank, and the night air coming in was cool. He had fallen to shivering violently again.

'There's a breeze. I'll just….,' Tom had said, and had pushed the metal door with his foot. There had been a solid, oily clunk. About to ask Tom a question about the painting, the thud unscrambled itself in Jem's mind. He had made a swift step to the door, depressed its handle and had discovered it wouldn't open.

'What – what have you locked it for?' he quavered, rattling the handle up and down.

'Huh?' Tom had grunted, pushing his hands through his tough, greying hair.

'The door!'

Tom had shrugged and patted his jacket pocket. An extraordinary expression came into his face.

'Oh, God!' he had gurgled, a momentary soberness penetrating the whisky-fog. He'd turned to Jem with a face almost comically agitated. 'You heard that clunk?' He had started fumbling in each of his pockets. 'Oh no! I haven't got them.'

'Got what?'

'My keys. They're still outside – in the lock. That door…. It's a simple sprung latch. It needs a key to get in and out. The door came from the wine cellar in the house.' Jem had goggled at him as his meaning penetrated. 'I always have the key…. I mean I keep the key on my car key ring, but I've left it on the other side.'

Jem heard a rhythmic pulsing, and realised it was his own panicky breath.

'Did you hear what I said? I've left the damned key in the lock outside. I've never done that before!'

Jem had found his voice – shrill with terror and exhaustion.

'You mean we're locked in! What are you going to DO?'

The ceiling light gave a flicker and then became even more feeble.

Tom had stared at him.

'I don' know. At this time of night…. I need time to…. They'll find us in the morning. Garland'll see the car. Look, I need time with you, Celia…. I mean….'

A choking panic, unlike anything he had ever felt, mastered Jem. He noted the fact that his heart had leaped, stopped and re-started again. Locked in! He had moved one way, then the other, the long dress swishing. The fur coat slipped from his shoulders to the floor. He had two coherent thoughts: he was locked in for the night with this drunk, and Rick had been knocked over and he wanted to be with him.

'Oh! Ooh! Oooh!' he had wailed.

Tom had come to him.

'Don' – don' be afraid, Miss – Cleo. Don't, darling. I'm here. They'll know by morning. You're safe – safe with me.'

He had tried to enfold Jem in his arms. Tom's eyes had been closed, his eyelids shadowy under the expiring light. His face was a mask of giant pain. Had Jem known about them, he would have been reminded of Orson Welles, or Mount Rushmore. 'Darling girl,' murmured the big man. Jem mastered his instinct to struggle away. Tom was in a moment of transcendence: his Celia was with him; his breathing had slowed. Jem had clung to one central determination: he MUST remain Julia. Earlier, he had almost come clean and revealed who he really was. He hadn't done so because of Tom's drunken unpredictability. As a woman – Celia's double – would he not be safe? As a young man, much less so? Held closely to Tom's jacket in the cold shrine, Jem was quiescent – and he was surprised to find that it was as much out of pity, as out of fear.

'Do you mind,' he had asked, several minutes later – his voice light and Julia-ish, 'if I lie down? I'm frightfully tired.'

'Oh, yes. Of course. I hadn't meant it to turn out like this. Why not use the bench? Have my coat as a pillow.' He had groped in his coat pocket and brought out a flask. To Jem's dismay, he took a long swig from it, and drew his hand across his lips. 'Hair of the dog. Ha, ha. Would you like a nip?' Jem shook his head. Tom had gurgled another long gulp, and snapped the flask shut. He had then peeled off his coat, puffed it up and, once Jem had lain down on the cold stone, placed it under Jem's head, tucked the fur coat round him and slumped to the floor by his side. He was silent for some time, then a snorting groan repeated regularly told him that his host had fallen asleep.

After a time, the battery light had grown dimmer and dimmer until it was a tiny orange glow-worm above the prone man's bulk and the elegant boy on the bench.

Then it had gone out.

In the hospital, Rick drifted in and out of drugged unconsciousness. He could feel nothing below his right knee, and the tips of his fingers seemed to have no shape. He kept replaying the astounding crash of the gate on his arm, and the slow-motion of the trolley, rolling, rolling. The roman-candle of agony that had followed interested him less – it seemed someone else's pain, someone else's screams. He was chiefly occupied by a worry that one of the St Matthew's party would find the photographs when packing away his things in the sleeping-car. If Jem had got there first, all would be well. If he hadn't.... and the last he had seen of Jem was a frightened face in a car being whisked away into the darkness.

The previous night, after Jem had returned from Mon's quarters, Rick had produced a camera.

'That's a Polaroid, isn't it?' Jem had asked.

Rick had nodded.

'I want some souvenirs. Of us. You know.'

Jem's skin had flamed with instant, violent lust.

'You want to take photos of us – of me – doing it?' he had gasped.

'Yep. I take them of you, you of me, and then we get all sexy looking at them and go at it again.'

They had photographed each other until they had used up most of the supply. Jem had liked best one of Rick kneeling provocatively in front of him, both hands caressing himself, his head back and his mouth bowed in a kiss. He had slipped it into his wash-bag, knowing that it would propel his self-pleasurings for weeks into the future. Rick had been in ecstasies over one that Jem had begged him to tear up. Jem had recovered from physical exhaustion around three o'clock and had been ready for more pleasure in the dawn. Lying back, half-reclining on the upper berth – with legs drawn up and as far apart as the narrow confines permitted – he had been caught on film during ejaculation. A jet of semen was suspended in the air. But what disturbed Jem was the angle of the shot: a pillar of flesh, a triangle of curls and fevered hands, so much in the foreground that they dwarfed the person behind them. He had been alarmed by the desperation he had read in his own distant face as he had fought to attain yet another climax after so many – a grim struggle with his own body in the effortful climb up the peak of sated nerves to the next euphoric surrender. Jem's soul had squirmed at the thought of *anyone* else seeing it: Mr Howard, Betsy, his *mother*, for God's sake! *Anyone!*

'Please, Rick! I want to tear it up. You *can't* keep it!' he had cried.

'Are you ashamed of it?' Rick had teased.

'Yes, I am!' had replied poor Jem.

'Why?'

'*Look* at it! I just seem, oh, depraved, with all control gone, mad with lust....'

'Well, you were, as I recall. That's what I like about it. You, with your usual shyness and quiet ways! It's amazing. And well worth keeping.'

No persuasion on Jem's part had prevented Rick from preserving the shot. He'd never seen such concentration on anyone's face, he said. It was so, so sexy.

Now Rick wished that, after the stimulation the photos had given both of them, they had, after all, ripped them up. Jem at climax was still under his pillow in the sleeping-car berth where he had slipped it. It was just bound to be discovered.

In and out of drugged mutterings Rick sailed.

'Poor thing. He's going on about photos again,' whispered the night nurse to the orderly.

'Nothing doing,' said Sir Alan. 'He hasn't brought the boy home. I thought he would, but....'

'Where else could he have taken him?' snapped Mon. He strove to keep his voice even and calm, but he would have given years off his life never to have accepted this ridiculous invitation to Nova Scotia. Dr Bennett would have backed him if Mon had put up enough real, or imagined, objections. Mon felt the guilt of one who realises that things are as they are because of him. It was to spend longer with Jem, rather than face the beginning of the long, lonely summer vacation, that he had done this. It was hard not to snap.

'Is that, um, shrine, the memorial thing to Celia, near here?' asked David. 'I only ask because perhaps he took Jem there. Showing him his double's temple, and all that.'

'The shrine's in the middle of the old railroad track bed,' said Sir Alan grimly. 'I suppose he could have gone up to it. Why he should still be there, God knows. There's nothing to see.'

Impatience roughened Mon's voice again.

'Well, come on then. Let's try. If he's not there after all, I'll have to tell the police about this as well.'

'I hope we can avoid that. Things are bad enough already.'

They got back to the narrow track and, a minute later, the headlights swung onto Tom's Cadillac.

'They *are* here!' cried David.

There was a silence over the car and the shrine that Mon didn't like.

'It's just a stone hut,' said Sir Alan. 'But they can't be inside. The window's dark.'

'But what's the car doing here?' asked Mon.

David got out and was striding towards the shrine, calling,

'Mr Althorne! Jem!'

Sir Alan swung his car's headlights across to the stone building and left them on. He and Mon joined David and each noticed the small bunch of keys in the lock at the same time.

Louise saw to the packing of Rick's and, later, Jem's things. She was deeply, painfully shocked by what she found in washing-bags and under Rick's pillow. Her opinions of both boys underwent, initially, a sharp change. She felt especially upset about Jem, whom she had come to like very much and whose unusual sincerity and kindness had marked him out in her mind from the others in the cast. Jem and Riccardo! Such dreadful photographs! How could they *do* such things?

Then it occurred to her that she, of all people – she, who had had no brothers and no boyfriends, and had entered her convent straight from her high school days – knew nothing at all about the private, the hidden lives of adolescent boys. Had she heard of Kinsey's research figures: that 95% of all boys are sexually active, at least on their own, by fourteen, and that 33% of all boys had same-sex erotic relationships leading to orgasm in their teens, she might not have been so bewildered. Then she remembered CoCo's tales of life at the school they both attended, and how a totally different establishment had been opened up to her. Perhaps this sort of thing was, well, normal.

She felt she had a great deal more to learn about young people and what drove them; about the needs they had, and the paths they took to fulfil them – and so, gradually, she withheld judgement. After all, they were both such nice boys: clever, amusing, well-mannered, charming, reliable, responsible. And they had been all of that while those – those *things* were going on, hadn't they? The only difference had been that she hadn't known about it. Absurd, then, to see them in a different light. What, after all, would *they* have thought about her night with David in her berth? *Judge not, so that ye be not judged* was what she found her brain framing as she collected the Polaroid pictures, shaking her head in mixed fascination and horror, as she examined them. Part of her deepest being responding to the black and white paper images; whatever it was, she stopped herself tearing them up. Sighing, she tucked them into Riccardo's copy of *The Duchess of Malfi*. David would know what to do. She would speak to him later. But she never did.

'Uurrgh. Uh, uh….'
Tom Althorne came to himself with a snort.

Why? What? Where was he? It was dark, and chilly too. He put his hand to his head. Of course! He was in Celia's shrine – with Celia's double. Had he fallen asleep?

'Miss Jakemar?' he said, the double's name returning to him. A gasp of breath came from the bench above his head. 'Has the battery gone?' asked Tom.

Jem pulled the fur coat closer to him.

'The light went dimmer and failed,' he replied.

'How long ago?' asked Tom, heaving himself to his feet.

'It seems ages, but it probably isn't,' whispered Jem.

'I'm sorry about this,' rumbled Tom. 'It's all turned out badly. I didn't want you to be…'

'I haven't been,' said Jem, without knowing what it was Tom hadn't wanted him to be.

Tom reached down to the bench and contacted the soft fur.

'I was so struck by your performance,' he said. 'And I know I got drunk at the interval. Do you accept my apology?'

'I do, of course,' said Jem, not trusting himself to say more. Then he added, 'I really would like to go back to the summer school now. Do you think there's a chance of being let out?'

'To be honest, no. Not 'til morning. Garland'll see the car, as I've said. But there must be hours to go. My God, you *are* shivering, aren't you?' He sat next to Jem on the chilly bench and put a clumsy arm round Jem's shoulders. 'Let me warm you up a bit. You don't mind, do you?' Jem said nothing but fought his trembling. 'I promise I didn't engineer this – like running out of gas in Lovers' Lane with a pretty girl – but I'm not sorry.' His breath reached Jem's face in the dark. Tom twined a finger in the tumbling curls. 'This wig,' he laughed. 'Take it off. You must be uncomfortable in it. It feels like pure nylon.'

'It is,' muttered Jem. He let Tom's hand pull it back and off. It fell to the stone floor.

'Goodness. You have got short hair,' said Tom, allowing his hand to run across Jem's scalp, 'Quite boyish.'

'Look,' began Jem, with a touch of male depth in his voice.

'You're so like her. So like her,' murmured Tom. 'Forgive me, but this means so much to me. Auld lang syne. See?' He ran the tip of his finger from Jem's forehead down his cheek to his lips. 'Forgive me,' he said again. 'I must kiss you once. Just for her sake. They're so soft.'

He cupped Jem's chin and tilted his mouth towards his own. In a moment their lips would meet. Jem was determined Tom should not kiss him; Rick's mouth was one thing, this old man's was another.

Tom, leaning in to him, instinctively covered Jem's breast with a hand. Jem squirmed away and the Drama department's "Marilyns" slipped round him.

'What the....?' began Tom, compressing his grip on the padded cup. Jem ducked under his arm and got off the bench, wrenching the bra from his hands.

'Let me go!' he articulated. 'You're not allowed to do this.'

Tom fumbled to his feet and caught Jem by the waist. He pressed his face forward, finding Jem's cheek with his lips. As Jem fiercely fought him off, he was again astonished by this girl's strength.

'Stop struggling,' he gasped.

'Keep your drunken hands off me,' breathed Jem.

Tom's head had cleared a little, but he was by no means sober. In a gust of self-pity he saw himself as the injured party. How dared this little tramp of an actress treat him with contempt? And she seemed to have been done up in disguise – probably a part of some cock-eyed plan.....to look like Celia. But why?

'Why are you wearing falsies and a wig?' snarled Tom. 'Quite the actress, eh? What are you like underneath, I wonder?'

He made a grab and succeeded in capturing Jem. In the absolute velvet of the airless dark, they swayed in each other's arms, Jem silent, not trusting his voice, and Tom breathing with greater and greater noise and effort. With his arm round Jem's waist, Tom was jamming them together, face to face, when Jem hit out as hard as he could, catching the gasping man on the jaw, just under his ear. With an inarticulate shout, Tom clawed at Jem's shoulder and, in a spurt of rage, moderate feeling gone, savagely ripped the delicate dress open. His hands were electrified by the soft skin under it. With primitive and near-dead passion re-ignited by drink, by rage at the stinging blow, and by the subterfuge of the girl and those who had put her up to it, he brought Jem to the floor, insensible to the indecency of his attack.

He knew that he was not likely to do anything sexual – it was long since he had been able to summon potency at will; drink had seen to that. But the mental thrust was there all the same. He needed to bring this lovely, cold and scheming girl to submission.

Jem, for his part, remained desperate to be Julia still. He heard Tom whisper hot endearments, wet urgings. His knees were on each side of Jem's torso, one hand capturing Jem's arms, the other tearing at what remained of the frock.

Jem knew that Tom would eventually discover what he was. He had to prevent that. He wriggled out from under the heavy man, staggering backwards. Tom threw his arms round Jem's hips, his hands on the back of Jem's thighs. He seemed to have difficulty arising from his kneeling position. His laboured breathing grew more alarmingly loud.

All this while, Jem had not spoken, just matched grasp for grasp. With a heave, using Jem as a support, Tom regained his feet. With a cruel grab he found Jem's cheek and clutched it, puckering his mouth.

'Kiss me! Kiss me!' he hissed.

Jem let his mouth hover for a second on his captor's. Tom's tongue forced his lips apart and his hand dropped to Jem's stomach. 'Come ON!' he grunted, almost to himself. At the tongue-thrust, Jem staggered back against Celia's altar. It rocked and they heard a vase tinkle to the ground, and its faded flowers spread under their feet. 'Jesus! You're a bitch!' cried Tom. 'That wig, the dress, the bra..... *Why* did you do it?'

Jem, misunderstanding, thought that Tom had twigged his gender at last.

'All right!' he screamed. 'So I'm like Celia! It's coincidence, that's all. Why do you suppose I never wanted to meet you?'

They stared towards each other's unseen mouths. Tom gave a squint of percipience, nodding.

'I don't believe you! You little cow! Why can't you admit you were put up to this?'

After roaring this question, Tom yanked Jem towards him again. There was a rending of material as Jem's heel caught in what remained of the dress, and it dropped away. In nothing but underpants, stockings and displaced bra, Jem fought against another assault, another kiss. Then what Tom had called him tore back into his mind: "You little cow". He was still a girl then!

When they had first been locked in, Jem had quietened the drunkard by being a soft and quiescent

Julia. He must try that trick once more; must feign collapse and surrender. He suddenly ceased his struggles, went limp and fell sideways through Tom's grasp. He felt the stone flags bang his head and shoulder. He began to cry, quietly, but with Julia-like intensity when she was at the moment of her death. A little part of him relished his performance, but most of his misery was propelled by self-pity and outrage.

Shocked by the instant cessation of struggle, struck by the slimness of Jem's figure as it slipped through his arms and rendered drunkenly emotional by the quiet sobs, Tom passed rapidly from fever to solicitation.

'Look,' he gasped. 'Please. I'm not going to hurt you. I only wanted to know who put you up to….. Oh, don't cry like that, dear. Don't!'

'No….one….put….me….up….to….to it,' sobbed Jem. 'I was given the part….at school….'

'At school?' echoed Tom. 'What school? What do you mean? Christ Almighty! Aren't you an actress?'

'I'm at school,' cried Jem, aware, as he hadn't been before, how young he really was.

'Dear God,' whispered Tom. 'A school-girl.' He thumped down on one knee beside Jem. 'There, there. Dear lass, please. Forgive me – please.'

With a great inspirational thrust of victory, Jem knew that the danger was past. Tom would not forget himself again. Once more, tears and helplessness – being Julia, being young – had achieved what violent struggles had failed to do.

With heavy, unhealthy gasps, his hand lightly on Jem's shaking shoulders, Tom went on, 'I see now about the wig, those falsies. I should have realised. How old are you?'

'I'm sixteen,' croaked Jem.

Tom's hand left his shoulder.

'Jesus Christ! I took you for twenty-four, twenty-five.'

'I'm in the eleventh grade at high school. We're all still at school.' Jem hated himself for not being able to keep his voice steady. It wavered in and out of his Julia semi-falsetto, but Tom didn't seem to notice.

'I didn't realise. No one told me you were all kids. I could see some were, but you, and the guy playing Bosola, and your Duchess and the Cardinal..... I assumed you were Drama students at college, at least. And I've, I've.....cuurrch!' Tom gave a peculiar retching cough. 'I've done....done this.... to you. Oh God, God, what have I started?'

As if in answer there was a click at the door.

The cool air swirled about them.

An engine idled outside and a spear of light pierced through the open doorway across the figures on the floor and lit from beneath the quizzical, painted smile of the dead Celia.

Sir Alan stepped across the threshold, Mon beside him. Mon's eyes flew to the near-naked Jem. His throat, before he could stop it, gave a single, hoarse cry of alarm, rage, pity and love.

'Tom!' came Sir Alan's crisp voice. 'That's a child you've got there. Be sensible, old chap.'

Jem tried to suppress his sobs but couldn't. Tom stood up in the beam, his shirt out, his hair on end, his face disturbingly mottled. Jem – the bra down round his waist, stockings ripped, make-up smeared and wig missing – slipped past him and ran to Mon's arms.

'Steady, old son,' said David, putting a hand on Jem's trembling shoulders. 'Okay now.'

Tom Althorne emerged from the shrine.

'I – I didn't know 'til a moment ago she was only sixteen,' he gasped. 'How could I have?' He felt it was imperative to make them understand, especially the two teachers. Sir Alan looked more severe than he had ever seen him. 'How could I?'

'What you seem to have tried to do would not have been decent if she had been thirty,'

'You know what I've been through. She....I....' He tailed off, and his eyes swivelled round to Jem. He stopped, his purple-lipped mouth wide open, his gaze growing more fixed.

Mon held his boy close, close – his eyes full of tears.

Oh, here were the years of his lost loves, the nights and mornings of yearning, the misery of his chemical need for Jem's body, the terrible grief when he couldn't have it, those months of long glances and carefully contrived meetings, those plans – fevered, mad, of assignations, of holidays together, of waiting until Jem was eighteen before living with him, of proposing marriage to Mrs Clarke (yes, he'd even, in his madness, considered that, although not sure if she were divorced yet, or not). There had been the singing happiness of rehearsals, of the ride in the Morgan, of this adventure in Canada, of his dreams that he and Jem were the same age, had the same life before them, could prove that love, glorious, lightning-flash love, had been prepared for them by a pitying God.

It was all there in the desperate clutch to his chest of the one creature on earth he could never have, and whom he had, in loneliness, sternly, irrevocably rejected in the name of decent sanity.

Jem, drawing his hand across his damp eyes, listening in astonishment to the whispered endearments that poured with the tears from Mon's face, feeling the strong encirclement of Mon's arms, knew then, if he'd doubted before, that his almost-instinct had been right about his teacher's unusual love of him. And he welcomed it. Mr Howard was old, of course, but so different from Tom Althorne. Tom was the ravisher, Mr Howard the saviour. In Mon's arms Jem was the beloved child again, and Mon the haunting spectre of his lost father.

As Jem stood, leaning against Mon, and Mon enwrapped him with devotion – each oblivious to the surreal glare of the headlights – Tom Althorne took a step towards them.

'Oh*! OH!* You're not....!'

He took in the figure, brilliantly white, like a paper cut-out in the light. Jem's male torso, legs, waist, shoulders – all bare, save where tattered shreds of Julia's dress hung like gossamers – smote him with the force of revelation. Everything fell into place: the muscles, the occasional deepish voice, the bra and wig, the extraordinary strength.

'Oh, *God*! You're not a girl at *ALL*! You're a....'

'Yes, a boy,' cut in Mon. 'Julia's part was played by a boy of sixteen. We didn't feel, after all the fuss you were making, that we could tell you.'

After the silence that followed, Jem spoke first.

'I'm sorry, Mr Althorne,' he said, clearly, and in his own voice.

Tom gazed at him, still held closely by his teacher.

'There is,' Tom said, 'no need for you to apologise. You have nothing to be sorry for. Indeed, I should and do apologise to *you.* What I did was unforgiveable and inhuman.'

He drew himself up, tucked his shirt in and pulled the door of the shrine shut behind him.

'It doesn't matter, Mr Althorne,' began Jem, finding that he was sobbing once again. 'I was as much to b-blame....'

'Mr Althorne....,' began Mon.

Tom pulled the shrine's key from the lock. He

faced Jem. He had attacked, kissed, and indecently assaulted a schoolboy. This lad could send him to prison, ruin him, and yet it was the lad who was apologising. Ridiculous.

'You are an honourable, decent young man. I hope you can forget how I behaved tonight and remember only what a fine performance you gave at our theatre.' There was hardly a trace of drunken slur in his speech.

'Tom….,' said Sir Alan.

Tom waved a hand at them. He started to say, 'Get off my land', got no further than, 'Get off …,' gave an odd whimper, dropped the Cadillac's keys, looked down stupidly at them and fell dead at their feet.

Jem, in shock, was put to bed in Sir Alan's house at Trevanaunce, with Mon in the room next door. Twice Jem cried out in nightmare, and Mon was there to comfort him.

All Jem could repeat over and over again was,

'I should have stayed dressed as Julia…. I should have stayed dressed as Julia….'

February 2020: IN PARADISUM

February nights are long and wait to claw sunlight from the world. Janek sensed the coming of shadows as he filed out of the abbey church.

'Ladies and Gentlemen, reception is in the guest lodge. Please follow me,' announced the hospitality master. One by one the funeral goers got into motion and made their way up the path. Jan hung back, waiting for the lovely woman to emerge from the porch.

Lindy Franitza twitched his arm.

'Look,' she said. 'Can't we skip this bit? It's cold and I want to get back and do some shopping.'

'I want to stay,' muttered Jan, his eye on the church door.

'Oh, Christ. It was bad enough having to come all this way. You said you didn't recognise any of these people. What do you want to hang around for?'

Janek turned to face her. For a second he felt hatred – rather than the weary tolerance more usual to him. He fished in his pocket and produced an electric fob.

'Go on, take it. Why don't you drive off now, if you'd like to? I'll get back later. '

'What? Go back to New York without you? Have you gone bananas?'

'Why not, Lindy? I just want to stay here a bit longer. I want to talk about him. I want to speak to some of these people – find out who they are. It doesn't matter about you taking the car. I can come back by rail, I suppose. Phone for an Uber at the station. Come on. I understand why it's of no interest to you, but it's my past – at St Matthew's, see? I just need to.....' He tailed off. Why had he thought of bringing her in the first place? He supposed he'd had absurd visions of saying to well-remembered faces: may I introduce my wife? And – even more absurd – of her being charming and supportive.

'I've a damn good mind to take you at your word,' she snapped. 'I really have had enough of monasteries for one day.'

Jan's hearing seemed to fail him. Her words faded as if being turned down by a volume control. A movement in the abbey church doorway caught his eye. The lovely woman! She was moving out into the waning light. She was with that Riccardo (Jan still couldn't bring back his surname) and his young helper. Oh, and again that tantalising movement he seemed to remember so well – that flutter of her hand to her breast! He turned to Lindy.

'Oh, for God's sake, go then! I've told you, haven't I?'

She grabbed at the fob, still amazed that he should be doing this.

'I hope you get stranded, you silly twit!' she hissed. The fact that she was stamping away from him along the trim path made no impression on him at all.

He kept his eyes fixed on the conversation in the porch.

'It – it's Janek Franitza, isn't it?' came a quiet voice from behind him. Jan turned. A plump grey-haired man was holding out his hand. Jan took it. He searched the grey-haired man's face for clues.

'I'm real sorry,' he said. 'You have the advantage on me. I'm so bad at names.'

The grey-haired man smiled ruefully.

'I expect I've changed. And you'll be pleased to hear that you haven't, Janek. It's Greg McManus. You came to my house for the cast party at the end of our play *The Duchess of Malfi,* back in the day. Remember?'

'Oh, Greg! Indeed, I do remember.'

Jan studied the heavy Irish-looking fellow in front of him, tried to relate him to the outrageous, extrovert teenager who had played Delio and the Old Lady so many years before, and failed.

'I expect you noticed Jonathan and Mark in the abbey,' went on Greg. 'They kept up with old Howard to the end of his life. They were in my year, 12th grade, when we were doing *The Duchess*, and you were 11th grade, I seem to recall.'

'I was,' said Jan. 'A year seems a long time apart, at school.'

'Oh, it does indeed. Well, now, shall we go along in? It's chilly enough out here.'

'I'm – I'm just waiting for….for….,' said Jan,

jerking his head back towards the church.

'Fine. Fine. See you inside. We'll have a lot to talk about.' Greg started to move off, and then turned back. 'By the way,' he went on, 'old Lomax is here, with Mrs Lomax. You remember when she was Miss Carrbridge?'

The oldish couple at the back, thought Jan, so *that's* who they are.

'I remember when they got married,' he said. 'You had left St Mat's by then. I would like to speak to them again. Oh, and Greg, you don't know if Rosa Voss is here, do you?'

Greg wrinkled his nose.

'Rosa?'

'Yes. Also in *The Duchess*.'

'I know who you mean. Good God, no. Well, I wouldn't know. I haven't thought of her in over twenty-five years. I certainly wouldn't recognise her.' He rubbed his hands vigorously, in the manner of the bluff Sligo farmer. 'Well, see you inside.'

Jan was left on the path.

The cold crept into his coat and again he sensed the onrush of night over the cold fields. I'm being idiotic, he thought. It's not even four o'clock yet.

The group in the porch broke up. Riccardo, leaning on his young man's arm, came carefully along the path. Jan sought his eye, noted the grim clench of his jaw and looked away again. Riccardo – oh, *what* was his other name? – hadn't recognised him. The young man gave him a polite nod.

'Steady, Rick,' he murmured as they moved on.

Jan – not quite knowing why he hadn't introduced himself to Riccardo but recalling how much he had disliked him at school – turned back to the porch.

When he reached its shadow he caught a single, gasping sob.

It was so perturbing and surprising that he froze, his body casting a slice of dark into the stone enclave. Because it would be clear to whoever was inside that he was there, he waited a second or two, coughed tactfully and stepped in.

The attractive woman was seated on a shelf of stone, her coat open, its fur collar fluffing her neck, her long legs in black tights stretched out before her, her right shoe half off. She looked very distressed, and Jan saw that her eyes were wet with tears.

'Oh, excuse me,' he began. 'I just came back to ask if you'd heard where the reception was....' He tailed off. Obviously he had stumbled onto the tail-end of something, and it was too late to back out. 'Er – are you all right?' he asked, feeling foolish, for she was clearly anything but all right.

'Oh. Oh, I – I – I'm fine. I've had a – a – a bit of a shock. Please don't worry about me. I know where the reception is,' she replied, in a husky voice.

Jan should have walked away – he knew that. She had as good as told him to mind his own business. But her mature loveliness was so heart-breaking, and her face....well, no, not just her face....but her body-language, her intonation, her demeanour...seemed so – so familiar to him that he just could not go away without finding out a bit more about her.

'I will go, if you want,' he said. He felt that she was hugging a secret from him, and curiosity vied with his attraction to her. 'But you must admit you *are* being rather fascinating – alone and upset. It rather brings out the knight to the rescue in me.'

She drew her legs up and twitched the coat round herself.

'*A parfit gentil knight*? Well, that's more than I got from my last conversation.' Her deep voice, warm and clear, had a touch of California in it – and, there it was again! – that familiar intonation and timbre. She applied the full force of her gaze to Jan and gave a gasp. Her hand went to her breast and her mouth fell open. 'I don't believe it,' she whispered. 'Well, of course I might have expected kindness from *you*. You were kind to me – always.'

An intimate and dearly remembered smile had appeared on her face. Jan realised that he too was gaping rudely. He *did* know her – but who...?

'Yes, hello there, Jan,' came the perfectly articulated voice.

'What? Do we know each other? I thought I *did* recognise you for a minute in there. Do we go back to St Matthew's days?'

'Yes, we do, you nutcase. And as soon as I

concentrated on you I knew you at once – even though it's been well over twenty-five years. You've got better-looking.'

Jan peered into the porch. The ochreous light softened her face. She was so beautiful in this glow that his heart stirred strongly. Then, with such a rush of recognition and shock that he felt he had been physically struck, he realised who she was. His mind irradiated with the image of an unusually handsome sixteen-year-old boy, delightedly snuggling into a fur coat in their school production over a quarter of a century ago. He felt sick and joyful at the same time.

'Jem! God almighty! It's *you*. Jem! Jem Clarke!' he cried.

'Yes. Or, as presently attired, *Julia* Clarke.'

'But – but, Jem…? He stuttered. 'W-Why are you dressed up? I mean, why…?'

'I often dress like this,' replied Julia quietly.

They stared at each other in silence. As pennies dropped, Jan heard himself say,

'Oh, I *see!* You'd had – a - …'

'No. you're trying to say "sex-change operation", aren't you? Well, no, I haven't. I'm a gay transvestite, not a trans-sexual.'

'Ah, er, yes. You look so very feminine, but….'

'But nothing. I'm sometimes Jem, sometimes Julia. It depends. Come on, give me a hand.'

Jan helped her up. She pushed the high-heeled shoe back on. Standing in front of him, she was his height, infinitely better cared-for and manicured, and looking a full ten years younger than he did.

Jan glared at her. All the anger and disappointment of the past stormed back into him.

'Why didn't you ever write to me?' he cried. 'You just disappeared.'

'Look,' said Julia. 'Do you very much want to go into the reception just yet? Can we sit, say, in your car and chat? This porch is freezing and, to tell you the truth, I've had a shock.'

'Of course,' said Janek. 'But it'll have to be your car, if you've got one here. Mine's been driven off back to New York.'

Something – the oddest thing – stopped him telling Julia he was married; something too complex for him to analyse.

'Sure. Mine's just over there.'

They walked over to a line of cars. Impressed, Jan watched Julia flick her tab at a big new Tesla electric sedan. 'Get in. I'm going to put the heat on to warm us up.'

They sat in the fine interior, the climate control inaudibly warming the air.

'Very nice,' said Jan.

'It's not mine. It's hired. But it's like mine. I've got one in L A. Saving the planet – you know.'

'L A? Jeez, I don't know where or how to begin,' said Jan. 'I've got so many questions and they want to tumble out together.'

'Go on then. Ask me something.'

'Okay. One: why didn't you keep in touch? I went round to your house on 172nd Street. I rang. I tried everything. Christ, Jem, you just walked out of my life.'

'I walked out of everyone's life, even my own,' replied Julia. 'It's nice hearing *you* calling me Jem again after so long.'

'And why *Julia*? Wasn't that the name of the girl you played in *The Duchess*? Why do you still use it?'

'When I did that part I think I was truly myself for the first time. That's why it has stuck. I become Julia when I need to, see?'

Jan hardly knew what to reply to this extraordinary comment, so he returned to his questioning.

'So, you walked out of life. Walked where?'

'You won't have known, Jan, but I had a complete breakdown. It was after all that business in Canada, that fellow Tom Althorne's death, other things. Everything. I know I came back with you all on the plane, and I probably seemed okay, but after I realised what had happened to Rick, I began to go a bit strange. I blamed myself, you see....'

'He's still badly crippled, isn't he?'

'I was very shocked today. I knew how serious his injuries were, and I guess I realised that he might never be the same again – but then I didn't *know*. I haven't been in touch since that time.'

'But, I'd have thought.... I mean given how close

you and he had got. At least that's what I believed back then.'

'You're right. I was totally, violently in love with him, Jan. I realised later how much when he was wrenched from me. We were torn apart in the springtime of love. We never had time to find out each other's bad points, or to get tired of each other. There was just this – this *glory*.... And then it was gone. After the accident we only met once more. He was in hospital in Halifax for some time. His father was awful about it all, I heard. He sued the school, sued everybody, even that museum trust and their railroad. It never got built, I gather. Anyway, he wouldn't let anyone from St Mat's near Rick and I –
I so wanted to be with him. We'd gone a long way between us, as I'm sure you sussed out....'

'I did. Funny. It hurts me a little, even now, to remember how I felt, Jem.'

'Why? What was it to you?'

'I don't know. I really don't. I just felt betrayed by you – back then. I can't explain.'

'My mother took Betsy, my sister – you knew her, didn't you? – and me to Florida to see my dad, and we stayed on there. So I only met Rick once more.'

'What was his other name? I've been trying to think of it all afternoon.'

'Parisi.'

'Of course! Riccardo Parisi, who played Bosola. Jem, I gathered from the expression on your face back there, when I came into the porch, that your reunion with him wasn't, hadn't been....'

'I was crying, Jan, when you came into the porch. After Rick was brought home to New York, I tried everything that a helpless, penniless seventeen-year-old *can* try to see someone again. I never succeeded beyond one terrible, awkward meeting at his house before I left for Florida. I'd climbed in at a back window. I thought his mom was out.... He couldn't walk on his own.... He didn't meet my eyes..... I don't know......'

Julia stopped, one finger tracing an arabesque on the steering-wheel boss. Such unhappiness, dating from so far back, thought Jan. So absurd, but so touching. He raised an arm and placed it along Julia's shoulders, patting gently with his hand. A phrase: *I shall arm you, thus* flickered in his brain. Jesus! That was it! It was a line of seduction from the old play!

Julia resumed, after a strange, near-silent sigh.

'The, whatever it was we had between us, has affected our whole lives. *The child is father to the man* as old Howard used to say. Rushing in to rescue me, he's maimed for life, and then....there's the other thing....' Julia paused. 'Can I speak honestly?'

'Of course.'

'I only ask because you used to be real strait-laced about certain things.'

'God, Jem, I was a kid. What did I know?'

'Rick told me, back then at that time in his house,

before his mom threw me out, that he thought what we had had between us was the sweetest and deepest experience of his life and that it had changed him forever. He then said that he wondered if his injuries were God's punishment for the pleasure of those forbidden sins. And then he muttered that I had better go. How Catholic Italian can you get? And that was it, until today.'

'And that made you miserable – now?' asked Jan, trying not to be dense.

'No. It's what has happened since. You know, he believed he could have been straight or gay, Jan. I made him gay, I'm convinced. Perhaps that was another piece of gelignite I handed him. But you know what was really awful today? He passed me with that young lover of his…'

'Lover? I suppose he is.'

'He is. And, Jan, he didn't recognise me *at all.* We spoke for a few moments. I said I'd known Howard for years, He said he'd known him as a kid. I thought there might have been a flicker of recognition, but all he saw was a middle-aged old bag…'

'Jeez, Jem, you're hardly a bag. You only look about twenty-five. But why did you turn up dressed as Julia? Why not as you were? Wouldn't that have made a difference?'

'Probably not. In his mind the far-off Jem was a nice-looking boy of sixteen – a dream from the past, you see. A dream forever young and forever lost. It's why I didn't, in the end, tell him who I was. Let the past stay in the past.' Julia sighed again, then seemed to sharpen up. 'As for dressing as Julia, it was partly to be incognito – not that I *was* from clever-clogs Franitza, of course – and partly because I had always known that old Howard had been excited by me in Julia's costume. As I too was. So, it was a sort of farewell tribute to him....' Julia paused with a wry grin. 'But don't let's talk about Rick anymore. I didn't know he'd be here, but I've had a sort of dream about meeting him again for years and years. Well, it got smashed today. I guess I'm not young enough anymore, but that boy of his is – just about. Maybe – sad thought – he's one of a long line of replacement Jem Clarkes.'

They were silent for a few minutes. Then Janek asked,

'I know you didn't come back to St Mat's. Did you finish your studies?'

'Oh yes, most of them, with a private tutor in Miami. A silver lining was that mom and dad got together again to look after poor, broken-down me, and they're still together. Funny how it works out.'

Jan felt he had let a thread slip somewhere and strove to catch it.

'This breakdown you had. What was it? A sort of post-traumatic stress thing?'

'I wonder sometimes if it was a broken heart. That is, if one can *have* a broken heart. I didn't talk. I didn't eat. I didn't smile. I didn't do anything for over a year. The agony of desire for him, Jan, was just…. I also discovered that I too was gay that summer in Canada. It was a shock, although I had suspected it about myself since I was fourteen. You know *him*…?' Julia nodded towards the abbey. 'When they carried his coffin past us at the end of Mass, it came to me that he'd had a kind of breakdown back then as well.'

'Really? How do you mean?'

'He left St Mat's during the vacation. He came on here as a lay brother. He and I never spoke again. The last thing I remember of him is being in his arms outside Celia's shrine.'

'Shrine? What shrine?'

'Ah, it was at the house of one of the museum patrons – that madman Althorne who drove off with me, remember? He'd put it up for his dead wife who, they said, looked like me dolled up as Julia. Anyway, you know what I was saying about Rick? I'm absolutely sure old Howard felt the same about me.'

'Jem, really! You make it sound as though half the guys connected with *The Duchess* were gay and falling for everyone else.'

'Take it or leave it. It hardly matters now, does it? But I know I'm right about Howard. Poor man, to have the bad luck to love me deeply when, unfortunately, he was older than my father, I was his sixteen -year-old pupil, I loved someone else, and, to cap it all, I was the same sex! But it couldn't stop the yearning. How could it? We meet, and we love.'

Julia closed her eyes.

'You've still got very long lashes,' said Jan, before he could stop himself making this observation.

'I remember,' went on Julia, as if he hadn't spoken, 'a look he gave me one evening, in his berth in the sleeping-cars. It haunted me later. And what he whispered to me when he held me….at the shrine….'

'Jem,' said Janek. 'I must ask you something.'
'Yes?'

'My brother Francis; was there ever anything….?'
'Want the truth?'

'Of course,' replied Jan – not sure if he did.

'Nothing. Nothing at all.' Julia sighed. 'But there might have been. I had fantasies, I admit. He was very nice-looking. There might have been if….'

'If you hadn't discovered he was such a little shit?'

Jan was nearly on the point of telling Julia about the death of the darling son he had lost, named after the brother in the United Arab Emirates whom he seldom saw, but, as when about to speak of his marriage, he swallowed the words. So, one fell in love out of a cold blue sky, did one? And the frenzy over-rode custom, sense, age, law, gender – everything? He doubted he had ever loved like that in the past. Would he in the future?

'Jem, what have you been doing all this time?'

Julia's eyes twinkled, and she averted them from Jan's gaze. She was enjoying this conversation with an old, old friend – it was so effortless. There was no need for pretence; the words and silences flowed into each other. But she doubted if Jan was ready for her answer.

'I expect you're wondering how I knew about Howard's death,' she said.

'I assumed you'd read about it in the St Mat's news-sheet,' said Jan. 'I did. They ran a piece on all the plays he had produced back when.'

'I didn't know there *was* a St Mat's news-sheet. No, I got a phone call direct from the Abbott.'

'You must be very special.'

'Because of what I told you about him and me, I always kept tabs on what he was doing here over the years. Actually, I sent a fair bit of money his way to help him in his various projects – he did a lot for those with mental problems – but he never knew the source of it. Only the Abbott did.'

'Lord! You mean he didn't know you were sort of tracking him and supporting him?'

'No. I thought it was better that way. But they let me know the moment he fell ill and kept me up to date almost every day.'

'You *are* grand, Jem. Quite the privileged one. But you haven't answered my question, old procrastinator. What have you been doing that gives you this money and special treatment?'

'Let's say,' said Julia hesitantly, 'that for a while I did what I discovered I was good at when I was sixteen. I applied for an acting job in L A as soon as I was eighteen and got it. The monks here knew nothing about it. Nor did my parents. Then I set up my own film company, and it was a success.'

'Your own company? In the movie business? Well, well. But you were a good actor, Jem.'

'I wasn't quite referring to *acting*, as being what I was good at, Jan. They were rather special movies,' smiled Julia.

'Oh, for crying out loud! *Special* movies? What did you actually *do* out there?'

Then Jem's words about his discoveries at sixteen came back to him, and the penny dropped. 'You don't mean you acted in *adult* movies?'

'Got it in one. I did indeed, for about four years, until I was twenty-two. Gay films.'

'Oh Jem, how dreadful that must have been for you!'

'Well, actually, it wasn't, you know. When I was nineteen, twenty, I really quite enjoyed it. And most of the other young guys in the biz I shacked up with were the same. It didn't seem odd at the time; addicted to dopamine and oxytocin, perhaps. In a funny way it stabilised me, gave me a focus and helped me forget. As they used to say in San Francisco: "Lust is Life". The world of gay movies is a fairly broad church, and I was lucky to have coincided with awareness of AIDS, so I didn't ever have to do what I didn't feel comfortable or safe with.

A lot of the guys who were in the industry ten years earlier were dying in their thirties. I specialised in what we called "vanilla sex" – you know, making love face to face, endearments, kissing – what most people might think of as "normal". At first I imagined I was with Rick each time, but then I came to love, just for the occasion, you understand, the young man I was with. Sometimes it was just business-like – a paid job. Most of my fellow actors were nice boys, good-looking, considerate. Many had private problems like me, but on the surface, with clothes on, I guess we looked like everyone else.'

Jan stared at his old childhood friend in fascination and horror. He could think of nothing to say.

'If you want more details, just ask.'

'I don't think I do. I'm speechless,' gasped Jan. His own slow career in life insurance sales which began in his twenties, his tepid marriage, his steady but unspectacular income, seemed to recede into a tiny microcosm of ordinariness, by comparison with this!

'Just to complete the tale then,' went on Julia, 'I set up my own gay movie company with three old associates I'd worked with and made quite a lot of money over the years. But when it all went belly-up with the advent of the internet – and after all, you can see anything you want on-line nowadays, so who needs grainy VHS tapes? – I set up a website and, five years ago, opened a clinic in Glendale which helps a lot of people, straight and gay, with mental issues and with gender identity problems. I find I need to help others now, Jan, to give them the help I didn't have when I was young and needed it.'

'You mean you help people in the LGBT area?'

'Trans, gay, gender-fluid. I don't know what's causing it – oestrogen in the drinking water, microwaves, diesel emissions – but there are more and more young guys and girls who need guidance in painful circumstances which their families, their churches, their schools just don't understand. It is getting better, though. Society is a little kinder.'

Jem sighed and put a hand on Jan's arm. 'I think I've told you enough for now. I'll just add that it's taken me years to find peace. All I want now is to knit the past and present together. That would be perfect.'

Julia sighed softly. The light had nearly gone.

'Are you still a Catholic, Jem?'

'Yes, in a way. You never quite lose it; but a sort of modern, liberal one. I do go to Mass occasionally. I think I believe more now than I did when I was seventeen – about Christ's message of love for others, about redemption and an after-life. I don't think about the medieval accretion of guilt and sin around love and sex. We had too much of that as children. How about you?'

Janek was about to touch on his collapse of faith at Francis' death, but decided not to – yet.

'Oh, about the same,' he muttered.

Jem turned to peer out of the windscreen. Jan drank

in his handsome profile and flawless skin. There was a sort of nobility in that face, he decided. What Jem had done over twenty-five years ago was disturbing, even terrible, but it was also honest. Jem had always been honest. And now – well! He seemed to have matched the late Brother Howard in concern for others. Jem had always been remarkable – and admirable in his way. With a strange rush of emotion, Jan wondered if he had, perhaps, in his own way, been in love with Jem back then. '*You take me upstairs on a peach-flavoured skateboard*,' he murmured, thinking of his desire to *be* Jem at fifteen.

'What?' said Jem, absent-mindedly. He turned to Jan. 'Look, do you want to go in there and talk to the others?'

'No,' said Janek. He knew he didn't have to – now.

'Not even to old Lomax and Miss Carrbridge?'

'Not even them. They probably wouldn't remember me. Oh, and by the way, Greg told me they're married now – to each other.'

'That's nice,' murmured Julia. 'That's a happy ending, I'm sure.'

She put a hand on Janek's arm. Knowing who she was – just Jem – did not prevent Jan feeling a warm attraction to her. How odd it was. How upset he had been with Jem. How it had all hurt, back then.

'I feel better,' said Jan, almost to himself.

'As you haven't got your car here, why don't you let me drive you back to New York?' asked Jem.

The Tesla was warm, opulent – a softly-lit room. Jan, in that moment, realised that he wanted to stay with Jem – with Julia – in that little room for a long time. An as yet unarticulated determination never to let Jem go out of his life again, however difficult that would be, hardened within him.

Neither had any premonition of what a far-away virus in China would mean for them in the years to come – and the happiness they would discover in the midst of death and personal and national tragedy.

Janek's hand strayed to Jem's cheek and he touched it once. How soft, how fragile.

Jem turned towards him and their eyes met, and each searched the other's face.

The grey air dimmed outside the car.

Jan nodded in answer to Jem's offer.

The glow from the dials played on them. I wonder if life after death is like this? thought Jan. The cares and hang-ups we live with all drop away and the softly-lit faces of our beloved ones smile at us, their arms outstretched in welcome.

Jem touched the accelerator and the car glided away from the dusky abbey, carrying them both onwards, the fallen leaves of last summer writhing under its wheels, the shy snowdrops glowing.

THE END

Other **Trans-Oceanic-Press** novels by Simon Potter, available from Amazon and Witley Press Bookshop, which you might like:

"Losing It All". 1960s London boys Anthony and Mike are fascinated by their grandfather's magnificent haunted Scottish house. When it is sold and becomes a school, Anthony is a pupil, then a teacher there, then becomes the owner. But the dark force has not gone……. ("Hilarious and touching" *The Month.* "Novels like this are the best sort of history" *BBC World Service*) ISBN: 978-1-9164295-2-9

"Together Forever?" Anthony's brother Mike has become rich but homesick in Los Angeles. He invests in a TV series and returns to England. His insane "schlock" artist lover, Mopsa, pursues him to New York then London with a grotesque plan to keep them together forever……. ("A well-observed page-turner" *Goodreads*) ISBN: 978-1-9164295-5-0

Simon Potter has written, adapted and directed over sixty plays and musicals for youth theatre. He lives in London, England, and his published work includes history, fiction, literary commentary, technical non-fiction, poetry and articles for magazines. He was awarded an MBE for services to education in 2016.